Chaos Challenged

Book Four: The Chaos Reigns Saga

Carol Hightshoe

WolfSinger Publications ❨ Security, Colorado

Chapter One

"Chaos take it!" Thynitic's voice echoed in the silence of her throne room.

She watched Drezmona after she sent her to fetch Kyrianna and bring the girl to her citadel. Watched as the demoness betrayed her, letting the girl leave with her friends. Even as the Lady of Chaos, she was finding it harder and harder to thread her way through the chaos swirling around her. Her own plans were crumbling and the thread of order she had clung to for so long was dying.

The goddess flung the glass she was holding against the wall and watched as the blood-red color of the Lorniwen blended into the black of the obsidian.

Both Kyrianna and Torliana had renounced her, stripping her of more of her power and sending her deeper into the chaos she had been born from. But, there was something neither of them could renounce nor deny—and that would be what brought them back to her. Or, at least she hoped it would. Things were moving too quickly out of her control. She needed to regain what control she could. She would start with Torliana and Brular

~ * ~

Torliana was trapped in a sightless and soundless prison. She could feel the floor beneath her feet along with the weight and waves of pain from the manacles on her wrists. She could smell the sweet incense Thynitic favored for the braziers in her throne room. Incense made from a flower that grew only in Kilenter Forest on Rhysia. The only senses left to her were touch and smell. That would be enough. Her hands and ability to wield magic might be restrained by the manacles she wore, but her feet were free. One way or the other she was determined to free herself from Thynitic.

All these decades serving the Lady of Chaos she had continued to believe Brular would have cast her out of the temple. She had failed in her trial to be named a Flame Dancer and had violated more than just a few of the rules of Mount Veri. Thynitic had spoken to her from the flames of her meditation brazier and warned her Brular would reject her and cast her out of the temple. His attitude when she had approached him after the trial had convinced her Thynitic was correct and she had called out to the Lady of Chaos, summoning a fog of chaos to consume the temple.

The results had been horrible. Vile magic infested the very walls, warping the bodies of some and twisting the minds of others. Demons stalked the corridors. Monks, clerics and paladins were caught in the madness that pitted one against the other as the order of the temple was swept away. All this she saw as she made her way to Brular's office where the bodies of his most loyal followers lay, slain by Rudalynth, Thynitic's most devote and powerful chaos demon, while he had been powerless to help them.

She had wanted to kill him at the time, for rejecting her, for his own blindness and lack of caring, but Thynitic wanted Brular sent to her. Torliana opened a portal to Thynitic's citadel and he had been taken by the chaos demons.

That day had been a source of strength for her all these years. It was her greatest victory. She had molded the chaos to her needs and her desires to bring down those she saw as her enemies. Now, it was her worst nightmare.

The man she had sent to the Abyss those decades past had come to her just hours ago. He had chased her like a mad animal through the planes and finally had a chance to vent his anger and pain upon her, but refused to do so. He had done something she would never have imagined him doing: He forgave her. As the Keeper of Mount Veri and a rited judge of Shokar, he forgave and absolved her of her crimes. He did this even as the demons reached through a portal to take him back to Thynitic. He forgave her for the destruction of Mount Veri, the deaths of those there that night and for the evil done.

He also told her he would not have cast her out; that the rules of the temple bound him as they did any other and he could not impose any such punishment, *even if he had wanted to*. Thynitic had lied to her and she had destroyed everything because of that lie. Because she did not have faith in the one person she should have trusted the most.

Instead, she had reveled in the torments the chaos demons and even she herself had laid on him during the years. Her heart still burned with the passion she had felt for him, but it had turned from love to anger and hatred at his rejection of what she had offered him.

She had seen in him, when he came to the temple, a paragon of law and structure. She was an elf, more ruled by chaos, but she had found no place among her kindred and had sought the temple of Hellavar to find some sort of balance in her life. Then that balance had been disrupted because she had been drawn to Brular, but it was only she who realized it. Even when she had invited him to stay while she danced to welcome the coming spring and the rebirth and renewal of life, he had failed to see. In her desperation she had gone to Rynalia, the Mistress of the Flame and head of the Brotherhood. She wanted to know how one as ordered as she was had found her passion and given herself to both her husband and Hellavar. She wanted to understand Brular and hoped to find the spark that might ignite the fires of passion in him.

Rynalia had told her Brular had been orphaned at a very young age and raised by the church. While only about forty years old, a short time to an elf, he had spent a human's eternity within the scriptures. She had likened him to a piece of wood scorched for decades and now difficult to ignite. Rynalia had then chided her on setting her heart on that which was least attainable.

How right you were, Mistress. And in the end, I betrayed myself and all of you because I couldn't see.

Her hands balled into fists as Thynitic's voice broke through the silence.

"Torliana walk forward. You are a bigger fool than that living scab of a priest. You thought to take my power for your own; thinking I wouldn't know. And then when that priest gave you his forgiveness, you had the gall to try and renounce me." Her voice became a mocking laugh. "All this time devoted to me and you think it can be all washed away by a touch and a moment of guilt. For all the power you have touched and held, you are still a fool. There are patterns within the chaos—you are where I want you to be."

Torliana took a breath. "I am a fool for believing in you." She took another breath. "If there are patterns within the chaos—and I am where you wanted me, then why was a simpering half-elf child able to evade your control?"

"Who says she did? Perhaps she is where I wish her to be also. However, she will need to be taught respect—just as you do. You can stop walking now."

She could sense a presence standing in front of her, then came the sting of a hard slap across her face. Her anger flashed and she lashed out with her right foot. To her surprise, she connected and she felt the crack of ribs. She spun on her right foot, brought her other leg up and around in a high arc that connected with what she hoped was Thynitic's head. She didn't have any real hope of defeating the goddess, but she would give a good accounting of herself before she fell.

Her motions flowed smoothly and automatically. One foot striking even as the other was again touching the floor. She didn't keep track of her strikes; only that they were connecting with her unseen opponent, who did not seem to be defending herself. *She's waiting for me to misstep; to make a mistake,* she thought. *Playing with me.* This only fueled her anger further, and she focused that rage and hatred into a kick that connected with what she thought was her opponent's chest. She felt the bones and flesh collapse then her foot press into the body, just before she felt it fall to the floor.

"Impressive, Chosen," Thynitic's voice came. "I shudder to think what you would do to someone you hate." Her voice was slow, each word deliberate.

"No!" She let herself fall to the floor. "Bru…" She choked on his name.

"K…Kee…Keeper." There was no reply.

She stretched out her right hand, her fingers touched his face and she felt a tingle go up her arm at the contact. The skin was rough and uneven, the jaw shattered.

She let the tears fall as she sat there. "Does he still live?" She asked as her fingers moved to his neck.

A hand moved to cover hers and again that tingle—this time in her heart. "I let my anger, like my fear and doubt before, betray us." The hand squeezed hers and she knew she was forgiven—yet again.

"What a pathetic pair you are," Thynitic said. "An aged priest who will not let the fires of passion into his soul and an elf who denied those fires for so long, only to let her herself now be ruled by them and lose all touch with reality. It was I your anger was directed at, Torliana, but you did not stop to think as you lashed out. If you had, would you have continued? Do you honestly believe I would stand there and let you attack me?"

There was a long pause.

"Nothing else to say. Then, I will leave you two together to think on what I have said."

Sounds returned and Torliana listened for a few seconds. There was no other sound in the room, other than Brular's labored wheezing. She knew that sound. One of his ribs had punctured a lung. He was dying and he had still forgiven her. Thynitic was wrong; the spark had been lit.

"Let him find his peace," she whispered. "Let him rest." His hand continued to clutch hers and he coughed as he tried to draw a breath.

"It will take him many long and painful minutes to die, Torliana. If you are merciful you will grant him a quick death." There was a pause and she could see Thynitic in her mind holding the blood-red amulet. "However, it will not be for long."

Torliana sat holding his hand for several minutes. She could sense his pain, so much of it. "At least I can spare you this," she said as she tried to release his hand.

He wouldn't let go of her hand. "Please, Keeper, I only want to help you." His hand held hers tight. She stopped trying to pull away. His hand moved slowly up to her face and his finger traced her lips. "You want me to talk to you?"

His hand dropped back down to hers and he squeezed once.

Torliana wiped her eyes and nodded. "What would you care to hear?"

His hand moved to her wrist and his fingers wrapped around it and squeezed, before they returned to her hand.

"Myself, then." She crossed her legs and composed herself. "I don't remember much before I came to the temple of Hellavar," she said. "All I remember was that I knew I didn't belong in Johran. I don't know what led me to Mount Veri, but something did." There was an increase in the pressure on her hand when she mentioned Mount Veri and she felt her breath catch in her throat. "Please, no. Not the temple. I can't. All the death and destruction I caused."

His hand tightened on hers—twice. The pressure was powerful and it demanded her compliance. His hand released hers for a moment then tightened again—twice. He guided her hand to his shoulder and squeezed again. "You want me to talk about you."

The single affirmative squeeze.

"I had come to the temple a few days before your arrival. The ritual of the Summer Flame was only days away and the Kindling prepared the courtyard. Even though I had been there only two days, I understood Rynalia was the absolute authority within the temple. The Keeper was feeling his age and had passed many of his duties to her."

She sat up straighter and left her hand on his shoulder. "You arrived on the day of the Feast of the Summer Flame. Several of the new clerics whispered about your arrival. Did you know they all spoke of you with such reverence and awe? The great bringer of law. Hellavar's blazing judge. He who presides over Tormasus' Lord High General and Dh'Mark's King were the things they called you." Her voice lost its melancholy. "You were a legend to the Kindling. They all wanted to see the incredible figure who made thieves cower and city-states bow." She grinned. "I think they were disappointed. You weren't seven feet tall and sheathed in radiant flame. You were an unimposing man who could hardly fill out the armor he wore."

She laughed. "When you slid off your horse, your stride was hobbled. I wondered if you even liked to ride." His hand squeezed hers twice. "So the High Judge roamed the entire eastern expanse of Shokar and was saddle sore the entire way." She laughed again as both their hands tightened. "That just creates a new picture of all those tales the Kindling told of you. The mighty judge laid low by his four legged steed."

She swallowed her laughter and let her left hand stroke his where it rested on her right. "Here was this man whose reputation held the Kindling almost in prayer to his great deeds and he was hardly worthy, in my mind, of training beside me. He was just a weak little cleric whose name preceded him. I was shocked when Rynalia first approached and greeted you with a bow of her head. I found it offensive to the Brotherhood that our Mistress would give deference to such an individual. I had seen how the brothers and sisters of the flame honed their bodies, minds and souls to perfection and harmony with their surroundings. I looked forward to the part of the Feast where they would dance among the flames. Yet, she accepted you as an equal without the least confrontation." She paused and took a deep breath.

"I did not see you again until that evening. You had traded

your armor for your robes and sat next to the outgoing Keeper as the Flame Dancers celebrated among the flames. I marveled at how they moved and jumped, becoming one with the flames. Their movements were euphoric, without hesitation, thought or fear. The crackling of the fire spoke to them and the heat caressed their bodies as they moved. I had been told the Keeper, as part of the ceremony, would summon living flame to take part in the closing of the dance. No one knew, did they, that you would take the Keeper's place that evening in the summoning?"

His breathing had slowed and grown more labored, but his grip was still strong as she felt it tighten and release twice.

"You rose and descended between the roaring flames as we waited. Then you waved your hands and spoke in the language of fire. The burning wood crackled with power as you spoke. I was ready to see a giant of radiant heat appear. Instead of being dumbstruck by a display of power; I was awestruck with wonder. The creatures were tiny and beautiful as they flew with sparks trailing after them. They were like hummingbirds of vivid orange and red flickering light. They fluttered around us and we were enchanted. I reached out and one responded by lightly caressing me. Its touch was like the warmth of a bath or the kiss of a lover.

"Everyone watched as the birds you summoned surrounded the courtyard in smoke. Then one of the Kindling called out 'eyes?' You had summoned sentient smoke that chased the Flame Dancers wrapping them in cloaks. You were then sheathed in your own blue flames and your voice elevated the fires even higher. Your arms rose to the sky and you dropped your head. With a flash of fire and the sound of thunder, something appeared behind you. The molten rock figure knelt with its left knee to the ground and its head bowed. It was eerie as both of your faces rose together and both sets of eyes burned with the same inner fire. It was a magnificent display; one I have never forgotten and will never forget. I have wielded power that surpassed your own, but have never had the control or mastery you possess; it has always evaded me."

She felt his hand go limp in hers. "After that day, I would never consider you weak. You were Brular Eglis, the burning bringer of order. Your face was the one that would stare back at me from the fires from that day forward until she took that from me."

Tears flowed freely as she continued to hold his lifeless hand. "I wish this was truly goodbye, Keeper; but she will never let you go. How many more times must I see you die? How many more times must you bear the consequences of my actions?" She remained there, in silence until the demons came for him, to bring him to Thynitic. She continued to sit there praying Resare would take pity on Brular and destroy his soul; anything to release them both from this misery. However, The Lord of Death had never done so before and she knew he would not do so now.

She collapsed on the floor. "Hellavar's blessing keeps your mind intact and Resare lets you return over and over again. Why do they damn you to her endless torment yet again?"

Chapter Two

Torliana leaned back against the wall. She wasn't sure how long she had been in this room after one of the demons had brought her here. This was one of the rooms reserved for guests Thynitic honored as well as providing a place of reprieve for those she tormented. It was not an act of mercy but further torment as they saw the contrast between what their pitiful lives were compared to the pleasures that could be.

The table in the room held exotic fruits, cheeses, meats and other tempting foods. The bed, which she had not slept in since she had been brought here, was exceptionally soft. There was even a choice of books to read by the well-padded chair.

Her tears came again. None of it mattered, he was somewhere in this place. Thynitic had him again and he had done the unthinkable. He had shown a lowly mortal the way to hurt her. She smiled through the tears; she had sought that power. She had worked hard to gather the power to challenge her. She had become her Chosen to grab and hold that power; power that would bring meaning to her life. *She knew what I was doing the entire time. She wanted me to do it. She wanted me to fail and thereby deepen her own power. She wanted me to take the power so it would consume me then draw my soul to her.* "It was all for nothing," she said. "I schemed away all these years of my life to be what? To be her? To feed her?"

Brular had fought both her and Thynitic, but not as the raving lunatic one might expect after everything that had been done to him. Instead, he had remained a controlled paragon of order. Even when he let his anger rule him as the man known as Ashe, he was controlled and calculating. *And, completely unnerving.* She smiled at the thought. *Kyrianna and her companions had found him unsettling even fearing him.*

Yet, through everything they faced, he never flinched. He had seen the worst life and even death could offer. He faced it all with complete impassiveness. Never would he let the order he served break. He summoned the efreeti and fed him from the bits of his own soul he had left to do the near impossible. He even summoned an avatar of Mykaylene to stand before her servants. She wished she could have seen what transpired. She felt it would have been like Mount Veri. He was the Keeper in every sense of the word. He would take up the mantle, even for a few he had only recently met and who didn't worship his god. "It would have been marvelous to watch," she whispered.

He had held to the order even as he was taken by Thynitic's demons. "You could have crushed them, Keeper. I have seen you. Everything is so clear and simple for you. You would have had them at your mercy in only the first few moments." She brought her knees to her chest. "And, I'm the one who destroyed it. He pardoned me. He absolved me. He forgave me." She slammed her fists against the floor. "How could he do that?"

The door to the room opened and a chaos imp flew in. "She summons you to her throne room," he said.

Torliana stood slowly, she cursed herself for not finding a way to break the magic on the manacles she was wearing. While in these rooms, they did not pulse with the pain used to hinder the wearer's power, unless the one bound attempted to use magic. As soon as she left the room, they would again activate.

She entered the throne room and glanced up at the ceiling, now at less than twenty feet above the floor instead of its previously towering height. "Have you finished with the self-pity?" Thynitic's voice echoed in the room.

"No. To do that I would have to grieve for him and myself for all of the years we lost to you."

"I see you have regained some of your spirit, but is your anger not misplaced." She pointed to the ceiling. "Look."

Torliana stared as the obsidian flowed and an image formed of a clearing. "Kilenter," she whispered.

The picture showed a wolf playing with a ghostly child. Kyrianna sat next to the unicorn Brular had summoned for her. The unicorn had been given substance by Brular who had also given hope to Kyrianna, even as he sacrificed himself to forgive her. *They should be grief stricken,* she thought. *Instead, they laugh and play.*

Thynitic frowned. "You didn't think they would actually come for him, did you?"

"No." *They have left him for dead. No not dead, that would be a blessing.*

"So, what now? There will be no rescue. Not for you. Not for him."

Torliana went to her knees. Thynitic was right. How could she possibly do anything to help him? "What do you want?"

"My Chosen."

Torliana's heart sank. "I tried to steal your power."

"You are not the first of my daughters to do so. However, you will be last. You are the last, who truly serve the chaos. Kyrianna has her role to play, but it will not be as my Chosen."

Torliana's voice broke. "For what?"

"You want to see him. You want to help him." Torliana looked up as the Lady of Chaos waited.

Her gaze went up to the ceiling and she knew it was the truth. There was something familiar about the ghostly girl, but she couldn't place the memory. They were not coming and of everyone in that group, she had truly believed Kyrianna would try. Now, it appeared it was up to her to do what little she could. What was left of her soul, she had forfeited a long time ago.

She bowed her head and began the litany. Her voice was broken and detached as she let the first passages escape her lips.

"Nowhere in all the worlds or planes is there no pain, torment or chaos. All we can do is accept those strikes which cannot be avoided and give back chaos and pain to those who offend. Kindness should be the only companion to pain and will increase the intensity of suffering and the chaos surrounding us."

She felt her voice gain strength with the familiarity of the words. "Do not ignore the sudden whim of compassion; let it always come, but only seldom as to give those who suffer a sense of hope. Hope is the consort to chaos and torment in their offspring. Unending torment destroys pain and this in turn destroys the chaos that nurtures us."

"Stop!" Thynitic's voice reverberated in the room. "Those words are an abomination created by Carrinna. If you do not wish to join her in her prison then speak the correct words."

Torliana paused. She knew no other words.

"If you are a true Daughter of Chaos and my Chosen, then you will find the right words." Thynitic stood. "If you cannot serve, then I have no further need for the fire cleric and will give him and the amulet to one of the demon lords as a gift."

Torliana let her mind turn inward as she searched for the words that would placate the Lady of Chaos.

"It is from chaos that we are born." She spoke the words slowly and held her breath. She struggled to hold the memory of words she had only read once on a scrap of parchment at the temple in Nydith. "Chaos gives life and creates change. It is only through chaos that we can see the truth. Chaos and passion call all to them. Mercy and retribution should only be meted out when deserved; not when dictated. Embrace passion, mercy and retribution. Embrace chaos. Embrace life."

"Very good. Let those words sink into your soul. Let their meaning become a part of you. When they do, you will understand."

Torliana lowered her head to the floor. *Nothing matters anymore. Why should these words hold any different meaning than the others?*

"Pathetic," a new voice called and Torliana looked up.

"Drezmona, I am surprised you would return after your failure to do as I directed." Thynitic waved her hand as if to dismiss a servant and Torliana smiled, glad the goddess' attention had been diverted.

"Really? You said it yourself: I have more plots and schemes working than any other denizen of the Abyss. However, that is not the reason I am here. I bear you a message."

"From who?"

"Carrinna."

Thynitic raised her hand and Drezmona was thrown against the far wall. "So your allegiances lie with her."

"No, Thynitic." The demoness forced herself back to her feet. "My allegiances lie where they always have—with myself. I have respected your guile in the past, but you have grown weak."

"Relay your message and leave."

"Carrinna sends her greetings to her mother and wishes to remind her there is little time left. You have let the games you are playing cost you power; power she has claimed for herself. The spark that has been captured will soon die."

Torliana shuddered at the demoness' final words as she vanished from the throne room.

Thynitic slumped in her throne; her eyes closed and her hand reaching for the empty throne beside her. Torliana thought she saw the glint of a tear on her cheek, but that couldn't be.

"Your first task." Thynitic said opening her eyes and throwing something at her.

Torliana caught it with one hand and looked at it. Her blood went cold. The bloodstones had already been set in the cold iron of the amulet that would be used to trap a soul.

"Not for you. You have not earned that—not yet. It is for Kyrianna; see to it."

She looked down at the amulet. Of all the things to ask her to do, this was the most vile. However, there was a reason she had agreed to serve. "Brular?"

Thynitic smiled. "Already?"

"You want her." She straightened her back as she faced the goddess. "I will see him before I start the first etching."

A door opened. "Go."

Torliana raised her arms. Pain radiated from the manacles.

"Don't play games. I will remove those shackles only after I am sure of your allegiance. If you want to see him—go."

Torliana hurried out of the throne room and ran down the corridor as her ears picked out the sound of Brular's screams. When she entered the small room, she felt her heart being torn in two. Veterak, Thynitic's master torturer, had strapped Brular to a stone table, with a large vat positioned above him. Acid flowed slowly and irregularly out of the vat and through a lattice of glass tubes that dripped it onto different parts of his body. She could see places where the acid had burned through his body to the stone of the table. Her body shook as he turned his head toward her. His eyes had been burned out and his tongue removed. She grabbed the wall to prevent any show of weakness before the demon.

"Release him!"

"I cannot. By her order, the restraints were placed so the only way to remove them is to dump the vat."

She looked at Brular and was unable to say anything.

"He dies by the acid; fast or slow, but he must die. I was told you would make that decision." He turned away and pointed to a lever.

She glanced at the manacles on her wrists. She could have used magic to protect him from the acid, but she was denied that power. She moved to stand next to him and her tongue stumbled over a language she had not used in many years as she spoke to Brular in the language of fire. "I cannot begin to take back what has been done to you. And now, she leaves me the choice of letting your torment last for days or killing you in a horrible manor." She turned away, grabbed the lever and pulled it.

Torliana collapsed as the acid cascaded through the glass tubes and pooled over Brular's body, dissolving it. There was a sharp pain in her heart—as if a part of her own soul was being ripped away from her body.

Thynitic walked into the room holding the amulet of soul binding that held Brular's soul and smiled. "His part is done," she said. "Start on her amulet."

She raised her head and glared at the goddess. "For what? To be given this choice again."

Thynitic shook her head. "I said his part is done. I have no more need of doing this to the Keeper. However, there are far worse things I can do if that is what it will take for you to complete the amulet." She reached down, grabbed Torliana by the neck and lifted her from the floor.

"Finish the first layer within three days," she said.

"Three days." Torliana rubbed her neck as Thynitic released her. "That would take a week by hand. You ask the impossible."

"You have one day for each stage of the first layer; the etching and the sentryl to be poured," Thynitic said as she reached out and grabbed the manacles. "Their power is restricted. You will be able to use magics that directly benefit your task and nothing more."

"Now I only have two days."

"Yes, Torliana, now you only have two days. However, if you succeed, I will give you one day of rest that you may spend with Brular. I will restore him and he will not be harmed while you are working."

Torliana looked down at the amulet she still held in one hand. The bloodstones glinted in the flickering torchlight of the room—accusing her. She hesitated for a second; she would be trading Brular's safety with Kyrianna's damnation. Her gaze went from the amulet to the horror of what was left on the table. *He has suffered enough; let another suffer in his place.* She nodded her agreement.

"Do the work carefully, Torliana. If there are any flaws in the amulet, it will be Brular who pays the price for your incompetence."

"I understand."

Chapter Three

Brular looked down at the smooth obsidian floor and watched Torliana working diligently at her task. She had spent the first day fueling powerful magics. He had sensed the power she was working with, but not the reason for it, until she finally placed the amulet on the desk, the etching completed. Even with magic, it had taken time and considerable power to complete the work as cold iron was resistant to magic. He had stared in shock at the bloodstones embedded in the metal as Torliana prepared the sentryl. She was creating an amulet of soul binding.

Now he understood why Thynitic had had him brought to this room. Torliana toiled on the amulet, expending much of her own power to create it and he knew why. She did it to shield him from Thynitic. "This is not the way," he whispered. "There is no freedom in this, Kindling."

Torliana stood and stretched her muscles as she waited for the sentryl to finish melting in the small pot. He smiled as she went through the same exercises she would have learned as a Kindling. Despite everything, she still remembered her training from the temple; perhaps that was something he could use to bring her back from the path she was now treading. Still, the movements were mechanical, there was something missing in them.

"Has she taken the last of your spirit, Kindling? In all this time, she never took that from you. Did I take it?" He walked the floor then stopped and looked down at the amulet. He understood the process. The deepest etching would be cut then filled with sentryl, the second cut and filled with platinum, finally a third that would be filled with silver. It was a layered net to trap and hold a soul. There was only one person he could think of who Thynitic would be doing this for—Kyrianna. "You can't think this is what I want," he said as he looked down at her. He shook his head again as he sat down to watch her and she began to pour the sentryl. He brushed the floor above her head hoping she would know he was close. Her actions were not her own, but those of Thynitic. He understood why the goddess let him watch this. It

15

was to show him Torliana was once again her puppet and this time he was the string being used to make her dance.

He knew the magic needed to carve the etching had been difficult and draining and now she would be laying the sentryl, a metal that had to be kept very hot or it would start to solidify as it was poured. Any occlusions or imperfections would mean the amulet was ruined if left in place. The layer of metal had to be seamless and smooth.

He turned away, he couldn't watch her do this. A small book on the pile near the desk caught his eye and he found himself picking it up.

The cover was black leather with a rearing unicorn etched in silver. In each of the corners were four other symbols. He knew two of them: The moon bow of Galolith and the chaos portal of Thynitic—deities of Kyrianna's world. The other two must belong there as well: a green star and red flame. He opened the book and watched as the elven script shifted and flowed so he could read it.

The book told of the birth of Thynitic from the primordial chaos of the universe, followed by the birth of a god named Neysinil. Neysinil was called the Lord of Order and the Consort of Chaos. He had never seen this consort or any evidence of any order around Thynitic in the decades she had held him. Where was Neysinil?

The name was familiar and he searched his memory to find the reason. Kyrianna and the others had mentioned the name as one they had heard in the temple where they met. None of them had recognized the name. The book also talked about Frayrith— the goddess Kyrianna followed and Galolith the last of the elven deities from her world.

The book contained information he had not found in the library of the celestials and he sat back in the chair as he continued to read. Knowledge was power; perhaps there was something in here he could use to stop Thynitic's plans.

Chapter Four

Andrinor opened his eyes as someone knocked on the door. The knocks were soft almost tentative and he shook his head as he looked over at Nirev. The dwarf was using his mug as a pillow and snoring. How he managed to hear the knocking over that, he wasn't sure. He pulled the pommel of his sword out of his belt and headed for the door. "Never know when someone in this city will want to visit us with guards," he said stepping over Falden and Jerietlan.

Andrinor looked down at the group that greeted him at the door. A man, woman and three children stood there.

"My Lord, I was told by a friend to come here with my family regarding a position in the household."

Andrinor only stared at him.

"Is there a Master Jhoro about?" the woman asked. "We were told to speak to him."

"Jhoro?" Andrinor shook his head. "I don't know that name."

"That would be me," a voice said next to him.

He turned.

"Down here."

Andrinor looked down and saw a mongoose perched on its hind legs. "How and when did you arrive?"

Jhoro waved his paw. "Later. I must see to the house at this time."

Andrinor stood there and stared at Jhoro. The mongoose finally made a shooing motion with his paws and Andrinor stepped away from the door.

"Okay," Jhoro said. "If you were sent by Lord Duvall, there was a phrase you would have been given."

"Pray for a safe return of all," the oldest girl said.

"Very good. Now, to the first order of business this morning: We have a situation in the dining hall. Four." He looked up at Andrinor. "Sorry, three…"

"What be going on out there?" Nirev's voice called from the

dining hall.

Andrinor nodded as the dwarf exited the room and raised his mug in salute.

"Amazing, the dead can rise," Jhoro said then turned back to the family. "Okay, two." He paused and looked at Nirev. "Are the others stirring?"

"Those two?" Nirev laughed then took a long drink from his mug. "They be practically dead and will be wishing they were when they do wake."

Jhoro nodded. "Very well. These are the things that will need to be taken care of first then. Please prepare a bath for both of them. The bathing chamber is upstairs. You may find the appearance of one of them frightening—I expect him to be treated the same as anyone else in this household. The rug is stained and may not be salvageable, but I do expect an honest attempt. Who is the cook?"

Both the woman and eldest girl raised their hands.

"Good. We need breakfast for twelve."

"There are only seven of us," Andrinor said.

Jhoro turned and shook his head. "Excuse me—I have seen you and Nirev eat. Please prepare enough for at least twelve.

"I believe it would be best if the girl started on breakfast. You two," he motioned to the couple, "should see to the rug. The two youngest will see to preparing the bathing chamber. Once the two from the dining hall are upstairs and in no danger of drowning, they can wake the others for breakfast."

"You have not even asked our names," the man said.

"A minor detail, Sir. Let's get this group on their way to the Abyss then we can finalize the details after that. I do assume Lord Duvall has already made arrangements for your payment for the position?" He didn't wait for an answer. "The servant's quarters are in the back. A nice little cottage that should be sufficient for your family. If not, you can stay in the common room upstairs, until I can have the cottage renovated."

He stopped and looked up at the man who was standing there with a blank look on his face. "Well what are you waiting for? The demons are waiting, and this group is late meeting them as it is. Just leave your bags in here." He gestured to the great hall. "I will give you the tour and get you settled in once the others have left. The kitchen and dining hall are this way." He turned and scampered into the dining hall. The family set their bags inside the great hall and followed.

"You didn't seem surprised by Jhoro, Nirev," Andrinor said as they headed up the stairs, the two youngest following them.

"I thought he might be a friend of yours," Nirev said. "Does the dragon warrior have a weasel warrior friend?"

"Actually, he's a mongoose," Andrinor said.

Nirev stopped and looked up at Andrinor. "Now, *that* be strange."

Andrinor looked down at Nirev who started laughing.

~ * ~

Kyrianna stretched, the first hint of dawn was rising in the east. She smiled as she inhaled the scents of the new day.

:*You seem happy*, Melissa's voice said.

"Why shouldn't I be?" She stood and adjusted her armor. "We need to get to the house, but there are a few things I need to get first." :*Kyri, can I play at the wedding?*

Kyrianna felt the heat rise in her cheeks. "Getting a little ahead of ourselves, aren't we?"

:*Well, I thought...* Melissa's thought's trailed off.

Kyrianna finished checking her gear. "I am not saying anything about a wedding yet. Let Tristan and I have our time of courtship. Many of the problems Hendandra is having are because her courtship did not exist at all." She laughed again. "The courtship is half the fun."

Kyrianna finished with her gear then turned and hugged Cewyr tightly as she removed the collar. "Return to your home for now," she said. "And thank you." The figurine secured, she headed for the grove dedicated to Dwycia.

She waited until the druid finished with his morning prayers before approaching. "Your pardon. I will be traveling to a far off place and wish to bring a statue, which I can dedicate to Dwycia."

He nodded and extended his hand.

"My apologies, but I do not know what is required as I am a stranger to this realm."

"If the shrine is to be placed in good conscience for those of faith then the cost is what you think it is worth," he said.

Kyrianna nodded and smiled as she extended her hand. He took it and squeezed with just enough force to give her the assurance she had responded correctly. He gestured to a simple hut.

When she entered, she saw three small, carved wooden figures. The druid selected one and handed it to her followed by a small vial. "This will purify the area where you wish to place the figure."

Kyrianna smiled. "My thanks." She turned to the doorway then stopped and turned back to the druid. "There are two others who travel with me who do not have what they need to dedicate a shrine to those they serve. One serves Mulog and the other Shyada. Are there those who serve among the Grove?"

He nodded and pointed toward a path that wound around to the north.

~ * ~

Kyrianna paused as a deep bell rang in the silence of the morning, the echo thundering around her. She followed the sound to a large stone enclosure; one that was shaped like a singers' alcove to focus and resonate the sound. A dwarf brought a large mallet against the bell again and Kyrianna brought her hands to her ears as the sound pounded her senses.

:*I think we found the right place,* Melissa said.

Kyrianna waited patiently and forced her hands away from her ears. Mulog was a god who expected to be heard and the act of trying to prevent that might be considered disrespectful. The last echo fading, the druid turned and descended the stairs. She looked at Kyrianna and the figure she held.

"Why does a follower of Dwycia stay to hear Mulog's challenge to Hellavar?"

"Challenge?"

"Hellavar rises in Mulog's sky without asking. He challenges him every day. Sometimes the clouds win; sometimes Mulog is bored with the contest and lets him have clear skies."

Kyrianna glanced up at the brightening sky. "I understand." She turned her attention back to the druid. "I have come to ask not for myself, but for a friend who journeys to challenge the Abyss itself. I wish to see he is provided with the requirements to dedicate a shrine to Mulog."

"Who is this worshipper? Is he an acolyte or possibly an anvil?"

Kyrianna paused unsure what to say then remembered Nirev's words at the temple. "He calls himself the First Hammer."

The druid took a step back. "First Hammer? I have heard and felt the power of Mulog strong in the city as of late. You are sure that was his title."

"Yes, and he proudly gave his measure of Sir Balthas with a crack of thunder and lightning against his statue in the Coliseum. You don't seem concerned he may have lied about the title."

"Few would dare to declare themselves a Hammer, let alone the First." The druid motioned for Kyrianna to follow as she led the way to an area beneath the structure. A granite statue, not much smaller than Hendandra was seated in the center.

"This is the shrine's centerpiece. You expect me to take it?"

"No, I expect the First Hammer to demand the strength of Mulog's power as is his right."

"This is too heavy for me to handle. How do I move it?"

"That I do not know, but it will aid him; therefore Mulog's strength will provide."

Kyrianna bowed. "I am sure it will. I will return to see the statue is taken to the First Hammer. There is another I see to as well. Can you direct me to Shyada's grove?"

He pointed to the west. "Just beyond the trees you will find the baths. Be wary as a large creature seems to favor sleeping there of late."

Kyrianna raised an eyebrow then smiled. *A large creature? I wonder?*

Kyrianna moved slowly and soundlessly toward the tree line. Sure enough, the shape of a large tiger could be seen. *So, you have been sleeping here close to your goddess, if not your wife.* She concentrated on her footsteps as she walked, but still saw him raise his head and an ear flick towards her. "Shydaran, it's Kyrianna," she called.

He placed his head on the ground.

She approached slowly. "She told me."

The tiger growled, but didn't move.

"She is confused right now, give her time. I'll be back." She turned as a woman walked past the two panthers guarding the entrance to the grove. "I need to speak to one of those who serve the grove."

This time, she did not try to hide her steps as she approached. The panthers looked at her, but did not move. She paused in front of one of the guardians and bowed her head, the cat's growling settled as it looked at her. She held her hand out to let him sniff it and was rewarded by him pressing his cheek against the palm. "You protect your mistress well. I would not think of harming her."

The cat nodded and she stepped between them and approached the pools. She scanned the area, but didn't see the woman. A discarded cloth on the ground told her she was looking in the wrong place. Kyrianna turned her attention to the water and saw a faint ripple. She knelt down and placed her hand on the smooth surface. It was warm to the touch.

"Have you come to join me?" a voice asked.

Kyrianna glanced down then looked away as she felt heat rising in her cheeks. The woman was nude and seemed not the least concerned that the water was perfectly clear.

"No," she said quickly. "I...I...have come to make a request."

She felt droplets of water splash on her arm and turned to see the woman with her arms against the side of the pool, holding her head and shoulders above the water.

"A request at so early an hour is hardly appropriate. This time is for rejoicing in a new day. You should savor the morning coolness and its beauty." She winked. "Preferably, with another."

Kyrianna's thoughts went to Tristan but she pushed them aside as she realized they could cause even more uncomfortable questions from Melissa. However, the idea of a swim in the pool did linger for a moment longer. "The offer is tempting, but unfortunately my road at this time does not allow for such luxuries. I do apologize for disturbing your morning prayers."

"I understand. What is your request?"

"A servant of Shyada travels with me and my group. I wish to provide him with the requirements to dedicate a shrine to her."

The woman grinned and nodded toward Shydaran. "You are a little tall to be his mate."

"You know about that?"

"His true form is not hidden from those with the goddess' sight. The way he acts shows he misses someone; someone close."

"His mate travels with us. I don't think she slept well either." She looked down at the woman. "Again, my apologies, but I am expected back."

The woman leaned back and kicked away from the side then

raised her hand and pointed. "Beneath that pedestal you will find several figures as well as a perfume to bless the site where it will be placed."

Kyrianna rose. "What is the typical offering?"

The woman laughed. "I believe you can guess what the offering is. However, I saw your face—you are not ready yet." She closed her eyes as she floated in the warm water. "When you are, return with your mate. There are private pools where the only witness is the goddess. Come back and enjoy the water and each other's company."

Kyrianna nodded then turned away.

"Wait."

Kyrianna turned back around to see the woman standing only inches from her. Her breath caught and she closed her eyes.

"Your modesty is refreshing and annoying at the same time," the woman said.

Kyrianna heard the woman's voice as she moved around her. "So you would interfere with the pursuits of him and his mate." There was something different about the woman's voice. Power resonated behind the words. Kyrianna felt a nail drag against her neck and she trembled as she remembered Hendandra's story of what had happened on Justula. "I know Thynitic's Chosen has already shown you pain," the goddess whispered.

Kyrianna opened her mouth to defend her actions, but the claw was replaced by fingers that caressed the back of her neck.

"What about pleasure?" Her voice was even lower.

Kyrianna's voice and thoughts failed her as only a gasp escaped. She felt the goddess' breath against her ear and wasn't even sure she was still standing as everything melted into the feel of the goddess' touch.

"Stay absolutely still."

Kyrianna didn't know if it was the threat of harm, the risk Shyada would remove the euphoria, or the power of the goddess that held her, but she held still as the woman pulled the silver sword from its scabbard.

:*Kyri, what's wrong,* she heard Melissa's voice say,

Shyada laughed. "There is nothing wrong." She let her fingers rub against Kyrianna's neck.

:*What are you doing to her?*

"I am giving her a taste." She traced a circle on Kyrianna's neck.

Kyrianna shuddered and inhaled sharply as a tingle went through her body.

"I am sorry little one," Shyada said. "However, I am not interested in an additional player at this moment. And, it would not be appropriate for you to be involved. You be a good girl and stay in the sword and I will send her to fetch you after I am through."

Kyrianna heard the sword hit a nearby tree and wanted to turn her head, but found she still could not move from where she stood. "Melissa?" The name came out as harsh whisper.

Shyada's fingers caressed the tip of her ear. "I am the one who speaks here."

Kyrianna nodded.

"You have found your mate and maybe a proper punishment would be to take something from you before you can give it to him."

Kyrianna felt her breath quicken and her mind cleared enough for her to protest.

"No." It was a plea, not a demand.

"Really?" Shyada's fingers again caressed Kyrianna's ear and pulled at it.

Kyrianna gasped as she realized what Shyada could do and what she was willing to let the goddess do in that moment. She brushed her cheek against the goddess' palm. Her body was giving permission, even asking. Her mind though, still protested. "No, please."

"It is too bad you have already found him. I could take that precious gift, but then I rob him of it." She sighed. "It would have been wonderful for you, but then what would the pair be with one constantly wishing for that moment again." She removed her hand and stepped back. "Look at me."

Kyrianna opened her eyes and found herself studying the woman before her. Her gaze moved over her body, seeing the curves and shadows, the water still glistening on smooth skin.

"You owe an apology for your actions last night." Shyada reached out, placed both hands on Kyrianna's face and pulled her toward her. Their lips met and Kyrianna froze in shock as her body began to tingle and her mind lost focus.

Shyada laughed as they parted. "You will have to do better than that." She leaned in again.

Kyrianna took a deep breath and this time relaxed and returned the kiss. She closed her eyes and felt herself held by a pair of strong arms as warmth caressed her body. In her mind, she saw Tristan and she felt her desire grow as she lost herself in the embrace.

When they separated, Kyrianna almost fell against the woman who nodded and smiled. "Definitely better. Do not forget, you are expected to return here to make an appropriate offering. Do not wait too long." She turned, took a few steps and dove back into the pool.

Kyrianna shook her head to clear the shock of what had happened. *Frayrith, what has she done?* She had to concentrate to force her thoughts back to where she was and what she was supposed to be doing. She found herself walking through some vines to see the silver sword embedded in a tree. It came free in her hand, and she paused as someone moved in the shadows of the trees. *Tristan?* She shook her head to clear her thoughts. This wasn't real, she needed to focus.

"Nothing to say?" Kyrianna asked as she felt Melissa in her mind.

:*I'm not sure what to say. Tristan told me not to ask any questions regarding the topic of maidenhood. But, this...,* her thoughts faded.

"He did. I will have to thank him for that." She paused trying to gather her thoughts. "Melissa, I really can't explain what happened at this time. When I understand it, I will try." Her gaze wandered to one of the pools and she again had to force thoughts of her and Tristan away.

She knelt before the statue of Shyada on the pedestal. "Shyada, sister of Dwycia who is kindred of Frayrith, I offer my apology for any offense caused by my actions last night. And, I will return here as you have directed. However, I stand by those actions. Would you have them put into a position to end up resenting the manner in which they first came to each other?" She stood, bowed her head again and picked up one of the figures and the perfume.

She saw the tiger rise and stretch as she approached and she held out the figure for him see. "Shydaran, I have a favor to request. I also requested a figure from the shrine dedicated to Mulog for Nirev. They have decided to give him their own statue and it is made of granite. Can you take it to the house before meeting Gwideon this morning?"

He nodded.

"Thank you." She led him to the shrine. "I think this will be a good day, for us both," she said as she rubbed his fur.

:*She will tell him,* Melissa asked.

:*Yes.* Kyrianna said in her mind.

Shydaran carried the heavy stature in his mouth as they walked back to the house. Kyrianna was amazed at his strength, even in this form.

"Thank you again," she said when Shydaran placed the statue near the door. She knelt down and lowered her voice. "Hendandra wishes to speak with you before we leave. I will send her to you and make sure you have a reasonable amount of time together. Watch for my signal."

Shydaran nodded then turned and left.

Kyrianna looked up and saw there were no lights lit in Myrith's room and grinned.

"Good, she's not up yet."

There was a flicker of light in the room. :*It is like she knows when you have been bad,* Melissa said.

"I haven't been bad. I am here and ready to go."

Melissa giggled. :*For once.*

"Granted." She pushed open the unlocked door and stopped at the smell of breakfast being prepared. "Who's cooking?" She really couldn't imagine any of the others using a stove, except maybe Myrith.

"That would be my sister, Jerania," a voice said behind her. "Could you excuse me, Lady...?" He paused and looked up at her.

She turned to see a young boy of about ten years. "Kyrianna. My name is Kyrianna. Lady is used only on formal occasions, please." She smiled and looked at the bucket of water he was carrying.

"Kyrianna." He lifted the bucket. "For Master Falden." He moved past her and up the stairs.

"I can help...." She let her sentence hang.

"Rourgen and no thank you. My father said I was to do it myself as the Lords and Ladies needed to get ready." He headed up the stairs.

"Interfering with the help?"

Kyrianna looked at the mongoose standing on the small table next to the door.

"Jhoro, who put you in charge?"

"Lord Duvall, I would have you know, and with Hendandra's blessing. You could ask him, if you don't trust me, but he is currently out seeing to other things."

She patted the mongoose on the head. "I have no reason to not trust you. I'm sure you will do a fine job." She moved to the entrance to the dining hall and gagged.

"What happened?"

"The mage could not hold all of the vile substance he took in," Jhoro said. "I'm surprised the stuff isn't poisonous."

The man and woman working on the rug looked up and shook their heads.

"That tears it," Jhoro said. "Dwarven spirits are banned from this house. They can drink it in the garden if they want, but only where the flowers and grass are already dead." He looked up at her. "I suspect it can work as an adequate weed killer."

She grinned and moved to the table. Footsteps caught her attention and she looked up as Andrinor came into the room. "Give me a hand with the table please," she said.

He nodded, grabbed one end and lifted. The servants pulled the rug from under the table.

"If you know someone who would want the scraps, then have them come for the rug as a whole. I would advise to either cut out or burn the stained area to kill the odor," Jhoro said.

Kyrianna headed toward the kitchen, Andrinor following her.

"On second thought, better tell them not to burn it. Who knows how volatile that stuff is."

Kyrianna looked up at Andrinor and grinned at Jhoro's last comment.

"I take it you had a good evening," he said placing a hand on her shoulder. "I did," she said as they entered the kitchen.

"Everything smells wonderful," Kyrianna said as a young woman busied herself preparing the food.

"Tastes good too."

Andrinor's voice was muffled and Kyrianna looked up to see him holding a loaf of bread, about half of it already gone.

"My apologies," she said to the girl as she elbowed Andrinor in the side. "We have spent so much time on the trail some of us indulge when we don't have blades at our necks. You must be Jerania. I am Kyrianna and my selfish friend is Andrinor."

The girl turned and bowed her head slightly. "I must also apologize. With such short notice, we were only able to buy a few fresh things for breakfast. Bread, ham and eggs are all I have had time to prepare."

Kyrianna looked over the girl's shoulder at what was on the stove. "Don't worry…" She stopped as crumbs dropped past her.

"Andrinor." She pushed him back and brushed the crumbs from the girl.

Jerania turned around and looked up at Andrinor a stern frown on her face.

"Unless you are here to help, get out and wait in the dining hall." She turned to Kyrianna. "I would also ask the Lady to wait in the dining hall as well. Father has made it clear that we are to see to you and your friends."

Kyrianna nodded her head. "Very well."

Andrinor pushed the rest of the bread into his mouth and offered his arm to Kyrianna. She grinned and placed her hand on his arm as he escorted her out of the kitchen.

The floor of the dining hall was now bare as the couple was busy setting the table.

"Yes, that will do. Table cloth is optional this morning," Jhoro said as he ran into the dining hall and looked around before scampering back out again.

"Where did you find him?" Andrinor asked.

"I didn't," Kyrianna said. "He's Hendandra's friend."

"That he is," Hendandra said behind them. "And what is going on here?" They turned to see her gesturing to their arms.

"A little joke," Kyrianna said.

"I got us both thrown out of the kitchen," Andrinor said.

"Already," Jhoro said from the doorway. "I will have to congratulate the cook on her efficiency."

Andrinor grinned and glanced toward the mongoose. "I like him."

The sound of metal caught their attention and Kyrianna stepped out the room to see Myrith and Nirev coming down the stairs.

"Good you're back," Myrith said to Kyrianna. "Now, I won't have to have someone go looking for you." She paused and looked around the room. "Who is this and where are the others?"

"These are the servants Lord Duvall hired," Jhoro said. "If

you will excuse me, I have other things to see to. Breakfast should be ready shortly."

Myrith's hand went to Conflagration as the mongoose darted away. "Kyrianna, please stop gathering more pets, companions or whatever else you are calling them. If you want so many furry friends, go live in the forest or on that island of Hendandra's."

Andrinor laughed. "I believe he's Hendandra's friend, not Kyri's."

"What?"

"He showed up our first night here and seemed friendly enough. Next morning he spoke to me. He seems harmless and quite intelligent. I told Tristan he could look after the house affairs and the servants."

"The servants are Tristan's doing?"

Hendandra nodded.

"Where are the other two?"

"Andrinor handles his drink like a dwarf. The other two? Probably feel like they be needing to be called back from the realms of the dead," Nirev said as he headed into the dining hall. "However, Jhoro has things in hand. They be currently being bathed and clothed and be down shortly."

Kyrianna sat down and claimed a couple of slices of ham for herself as Nirev reached for the platter. "Myrith, I have decided Shadow Seeker will not be traveling with us. I believe the Abyss would prove too dangerous for him."

The wolf whined from under the table and Kyrianna dropped a slice of the ham on the floor.

"My Lady," the woman who had been cleaning the rug earlier said. "Please use a dish, instead of dropping things on the floor."

"Thank you," Hendandra said. "The foul stuff the dwarf bought here last night ruined the rug—there is no need to ruin the floor also."

"My apologies." Kyrianna set a small dish on the floor with another slice of ham on it.

"Father," Rourgen called from the doorway. "The other two are ready."

"Stop the blasted yelling," Jerietlan said.

"Maybe I should turn him into something quiet, like a mouse," Falden said.

Myrith turned and glared at the two standing in the hallway as the boy hurried away.

Kyrianna grinned as the others stood and moved to where they could watch. She leaned down toward Shadow Seeker. "When you see me raise my finger, howl as loudly as you can," she whispered to the wolf.

:*You are in a better mood than you have been in a while,* the wolf said in her mind. :*This will be fun.*

"I…" Myrith started, but was interrupted as Shadow Seeker began howling.

Kyrianna swallowed her laughter as Falden and Jerietlan covered their ears and winced. "Shadow, quiet," she said.

Myrith turned and glared in her direction and Kyrianna dropped her head to hide her smile.

"I…." Myrith was again interrupted by Shadow Seeker.

"Shadow, enough," Kyrianna said.

"I…." Once again the wolf began howling.

Myrith spun around. "That is enough, Kyri. Take him outside—now!"

Kyrianna nodded, picked up a couple more slices of ham and went out into the garden with the wolf. She left the doors open so she could listen.

"Congratulations," Andrinor said. "That was indeed impressive. Next time, you two can drink with Hendandra, if she isn't too much for you." His voice was booming and his laughter echoed almost as well as Shadow Seeker's howls had.

"That was…" Myrith paused again.

Kyrianna pulled the unicorn figurine from her pack and waited as Cewyr appeared in the garden. The slamming of the door caught her attention and she moved to the corner of the house and watched as Tristan rode out through the gate.

"I cannot believe you two would do something so stupid!" Myrith's voice came through the walls. "We will need to be able to rely on your skills with magic and you drink yourselves into a stupor."

Kyrianna smiled until she heard Myrith say something about slurred speech and swerving fireballs. That image was too painful for her to find any more humor in Falden or Jerietlan's actions. She had heard too many stories about arcane magic that had gone wrong destroying those wielding it and their allies from the Chaos Wars for her think any of this was funny any longer.

As she walked back to the garden she thought about the amount of magic she now carried: She had the Ring of Hellavar's Favor; another that would allow her to alter her appearance; her armor had protective magics woven into it; her weapons had magic woven into them as did the arrows she had purchased yesterday. She also wore a set of bracers that improved her skills with the bow. Then there was the figurine that called Cewyr. She had begun to accept magic, and could see the benefits to using it— however Myrith's words were a stern reminder of the dangers inherent in doing so.

Chapter Five

Kyrianna rode next to Myrith as they followed the carriage carrying the rest of the group to the Coliseum. Her short bow rested across her lap as she watched the shadows along their route. Myrith was quiet as they rode, but no longer sullen or angry.

Three stone horses stood in the center of the field and she felt her heart skip at seeing Tristan standing next to them, speaking with Gwideon. Shydaran was lying in a patch of sunlight near one of the walls.

Tristan's gaze didn't pause as he glanced at her then turned his attention to Myrith.

Myrith slid off Riker and Tristan handed her two wands. "The first one is specifically designed for repairing damage to the horses and the other contains healing magics," he said.

"Thank you. Please accept my apologies for my rudeness this morning. The responsibility I have been given weighs heavily on me and I let my anger at the actions of others be directed at you when I shouldn't have."

Tristan put his hand on her shoulder. "I understand. It never happened."

"Thank you."

"Before we leave, I need to find a druid to grow the vines of my armor," Hendandra said.

Myrith turned to look at the smaller woman. "You cannot grow them?"

Kyrianna heard the concern in the paladin's voice. :*Melissa, you do have the appropriate magic prepared in case it is needed?*

:*That and some healing magic as well.*

:*Thank you.*

"I have ways, but I don't wish to waste the magic now. We may need it later. I will only be a few minutes."

"Very well. Be quick, otherwise I'll send the tiger to fetch you," Myrith called as Hendandra vanished into one of the hallways.

Kyrianna watched until she saw the doorway go dark, then

tossed a small rock toward Shydaran and nodded in the direction Hendandra had vanished. She smiled as he stretched then followed after his wife.

~ * ~

Hendandra waited in the shadows several feet from the doorway. She smiled as the tiger approached. "Come into the shadows," she whispered.

Shydaran turned to look back at the others then trotted into the darkness.

"Change, I wish to speak to Feric, not Shydaran," Hendandra said.

She waited as his body convulsed then shifted from the huge tiger back into that of her husband. Once the change was complete, she placed her hands on his face and found his lips with hers.

She felt his arms wrap around her waist and she broke the kiss and moved her head so her cheek rested against his. "It seems every time we see each other I am apologizing for something."

"You do not need to," he whispered.

"Yes, I do." She paused and rubbed her cheek against his. "I should not have let you leave last night; at least not without giving you an answer."

She turned and brushed her lips against his, but only enough to gather his attention as she pulled away. "I have been too busy trying to figure out what all this means; instead of just feeling what is there." She leaned forward and let her lips brush his again then she spoke with her mouth still next to his. "I love you, Feric."

She felt his arms pull her forward and she didn't resist as she let his lips find hers. They stayed there for what felt like hours, but she knew was only seconds, as neither wanted to break the embrace. She felt the hunger of that night in the jungle, but it was different. Where previously it had made her blood boil, now it was like a cool breeze that made her tingle. Nothing else mattered in these moments, only him.

When they finally released the embrace, Hendandra smiled. "They will miss us soon." She never took her gaze from his eyes. "I need you to grow the vines."

He smiled. "Close your eyes."

She heard him whisper the spell, then felt him place his palms on her cheek and throat as his finger extended over her ears and touched the necklace. She could feel the vines grow and weave across her body. She had felt the sensation before but never had she let herself believe it was his strength that surrounded and protected her—not just the vines. As the vines finished their weaving, she moved forward and let the hunger have her for just a moment as they kissed again.

"I love you," she said as she withdrew. "We need to go. I want to be done with this journey as quickly as possible," she said. "I want to return to our home and the beach." She kissed him again. "Before they come looking."

He nodded and she watched him change back then trot back out onto the field. She didn't care if Myrith complained she had been gone too long. The only thing she truly cared about walked on four legs now. She knew this last embrace would have to hold her dreams until they returned.

~ * ~

Kyrianna nodded as Tristan glanced again at her and Cewyr. His gaze seemed to be focused on the unicorn and he closed his eyes and turned away without acknowledging her.

:*He doesn't know,* Cewyr said. :*He thinks you've made your choice.*

"Chaos!" Kyrianna smiled as the others turned to look at her. "We never thanked Tristan for last night," she said as she slid off Cewyr.

"I got drunk," Nirev said. "That be considered proper appreciation in Domar."

Falden glared at her.

"I was a captive," Jerietlan said with a smile.

"I was holding him captive," Andrinor said.

"Perhaps you should be the one to relay our thanks, Rangerette," Myrith said.

Kyrianna looked at Myrith and smiled. "Perhaps I should."

"Lord Duvall, a moment please," she called as she hurried to catch him.

He stopped and turned to face her. She saw his gaze go to Cewyr again. "There is no need for formalities," he said.

She offered him a half bow. "However, I must apologize for my friends who have not thanked you for your generosity."

"That is hardly necessary, Lady Kyrianna."

She felt her breath catch at the formal tone in his voice. She couldn't let them separate like this. He had to know. "It is not only necessary, it is also required," she said. Her hands went to his shoulders and slid around the back of his neck as she lifted herself up and pressed her lips to his. She could hear the others laughing behind her and was glad they had this moment before they left. She felt his arms wrap around her and she let the kiss linger far longer than she knew a *lady* should.

Her skin began to tingle and she felt heat rising in her body. She pulled away and saw the smile on his face, and also the apprehension in his eyes. She reached down and slipped her dagger from its sheath. She turned the weapon in her hand and presented it to him, hilt first.

Tristan looked at the rearing unicorn inlaid in silver and gold and his fingers touched the matching design on the inside of her right wrist. "The dagger originally carried another symbol," Kyrianna said. "It was changed when Frayrith's avatar touched it after she accepted my pledge. I give it to you now as my promise I will do everything I can to return."

Tristan took the dagger, nodded then looked over her shoulder, the look on his face was pleading. She didn't have to turn to know he was looking at Cewyr. "The magic that bound her to me, has also removed the need for me to be forced into making a choice," she whispered. "I am free to follow my heart in this." She placed her hand over his holding the dagger. "I intend to return to you Tristan Duvall."

"Kyri," Myrith called. "We need to be leaving."

Kyrianna nodded then leaned forward and pressed her lips to Tristan's. She gasped as a shock went through her and she pressed her body into his. Her mind became lost in thoughts of the pools with her and Tristan together.

"No!" Kyrianna spun around as she was pulled away from Tristan. Her fist slammed into Myrith's armor. "That. Was. Stupid," Kyrianna said through clenched teeth. She held her hand against her chest as she fought to keep from screaming.

"You have already made us miss two days; it will not be a third," Myrith said pushing her toward the group. "Jerietlan, make sure her hand is properly healed."

Kyrianna paused and looked back at Tristan.

"Go on, I will be waiting," he said.

"Tristan, I will endeavor to see your lady is able to return as soon as possible. However, we have delayed too long and need to be leaving."

"I understand." Tristan said with a nod. "Mykaylene's blessings go with all of you."

Kyrianna waited as Jerietlan placed his hands over her injured one and the warmth of his healing power flowed into her hand, mending the shattered bones. "Thank you," she whispered. "I only hope this is not a sign you will be using your gifts extensively on this journey."

Myrith turned back to face the group as Tristan moved to the side. "If that is everyone, we need to be leaving. Urric, you have discussed where we will be going with Falden, correct."

"I have," the skull said.

"What can we expect and what terrains will we be traveling?"

The skull's eye sockets glowed and pulsed in time with his words. "The layer of many portals is a vast gray waste with horrid forests and putrid swamps. I have directed the one who will take us to a relatively safe location. By this, I mean away from any major cities or strongholds. This location was chosen not because it was close to a portal but because of the nature of our travel. The spell should land us maybe a league or two or possibly as many as two hundred from our destination. You have angered a goddess of that plane; I do not wish to tempt fate and have us guided to a place of her choosing."

"That would probably be a bad idea," Falden said.

"Indeed it would. Travel through the Abyss with this group will be hazardous enough without interference from one such as Thynitic. The knight, cleric, dwarf, horse, unicorn and tiger all radiate auras that will draw too much attention in that environment. The ranger may be marked as well so agents of the Lady of Chaos can find her."

Kyrianna's head jerked up and she caught her breath as she remembered Drezmona's words. 'I understand she is having an amulet made for you.'

"The thief has a problem with another goddess, who has been known to have followers on that plane as well."

Hendandra glared at the skull.

"In truth none of that concerns me as much as the dragon warrior." Urric paused for several seconds as the others turned toward Andrinor. "His aura may prove to be a serious problem. Any native dragon kind may be able to sense his presence, similar to the demons being able to sense the knight. The mage has nothing, I believe, that will draw undo attention and the Gray will be treated impartially at worst and feared by most."

"What be making him so special?" Nirev asked.

"Unlike most here, he does not serve a god of light, but instead one of neutrality. He is a warrior in service to Resare, the God of Death and Undeath. While, Resare himself holds no power over demons, his high priests can animate and compel a demon's essence to service. The demons respect power. The fouler undead of the plane will see Gwideon as a force of their own destruction and will avoid direct confrontation for the most part. Now, that is not a guarantee as nothing is certain in the land we will be going to.

"There are several paths for us to take once there. The exact journey will be determined by where we land. If all goes well we will only visit five layers before the sixty-third. However, if we are unlucky we could be running from one layer to the next blindly."

"We will handle that when it comes," Andrinor said.

"Be advised, if we are unlucky enough to enter an area where the demon wars are raging on the field, we would be fools to stay. These battles involve thousands and we will find no true allies there.

"Have you made your peace with your gods?" Urric asked. "Because you may see them soon."

Kyrianna glanced at Tristan as a shudder went through her at Urric's words.

Chapter Six

Brular laid the book on the table and closed his eyes for a moment. Not even the information he had gained from the celestial library had mentioned any of what he had just read. Was this a trick on the part of the Lady of Chaos? It did seem possible. If it were true then there was a greater threat to them than her whims. He had learned about Carrinna, the first Daughter of Chaos, from his previous research. He had thought she was the daughter of Thynitic's avatar and one of the midnight elves of Rhysia. However, this showed her to be the daughter of both Neysinil and Thynitic's avatars.

What he found most troubling was that Carrinna was the one who had written the Book of Chaos, the book that became the cornerstone of Thynitic's worship. The book that had shaped her worship and consequently the Lady of Chaos into what she was now. As the daughter of Thynitic and Neysinil, she should have served the balance between the two; instead, she had followed the darkest paths of chaos. It had been her influence that eventually replaced the freedom Thynitic represented with pain and diminished passion in favor of retribution. She had been the one to write the litany Thynitic's followers now recited—even if it had taken them several centuries to make the change.

"Neysinil," he whispered the name. His essence had been trapped by Carrinna in an amulet of soul binding. One that been created to draw the god into it and hold him there until he eventually perished. "If he were to be released and restored, would he be able to bring Thynitic out of the madness she is trapped in?"

Brular followed the strict dictates of order, but understood the need for balance. Things were beginning to make sense to him now, but was it too late for any of it to be corrected?

He looked down at the floor and watched as Torliana continued her work on the amulet. Sentryl was fickle and tended to cool quicker than other metals. It would leave voids in the layering if not handled properly. Despite the system she had rigged to heat the metal as it flowed from the melting pot to the amulet it still appeared to be very difficult to maintain the smooth layering that was required. Torliana leaned close to the amulet as she turned it, allowing the metal to flow into the grove. She had done nothing to protect herself from the fumes of the sentryl and he could see her body shake as she fought to keep from coughing. He knew she was almost finished with this stage and wouldn't let anything cause her to have to start over.

Torliana set the amulet on the pedestal then stood and stretched before she sorted through a set of files and laid them out on the table. Brular knew she would only be doing a general smoothing of the sentryl once it cooled, as she would wait until after the final layer was completed to smooth everything so it was even and seamless.

"I see you found the book I left for you," Thynitic's voice said from the doorway.

He looked up as the goddess stepped into the room. He studied her face and movements as he compared what he thought he had known of her with what he had learned. The thing that surprised him was the dull black of her eyes. There was no fire or passion in this woman, like there had been in Torliana at one time.

"Where is he now?" he asked.

"Bound and dying. I have little time left to release him but I cannot undo what she has done any more than I change what is now a part of me." The goddess sat on the bed and looked at him. "I am no longer even sure which plots are mine and which are hers. I hear of things I am involved in but cannot remember."

"She is imprisoned," Brular said.

Thynitic laughed then shook her head. "She has gained too much power to remain trapped in that place, though she now calls it her home. A prison you can walk out of at any time is no longer a prison is it?"

"No, it is not."

"Come, Torliana has finished her task and there something I need to test before I allow her to spend time with you." She stood then turned and looked down at him. "You are not to tell her anything about the Book of the Four."

He raised his head. "I will not lie to her. However, I will not volunteer the information."

She nodded. "I understand. Come."

He followed Thynitic to her throne room and watched as one

of the chaos imps opened a door for Torliana into a large room, identical to the one he had been in.

~ * ~

Torliana hesitated before she stepped into the room. She had expected to see Brular as he had been, scarred from the many years he had endured in this place. Instead, he stood before her as the man she remembered from Mount Veri, unscarred and still strong. Thynitic had restored him to what he had been before she had cast him down into the Abyss.

The door closed behind her and sealed as she stepped into the room.

He did not speak and turned away from her.

"I do it for us." Her voice sounded tired and small in her ears.

He turned his back on her.

"She has taken your voice this time," she said. "She is taunting us at every turn." She frowned as he ignored her.

"We have only the few moments she will let us have. Moments I am earning from her with the vile task she has given me."

She clenched her fists tightly as he continued to ignore her. "I waited all these years and this is how you treat me after giving me hope." She didn't fight the tears that were now flowing.

He turned and looked at her, then smiled as he held his hands out and took hers.

"I make that vile thing to be here—the only thing that has any meaning for me now. I know you hate me for it. I hate myself for doing it. I am creating the same thing she has trapped you with, in order to trap another. I know it is wrong, but it is the only way I have left to stop what she has done to you."

He pulled her close to him and their lips met. She felt his warmth as his arms held her tight. Her breath caught in her chest as the emotions overwhelmed her. All these decades, since she had destroyed Mount Veri, she had felt nothing except hatred and anger; now it was as if those years had waited for just this moment.

She glanced at the bed and took a slow step toward it. He smiled and squeezed her hand as he took the next step and pulled her with him.

A chill went through Torliana. Something wasn't right. While

Brular acknowledged he had failed to see what she felt for him at the temple, he had never admitted he felt the same way about her. Though his actions told her he did when he forgave her. That he did not want her to risk breaching the contract by trying to fight the demons when they came spoke to his feelings more than any words could have. She hesitated at the insistence she felt in his grasp. She shook her head and stopped moving. He turned toward her then yanked her toward him.

This isn't Brular! He would never have tried to force her. She felt herself grow cold at the thought, and she knew she was right. This wasn't Brular. She relaxed slightly as he yanked on her arm again and let herself be pulled toward him. Her forehead slammed into his nose and he stepped back from her. She raised her foot and spun quickly catching him in the head again and sending him to the floor.

He stood quickly and she watched as his eyes darkened with rage. She ignored the pain from her manacles as she began her spell. With the final word of the incantation, ice and snow flowed from her hands to surround the creature posing as Brular. When the storm died, only a frozen husk lay on the floor. Her hands trembled as she reached down and touched the face.

At her touch, the magic faded and she nodded at the sight of the small horns on the creature's head. An incubus; one whose power had been tempered as it had not enthralled her with its kiss. *A test of some sort? Or just Thynitic playing one of her sick games?* She glanced up at the mirror and saw her reflection. She was tired, dirty and emotionally drained. "For what?" she asked her reflection. "For nothing!" Her fist slammed into the mirror shattering it.

~ * ~

"The weaving is complete," Thynitic said.

Brular stood at the bottom of the stairs and watched as Torliana leaned against the table and cried. Even though her enemy lay dead at her feet, she was the one who was defeated. There was something else here, something he was missing, just as he missed Torliana's feelings for him in the past. "She is stronger than you thought," he said. "She cast even through the pain." He turned to look up at the Lady of Chaos.

"Yes, she did." Thynitic smiled and nodded. "It is a strength she did not have before. A strength she now has because of you."

She saluted him with her glass of wine then sipped the blood red liquid. "You wish to see her?" she asked after a few moments.

"Yes," he said.

"Very well." She gestured toward the wall.

As he approached, Brular felt a tingle of magic in his arms and he stopped and looked down at the heavy manacles he wore. They were still there. He glanced back at Thynitic.

"You may cast a single spell, to prove to her you are indeed who you are. I suggest you think carefully about the magics you will call on as the wrong spell will bring harm to her."

He nodded and turned back to the wall as the portal to the room Torliana was in opened and he entered. Torliana looked up at him and he saw her eyes widen as she took a step back.

"Torliana," he spoke her name, but heard nothing in the silence of the room. Thynitic would not allow them to speak to each other. He stared at her eyes as she continued to watch him. Those windows into her soul told him she wanted it to be him, but she was scared to let anyone near her again. He nodded and moved to the two chairs. He slid one to face the other, took a seat and waited.

She looked at him and he saw the hesitation in her body, but she finally moved to take the other seat, a flicker of hope in her black eyes. He reached for her hands and he saw her tense, but she didn't pull away. He smiled as his fingers tapped a rhythm on her palms. She looked up at him and he watched the confusion on her face change to a smile as her own fingers copied the slow rhythm of the drums of the Feast of the Summer Flame. He concentrated on the small amount of magic Thynitic had given him access to and watched as Torliana's eyes widened and her face lit up at the appearance of the tiny firebirds in the room. In his mind he could see her again, for the brief moment she had been one with the flames during her testing. It was an image he wanted to see again, when she finally completed the test and became a Flame Dancer. In his heart, he knew it would happen, *if* they were ever able to escape this place.

The ceiling started to glow and Brular looked up as it rippled. The scene showed Kyrianna sitting on a unicorn. *Cewyr,* he thought. She swung herself from the unicorn's back and walked quickly to embrace a young man whose clothes marked him as a noble.

Brular felt Torliana tense as she looked up and he wished she could hear his words, even though they would do no good. He could feel the anger and hatred radiating from her. Anger that Kyrianna had escaped Thynitic and she could not. Hatred that Kyrianna appeared to have found happiness and she was trapped in this place. He understood the emotions all too well and knew how they would continue to poison her if she didn't let them go now, while she was still able to.

The image faded and Torliana looked once more at him as he shook his head. She did not respond. He slipped from his chair, knelt in front of her and reached up to wipe the tears from her eyes.

She looked up at the ceiling then back at the corpse of the incubus. Her eyes were hard when they returned to him. He pulled her to him and held her as he felt her body convulse with her sobs. When she raised her head again, her eyes seemed to stare through him as if she could no longer see him. Her eyes were sunken and hollow—the eyes of the damned. He had seen these eyes once before. For a moment, he was back at Mount Veri as those same eyes turned away from him and Lord Hellavar in that twilight hour so long ago. A night when his own eyes had been blind. She dropped her head and he reached out to cup her chin and brought her face up to look at him. He shook his head. "You are not alone," he said in the silence of the room.

"Not alone," he watched as she mouthed the words back at him and smiled. He continued to hold her as she drifted off to sleep.

Chapter Seven

Kyrianna frowned as the disorientation of the teleport faded and she looked around to see a swarm of small demons around her. "I don't think this is where we wanted to be!"

"They're called manen," Falden yelled. "Their blood is similar to acid. I suggest everyone get out of the area and use any weapons that can be used from distance to avoid injury."

"Good idea." Kyrianna flinched as Andrinor's blade cut through one of the demons and she felt the acid burn her arm. She kicked Cewyr who bolted away from the demons.

Falden nodded and raised his hands as Myrith and Gwideon finally joined the rest of the group. A shimmering light appeared over the demons then they fell to the ground screaming before they were still.

"While most demons can handle fire, cold and acid they are very susceptible to the disruptions certain sounds can create," Falden said.

"What sound," Andrinor asked. "I heard nothing."

"Of course you didn't. That spell was specifically targeted at the demons or you would be dead as well." Falden turned toward Gwideon and looked at the skull. "I doubt you meant for us to drop in the middle of a demon hoard."

"While we are within the area of where I directed you to bring us, I felt something interfering with the spell," Urric said. "It was no coincidence those creatures were waiting for us."

"How did they find us so quickly?" Jerietlan asked.

"That I do not know," Urric said, his eye sockets glowing. "But as I mentioned, some of you have angered deities who have specific reason to target you and may have marked you in some way so you can be tracked." The light in his eye sockets moved from Hendandra to Kyrianna.

:From what Hendandra told you, I doubt Rhyra has marked her. She made her attempt in Irrmar, it is doubtful she will risk Shyada's wrath again, Cewyr's voice whispered in her head. :You need to tell Myrith about the whip.

44

"Could it have just been that someone was watching for teleport magic?" Kyrianna asked. "We haven't exactly hidden the fact we were coming here."

"And those with an interest would also have a general idea of the best route as well, if as you say there are so few portals to the layer where her citadel is located." Myrith paused and looked around at the group. "We've spent too much time here, we need to get moving. Where do we go next?" she asked.

"There are two portals on this layer to our next destination. One is approximately seventy-five leagues from where we are; the other is approximately two hundred and fifty. The choice is yours."

"Let's get there as quickly as possible and get this over with," Andrinor said.

"I agree," Hendandra said.

She is watching us; I doubt the whip had anything to do with us being brought here, Kyrianna thought as she nodded her agreement.

"Gwideon, you, Hendandra and Kyri will take scout positions in front of the rest of us. I want to avoid any more surprises if possible," Myrith said.

"Then you had better return to your home," Urric's voice said. "You are on a layer of the Abyss. Home to many of those who tread the darkest paths—the bigger surprise will be if there are no surprises."

Kyrianna glanced out over the desolate landscape. There were no landmarks other than a line of high rocks in the distance. "How do we know which way to go?"

"There are magics that will give you an overview of the area—almost like a map," Urric said. "Perhaps you should use them—if you know them. Of course *you* could always ask Thynitic for help in reaching her citadel. I am sure the Lady of Chaos would provide it."

"Enough!" Myrith stepped in front of Gwideon and grabbed the skull. "I will not tolerate that tone or your harassment of any member of this group."

"I don't know the magics he speaks of," Kyrianna said. "But perhaps there is some merit in what he said."

"What?"

"She wants me. Perhaps we can use that to our advantage and get her to guide us to her citadel."

"No!" Myrith raised Conflagration. "Have you lost your mind? I will not let anyone, particularly you, try that."

Kyrianna nodded. "It was just an idea. As it is we still need a direction to follow and a way to make sure we are following the proper path."

"We will need to parallel the ridge until we reach a road," Urric said. "That road will lead us to one of the bridges that cross a large gorge. Once across, the path will lead us to the portal we currently seek."

~ * ~

"What is it?" Myrith reined Riker in as they approached Kyrianna who was watching something.

"I don't know, but it's big and it has been shadowing us for some time now." She pointed to a large creature moving in the shadow of a rocky outcropping.

"It is quite a distance away, perhaps it appears to be shadowing us but is only following a similar path at this time," Myrith said. "We still have a long way to travel ourselves and should be moving."

"No Lady Lake," Gwideon said. "Whatever it is, it is now moving toward us. We should wait and see what its intentions truly are." He slid off the tiger and drew his sword as he waited.

Myrith slid off Riker, drew Conflagration and watched as the shape grew closer. She drew a sharp breath when she saw what came toward them: a spider, one even larger than the one that had stood with Drezmona, approached. She glanced back at Kyrianna; the girl had gone pale at the sight and no doubt the memories it invoked.

"There is magic guiding it," Falden said. "It is seeking something."

"Or some*one*," Urric said.

An arrow flew past Myrith. "Hold!" She spun to face Kyrianna. "We don't know it's seeking us."

"If it wasn't, it is now," Falden said. He raised his hands and several bolts of arcane energy struck the spider.

Myrith swung Conflagration as one of the spider's legs stopped in front of her. Razors covered the leg and she stumbled back to avoid being sliced open. As she studied the creature, she saw it was made of some sort of stone. "What is this thing?"

"It is a construct. Similar to a golem—most magics will have little effect on it," Falden said.

"Hendandra?" The smaller woman had dropped to the ground and was somersaulting behind the creature. The tiger charged after her.

"Chaos!" Kyrianna yelled. A strident neigh followed the girl's curse.

Myrith glanced up to see the spider holding Kyrianna in one of its pinchers. "Or someone," she muttered.

Even as she blocked the razors on one leg, the ones on the other front leg were slicing into her armor. She felt herself growing cold as she stumbled back again. Andrinor stepped in front of her, pushing her back several more feet. The young man was also bloody and swaying on his feet.

"Chaos!" Myrith dodged the sword that fell next to her and looked up. "Kyri?" The girl was limp in the spider's pincher.

"It's trying to leave!" Andrinor shouted.

Myrith jerked her attention back to the spider and away from her friend. It was starting to back away from the group. *So, Kyrianna was its target and now that it has what it came for it thinks to escape. That is not going to happen.*

She called the flames to Conflagration and charged past Andrinor. She fueled the blade with her own power and saw the flames change to a brilliant white.

Her first swing of the blade sent pieces of rock flying. She swung again, more rocks. She could see where the chips had come from and she focused her strength and swung again. She could hear Nirev's voice chanting it the background and as her blade hit again, the sound of thunder echoed across the area and the spider shattered. She raised her shield to protect herself from the falling debris.

She crawled from the rumble and saw the dwarf standing several feet away, his hammer held high and a smile on his face. "The power of the storm crumbles rock and stone," he said.

Myrith nodded as she forced herself back to her feet. "Kyri?" she called. She looked around, everyone except her and Andrinor were standing outside the pile of rubble; there was no sign of Kyrianna.

A neigh caught her attention and she hurried to where Cewyr stood behind a large pile of rocks. The unicorn had her horn laid against one of the rocks. "She is still alive," Cewyr said.

"Andrinor, Nirev give me a hand," Myrith called grabbing one of the rocks.

It didn't take the three of them long to dig the girl out. Kyrianna was unconscious but still breathing as Nirev pulled her out. She focused her healing energy but was stopped from touching Kyrianna by the unicorn's horn.

"See to your own injuries, Myrith. I will see to hers," Cewyr said.

She nodded as she watched the unicorn's horn glow before she touched it to Kyrianna's chest. The girl coughed and drew a deep breath. "Chaos," she muttered.

"It would appear Urric was correct, Rangerette," Myrith said. "She has you marked in some manner. The question is how."

"Blood magic," Falden said.

"What?"

"Remember when Thynitic appeared while we were trapped in that place created by Torliana. She scratched Kyrianna's face and caught the blood in her hand. Blood calls to blood. She could be using that to track her."

"You know, you really need to learn to hang onto your weapons better," Hendandra said as she handed Kyrianna her sword.

"Thank you." She took the sword and sheathed it. "Falden is there any way to block her seeking?"

"There might be one way, but it is not practical in our circumstances." He paused for a moment then shook his head. "The only thing I can think of would be to surround you in an antimagic field. That would block all magical links and interfere with her seeking. But, it would also mean all of your enchanted items would lose their magic; not that you are carrying that much."

Kyrianna took a step back and Myrith watched her face go pale as she seemed to lose focus for a moment. "Kyri?"

"Still a little weak, I'll be fine." She shook her head. "I agree; that is not a practical solution in these circumstances."

Myrith nodded. "We still have a long way to go, let's get moving."

~ * ~

"How long?"

"About four hours," Kyrianna said. "I know Riker doesn't

tire, but Cewyr needs rest, and Andrinor probably does as well, but I doubt he will say anything."

Myrith glanced around at the others. Kyrianna was right. They needed a break. Between her healing abilities as well as the skills of Jerietlan and Nirev, they were recovered from the serious wounds they had suffered in preventing the spider from abducting Kyrianna, but they needed rest. She didn't want to call a full halt and have the shield keep opened yet, they still had too far to travel and time was critical.

"We need to take a short break," Myrith said. "Keep a sharp watch."

"There is a field of geysers a short distance away," Urric said. "There are no paths through it and the distance around would double our travel, I recommend we find a way across first then take a short rest."

The others only shrugged and Myrith looked at Kyrianna. "Any objections?"

"Not at this time." She patted the unicorn's neck.

~ * ~

Myrith stared at the area in front of them. "How are we supposed to get across this?"

"I can cast a spell that will allow each of us to float over the area," Falden said. "However, we don't know how large it is and it will be difficult to fight if we are attacked in the air."

"Couldn't you open a portal like the one that brought us here?" Hendandra asked.

"The problem with that type of magic is that I must know exactly where it is we are going. I could make a guess as to the distance, but that could land us in the middle of the field or trapped in a rock. And if Thynitic or her agents are still watching us, I don't want to think about the consequences of her interference."

"I can carry a couple of people at a time over in my dragon form."

"I believe Shydaran can carry Hendandra and I across without any problems," Gwideon said.

Myrith turned to see a golden shimmer surrounding the tiger and his riders.

"Kyri, I suggest you dismiss Cewyr for now, you can call her back once we're on the other side," Myrith said as Riker vanished.

"Andrinor, can you carry one of the stone horses and its rider in your claws and a rider on your back?"

"Yes."

"Good. Shydaran can take Gwideon and Hendandra. You can carry me and Falden on the first trip, Kyrianna and Jerietlan on the second and pick up Nirev on the last."

"I believe Shydaran can carry one additional person. Perhaps he can take Kyrianna with us and that will save Andrinor a trip," Hendandra said.

"The protections around you are already in place," Myrith said. "It might disrupt them to add another person at this point. We'll do it this way."

Andrinor nodded and Myrith stepped back as his body convulsed and he changed into a silver dragon.

"Let us hope there are no dragon kind in the area who want to investigate this," Urric said.

Andrinor hissed and exhaled a cloud of ice. "We will deal with that if necessary." He lowered his head. "In front of the wings please, Myrith. If you have a rope, you might want to loop it around me so you have a handhold."

Myrith used the dragon's leg to climb up. "I think I'll be okay," she said.

"Hang on."

Andrinor launched himself straight up and Myrith fell against his scales as she clung to his neck.

"My thanks," Myrith said when they reached the other side and she slid off Andrinor. The dragon only hissed with laughter as he leapt into the air and headed back.

She drew her sword and waited for the others to arrive.

"Myrith," Falden called. "Over here." He gestured to a small rock outcropping. "I can ward this area so we can take a short break before pressing on."

"Good. Kyri was concerned about Cewyr and doing the ferrying like this will be hard on Andrinor—even if he won't admit it."

"I will ask Jerietlan if there is restoration magic he can cast over the area that might aid us."

"Thank you." Myrith turned as Andrinor landed again, released Jerietlan and his horse and Kyrianna slid off his neck."

"The tiger is not far behind, I'll be back with Nirev shortly,"

Andrinor said.

Myrith waited until the dragon was again in the air. "How is he doing?"

"He is tiring, but he should be able to make this trip without too much difficulty," Kyrianna said. "Have you tried calling Riker?" She asked as she held up the unicorn figurine.

"Not yet." Myrith paused. "Riker." The ghostly horse appeared.

"Cewyr." The unicorn appeared next to Riker.

"Falden will be warding the area over there so we can rest." Myrith pointed to the rocks.

She waited as the rest of the group arrived. Andrinor staggered as he changed back and she placed a hand on his shoulder to guide him to the area.

"Restorative magics have been cast," Jerietlan said.

"We'll rest about an hour then head on," Myrith said. "Gwideon, Hendandra and I will keep the watch."

"Lady Knight, I suggest ye be one of those who takes yer rest at this time," Nirev said. "I saw the amount of blood ye lost to the spider. I will keep the watch with the Gray and the sharp-eyed thief."

"Very well."

~ * ~

:*Will you tell her about the whip?* Cewyr asked.

:*It's possible Falden's explanation or even bad luck is the reason why we ended up in the middle of those demons and the construct found us. There have been no other signs we are being tracked since that.*

:*You should still tell her,* Melissa said. :*She hates people keeping secrets—particularly ones that could affect everyone.*

"I know," Kyrianna muttered.

"Rangerette?"

"Huh?"

"Are you okay?" Myrith placed a hand over hers and frowned.

"Just listening to Cewyr."

"We need you here and paying attention to what's going on around us."

Kyrianna nodded. "My apologies," she muttered.

"Hold," Myrith said as she pointed to her right.

Kyrianna followed the gesture to see a rider coming toward them from a small encampment. He stopped several yards away and a second rider slid off the horse and approached the group. The other remained on the horse and held a short bow at the ready. Kyrianna readied her own bow watching for any movements on the bowman's part.

Kyrianna frowned as a chaos imp approached and offered her a deep bow before turning to Myrith. She turned her attention back to the person on the horse; that was where the threat would come from.

"We appreciate your offer of hospitality," she heard Myrith say. "However, tell your master we will be declining."

"I will deliver your message," the imp said offering Myrith a slight bow. The imp then turned to Kyrianna and bowed again before taking several steps back then turning and returning to the horse.

"Any idea what that was all about?" Myrith asked.

"None."

"Good enough, let's move on."

~ * ~

Myrith reined Riker in and stared at the chasm in front of them. A bone structure served as a bridge from one side to the other. In the center of the bridge was a group of cloaked and hooded figures. "Now what?" The idea of crossing the bridge was bad enough, the aura of darkness surrounding those in the center made it even worse.

"There are other bridges, but the next closest one is probably twenty leagues away," Urric said. "Then we would have to return to this spot to continue following the road."

"Forty leagues out of our way," Kyrianna said. "Another day or more of travel."

She placed a hand against Cewyr's neck. "She's heating again and needs a break."

"Let's figure out what these creatures are and we'll take a short break on the other side of the gorge."

A loud shriek cut the air and Myrith looked up to see Falden's hawk circling above them. The hawk swooped down and headed out over the bridge. "Falden call him back," she said.

One of the hooded figures raised his head and looked at the

hawk. Talon gave a strangled cry and fell into the chasm.

"Falden?" Myrith reined Riker around next to the mage's stone horse. "Falden?"

Falden ignored her and raised his hands as he stared at the figures on the bone bridge. The bridge shattered and the figures followed Talon into the blackness that filled the chasm.

Myrith placed a hand on Falden's knee as he turned to look at her. His green eyes where black with rage and she pulled back from him. He shook his head and snapped his fingers. A portal opened in front of him and he rode through it.

Myrith saw Falden appear on the other side of the gorge and she motioned for the others to hurry through. Everyone was looking tired. They had the fight with the demons when they arrived and then the fight with the spider. They had ridden for about four hours before the previous break and she estimated about three hours since that break. Another short break would be good and then a couple more hours on the road before she asked Jerietlan to set up the shield keep for the night.

The portal snapped shut behind her and she looked around for a suitable place for the group rest. This area was too open and too close to the chasm. They would have to continue a while longer. She knew the ones who were riding were getting tired. Sitting a horse properly wasn't as easy as it looked and even her own leg and back muscles were sore at this point. She couldn't read the tiger well enough to know how tired he was carrying both Gwideon and Hendandra, but he seemed to be okay. Andrinor was keeping up with the pace set by the tiger and Cewyr, but she had seen the slight stumble when he stepped through the portal. Kyrianna had already told her Cewyr was heating and needed a break and she had no reason to doubt the girl's assessment. There just wasn't any place here she was willing to let the group take a break.

"Jerietlan," she called. "Brular cast magics that removed Andrinor's exhaustion would those help Cewyr and Andrinor now? And can you cast them?"

Jerietlan looked at Andrinor and Cewyr. "I can, but simple healing energy may be enough in this case."

"I leave it to you. They need rest, but this is not the place and I want to get some more distance before we break for the night."

Jerietlan bowed his head and she watched as he first approached Cewyr. The cleric stood there for several minutes talking to Kyrianna before he laid a hand on the unicorn's neck. He bowed slightly then walked past Andrinor, placing a hand on his arm as he did.

"Thank you," Andrinor said.

Jerietlan turned and nodded.

"Kyrianna any idea how far we've traveled?"

"Cewyr has maintained a steady pace when we've been moving, so I would estimate about twenty-one leagues."

"Do you think we can handle a couple more hours?"

"Cewyr says she can and Andrinor should be fine now." She paused and glanced around at the others. "The problem is we have people who haven't done very much riding in their life. I have ridden more than you and I am feeling the strain. What about you?"

"My back and legs are sore."

"In the morning they will be even worse. The longer we ride today, the harder it will be to move tomorrow. It becomes a balancing act, Myrith. If you push too hard today, we will suffer for it tomorrow and make even less progress."

"How much longer could you ride today without serious risk to your riding tomorrow?"

"I am not a good meter for you to use. My family breeds horses and my father, in addition to being arms master for the guard, trains all of their riders. I have been riding most of my life. I could handle three to four more hours, and I suspect Gwideon would be fine as well—he has the look of one who rides a lot. However, I doubt you or the others could. You had starting training with Riker at the Coliseum, so would probably do better than the others, but you are probably safe using how you feel as a guide."

Myrith nodded.

"Just don't think they're as stubborn as you are," Kyrianna said grinning.

"You think I'm stubborn?"

"Yes, I do."

Myrith smiled. It felt good Kyrianna was joking with her. Their friendship had suffered because of what had happened in that vile place of Torliana's creation. She still thought of Kyrianna as her dearest friend, and hoped the girl felt the same way. The nagging suspicion there was some connection between the two of them came back and she shook her head to clear it.

"If I'm stubborn, it's only because I've found that is the only way to save you from whatever trouble your rashness has gotten you into," she said.

Kyrianna's eyes went wide and the color drained from her face. "What?" Myrith reached for her friend's arm, but the girl pulled away from her. "Rangerette, did you do something?"

Kyrianna shook her head. "No, I was just remembering the last time you had to save me from my rash actions. Do you think she has finished the amulet?"

"No! And she won't get the chance to do so." Myrith kicked Riker and he headed down the road, away from the chasm. "Let's get moving."

~ * ~

"This looks inviting," Kyrianna said looking at the high walls in front of the group.

"The road should follow a path through the Rock Palace," Urric said.

"Rock Palace?" Myrith stared up at the walls.

"It is the name of this area. The rocks create a warren of passages and caves. However, as I said the road should lead through it. If we stray off the road, we could end up wandering around in there forever."

"I will ask Frayrith about the magic he mentioned when I pray in the morning,"

Kyrianna said. "Being able to see the area like a map should help to prevent that from happening."

"Kyri!" Hendandra yelled. "Under you!"

Cewyr neighed shrilly as several clawed hands erupted from the ground, clawing at her legs.

Kyrianna drew her short sword and slashed at one that grabbed her leg and was pulling her from the unicorn's back.

"By the power of Resare, leave this place and return to the realms of the dead." Gwideon's voice echoed against the rocks and a bright light surrounded Kyrianna, Cewyr and the clawed hands.

Kyrianna felt herself grow cold for a moment then the light vanished and she turned to stare at Gwideon.

"You are one who has died and been brought back," Gwideon said. "I did not know this or I would not have called on that power without asking it to exempt you. Fortunately, there was someone protecting you; I cannot tell if it was Resare or one of your own patrons."

:*Melissa?* Kyrianna ignored the knight for a moment as she tried to sense the ghost's presence.

:*I'm fine. There was something in his command that protected me and that is what protected you. He knows this, but will not reveal my presence without our consent.*

"I understand," Kyrianna said. "Thank you." She slid off Cewyr, sheathed her sword and began examining the unicorn's injuries. All four legs had been slashed by the claws and there were several deep cuts on her belly. Kyrianna placed her hands on Cewyr and called on her healing gifts. The wounds closed enough to stop the bleeding, but they were still black and ugly. She turned to look at Gwideon.

"They were dread wraith claws. They had to be summoned and animated by someone who directed them to attack. The wounds will continue to fester and will eventually consume her flesh turning her into a wraith if they are not healed with sanctified magics."

"The great hall of the keep has been consecrated and sanctified," Jerietlan said. "Any healing magic cast there should heal her properly."

Kyrianna looked up and nodded. "Thank you." She turned her attention back to Cewyr.

:*Kyri, you need to get rid of the whip*, Cewyr's voice whispered in her mind. :*This was a specific attack on you.*

:*And it could be because she has access to my blood.*

:*Kyri, do you honestly believe that?*

:*We've had this discussion before*, Kyrianna sent her thoughts to the unicorn. :*I understand how you feel about it, but I am determined to give it back to Thynitic personally.* She paused as tears stung her eyes. :*Please help me.*

Kyrianna slapped at Cewyr's nose as the unicorn pulled her hair with her teeth. :*You're placing your friends in greater danger by carrying it, if that is what she is using to target you.*

:*At least tell Myrith about it, like Tristan said you should*, Melissa said.

:*She is not going to like it, but I will tell her.*

"Kyri, what are these?" Hendandra reached for a red gem on the ground near Cewyr's hoof.

Kyrianna grabbed Hendandra's hand then released it quickly at a low growl from Shydaran. "Those are called Frayrith's Tears. They are formed from the blood of a unicorn."

"Oh." Hendandra opened her hand to reveal three more of the gems. "Here, you should have these also."

"Thank you."

"Come on you two," Myrith called.

Kyrianna picked up the last of the gems then turned and headed into the keep with Cewyr.

Chapter Eight

Jerietlan stood in the middle of the great hall as the others came in. "First things first; Myrith, Kyrianna and Andrinor; you three get out of your armor and give it to Nirev. There are magics in the smithy so it can be repaired by morning. I suggest the ladies get first shot at the showers as both Kyrianna and Myrith are covered with blood. As soon as they are done, Andrinor, you need to get in there and get the blood off your body as well.

"Nirev, leave the stone horses in the stable area. Cewyr, Riker and Shydaran can move about as they please. I suggest Cewyr remain here in the great hall tonight. I will tend to her injuries while you are bathing, Kyri."

"Thank you." Kyrianna turned to Myrith. "A shower is a good idea. Nirev, our armor will be outside the bathing room, you can pick it up there."

~ * ~

"Myrith, can we talk privately?" Kyrianna wrapped a towel around her hair. They had both left their under tunics and pants to soak in one of the basins and were wearing long tunics. She picked up her swords and belted them on as Myrith did the same with Conflagration.

Myrith nodded as they headed out of the showers and down the hallway.

"Good, you two are finally finished," Andrinor said. "Hendandra is already finished with her dinner and asleep."

"She didn't have her hair tangled with her own blood," Kyrianna said.

"Point taken. There is still quite a bit of food left. However, the tiger hasn't been in there yet, so you might want to hurry." He bowed slightly then entered the shower room.

Kyrianna opened the door to the scribe's room and stepped inside. She waited for Myrith to follow her then shut the door.

"What's wrong?" Myrith asked.

"This." Kyrianna opened her pack and pulled the whip out.

"Kyri?"

"This was my mother's when she served Thynitic. I told you about what happen when Torliana held me." Myrith nodded.

"Thynitic told my mother if she returned to her, she would see I was released. It was a lie. A lie told so she would travel into Kilenter without the sword Frayrith had blessed. She was carrying this when she was attacked. My brother found it when they tracked the group that killed her. I brought it with me in order to return it to Thynitic personally."

"Kyri, if you are doing this because of a need for revenge or retribution, I cannot allow you to do that. You saw what traveling that path did to Brular. You have held Thynitic's power; do not let yourself be drawn back into her grasp."

Kyrianna nodded. "Yes, there is a part of me that wants to hurt her for what she did. However, this is more symbolic. I don't intend to use the whip, only return it. I want her to know she has lost all hold on me."

Myrith looked down at the whip then back up at Kyrianna. "I still don't understand what's wrong."

"Cewyr thinks Thynitic is using the whip to track me. I don't want to be rid of it because I do intend to return it to her. But, *if* Thynitic is able to track it, is it safer leaving it here in the keep or carrying it? Perhaps Falden can shield it somehow."

"Kyri, I doubt it matters whether you're carrying the whip or not. You've been touched by Thynitic's power; she can probably track you because of that. I can sense nothing unusual about the whip."

Kyrianna stared her for a second. "It should be radiating—" Her head jerked up as a loud crash came from the direction of the dining hall.

Myrith reached for the door. "Now what?" She paused and turned back to face Kyrianna. "The keep is supposed to be secure, if it makes you feel better—leave it in the storeroom or secure it in one of the chests." She opened the door. "I had better see what that noise was."

Kyrianna grinned as she heard Myrith starting to yell at Shydaran in the dining hall. She entered the great hall and headed for the far corner where the entrance to the storeroom was. She looked at Cewyr dozing with her head down. The injuries she had taken to her legs had been healed, but they had left several scars.

Riker stood near the unicorn and bobbed his head in greeting.

"Thank you for watching over her," Kyrianna said offering the spirit horse a bow. Riker nodded his head in return.

Her hand hesitated as she reached for the wall. If the whip wasn't radiating then what was the point of leaving it? They had no idea when they would reach Thynitic's citadel, after all the goddess had interfered in their travel once. She could bring them to her at any time. If she wanted to be able to return the whip, she would need to have it on her.

She put the whip back into her pack.

"Did you talk to Myrith?" Cewyr asked, interrupting her thoughts.

Kyrianna set the pack on the floor and placed her hand on Cewyr's neck. "I did. She said she didn't sense anything from it and left the choice to me. But, I'm worried—Tristan told me the whip radiated with a vile aura. Myrith should have been able to sense it."

:*Remember Ash?* Melissa's voice said. :*When he first met the group, he shielded his aura—Myrith never detected the darkness there until he dropped the shield.*

"Kyri, shouldn't you put that vile thing away instead of carrying it?" Cewyr pulled away slightly.

"I put it in my pack." Kyrianna glanced down to see the whip hanging from the hilt of the unicorn horn sword. She pulled it from the weapon and dropped it on the floor and kicked it away from her. "How..."

"Kyrianna?"

She glanced up to see Myrith standing in the doorway. "You started to say something when we were interrupted by the noise from the dining hall."

"Tristan told me the whip radiated a vile aura similar to Gwideon's sword."

Myrith frowned and glanced at the whip hanging from Kyrianna's sword. "I sense nothing," she said. "However, in that case, I believe you should put it in the storeroom until Falden can examine it."

Kyrianna nodded and turned to retrieve the whip. Her hand brushed against it and she jerked the sword from the sheath dropping the whip.

"Kyri?"

"I just dropped that thing on the floor. How did it get back on my person?"

"Falden is in seclusion—but I'm going to go get him," Myrith said. "Secure that thing in the storeroom."

Kyrianna nodded, picked up the whip and reached for the area of the wall that would open the storeroom. She hung the whip on a hook on the wall and turned to leave.

"You shouldn't have decided to leave me behind," a voice said behind her.

Kyrianna turned as she readied her swords. "Chaos," she whispered when she saw the chaos demon standing there holding the whip.

"Myrith!" Her voice was only a harsh whisper in her ears.

The demon took a step forward and Kyrianna raised her swords. "I find it amusing you think you can fight me," the demon said. "However, I cannot stay. Therefore, I will bring you someone to test your skill." He raised his hand and Kyrianna watched him vanish to be replaced by a demon with a snake-like torso and tail, and six arms—each one holding a scimitar.

Kyrianna took another step back and stumbled over her pack. As she struggled to maintain her balance, she felt the sharp blades slicing into her arms and chest. Her left arm went numb and she heard her blade hit the floor. She turned to run and felt the demon's blades hit her back. She was trembling as she exited the storeroom and saw Cewyr standing there. Only it wasn't Cewyr. The unicorn in front of her had wings and its horn gleamed bright silver.

The winged unicorn reared and neighed then lunged forward slashing at the demon with her horn. Kyrianna turned and had her other sword slapped out of her hand by the demon's tail. The tail wrapped tightly around her and she fought to keep breathing.

"Kyri!"

Kyrianna heard Myrith's voice echo in the room before she lost consciousness.

~ * ~

Conflagration was in Myrith's hand and she charged toward the demon holding Kyrianna. A roar stopped her and she turned to see Shydaran charging through the doorway. The tiger leaped onto the demon placing himself so his body blocked Kyrianna from additional attacks. He turned and looked at Falden who raised his hands and unleashed bolt after bolt of arcane energy at the demon. The air of the room was charged with the power Falden was unleashing.

Shydaran continued to claw and tear at the demon, without any concern for the arcane energy dancing around him. However, it seemed whenever a bolt of energy came close to Kyrianna, he would shift and prevent the unconscious girl from being struck.

With the energy Falden was throwing at the demon and Shydaran clawing at it Myrith could see no way to safely attack the creature without risking harm to Shydaran or Kyrianna. She moved to the side and stood at the ready. A quick glance showed her Gwideon had mirrored her position on the other side of the demon.

There was a pause in Falden's arcane bolts and Myrith saw Shydaran lunge at the demon's throat. The tiger's teeth connected and the demon dropped to the floor. She dropped Conflagration and rushed to Kyrianna, only to have the winged unicorn step between them.

"I will tend to her," she said.

Myrith nodded. She had heard both Cewyr and Riker's voices in the voice of the unicorn when it spoke.

The sound of Jerietlan chanting caught her attention. "Move away from the demon," she said. She ignored the unicorn and grabbed Kyrianna. Shydaran leapt off the demon as flames flowed from the ceiling to destroy the body.

Myrith carefully placed Kyrianna on the floor and nodded as the unicorn lay next to her, one wing draped protectively over the girl. She looked at the group in the great hall, everyone was there except Andrinor. *Probably still in the shower*, she thought. She stepped into the open storeroom and picked up the whip. Now, she could sense the darkness that infused the weapon. Why hadn't she been able to sense it before? It was very similar to the aura that surrounded Drinker, but there was something else there. She paused as she glanced at Gwideon. Yes, she could sense the magic on Drinker and it was similar to what was on the whip. Had it been the whip she had originally sensed when Kyrianna had returned to the Coliseum? She had assumed she was only sensing Drinker's enchantment because Gwideon was standing behind Kyrianna at the time. That assumption had allowed Kyrianna to bring this vile thing with her and had almost cost her friend her life as a result. She would not make that mistake again.

She walked out of the storeroom. "How is she?"

The winged unicorn looked up at her. "She is healed of her injuries, but she is still unconscious."

The unicorn stood up and moved away from Kyrianna a few feet. Myrith watched in awe as Riker seemed to float out of the unicorn's body and they were both surrounded by a golden light. When it faded, both Riker and Cewyr were standing there. The unicorn returned to stand protectively over Kyrianna and Riker came to stand next to her.

"We will need to talk later," Myrith whispered to Riker, who only bobbed his head in response. She tossed the whip at Falden. "Destroy it!"

Falden caught the whip, looked at it then back up at her. "Why?"

"I believe there is some connection between it and that demon. Destroy it now!"

Falden nodded and summoned a small fireball to consume the whip.

"What are you doing?" Kyrianna's voice was a harsh whisper.

"I ordered it," Myrith said. "That thing hid its nature from my senses and when you tried to leave it in the storeroom a demon appeared that tried to kill you. It probably would have succeeded if Falden and I hadn't arrived when we did." Myrith started for the hallway. "Get some rest; we have a long day tomorrow."

"No!" Falden yelled. "I demand an explanation for what happened here, and I will have it before anyone leaves this area." He turned to look down at Kyrianna then back up at Myrith. "We walk lands of hellscapes and demons and then when we seek to rest something enters that could only have been drawn here from within."

Kyrianna forced herself into a sitting position and pulled her knees to her chest. Myrith shook her head as the girl dropped her head without saying anything. Kyrianna was the only person who knew what had happened to bring the demon here. She took a step toward the girl, but stopped when Cewyr moved behind Kyrianna and lowered her head protectively. There was no fear to be seen in the unicorn's eyes, only caution.

"Falden!" Myrith reached for Conflagration as a bolt of arcane energy streaked across the room to strike the archway where Hendandra and Shydaran were standing.

"Stay where you are," Falden said. "You leave once I am satisfied, not before."

Myrith nodded as Riker moved to stand between her and Falden. The mage was letting his emotions control him and was becoming very dangerous as a result. Jerietlan stood next to her, leaving Kyrianna alone with Cewyr as Nirev was now standing with Gwideon.

"Beware," Gwideon said looking from Falden to Kyrianna and back. "Anger and fear can lead down many dark paths."

Falden laughed. "Do you think you scare me? You are a puppet of your god." He waved his hand at the rest of the group. "All of you—nothing more than puppets." He looked up at the knight of Resare. "Why should I fear you?"

Gwideon took a step forward. "If one of us attacks the other, then one of us may die. I have faced far worse opponents than you Falden and have survived. However, if you do kill me what will you say to Resare when you stand before him on your way to Rhyra?"

Myrith saw Falden blink slowly, but he continued to face Gwideon, without any other betrayal of fear in his stance.

"Those who slay his willing servants are doomed to become one of his unwilling servants in return." Gwideon didn't move as he watched Falden.

Falden took a small step back and turned toward Myrith. "I have not heard an explanation yet. I am tired of the rash actions of others who do not think about the consequences of their decisions. This thing had to be summoned. What summoned it?" His voice rose and reverberated off the walls of the hall.

Kyrianna forced herself to her feet and faced Falden. "Leave the rest alone. They know nothing about this," she said. "Your anger should be directed at me. It was summoned in by a chaos demon. One that, I believe, was following the orders of Thynitic when it somehow managed to inhabit the whip you destroyed." Her voice broke and she dropped her head slightly. "A whip that once belonged to my mother when she served Thynitic," she whispered.

Kyrianna raised her head back up and Myrith frowned at the anger Falden was directing at her friend.

"I didn't know he was there. Tristan told me he sensed a slight aura of darkness around it, but told me it was the same type of magic that is on Gwideon's sword. After some of the events of today, I began to suspect Thynitic was using the whip to track us and spoke to Myrith just prior to bringing it here. She didn't sense anything wrong with the whip and wasn't concerned when I said she should have."

Kyrianna took a deep breath. "At Myrith's direction, I was leaving the whip in the storeroom until you could examine it further. That is when the chaos demon appeared. He said I shouldn't have decided to leave him behind. Then he vanished and the other demon appeared."

Myrith saw the tears and the haunted look on Kyrianna's face.

"I'm sorry." Kyrianna's voice was only a harsh whisper.

"You are a fool!" Falden took a step toward Kyrianna but stopped as Cewyr lowered her horn. "You should never have brought it in the first place. You have said you come from a place where arcane magic is hated and not used, so you have no knowledge of it. You were warned, that something was wrong. Yet you decided to ignore that warning and bring this vile item with you. Why? What possible value does it have to justify such folly?" Falden looked around at the rest of the group. "You are all so naïve! Do you not understand the powers that surround us? We are all nothing more than pawns in a play we didn't write."

His arm shook as he pointed toward Cewyr. "You and your precious unicorn." He turned and pointed at Riker. "You and that silly pony you hold so dear. Think you are any match for me? Today you all cowered at the sight of creatures in rags. It was only I and my companion who showed the courage to face the unknown. Talon gave his life for you and you walked on as if nothing was lost. Yet, I lost everything." Falden's voice broke and he dropped his arm.

Kyrianna nodded. "And I grieve for his loss."

Myrith frowned when the girl took a deep breath and then took a step toward Falden.

"However, it was also unnecessary. We had only paused for a moment to evaluate the situation, Falden. We were not cowering. Myrith asked you to call him back before he was struck yet, he still flew toward the creatures on the bridge."

"Kyri…" Myrith's voice was harsh.

"No. He wants to complain about rash actions, then he must also acknowledge his own. Yes, I know I have acted rashly but there are others here who have also done so. We all must take responsibility for our own actions. I have stated I brought the whip—yes it was rash. It was also motivated by pain and the loss of someone I also held dear—my mother. She was taken from me by Thynitic and while I was being held by Torliana, I was forced to watch what happened to her."

"I have stated that I approached Myrith regarding the whip—she sensed nothing. Because of my concerns, she went to ask you to come and examine the whip. Unfortunately, the demon inhabiting the whip had other ideas and choose that moment to reveal himself and summon the other one in." She took another step toward Falden and held out her hand. "I share your grief, may it soon pass as we remember the happy moments we had with the one who is gone."

Jerietlan walked over and placed his hand on Falden's shoulder. "He will be missed. I truly wish there was something I could do, but I would need at least a piece of his body."

Falden nodded.

Myrith took a slow breath as the mage seemed to relax. Perhaps they were through the worst of his outburst. The Gatekeeper's words came back to her: 'See you learn to curb your own rashness even as you condemn it in others.'

"Jerietlan's correct," Hendandra said. "He will be missed. Remember when we all raced to free him at the estate and Laraf was attacked by that giant spider?"

Myrith saw the briefest smile on Kyrianna's face then she went pale. *Why did she have to mention the damn spider?*

"What's going on?" Andrinor asked as he stepped into the room.

Nirev slapped the handle of his hammer. "The blasted elf brought an item possessed by a chaos demon into the keep and when she tried to leave it in the storeroom it got upset and summoned another demon in to kill her for her stupidity. Right now, the mage be trying to decide if he be going to do the same."

"Nirev!" Myrith turned toward the dwarf.

"He's right," Kyrianna said.

Myrith turned back toward her friend. "Kyri?" She started to step around Riker.

"The responsibility of bringing that thing here and the events that have transpired is mine as is all the pain you have suffered from Thynitic and Torliana. I accept that and I will have to live with memories of it for the rest of my life. Memories and images…." She looked at Falden then Andrinor and shuddered. "Memories and images I still see when I close my eyes at night."

"I know your heart is heavy Kyri," Myrith said glancing from Kyrianna to Falden. "However, we cannot let ourselves be troubled by the past. Powers far beyond you and I have dictated our course so far. As Falden said we are trapped in a play we did not write. However, I believe it is possible for us to write the next act, but only if we do it together" She gestured to everyone in the room.

Gwideon walked over and glanced down at the pile of ash that had once been the whip. "How long were you in possession of the whip?"

"Three days. Why?"

"Three days. You said he was a chaos demon: one with the power to summon another demon into a place that should have been shielded against such things. He could have taken you to Thynitic at any time if that was his intention. I suspect he was working to exert control over you with the intention of possessing you."

Myrith grabbed for Kyrianna as she took a step back and stumbled. Cewyr pressed against the girl holding her up. Myrith could see the inner strength she had called on to face Falden was gone and Gwideon's pronouncement about possession had hit her hard.

"Easy Kyri," Myrith said. "He obviously didn't succeed or he wouldn't have needed to summon in the other demon." She turned around to face the rest of the group. "In order to prevent other things from entering in, we will not be looting anything that is not absolutely necessary. I can't control the items each of you already has, but you will not be picking up anything else."

"What!" Hendandra yelled. She stepped out from behind the tiger, her hands on her hips as she glared at Myrith. "That is unfair. How are we to replenish our supplies? What of the treasure and equipment we leave in the hands of our enemies to be used again?"

"And here we are, yet again," Falden said. "What do you understand about the supernatural and the arcane? Nothing! You are like a child in many ways, Myrith. You think in absolutes. Nothing is absolute." He nodded toward Gwideon. "Not even death."

Falden gestured at the burned area on the floor as well as the small pile of ash. "A simple anti-magic field will expose any creature trying to possess one of us or something we are carrying. I suggest all be subjected to it," Falden said.

Myrith nodded. "So be it. I will rescind the order on looting as long as it is checked and then only as we have time to claim such treasure. We still need to move fast—we will not be going out of our way to grab anything."

Gwideon nodded and she saw his gaze go to Kyrianna and the silver sword she carried. Kyrianna's grip tightened on the sword and she slipped behind Cewyr.

"Falden cast your magic." Myrith said.

"Myrith, wait!" Kyrianna's voice was a harsh whisper as she stepped around Cewyr, the silver sword in her hand.

Myrith turned to see Kyrianna was paler than she had ever seen her before and her eyes were wide and ringed white as she shook her head.

"Your sword?" Gwideon held out his hand.

Kyrianna trembled as she pulled the sword to her chest.

"Do you think the chaos demon has not revealed that secret to the Lady of Chaos? How safe you do think she is hidden from those she travels with? She has nothing to fear from them." He took a step toward Kyrianna. "And if you don't, I will draw her out myself."

Kyrianna turned toward Myrith.

The older woman felt her frustration with the night's events building. First, the demon that shouldn't have been able to get into the keep; then Falden's tirade. Now, when they might have a way to know if any other threats were among them; Kyrianna had told her to wait. Now this with Kyrianna and Gwideon.

"She cannot manifest here, she is not that strong. She is only a child, Myrith. I beg you not to force this on her."

"Child, manifest? What are you talking about?"

"Do you remember the body of the girl we found in the hedge maze of the Duval Estate? Her name is Melissa and she has been with me since we left that place, though I did not know it until those last days with Torliana. She is only a child and should not be put through this kind of trauma. She only did this because she had been alone for so long and she could sense my own loneliness as well. She had no one left she could call her family and neither did I at the time. Myrith, I beg you not to force her to go through this."

Myrith nodded. She did remember the child. She also remembered how Nyssa's spirit had merged with Kyrianna's body after they told her about her daughter's death and Kyrianna had carried that spirit to the chapel so mother and daughter could be reunited. That same child had been the one to thank Kyrianna before they left the estate.

"You're sure it is Melissa and not something else that is seeking to deceive you?"

"I am; as is Tristan."

"Very well. I need only your word. The sword is exempt."

"Thank you," Kyrianna said.

Gwideon shook his head. "The spirit herself should state her case." He turned toward the rest of the group. "Maybe she should speak to those with whom she travels. That way no questions or suspicions can remain."

"I agree with Kyrianna," Hendandra said. "Melissa was only a child when she was killed. She should not be subjected to this. Let her be."

"She cannot manifest here," Kyrianna said.

"Jerietlan," Gwideon called. "There is a spell that will allow you to draw a spirit from the ether. Do you know it?"

The cleric seemed to ignore the question.

"Jerietlan!" Myrith said.

"What?"

"The spell to draw a spirit from the ether to our plane?" Gwideon asked.

"Yes, I know it."

Gwideon nodded then turned back to Kyrianna. "The magic is available, so she can manifest. Will she do so?"

Kyrianna smiled and nodded. "She says she would like that." She held the sword out.

Jerietlan chanted for several seconds then gestured toward the sword. The figure of a young girl appeared in front of the weapon. The dress she was wearing had a tear over her heart and the front of the dress was stained dark.

"I am Melissa Duvall, daughter of Nyssa and Rhinehart," she said as she curtsied. "Sister to Larissa, Christian and...," her voice trailed off. "And Mikyl," she finally said. "I thank you again for freeing us from that horrible existence. I have been a witness to your strength and courage these days and I am honored to travel with you."

She looked at Hendandra and smiled. "It was I who guided Kyrianna's hands across the keys last night. I hope we can play together another day."

She curtsied again to Myrith. "My father would have been proud to know you Myrith, Sword of Mykaylene."

Myrith knelt before the girl. "It is I would have been honored to have known him, just as it is an honor to know you," she said. She glanced up at Kyrianna and was surprised to see her friend's hand resting on the ghost's shoulder and there actually appeared to be contact between them.

Riker moved past her to lower his head to Melissa's face. She wrapped her arms around him. "I have missed you too," she said.

"You were not able to sense the chaos demon either?" Jerietlan asked.

"I could not. He hid very well."

"Then how did Tristan know?" Myrith asked as she stood back up.

"You said he sensed a power, but it was weak," Gwideon said.

Kyrianna nodded. "Yes. But if he sensed anything—why not the demon?"

Gwideon smiled. "Thank your goddesses for the thing's stupidity." He turned to Myrith. "You sensed a weak power before you ordered it destroyed?

"I did, but it also had the sense of something powerful having touched it. Why?"

Gwideon gave a short laugh. "The thing made a mistake. It possessed an item with an evil aura. It needed to suppress that aura to insure the item didn't radiate at all to Myrith or Tristan's senses. It was luck." He stared at Kyrianna. "Tristan found the whip in your room and not on your person, I suspect."

"I wasn't about to hide that thing under my skirts," Kyrianna said. "However, he told me he originally sensed it when I visited him after returning from Rhysia. Then, after the party when it wasn't with my gear he looked for it. Both times he was able to sense it."

Gwideon nodded. "Keeping a separate aura shielded is not an easy task at all. The demon must have thought it need not shield itself as you had done its job for it. If the enchantment was like Drinker's it is only noticeable within a few feet or closer if under direct scrutiny."

"Then that is what I sensed when you arrived at the Coliseum, Kyri," Myrith said.

"What?"

"Lady Lake?"

"When you arrived I automatically checked your aura and sensed something that felt very similar to what I sensed on Drinker. As Gwideon was standing a few feet behind you, I assumed I was sensing Drinker and dismissed it. Something, I apparently shouldn't have done."

"Myrith, I never left the group standing around you at the Coliseum," Gwideon said.

"But I saw you there."

"The demon was caught by surprise by Lord Duvall, but he must have sensed you before he had time to shield the aura and therefore created an illusion you would accept."

"Perhaps he was smarter than you originally gave him credit for," Andrinor said.

"Not unlike the way many people see you," Gwideon said. "I am done; Falden may cast his spell whenever you are ready."

"Melissa." Kyrianna touched the sword to the girl's shoulder and she faded back into it. "Falden wait a few moments, please. Myrith I need to speak to you before you do this."

"I already said the sword was exempt and you have shown us the spirit it houses."

"Myrith, you cannot subject Shydaran to an anti-magic field." Her voice was low and Myrith had to lean close to hear her.

"Why not?"

"You are correct, he is something other than what he seems to be. He is a druid of Shyada. However, he has been instructed by her to not reveal himself to anyone. Because of my knowledge of nature, I was able to discern certain things about him that I confronted him with during our talk at the Coliseum." She paused and Myrith followed her gaze to the tiger who was watching them as his claws dug into the floor. His growling had increased and he seemed ready to pounce.

"Shyada required him to not tell anyone about his true nature and I considered myself bound by that as well. However, I do not want to see him forced into betraying his oath to her or us being forced to fight him over this. I suspect I will have to answer to Shyada for telling you this, but I had to say something."

"If the blasted beast could take direction, I could have him dig new tunnels for the dwarves of Domar," Nirev said slapping the handle of his hammer with his hand.

Andrinor held out the pommel of his sword and two blades appeared. "Keep out of its reach Nirev or Jerietlan will be bandaging you all night."

"Very well. I will trust your judgment in this," Myrith said placing a hand on Kyrianna's shoulder. She looked back up at the tiger. "I would not have you break your oath to your goddess. It is obvious you intended to take that secret to the grave as well as few of us if necessary. You fought bravely this day and took more wounds than any except Kyrianna against that demon. You held the demon and protected my friend from its blades, and for that I am grateful. However, that you would then turn around and threaten those you journey with when all we do is seek to understand what is happening creates suspicion and distrust. Your actions lead to nothing but more questions of your motives."

"Talon?" Falden's voice interrupted Myrith.

"Now what?" She saw Jerietlan holding the body of the hawk in his hands. "Explain this."

Falden took Talon from the cleric. "And what happened to your face?"

"She left a mark then?"

"Stop mumbling and explain," Falden said.

"Shyada. I tried to call a true image of what the tiger is and she appeared before me. She clawed my face with the lightest possible touch, but it still sliced deeply. I think she did it to demonstrate her displeasure and to show what she is capable of."

"But why?" Myrith glanced at Shydaran. This was no coincidence. They were considering putting the tiger into an anti-magic field, which would have shown him for what he was. Jerietlan was casting magic to see the truth of the tiger, then Shyada appeared and stopped him. She didn't like what was happening here. This place—supposedly a safe refuge—had too many strange things happening within its walls.

"She told me Shydaran was one of hers and she sent him here to learn from us. However, she did not say what it was he was to learn." He paused for a moment. "She also warned me that we are not to try and penetrate his disguise lest he devour us."

"What?" Myrith stared at Jerietlan. "You said he was holy. How could Shyada allow that?"

"She is the goddess of predators," Kyrianna said. "There is no evil in the killing to eat. We do it all the time. Tigers and other large predators occasionally feed on those who walk on two legs. She has extended that to him." Kyrianna shuddered. "He can treat us like food, if he must. In nature that is not evil; it is life."

"The scar is a reminder," Jerietlan said, "to remember her words." He turned toward Falden. "We knew he was dead."

Falden looked up then handed Talon back to the cleric. "Look at his belly."

All of the feathers had been plucked and there were runes drawn on his flesh in blood.

"What are they?" Myrith asked

"I was hoping one of you could answer that. They are not arcane," Falden said.

Jerietlan studied the symbols. "Linked life. Linked…"

"…Forever," Gwideon said.

Kyrianna looked down at the bird then up at Jerietlan. "What did Shyada say about Talon, if anything?"

"She said it was more important to protect your friends in death than in life." He looked at the symbols again. "I understand what they mean, but not their use."

"They are used to re-establish a link with the whole of a being. In this case someone was preparing your familiar's body so it could re-link with you, Falden," Gwideon said.

Myrith frowned at the coldness in Gwideon's voice. No emotion, no acknowledgement of the pain Falden had already expressed and was feeling again.

Falden took the hawk back from Jerietlan. "Why would Shyada do this?"

"I do not believe Shyada did this." Jerietlan place a hand on Falden's shoulder. "Why would she have given him to me if she had?"

"We are in the Abyss and we lost sight of him," Gwideon said. "Any number of the denizens of this place could have done it with the proper knowledge. But, I suspect Thynitic's hand in this. She is the one who is credited with the creation of the first lich." Gwideon turned away.

"No!" Kyrianna stepped back. "Thynitic abhors the undead as much as Shyada does were-creatures. They are a corruption that she did not have a hand in."

"How do you know that?" Gwideon turned back to look at her.

Myrith felt a chill at the sound of Kyrianna's voice. There was an undercurrent of power there. Gwideon said the demon might have trying to possess her—could he have left part of himself behind when he left. There was no doubt in her mind now, they had to have Falden cast the anti-magic field. She had to be certain.

Kyrianna looked at him. "She is of my world. While what I have learned of her in the past is very limited, I do know she had nothing to do with the creation of undead creatures, such as lichs. I would ask how you know she is credited with the creation of the first lich as she is not a deity of Shokar?"

Gwideon inclined his head slightly. "The texts I have studied regarding some of the fouler undead, such as lichs, indicated she had a hand in their creation. I do not question them as they are part of Resare's church."

"The texts we rely on are often written by those who claim to serve the gods, but sometimes they have their own agendas. It can be almost impossible to tell the difference until whatever damage they wanted done is done," Kyrianna said.

"What could this link have done?" Falden asked.

"Your familiar could tap into your senses, your thoughts and even your magic. It would have become a weapon against us. The rites to create such a thing usually take days, however the person who did this completed the runes within a few hours. Shyada has saved you both from that corruption."

"Why would she do that?"

"Because she is the goddess of predators," Kyrianna said. "Talon is one of hers." Kyrianna's voice dropped to a soft whisper. "You should be grateful."

"I am." Falden hesitated as he stroked Talon's head. "What do I do now?" Let him rest in safety or bring him back to this foul place."

"That is your decision," Myrith said. "Know all of us would welcome him back if that is what you desire." She paused and took a deep breath. "We all made mistakes this day and I have no intention of letting that happen again." She turned toward the tiger. "You are excused. I know the only item you carry is the saddle Gwideon uses and it was created by his Gatekeeper. Go, Kyrianna's explanation has satisfied me and your goddess has shown the truth of those words to us all. However, do not threaten another member of this group again or we will see if steel can humble your claws."

Shydaran lunged forward so only a few inches separated him and Myrith. She did not move as she stared into his eyes. Eyes full of rage, hatred and intelligence. She refused to show any fear before the tiger and she would not allow him to think he had humbled her with his show of force and ferocity. He finally turned and left the room.

"He is powerful," Andrinor said after the tiger left.

"And potentially the biggest threat to us all as he has no regard for our safety or even his own," Myrith said. "I want all items that everyone is carrying brought to this room and subjected to the anti-magic field. The tiger and Kyrianna's silver sword are exempted."

"I object to that," Andrinor said.

"Why and for what?" Myrith asked. She knew he wasn't challenging her as Shydaran had, and she had already made two exemptions. But, it was still frustrating to have to listen to someone else who had something to hide.

"My bone blade was cut from the rib of my goddess' Shokarian avatar. I will not question its origin or nature by agreeing to this."

Myrith drew Conflagration. "What do you say to this testing?"

The sword flamed as it spoke. "The field is nothing. It does not dispel and as such no real harm can come to an enchanted item. As to what it might have done to the spirit, I know not. I have fought in Krella's hands as she wielded my inert steel against abominations from within Brular's own anti-magic field."

"That is not the point," Kyrianna said.

"I care not if an enchanted weapon, such as yours, tells me

this testing cannot harm it. It is a remnant of my goddess and I have no intention of defiling her presence by questioning its sanctity." Andrinor said.

Myrith nodded. "Very well. However, with the risk of unknown elements, we now sleep with watches. Kyrianna, Andrinor and Gwideon; we shall rotate."

"You be not including me—why?" Nirev asked.

"We begin to rely on your spell power more and more. Your hammer and mind need to be rested."

"And the tiger and Hendandra?" Andrinor asked.

Myrith looked around; neither of them were still in the room. "That is why," she said gesturing to where the thief and tiger had been.

She waited as everyone went to gather any gear or equipment they didn't have on them.

"Let's get this over with," Kyrianna said as she removed Cewyr's collar.

:*The unicorn should be exempted as well*, Riker's voice said in her mind. :*I will vouch for her*

"Very well. Cewyr you need not be subjected to the field either."

The unicorn moved to stand next to Riker and the two weapons that had been placed outside the area where the magic would be cast.

"I'm back and I have all of my stuff with me," Hendandra said.

"Is that everything?" Myrith asked.

"I suggest we see to cleansing the taint of evil that has been placed on Talon before summoning the other magics," Jerietlan said. He opened a silver flask. "Holy water should cleanse the vile runes.

Falden nodded and handed the hawk to Myrith. "If you would."

Myrith looked down at the bird in her hands and nodded. After all of the harsh words spoken in this room, that Falden would entrust her with seeing Talon's body was purged of the evil that had tried to take control of it was an honor. She and Jerietlan first removed the runes then the cleric called on Mykaylene to drive out any remaining taint of evil from the body.

Falden waited until they were finished then began chanting.

"It would appear our only interlopers have made themselves known," Falden said after a few moments. "I will be in the lab this night. I expect to not be disturbed." He left the room.

"I still want watches posted," Myrith said.

"I would like some time to meditate and another shower. If another is willing to take the first watch, they can find me in the shrine when it is time for the second."

"Very well. I will take first, Kyrianna second, then Andrinor and Gwideon."

Kyrianna nodded. "You realize your armor, mine and Andrinor's is all in the smithy awaiting repair and wasn't checked."

Myrith frowned. "We will deal with that tomorrow as I will be asking Falden to summon the field each day when we return to the keep. We will just have to be wary."

"Agreed. I will see you in two hours."

"Kyri…" Myrith held out her hand.

Kyrianna took the offered hand. "What?"

"I'm sorry I didn't realize what you were saying about the whip."

Kyrianna nodded.

Chapter Nine

Hendandra lay on the cot in the barracks and tried to sleep, but was unable to find a comfortable position. The cot was hard and one of the least comfortable things she had ever tried to sleep on. There were even some rocky areas she remembered as having more give than the thing she was now laying on. She picked up her pillow and blanket and left the room.

She opened the door to the scribe's room and saw Shydaran lying on the carpeted floor near a fire. The light from the flames danced across his fur and highlighted the colors. She approached slowly and placed a hand on one of his ears. She smiled when he jerked his head up; she had managed to sneak up on him. He relaxed and her smile vanished.

"We need to talk, husband," she said.

He shook his head.

"You will not speak because of Shyada's command?" He nodded then brushed his head against her shoulder. "Even though you have dropped your disguise for me before this."

Hendandra knew he was asking for her understanding in this, but she wasn't ready to give it. She looked down at the heart token she wore and cradled it in her hands. "I need to hear your words."

He closed his eyes as he let his head drop back to the floor.

She began to untie the knot in the cord holding the heart token. As she did she remembered a small voice whispering in her head. "Melissa."

Shydaran's eyes opened and he growled.

"Quiet!" Hendandra said. "If you won't talk to me, then talk to her."

He reached up and grabbed the heart token in his mouth and she nodded at the anger she saw in his eyes.

"Not the heart token. But, then what? She cannot hold herself in an enchanted item and Isdela wishes me not to wear or carry metal. What do I carry her in?"

He released the heart token and it dropped to hang low against her belly, then stood and moved to the pile of wood near the fireplace and sliced a piece off with his claws that slid across the floor to stop next to her foot. He growled and shook as he walked back to her and covered the wood with his paw. When he lifted it, a small wooden ring lay on the floor.

Hendandra picked it up and placed it on the ring finger of her left hand. She knew he wouldn't understand the significance of the placement, any more than she had understood the significance of the heart token when it had been given to her. "Stay here," she said opening the door. "I won't be long."

Kyrianna had said she was going to take another shower when they finally got through with that mess in the great hall. She didn't blame her either. Kyrianna had been covered in blood from the cuts she had taken as well as the ichor from the demon that had come from Shydaran's claws and teeth tearing into it.

She walked into the shower, without knocking and saw Kyrianna drop the towel she was holding and grab for her sword. Cewyr also jerked her head up and turned with the point of her horn lowered.

"Oops. Sorry," Hendandra said as Kyrianna wrapped the towel around her body. "A little jumpy are we?"

Kyrianna jerked her head up then grinned. "After what just happened, I wouldn't say I was little jumpy—only cautious."

"Kyri, I need to ask a favor."

"What is it?" Kyrianna opened one of the shower stalls and passed her hand over the rune that started the water flowing.

Hendandra stepped back and opened the door to look down the hallway. There was no one there and she shut the door. "I need to talk to Feric. I cannot let what happened today go without us speaking to each other."

Kyrianna looked up and nodded.

Hendandra held up her hand with the wooden ring. "Would Melissa tell me his words that he cannot speak?"

Kyrianna picked up the silver sword and held it for a moment then laughed as she held it out to Hendandra.

"What did she say?" Hendandra asked as she touched the sword and felt a chill pass through her and into the ring.

"I am always willing to assist Princess Hendandra."

:*Where did you find this?* Melissa's voice whispered in her head.

:*Feric made it from a piece of firewood,* she answered. She looked at Kyrianna and nodded.

"I'll be by for her when I finish in here," Kyrianna said.

"Thank you. We will be in the scribe's room."

Kyrianna offered her a bow and had to grab for her towel when it slipped.

Hendandra giggled as she closed the door and returned to the scribe's room.

Shydaran looked up as she closed the door then moved to sit next to him. "Melissa, please tell me what he says," she said placing her hand in the tiger's cheek.

:*I will*, Melissa answered. There was a pause. :*Feric, this wasn't my idea. I came because she asked me to.*

"Stop it!" Hendandra spoke in halfling, even though she knew the girl would understand her thoughts and meaning. "Melissa is here so we can talk and you can keep your disguise as Shyada commanded."

:*As you wish.* Another pause. :*He is not happy with the arrangement.*

"Take it up with Shyada. The two of you have forced me to this," she said. She stopped when he turned away from her and took a breath. *Too much anger*, she thought. *He is only following the commands of his goddess. But what about me? What about my desires? What about my friends?* She knew this was the crux of the problem. He didn't care about her friends, only her. His loyalty was to Shyada, Justula and her—no one else. To him, they were the same as the people who enslaved and killed his people. How could she make him understand they were her friends and just as important to her as his tribe was to him?

"I'm sorry," she finally said. "That was wrong."

He stopped, but still didn't turn back to look at her.

"So is it my destiny to watch you and Myrith come to blows eventually?"

:*She is a fool.* Melissa's voice was strong and steady as she spoke and Hendandra could hear Feric's inflections in her voice. :*She thinks she leads, but she knows nothing of leadership. She overreacts and dictates the actions of others without any regard for anything else or the consequences of such actions. We would be better off without her or any of them.*

"Really? Do you think you could have harmed that demon? Never mind, I know your answer before you even speak. You think you can handle anything. You will be saying that even as I watch some demon tear you apart." Her voice broke.

He turned back and nudged her head with his own. :*I will not go.* It was Melissa speaking—not him.

"Feric, did you not realize the demon was resisting your attacks? It was hardly harmed," she said as she let her face slide against his fur.

:*That was never my intent. I could have cast the same spell that allowed me to carve up the floor to find her flesh. The larger concern was protecting Kyrianna. That thing could have used her as a shield against us.*

Hendandra nodded as she stroked his head. "Thank you for protecting her."

:*You truly feel that way?* There was a pause. :*She leads Thynitic to us. She has tempted my own goddess' wrath, not once but now twice, as well as my own. I should have let that demon bitch kill her.*

:*Hey, that wasn't very nice!* Melissa's voice was full of anger and Hendandra felt the ring turned colder on her finger.

Hendandra pulled herself in front of his eyes and put both hands on his cheeks as she pulled him down so they were eye to eye. "Both of you watch your language and your tone. Feric, I will not have my husband teaching an eight year old girl to swear."

:*Swear? That is the appropriate term for a female of many different species. Is it not the correct one for a female demon?*

She slapped the tiger on the nose. "You know it is not. You who are a great hunter and the protector of Justula—do not try to convince me you do not know the proper term for a demoness."

:*Actually, I hear that quite often. Myrith and the others seem to use it almost like it is Thynitic's nickname.*

:*Would you like me to repeat that to Kyri or Tristan?*

:*No,* Melissa said. :*But he should not have said that about Kyri.*

:*I agree.* Hendandra frowned as she reached up and twisted the tiger's ear hard. "You listen to me. Kyrianna is my friend. She and the others are my family and we need them here. You said you would follow Myrith and I expect just that. I realize you need to follow Shyada's commands, but I expect you to listen to your wife as well."

He pressed his head against her hand. :*I serve her, but will obey you.*

Hendandra let go as his nose touched her neck and she pulled back with a shiver. She heard Melissa giggle. :*What did he say?*

:*My wife has her own fury and claws.* She giggled again. :*And a wonderful scent.*

The tiger leaned forward and gave her a lick on her cheek.

"Stop that." She pushed him back. "I don't need a bath." She smiled and let her hand stroke the tiger's cheek as she stared into the fire. The tiger stood and moved so she was able to lean back against him. She sank back into his fur, rotated her body to have her face against it and felt its softness embrace her body. She smiled as she thought of the beach and of them both watching the sunset.

:*It's beautiful*, she heard Melissa say.

:*Yes, it is.*

:*He has similar thoughts.*

Hendandra opened her eyes to look over his shoulder at the profile of his head.

:*What does he dream of?*

:*You*, Melissa said.

Hendandra closed her eyes and shifted her had to get more comfortable as Melissa continued talking. :*You are running through the woods. From him, I think, but it appears to be a game. You seem to race through the jungle to a cliff. You climb the cliff together, but you are just a bit quicker than he.*

Hendandra could feel herself slip closer toward sleep. "What else?"

:*He is with you on a rock ledge and uncoils a rope.* She gave a little laugh. :*He is placing his arms around you with the rope. You are smiling and laughing. He is looking into your eyes.* Melissa paused.

"Is there more?"

:*I can see the moon reflected in your eyes. It is as if he is transfixed. The image is as if it is frozen in his mind.*

"Is it a spell of kind?"

Melissa laughed. :*No, I don't think so. Well not in the divine or arcane sense anyway. If it is a spell, it is one you cast over him. I think he just never wants to forget that moment.*

~ * ~

Kyrianna paused at the door to the scribe's room. She bowed her head slowly as she opened the door and looked at the tiger who wrapped his tail protectively around Hendandra as he raised his head to look at her. "Feric, I apologize for the anger I caused you, however, I stand by my actions. I gave Myrith no specifics about who you are, and I wouldn't have. My intent was to prevent the forcing of an issue I saw leading to a fight between you and the others. No matter who won that fight, we would have all lost—particularly Hendandra." She paused for moment and glanced at Hendandra. "Myrith leads this group and she needed to know why Shydaran should not be subjected to the anti-magic field in a way she would accept. I tried to provide her with that. I know Shyada will demand something from me for my words and actions and I will accept her judgment when we return."

The tiger looked at her for a moment and Kyrianna thought she saw a hint of surprise in his eyes. He nodded his head once then lowered it back to the floor.

"Sister, it is time to go," Kyrianna said as she drew the silver sword.

"Thank you, Melissa," Hendandra said softly as she held her hand out.

Kyrianna touched the sword to the wooden ring and felt Melissa's presence as she moved from one to the other.

:Thank you for another look at your island, Princess, Melissa said.

Kyrianna saw Hendandra grin as she rubbed her face against the tiger's fur.

"Good night to both of you," she said as closed the door.

She smiled as she walked to the shrine. She wasn't sure whose relationship had the toughest time right now. Feric and Hendandra could be near each other and would be able to share moments such as they had now, but they also had a secret to protect. They had to be careful, but at least they could touch and be near each other. She and Tristan had only acknowledged their feelings before she had to leave to come to this vile place. And, now they were separated; for how long she had no idea.

Cewyr stayed close behind her as they entered the shrine and she smiled again. It seemed the unicorn wasn't going to be caught more than a foot or two from her again.

She knelt in front of the shrine and focused her thoughts on Frayrith and Dwycia as she sought guidance for the coming days and the strength to see the task through. She had been serious in telling the others she would confront Thynitic if the opportunity presented itself. However, the powerful desire she had felt for revenge at seeing her mother's whip was gone and she wondered if some power of Thynitic or the chaos demon had been what had driven her to bring the weapon. *No!* She chided herself for trying to find a way to blame her actions on another. It was in her nature to act rashly and she doubted that would ever really change.

~ * ~

Myrith looked at the ghostly horse for what had to be the hundredth time that evening. She had hoped her personal war with her own impatience and curiosity would resolve itself, but it didn't appear to be happening. Gwideon had gone to sleep several minutes ago and she wasn't due to be relieved by Kyrianna for almost two hours.

She turned toward Riker, who stood by one of the walls of weapons. She let her gaze track back to the door to see Gwideon watching her; judging her. "Go back to sleep," she said. "Your watch is not for several hours."

He stood and readied Drinker. "It would seem your watch has not yet begun."

She frowned. "I will deal with my own problems later. We agreed upon the order of the watch."

"It is not the order I question, but your attentiveness. Your eyes spend an equal amount of time on the horse as the door. I cannot read your thoughts, but I doubt your mind is even on the task when you do look to the entrance." Gwideon picked up his helm and placed it on his head; a stark contrast to his leather armor.

Myrith looked at the man as he took a position at the door. He looked at her with those eyes that seemed to have stared into death itself. "It is said you should face your own demons before you face another's. For those demons from within will feed on your doubt and own perceived failings and then the battle is already lost. That is the reason Kyrianna sought to have you officially recognized by the Coliseum." He turned towards the door and stood like a statue. "I cannot help you with the inner battle you are fighting now, Sword of Mykaylene; that one is yours and yours alone. When you are ready, you can take your watch. Until that time—it is mine."

She looked at him and knew he was right. She might miss something in her current state of mind. A single sound could be the difference between her blade being the first to strike or feeling her own blood spilled. She risked both herself and the others.

She lowered her head as she turned away from him and toward Riker.

As she took the first step, she heard him behind her. "Most of our internal demons are of our own making, Lady Lake. In many ways, they are more evil than even the vile thing we fought this night. Don't let them win."

She didn't look back. "I have no intention of that," she said as she walked across the room to where Riker stood.

:*We have traveled together these months and yet you surprise me again and again. Nothing could have prepared me for that.* She took a moment to find the word. :*Melding.*

~ * ~

Kyrianna finished her prayers and looked up at the figure of Dwycia. She wished she had brought one of Frayrith as well, but she had not thought to do so before leaving Nydith. She stood and looked at the unicorn she called friend and felt the silver sword at her side. The day had been eventful and frightening. Of all the places in the keep this was the only one where she felt safe. She knew it was not her body she worried about the most, but the very sanctity of her soul, which Thynitic sought to steal a piece of. She sat next to Cewyr and leaned against her. In some ways, she knew what Hendandra felt laying against the tiger. The heat and beating of Cewyr's heart were comforting. She took a deep breath and placed her hand on Cewyr's neck. "Please tell me what happened in there."

~ * ~

Riker's words were plain and clear in Myrith's mind. :*I wish I could have known myself. However, I had no such luxury. It was as if the course was as clear as an endless field in that one moment.*

~ * ~

Cewyr looked at her and bobbed her head. :*I heard you scream in my mind and felt your terror. It was the forest all over again. Everything was collapsing.*

Kyrianna felt Cewyr's concern and love wrapped around the words.

~ * ~

:*Myrith do you know what it is like to see everything you know and love taken so suddenly and relentlessly, by one you trusted?*

~ * ~

:Kyrianna, I died at the hands of your mother; a woman who had at one time been a protector of the forest and those who lived there. I do not know which hurt the most: the spell she wove, the fact it was one of our own, or what I did that night.

~ * ~

:Do you think after that knife opened my neck the horror of that night stopped?

Myrith swallowed hard. She had never considered all the events of that horrible night and the effects they would have had on her companion.

~ * ~

:I took his life. The very man whose name I carry was killed by my actions. What higher crime can I find myself guilty of?

The melancholy in Cewyr's mind was now overwhelming Kyrianna. She could remember the images from the visions. She could see the carnage. She had tried to wipe it from her memory as a bad dream. It was a dream to her, but reality to her friend. It was a sick desecration and blasphemy.

~ * ~

:I heard it all, Myrith, and I was powerless. I heard Melissa's screams. And she did scream; none but I could hear her. Her mother was already dead and her father was in the study with its thick walls that blocked the sound. Her sister was too close to the pounding shore to hear her.

:The same little girl who had rode upon my back with her father needed me and I could do nothing.

Riker locked his gaze with hers. Myrith had always thought it was his ghostly nature that made his eyes appear empty; now she knew it was sorrow, and guilt born from a failure to protect the ones who needed him.

~ * ~

:I have been given a second chance by Frayrith to atone for my actions. When I heard your screams, I would not leave—no matter the odds. Even if it had been Thynitic herself, I would have stood by your side.

"It wasn't your fault." Kyrianna swallowed hard. "It was my mother's and Thynitic's."

The unicorn brought her gaze to hers and her voice echoed in Kyrianna's head. :*And is that the same argument you use to judge yourself for the day Falden and Andrinor tasted her sick whim?*

Kyrianna couldn't fight the tears. "I was the one who challenged her to demonstrate her power. They would not have been hurt as they were if I had not done that."

~ * ~

:*I heard her over and over again, night after infernal night. It is the ones you care about, the ones closest to you that matter most; is it not? If you fail them, you become trapped in a hell it is almost impossible to escape from.*

She knew the horse had served many years as Rhinehart Duvall's steed, but she had never thought of the years he had been trapped in that cursed stable. The little girl's screams mocking his very existence. She lowered her head. "I could not possibly understand your pain, my friend."

:*I pray you never have to.* Riker brushed his muzzle across her cheek.

~ * ~

Kyrianna placed her hands against Cewyr's face. "That still doesn't explain how."

Cewyr's eyes never moved. :*You serve your gods and we also have those we serve. They are known simply as the Guardians and they watch over those who serve the great balance as a part of nature. Both loyalty and purity of deed is held in highest regard. Frayrith guided me back to take my place at your side, but it is the Guardian of the Fields who truly watches over those equines who serve the path of light.*

~ * ~

:*That was the past, Myrith. We have the present and the future to fight for. Mykaylene came to you and the other gods showed their favor to each of your companions. The Guardian of the Fields now blesses me. She has seen the horror that was my tomb. She has seen I am bonded once more to one who serves the light. When Kyrianna was beset by the demon, it was like that day once more. The creature dwarfed my power as it did that of Cewyr. We would have been nothing but an annoyance to it. Kyrianna would have been lost regardless of our efforts.*

:*I heard her neigh; it was as if it called to my soul. I gave myself over to that call and felt a heartbeat and warmth. I did not realize how much I missed that sensation. When I opened my eyes, it was as if I was reborn and I also heard every thought and could sense every one of Cewyr's memories.*

~ * ~

:*I felt cold, but I heard the Guardian's call. I dared not move and then it was as if Riker's mind was there with mine. I could see his pain and the horrors he has endured and I knew he saw mine as well. But, it was as if a chorus spoke in our thoughts. 'Not again, not ever again.' I could feel the Guardian's power course through me; as if Riker acted as a channel directly to her.*

Kyrianna only stared at Cewyr, not saying anything.

:*She has seen two of her charges killed in the most horrible manner. I don't think she is willing to add to the burdens we already carry.*

Cewyr lowered her head and pressed her muzzle against Kyrianna's cheek. :*I could not bear to see Thynitic take you back. Riker knew that as well. I think…no, I know he will not let another of his family be destroyed as the others were. He is here because he needs to be here. He wants to be here. He journeys with Myrith, because she is taking him where he needs to go. He is looking to prove himself once more and seeks to show to himself he is worthy; then and now. He comes to find redemption and if not that— punishment for his failure to protect those entrusted to him.*

Kyrianna nodded. That was something she understood.

:*What is the road we walk, Kyri? That of salvation of another or of our own damnation?*

"Frayrith spoke of redemption, rebirth and renewal," Kyrianna whispered. "I hope it is one of those three. Otherwise…," she let her voice trail off and shook her head slowly.

~ * ~

:*I saw Kilenter, her home. I saw her as her horn pierced the heart of the one who was her protector and she broke her own neck.*

:*I have seen everything I hold dear dashed upon the rocks; as has Cewyr. The Guardian of the Fields has seen the blood of her children spilled for far too long. She grants me, this poor shade of one of those children, the ability to channel her power to another of her beloved children so that together we are stronger.*

Myrith shook her head and leaned back as she tried to understand what Riker was telling her. "And what of us when you are joined?"

:*The Guardian would not break a bond that gives strength. When I joined with Cewyr, you and I were still bonded and therefore you were bonded to her as well. She would have allowed you to take her back to take the fight to our enemy by land or air; just as I would allow Kyrianna to do if you were unable to.*

Myrith nodded. "But what if I need you and Kyri needs Cewyr? Do you control this power?"

:In some ways I control it. But, I ask you, do you control yours or does it control you?

Myrith sighed and placed her hand on Riker's cheek. She didn't have to answer, Riker knew her answer as well as she did. She did control her gifts, but it was the presence of those gifts that drove her to fight the way she did. Was it really hers to control or did it draw her to this place to fight a near impossible battle? "I do not like it, but I cannot deny you your place on the field or the gift you have been given. I wish only to share it with you. I depend on you as much if not more than I depend on the bond of friendship I have with Kyri. I do not wish to share or lose you to this power or what it may drive you to do."

Riker turned his head to glance at Gwideon. *:You would not let Kyri sacrifice herself before, because you knew it was a rash choice; one that would not have made a difference, but, what if he held the line to let you and the others escape, what would you do?*

She dropped her head at the simple logic of the horse's question. "I would let him serve his god and his beliefs and see the others to safety," she whispered.

:I ask for nothing more or less.

She raised her head and nodded. "I understand."

:Myrith, Kyri does not know the full extent of the road Frayrith has placed her on. Even if we succeed in this task, there will be more she will have to face.

"What?"

:I do not know. I only caught glimpses of things in Cewyr's mind. I am not sure even she knows the full extent—but she is bound by Frayrith in her duty to protect Kyrianna.

Myrith nodded the turned and walked back to the main doors of the keep. "I will have my watch now, Sir Gwideon, you should return to your rest."

Gwideon only nodded and didn't ask her any questions. He respected her privacy in the matter and she found it one more reason to respect him.

Chapter Ten

Kyrianna nodded as Andrinor's eyes opened. "The watch is yours," she whispered to prevent waking the others. Though, how anyone could have heard her over Nirev's snoring she wasn't sure. She glanced around the sleeping quarters. Nirev, Jerietlan and Andrinor were the only ones there. Hendandra would still be in the scribe's room with Shydaran and she suspected Falden was still in the lab. Myrith and Gwideon had set up their bedrolls in the main hall so they were near the doors and could react if the person on watch needed assistance.

"Get some rest," Andrinor said placing a hand on her shoulder. His gaze moved away from her toward the hall for a moment. "I swore to you that my life, my blade and my soul were yours; I failed."

"How could you have known? We thought this place was safe. And it should have been."

"That does not matter. I should have been there and I was not."

"Andrinor, I do not consider you forsworn of your oath and you shouldn't either. If you had known what was happening you would have been there and that is what matters." She grasped his forearm.

"Thank you." He bowed his head slightly. "You should get some rest."

She smiled and turned toward the door then stopped and turned back to face him. "Why did you do it? Why did you swear that oath? Even if we are from the same world, we are not kin nor do we follow the same deities."

"True, but you could be. You remind me of several of the young women of my home. Besides, you need someone to look out for you until you start learning to think before you do something stupid." He grinned and cocked his head to the side.

Kyrianna nodded and grinned also. There had been no malice in Andrinor's voice despite the way his words could have been taken.

Kyrianna left as Andrinor headed for the main doors of the keep. She took a few minutes to check the rest of the rooms before returning to the shrine.

Before unrolling her bedroll she took a few minutes to scribble her notes into her journal. This was becoming a familiar ritual for her and she felt herself relaxing as she blew on the paper to dry the ink before closing the book.

Resting against Cewyr's flank, she let herself drift off to sleep.

~ * ~

"Tristan!" Kyrianna sat up, her hand reaching for the dagger that was no longer on her belt.

"Kyri?"

Andrinor stood at the entrance to the shrine. She felt her cheeks heat as she shook her head. "It was only a bad dream."

Andrinor grinned and shook his head. "You call out Tristan's name and say it was a bad dream. That does not make any sense. Although, after the day you had, perhaps it is understandable your dreams have been warped. Do you wish someone to talk to?"

Kyrianna nodded.

"Dreams can mean many things," Cewyr said. "They can also be nothing more than jumbled thoughts and images the mind is trying to sort out with no special meaning. Do not let them control you."

"She is correct," Andrinor said. "However, it can sometimes help to share that which scares and upsets you with another, even if there is nothing specific to be learned."

Kyrianna nodded and looked from Andrinor to Cewyr. "The dream started simply enough," Kyrianna said as Andrinor sat in the doorway. "It was the first time I saw Tristan followed by more memories of him."

Andrinor grinned.

"What?"

"Anyone who saw how you looked at each other last night or when you took your leave of each other at the arena could have no doubts about how you feel. Now you are separated, it only makes sense he would be in your dreams. As you are probably in his."

"And is there someone in your dreams, Andrinor?"

Andrinor only smiled but didn't answer

"Fair enough, it is none of my business."

"Indeed; it is not." He paused. "However, I am the one who asked you first and the answer is yes." He reached out and placed a hand on her shoulder. "Now if your dreams were of Tristan, why did you cry out as you did and awaken reaching for a weapon."

Kyrianna took a breath. "I lost him. He was taken from me by something I couldn't see." Her voice broke. "Pulled into darkness, like Torliana was pulled through that portal. Only this felt more permanent and like it was my fault. That I could have prevented it from happening—protected him somehow."

"Did he want to come with us?"

"Yes."

"And what did you tell him?"

"That I would not risk Thynitic trying to get to me through him."

"And what did he say?"

"That I risk letting her win anyway by stopping living."

"I think we've gotten to the reason for your bad dreams," Cewyr said. "Combine your concerns about someone hurting Tristan to get to you with the events of today…"

"And it's easy to see how my dreams could be easily twisted and warped." She smiled at Andrinor. "Thank you for listening."

He nodded, squeezed her shoulder then stood. "May the rest of your night pass more pleasantly," he said.

"And yours."

She listened to his footsteps as he returned to the great hall then leaned back against Cewyr. The dream had been so real she could still feel the emotions it had brought as well as her own desires. She had only talked about one part of the dream. She doubted she could have discussed the rest of it with Myrith or Hendandra and definitely not with any of the men in the group, even Andrinor.

:*Kyri?* Melissa's voice whispered.

Chaos! Kyrianna thought. How could she explain the images in her mind and the way she felt to a child such as Melissa?

The dream had started as she had told Andrinor, with the first time she had seen Tristan at the Wailing Banshee in Duvshire and progressed through various other memories: Racing from Tyrel's cabin because she realized the assassin was after Tristan.

Her heart almost stopping when Mikyl captured Tristan at the estate. Then again at Myrith's ordination, when Tristan stood to accept Balthas challenge. Each memory had shown her how deep her feelings were—showing her the Reishalli had been growing since the first time she had seen Tristan.

Then had come the memories of their last night, when she had finally acknowledged how she felt as well as her visit to the Pools of Shyada. That was when the dream had changed. She remembered thinking of sharing a swim with Tristan after her encounter with Shyada, but she had pushed that thought out of her mind at the time. In her dream, he had been there—inviting her to join him in the water and she had found herself doing so, her body still reacting to the goddess' touch. When she entered the warm water, the scene had changed leaving her in darkness. A flash of light showed Tristan being pulled through a portal, but she had been unable to move; unable to do anything but watch. Then a female voice spoke, whispering, "Be careful on the road you travel, or he may be destroyed from losing you." That was when she woke up.

There had been something almost prophetic in the way those words had been spoken and it scared her.

:*Kyri, it was just a bad dream*, Melissa said. :*Why would it bother you to discuss it?*

:*It scared me that badly.*

:*Oh.* Melissa's voice faded then she started humming.

Kyrianna leaned against Cewyr and let the humming lull her back to sleep, grateful Melissa hadn't asked any other questions, even though she could feel the girl's curiosity, wondering what she was hiding.

Chapter Eleven

"Looks like there is only one way into this place," Myrith said after Jerietlan closed the keep doors.

"So, do you have enough favor with your goddesses to cast the magics I mentioned?" Urric's voice echoed off the high walls. "Or with everything that happened did you forget to ask."

"Urric!" Myrith reached for the skull, but stopped as Kyrianna stepped between her and Gwideon then knelt down at the entrance to the Rock Palace.

She tried to keep from fidgeting as Kyrianna mumbled something she couldn't understand for several minutes then began drawing in the dirt.

"This is where we are," Kyrianna said pointing to a small rock. "The road through the Rock Palace will be easy to stay on as I see no major branchings off it. Travel will be slow because of the terrain. Once we are through, the road continues for a couple of leagues before coming to a large river. The road splits on the other side of the river, one path going through a forested area and the other through a swamp. The forest path looks to be twice the distance of the swamp, but I would feel more comfortable there than in the swamp."

"We'll make the decision when we get there." She looked around and saw several nods of agreement. "Everyone ready?"

She waited as people checked their weapons and packs. Kyrianna now sat on Cewyr, her short bow on her lap. She started to climb on Riker, then stopped when she saw Falden standing a little ways from the group.

"Falden?" She took a step toward the mage.

The mage turned and she found herself staring at the small body he was holding—Talon, his familiar. "His soul is at peace, I will not drag him back here," Falden whispered.

"The choice is yours and we will honor it," Myrith said.

Falden raised his head. Flames flared up in his hands quickly consuming the body of the hawk.

"Let's get moving." Myrith mounted Riker and looked up at

the high walls.

"A good place to be staging an ambush, I suspect," Nirev said.

"Agreed. Kyri, since you have knowledge of the route, you take the lead."

"I'll take the rear guard," Gwideon said.

"Hey, I don't want to be in the back—too much dust being kicked up by the rest of you."

"You can ride with me and Cewyr," Kyrianna said extending her hand to Hendandra.

"Rangerette…" Myrith gestured toward the opening in the walls, "…if you would." Kyrianna nodded and tapped Cewyr with her heels.

~ * ~

"This place is too quiet," Kyrianna said.

"Too quiet?" Nirev said, his voice booming in the silence. "I wouldn't have thought ye to be one who preferred a fight over a quiet stroll."

"She's right. This is an unnatural quiet," Andrinor said.

Myrith stopped Riker and turned to look at Andrinor. "Explain."

"The sounds of our movements are muffled, including Cewyr's hooves. Nirev's voice didn't echo as it should have just now. Something is preventing sound from carrying in this place."

"But, it's only us being muffled," Hendandra said. "Kyri and I have heard rocks shifting above us."

"So someone is aiding us in getting through this place by hiding the sound of our movements." Myrith's grip on her sword tightened. "I don't trust that."

"Neither do I," Kyrianna said.

Myrith frowned as her friend took several quick breaths. "What?"

"I have a feeling it is Thynitic doing this. But, why would she be aiding us?"

"Are you that naïve?" Urric's voice said. "She wants you. She tried taking you away from your friends yesterday and failed. She has apparently decided to help you come to her—for now."

"Gwideon, control that thing or I will smash it." Myrith said.

"Urric is currently in service to Resare, even if unwilling. You risk Resare's displeasure if you do."

Myrith shuddered at the calm in Gwideon's voice. There no doubt in her mind, he would defend the skull to the best of his abilities. "Then I will answer to Resare for my actions," she finally said. "I will not have that thing continuing to taunt Kyri. Now, control it." She didn't wait for an answer as she turned toward Kyrianna.

"Kyri, remember what Brular said: She is the goddess of chaos. She will give her greatest enemy free passage simply because of a passing thought. For her to be doing this to specifically aid you is not in keeping with her character. You are important to her; we have seen that, but..."

Kyrianna nodded. "She is one of the divine and trapped by her own nature."

"How much longer?"

"We have been in here long enough the images have faded, so it shouldn't be too much longer now."

"Good." Myrith looked up at the gray sky above them and took a deep breath. She was worried. Kyrianna hadn't said anything, but Myrith knew she would still be blaming herself for the events of the past evening and then with Urric taunting her as he was, the girl would be easy prey for Thynitic if something happened. That would put them all at risk. "Let's get moving."

~ * ~

"Hold up a moment," Myrith called as the walls opened up and they found themselves in an area of low hills. "Rangerette, what can you recall of this area."

"Nothing but these foothills for a couple of leagues. After that we come to a river."

"That river flows through all the layers of the Abyss," Urric said. "The road should take us to a ferry station. I hope you are able to pay the toll."

"What be the price?" Nirev said.

"It changes depending on who the ferryman is, so I will not be able to give you that information. The problem is most will want some type of vile drug and I doubt any of you are carrying such items. It is also possible the toll can be paid with a few drops of blood as well."

"We will deal with that when we get there. If we cannot pay, then we will find another way," Myrith said.

"Myrith," Hendandra called, "over here."

She turned to see Hendandra and Kyrianna looking over a nearby hill. *Chaos*, she thought. *I didn't notice them moving away from the group.*

"What?" She asked as she joined them.

"There." Kyrianna pointed to a large group of demons standing around a woman in robes.

"This can't be good," Myrith said as the woman said something and half of the demons left the area. She then moved her hands through several complicated gestures. "She told them to have the camp prepared for the arrival of Chaos' Daughter," Falden said.

Myrith jerked her head around to stare at the mage. "Chaos' Daughter?"

"That is what she said. Now, she is casting a spell of divination." He paused as the woman began speaking and pointed in their direction. "She told them the enemies of chaos were behind this hill and ordered them to destroy them."

"Let's get back to the others."

"Wait," Kyrianna said. "She's chanting again."

"She is targeting the demons," Falden said.

Myrith watched as a cloud of ice surrounded the group of demons. When it dissipated, all of the demons were dead.

"Amazing, she is very powerful," Falden said.

"If you oppose Thynitic, you are welcome in my camp," the woman called.

Myrith stood, Conflagration in her hand. "To whom do you owe your allegiance?"

"You would not know her. She is one that does not make a show of her power or position, yet she is opposed to the Lady of Chaos. Perhaps that is all the endorsement you should require. I can see you safely through the demon camps and across the river."

Myrith glanced toward Kyrianna as the girl gasped. "What?"

"That is exactly what Bukon told me, when I asked him who he served."

"We counted him as an ally," Falden said.

"True, but I am not ready to say the same about this woman." Myrith paused and looked around at the others. "However, she claims she can get us past the demons, we will hear her out."

She motioned for the rest of the group to follow her as she walked over the hill and toward the woman. The woman was a little shorter than Kyrianna, with hair the color of honey and dark brown eyes.

"Well met on the journey," Myrith said.

"Well met. I am Grania."

"You said you serve one who opposes the Lady of Chaos," Kyrianna said.

"Her name is Carrinna. Because you also oppose Thynitic, as she does, she has directed me to provide what aid I can."

"Kyri, have you heard of this Carrinna?" Myrith asked.

"No."

"Carrinna is the daughter of Thynitic and Neysinil," Urric said. "She attempted to seize her mother's power and was imprisoned for her troubles."

"For several centuries now, she has let Thynitic continue to think she is still imprisoned, while she is rebuilding her power to challenge her once again," Grania said. She straightened her back and took a step toward Myrith. "You will not be able to pass through the demon camp between here and the river without my help. Many of the denizens of this region have already been alerted to your presence and are waiting for you.

"And how will you be aiding us?"

"I can escort you through the camp as well as offer advice."

"Advice?" Hendandra looked up at the woman and frowned. "Believe it or not, we're actually pretty good at handling ourselves and getting to where we need to."

"If that were not true; you would never have made it this far. However, to pass through the demons you will need the help I can provide. We need to change your appearances as well as several of your auras—the horse and the unicorn included. You carry weapons which will also attract attention; those will have to be hidden." She paused and seemed to study the group. "If everyone would separate a bit so I can examine you properly."

"You," she pointed to Hendandra. "I sense nothing on you that should cause problems."

She raised a wand and a gray mist surrounded Hendandra. Kyrianna stepped in front of Shydaran as he started growling. "Wait," Myrith heard her whisper to the tiger.

The mist faded and Myrith frowned at the darkness she felt in Hendandra's aura. She looked closer and saw it was only an outer layer being used to hide the girl's true aura. She smiled at the streaks of gold she now saw mixed with the various shades of gray that made up Hendandra's aura.

Grania turned to her next. "You will have to find a place to hide your sword and shield."

Myrith pulled one of the ghostly blankets from Riker's saddlebags and placed it on the ground. With care she placed Conflagration on the blanket along with her shield then waited as Grania's mist surrounded her. When it faded she looked around at the others. "Anything else we need to remove, place on the blanket. Riker can carry it for us."

Grania continued with the others. The magic she was using created only subtle changes in each person's appearance, so they could still recognize each other. Shydaran growled and shook when Grania turned toward him and raised her wand. The woman paused and Shydaran's form slowly shrank into that of a weasel. He then ran over to Hendandra then wrapped himself around her neck when she picked him up.

Myrith frowned as several more weapons were placed on the blanket including Nirev's hammer, Jerietlan's shield, Andrinor's buckler and sword.

"This is ridiculous. You are asking us to walk unarmed into a demon camp on just your word you can get us through," Kyrianna said drawing both of her swords before Grania could tell her to do so.

"Your bows and quiver also," Grania said. "Your friend is not unarmed; she has another sword she can use. The Grey did not have to relinquish his weapon either." She nodded toward Gwideon. "Do you not trust your friends to protect you if necessary?"

"Myrith, there has to be another way." Kyrianna still held her longbow and quiver in her hands.

"Who has an extra weapon for Kyri?" She knew the primary problem—Kyrianna was unarmed. They knew she was being targeted by Thynitic; there was no way the girl could be comfortable walking into a demon camp—unarmed. She looked around. Those she knew carried extra weapons had had to give up their primary weapons and were now using those extras.

"Don't you trust your friends to protect you?" Grania asked again as she smiled and tilted her head to the side.

"I trust my friends with not only my life, but my soul. It is *you* I do not trust." Kyrianna left her weapons on the blanket.

Myrith watched Kyrianna bite her lip and shake her head. She was worried also. The woman had told the other demons to prepare the camp for the arrival of Chaos' Daughter, and now had effectively disarmed Kyrianna. Something wasn't right.

"One other thing." Grania grabbed Kyrianna's arms, her hands covering the marks from Frayrith and Dwycia. "I hope this will hide these, or you may have to be literally unarmed." She began chanting and a black glow surrounded her hands and Kyrianna's arms.

When she released her grip, Kyrianna jerked away from her and took several steps toward the woman her fists balled tightly.

"Kyri!"

"What did you do?"

"It is only an obscuration. It will fade in about twelve hours."

"Let me see." Myrith reached for Kyrianna's arm. The girl held her arms out and Myrith frowned at the chaos portal now glowing on both of her wrists. "You say you oppose Thynitic, yet you put the Lady of Chaos' mark on her. This makes no sense."

"I am doing what is necessary to get you past the demons and across the river. She raised a different wand and pointed it at the three stone horses, which shrank in size to look like small toys.

Nirev picked up the horses and put them in his pack.

"Is that everything?" Myrith looked around at the others and waited a moment before securing the blanket to Riker's saddle. "I'll call you when we get across the river."

She looked over at Kyrianna and Cewyr. "You should probably dismiss her as well."

Kyrianna nodded, placed a hand on the unicorn's neck as she vanished leaving only the small figurine.

"What else." Myrith looked at Grania.

"Only her appearance." She turned to Kyrianna.

"I can handle that myself; I have had enough of her magic." She indicated the slender ring she wore on her left hand.

Myrith watched as Kyrianna's features shifted only slightly and her hair and eyes darkened to black.

"I thought you knew nothing of Carrinna," Urric said. "Now,

you look enough like her to be her twin."

"What?"

"It is a good disguise and one that will help us pass through the demon camp," Grania said.

"Let's get going," Myrith said.

~ * ~

"Chaos!" Kyrianna stopped, her left hand going to her right wrist.

"Kyri?" Myrith reached for her friend's arm, but stopped as Grania stepped between them.

"A sharp pain, followed by burning," Kyrianna said pulling her arm away from Grania. She almost doubled over holding her arm as a shrill scream came from the demon camp ahead of them.

"The obscuration is still place," Grania said. "I do not sense anything interfering with my magics."

"May I?" Falden held his hands out.

Kyrianna nodded and held out her arm. Myrith frowned at the grimace on the girl's face as Falden passed his hand over the mark.

"It is the mark of Frayrith that is reacting to something. Unfortunately, I cannot sense what the problem is." He bowed his head. "Sorry"

"Andrinor, stay close to her," Myrith whispered. "I doubt this was a coincidence." She glanced toward the camp.

Andrinor nodded.

"I want across the river as quickly as possible," Myrith said.

Grania bowed and Myrith shuddered at the smile on the woman's face as she took the lead and they followed her into the demon camp.

"My lady," a small imp approached and bowed to Grania. "If you had sent word, we would have had food and a place to rest prepared for you and your guests."

"No need. My guests are in a hurry."

"Very well." The imp stopped then bowed to Kyrianna. "Chaos' Daughter honors us with her presence in our camp." He gestured to two other imps who vanished into a nearby tent.

Chaos' Daughter! Myrith turned to see Kyrianna had gone pale at the imp's words. Now, she understood why Grania had thought Kyrianna's disguise was a good one. *The witch planned for this.*

Daughter of Chaos, she thought. *That is what the damned imp called her. Brular also said that was the title her mother had before she renounced Thynitic.*

Two chaos demons exited the tent and Myrith heard Kyrianna draw in a breath. She followed the girl's gaze to another of the demons still standing by the tent. There was something familiar about the creature. This was the same demon they had faced in that first temple as well as later being disguised as Argrala. The demon only stood there watching them—waiting.

The two approaching demons knelt and one of them held out a gold goblet filled with a green fluid. "For your refreshment," one of them said.

Myrith could see Kyrianna's hands trembling as she took the goblet. Grania leaned over and whispered something in the girl's ear.

"May chaos guide you," Kyrianna said before she took a long drink from the goblet.

The demons stood, bowed and returned to the tent.

"Hold," another voice called. "I would challenge that one for the honor of being one of the Lady's guards."

Myrith turned to see a creature standing there pointing a sword at Andrinor. This wasn't a chaos demon. This demon was shorter, but just as powerfully built as the chaos demons. His horns were shorter, and his wings more closely resembled a dragon's. Her breath caught in her throat as she realized this was a half-dragon demon-spawn. He carried a battleaxe and a broadsword.

"Abomination," she heard Andrinor mutter and she felt a chill flow off his body.

"Don't. If you change form, you'll bring all of them down on us."

"My Lady is in a hurry and does not have time for your games," Myrith said.

"I accept the challenge," Andrinor said stepping past Myrith.

"We don't have time for this," Myrith said.

"I will not let that abomination live," Andrinor said.

Myrith glanced at Kyrianna who was staring blankly in their direction. Grania was standing next to her, a thin smile on her lips.

"My Lady," Myrith said offering Kyrianna a slight bow. "We do not have time for these games."

"If she interferes, it will damage her disguise," Grania said. "Rudalynth," she nodded toward the demon still by the main tent, "is already suspicious. That is why he is watching her."

"The challenge has been made and accepted," Kyrianna said.

"Kyri, that's Andrinor! Your friend! You have to prevent this. We will deal with any problems."

Kyrianna shook her head slowly. "The challenge has been made and accepted."

Grania raised her hands and a shimmering ring appeared on the ground circling Andrinor and the demon. Myrith's hand went to her sword, but was stopped by Gwideon. "Do not interfere," he said. "Rash actions on any of our parts will get us all killed."

~ * ~

Andrinor held his sword in front of him as he studied the demon. It was of the gold, like Vyroris; and he could feel the heat already surrounding him. He would have to end this fight quickly. Still, he had learned a lot during his time in Tormasus; he would wait for the abomination to make the first move.

The demon-spawn roared and a burst of flame rolled toward Andrinor. He dodged to the side, only to find himself blocked by the blade and ax. The demon-spawn was fast. But, he was of the silver and faster. His weapon seemed to move on its own, a blessing of the magic contained in the brands he had been given, as he moved around the creature. He looked at the demon-spawn as it took a step back and glanced toward the chaos demon standing by the tent. The demon shook his head slowly and Andrinor saw the demon-spawn's eye widen slightly. No one else would have seen it, but there was a sliver of white ringing its eyes—fear.

Andrinor took advantage of his opponent's distraction and swung his sword. The demon-spawn brought his sword up to block then roared as Andrinor's blade cut into his wrist.

The scales were strong and Andrinor had to jerk his weapon hard to keep it from being trapped by them. The demon-spawn dropped the sword and took a stumbling step back.

He's not used to something being able to hit him, Andrinor thought. He realized the demon-spawn's breath attack and its speed were the main advantages it held over opponents. That was information he could use.

He glanced down at the ring that surrounded them; there was

a shimmering distortion that rose up from the ground. He darted to the side and used his sword to toss a rock at the barrier. There was a loud pop and all that was left of the rock was a handful of dust. If he crossed the barrier before it was dismissed, he would end up the same way. Perhaps there was a way he could force the demon-spawn into the barrier.

"Pyremar's Fires!" He spun away as the axe sliced the air where he had been standing.

The demon-spawn hissed as he shifted his weapon and Andrinor's left arm went numb as the haft struck his elbow. He swung his sword around blindly, as he continued to move away from the demon-spawn. The distortion that marked the ring surrounding them brightened and Andrinor saw the ring shrink around him and the demon-spawn.

He had to end this fight, before it was ended for them.

He took several steps back and planted his feet as he faced the demon. The creature may be an abomination, but it wasn't stupid, he knew he wouldn't be able to lure it into charging him and then trick it into the barrier.

He jabbed his sword backward, letting the barrier destroy the second blade. Now he held what was basically a long sword. He took a deep breath as he saw the demon-spawn's chest expand slightly. The ring was now small enough he doubted he could avoid the fire. He focused on the power he had been given by Ghainaess. His blood chilled with the power of the silver and he whispered a prayer it would be enough to protect him.

"Chaos!" He yelled as he charged the demon-spawn and felt himself engulfed by the flames it expelled. He forced his sword into the creature's chest and twisted. The flames grew hotter and he released the sword as he fought to stay on his feet. He swung his right fist and the claws on the gauntlet slashed the demon-spawn's throat.

The flames stopped as the creature fell back into the barrier and was destroyed.

Andrinor forced himself to remain upright and he turned toward Kyrianna and the others. He brought his arm up in salute. "My Lady," he said dropping to his knees.

"The challenge has been met." Kyrianna raised the goblet she was still holding. "You hold the favor of the Daughter of Chaos." She turned to Gwideon and Myrith. "See to his wounds. Then we must leave."

~ * ~

"Do not call on your goddess, yet," Gwideon said as he knelt next to Andrinor.

Myrith was amazed to see the young man was still conscious as he lay on the ground. Most of his skin was blistered or blackened. Smoke was still coming off his chainmail and she grimaced when she saw where it had fused with his skin. "He needs healing magic," she said.

"That is obvious. However, for you to call on the gifts your goddess has given you will expose us. There is no way to hide that power from such as these." He held out a vial of a blue liquid. "This should get him back on his feet, so we can get away from here and then deal with everything we will have to deal with." He glanced toward Kyrianna then back at Andrinor.

Myrith nodded and held Andrinor's head gently as Gwideon brought the vial to his lips. The young man moaned then started swallowing the potion. She swallowed herself, to keep from gagging at the stench from his burnt flesh and hair. She glanced back down at his face and frowned. Covering his eyes was a layer of silver scales—also burned.

"Andrinor, can you see?" she whispered.

The scales seemed to fade and she found herself looking into Andrinor's ice blue eyes; eyes. They were clear and apparently untouched by the flames. Andrinor nodded slowly. "That is the one part of my body, I believe was untouched by the heat and flames," he said.

She nodded as she and Gwideon helped him to stand and they walked back to the rest of the group. "My Lady," she said. "It is time we were leaving."

Kyrianna only nodded. Myrith frowned at the glazed and distant look in her friend's eyes. There was something wrong. She glanced at the goblet as Kyrianna handed it to the imp that approached and bowed. There was still some of the green liquid in the cup. She frowned at the color—it reminded her of something that was dead and decaying. She followed Kyrianna and Grania as the woman escorted them away from the camp. They were within sight of the river when she signaled for them to stop and turned to place her hand on Andrinor's chest. The young man took several deep breaths as the healing power she had been given flowed into his body.

"What was in that drink they gave her?" She heard Gwideon ask.

"Sylvenis."

Myrith patted Andrinor on the shoulder, her power exhausted. "Thank you," he said.

"You allowed her to drink sylvenis," Gwideon said. "Why?"

"It was necessary to maintain the disguise," Grania said. "They thought she was Chaos' Daughter, she needed to act as they expected. Rudalynth was watching her very closely; no doubt suspicious of us all. He has served Thynitic for many centuries and probably knows who each of you are. He could sense the magic surrounding us, even if he couldn't discern what it was. However, the last thing we needed was for him to try and pierce that magic with his own."

Myrith turned to Gwideon. "What is sylvenis?"

"It is a drug that creates a unique blend of euphoria and pain. It is highly addictive and almost always fatal." He paused and lowered his voice. "It is made by distilling the pain felt by fey creatures when they are tortured and killed."

"That scream we heard." Myrith's grip on her sword tightened.

"A dryad, most likely," Gwideon said.

"Her patron is a nature goddess, that explains the pain she felt," Falden said.

Myrith brought her sword up and held it at Grania's throat.

"You still need me to get across the river," Grania said. "And, I have the means to prevent her dying from the pain of withdrawal."

"Then give it to her."

"Not until we are across the river. A few drops of her blood for each of us should suffice to pay the toll. I will release her from the drug once we are across—not before." She placed her hand on Kyrianna's arm and started walking toward the small dock.

"Myrith, there is no antidote to this drug that I am aware of," Gwideon said.

"Cewyr," Falden whispered.

"Unicorn horn? Perhaps." Gwideon shook his head. "I doubt Kyri allow it?"

"That will be Cewyr's decision, not Kyri's," Myrith said. She didn't sheath her sword as she followed Kyrianna and Grania. The witch had planned all of this. No doubt the woman would have created the same disguise for Kyrianna if the girl hadn't unknowingly done it herself.

"She sent the demons to prepare the camp for the arrival of Chaos' Daughter," Falden said. "She would have known they would offer her the sylvenis. This was not a coincidence."

"What about the half-dragon who challenged Andrinor?" Myrith asked.

"Also not a coincidence," Andrinor said. "When he failed to kill or even hurt me in his initial attack he looked to the demon she called Rudalynth almost as if he were asking to be released from the challenge. I saw fear in his eyes at that moment."

Myrith glanced toward Kyrianna and Grania. "Stop!" She darted forward and grabbed the dagger the woman was holding at Kyrianna's neck.

Grania smiled and took the small bowl the cloaked ferryman was holding. "Either you do it or I will," she said.

Myrith's hand tightened on the dagger and she took several quick breaths.

"Ten drops for each of us," Grania said placing the bowl on Kyrianna's shoulder and tilting it against her neck.

"I'm sorry," Myrith whispered. "But, I won't risk her hurting you any more than she already has." She pressed the tip of the blade against Kyrianna's neck, finding the vein and opening it just enough for the blood to drip into the bowl. Ten drops for each of them, each one of them an accusation she had failed to protect her friend during this journey.

Grania handed the bowl to the ferryman who turned and gestured to the small ferry. Myrith's hand shook as she placed it against the cut and pleaded with Mykaylene to grant her a tiny portion of healing power to help Kyrianna. It was enough to stop the bleeding. She grinned as Shydaran, still in the weasel form, jumped onto Kyrianna's shoulder and wrapped himself around her neck. His fur was warm and she thought she saw Kyrianna's eyes clear a bit before she stepped onto the ferry.

"Witch!" Kyrianna spun around to face Grania as the ferry left the small dock.

Grania raised her right hand and a bolt of lightning struck

Kyrianna in the chest.

The girl dropped to the deck.

Myrith swung her sword, only to connect with Gwideon's as Grania vanished from between them.

"She has two ways to die," Grania's voice called. "Screaming in pain from the withdrawals, which should start in a few hours, or by your hand. Either way she will never serve Thynitic as the Daughter of Chaos, which I believe is what you want. As it is also what Carrinna wants; this will just ensure it never happens."

"Jerietlan?"

The cleric looked up and nodded. "She's fine, for now. The drug seems to have been slowed and she is coming around."

"Let's go." Myrith said when the ferry stopped and the cloaked figure gestured to the bank. She and Gwideon helped Kyrianna to her feet and off the ferry. As soon as the last of their group was off, the small vessel vanished.

"Kyri?"

The girl shook her head. "Give me a minute." The illusion she was wearing vanished and Myrith frowned at how pale Kyrianna was. Her hands were trembling as she pulled the unicorn figurine from her pouch and Cewyr appeared. The unicorn touched her chest with her horn and Kyrianna stopped shaking.

"I've heard it said unicorn horn is a universal antidote for poisons and drugs," Falden said.

"No!" Kyrianna placed a hand on Cewyr's neck. "That would hurt her. I will not allow it."

"That is my decision," Cewyr said.

Kyrianna wrapped her arms in front of her chest, her hands rubbing her arms.

"That it is. But, I would not have you do this."

"It will take time to make the elixir," Falden said. "And I will need the use of an alchemy lab."

Jerietlan raised the tower shield. "I seek safe rest My Lady...,"

"No!" Kyrianna slapped her hand against the shield. "We will not delay any further because of me."

Cewyr looked at Myrith and nodded her head.

"Very well," Myrith said. "Riker."

The spectral horse appeared and she pulled the blanket with their weapons from the saddle. "Let's get going. Rangerette, you said the swamp route would be shorter than the forest." Conflagration blazed with fire when she picked the sword up.

"It's about half the distance, but I would be more comfortable with the forest. There are too many things that can hide below the surface of the water."

"I agree with Kyri," Andrinor said.

"Myrith," Hendandra said nodding toward the nearby trees.

She followed the girl's gaze to see an elf standing there, a scimitar in his hand as he watched them.

"Well met," Myrith said.

"Who are you that you think to invade my forest?"

"Your forest?"

"I am its defender. It is my forest."

Myrith nodded. "We meant no insult or trespass. We are only following the path through this area. We will not harm anything that leaves us in peace as we travel."

"And I am to trust your word?" The elf shook his head.

Myrith watched the light play on the elf's hair—hair that was a shade or two darker than her own flame red, but streaked with silver. His eyes were black and his skin had a golden hue to it. There was something else also—an almost ethereal look to the elf—as if he wasn't completely there. It was same thing she saw when she looked at Riker.

"It is all we can offer." Myrith held her hand out.

The elf looked at her hand then his gaze moved to the rest of the group. She held her breath as he seemed to study Kyrianna for a moment. "Who did this to her?"

"A witch named Grania," Andrinor said.

"Grania." The elf cocked his head to the side. "She serves one who would destroy order and usurp the Lady of Chaos."

Myrith's grip tightened on Conflagration and she saw Cewyr take a step forward, putting her between Kyrianna and the elf.

"I am called Raelis," he said turning his attention back to Myrith. "If you will help me with a problem I have, I will guide you to a portal that will shorten your journey through the forest considerably."

"What be this problem?" Nirev asked.

"A group of trolls are destroying one of the sacred groves. Will you help me stop them?"

"Sacred to whom?" Falden asked.

"Does that matter?" Kyrianna asked. "They are destroying

something that does not belong to them."

Shydaran, back in his tiger form, roared and Myrith nodded. "We will assist you," she said.

~ * ~

Myrith glanced at Kyrianna as they came out of the trees into an area almost a half league across filled with stumps where six trolls were stacking the felled trees together. The girl's hands were shaking but she wasn't sure if it was from the drug or anger at the devastation they were looking at.

"Wait," Falden said as Myrith started to kick Riker. The mage spoke softly as he raised his hands and a small bead of fire streaked forward to explode in the midst of the trolls.

She heard Jerietlan also muttering and a column of fire flowed from the sky as Falden's fireball faded. When that was gone also, the trolls began laughing as they each picked up a large spear and waited.

"Protected from fire?" Kyrianna said, shaking her head. "These are not normal trolls."

"Then we will see how they fair against ice," Andrinor said.

Myrith shivered as a blast of cold air preceded Andrinor, in his dragon form, leaping past her to claw at one of the trolls. She kneed Riker forward and guided him around to where one of the trolls stood chanting. The troll stopped chanting and watched her as she approached. As she raised Conflagration, the troll swept the staff he was holding at Riker.

"Riker!" She found herself sitting on the ground, the ghostly horse gone.

The troll lifted the staff as if he meant to break it. She pulled her feet under her and lunged forward. Conflagration slid into the troll's throat and he dropped the staff.

She took a stumbling step back and stared at the piece of wood resting on the ground.

"Riker?" Her voice broke as she reached for the staff.

~ * ~

"Myrith, you must see to the others."

She looked up to see Cewyr standing before her. The unicorn's horn was glowing as she touched it to the staff. There was a burst of light and the winged unicorn that had fought the demon the previous night was now standing before her. "Riker?"

"He is here," Cewyr said. "It is called spirit wood and will trap and hold any non-corporeal being. If the troll had destroyed it, Riker would now be lost as well." She paused and turned to the fight. "The others need your help or this battle will be lost."

Myrith gasped. How long had she been standing there, staring at the staff and ignoring the others? She jumped on Cewyr's back and quickly assessed the situation. Gwideon and Jerietlan were facing one of the trolls. There were three of the trolls around Andrinor, still in his dragon form, Kyrianna was on the ground and Andrinor held his tail over her, protecting her. Shydaran's claws were ripping into another of the creatures and Nirev was facing the last. She frowned at the amount of blood on the ground around Nirev and on his armor. It appeared it was only through sheer will the dwarf was still standing. The elf was hanging back, a bow in his hands as he fired arrows at the three facing Andrinor.

She cringed as a bolt of lightning streaked through the sky. It didn't seem to bother the trolls it struck. :*My Lady, these aren't normal trolls, but they must have a weakness.*

:*You have tried fire, ice and lightning. What else do you have?*

Myrith's head jerked up as Andrinor roared. His normally bright scales were dull where his blood had dried on them. Her gaze caught the small green horns next to his silver ones.

"Acid," she cried. "Falden, can you drop a ball of acid on them?"

The mage nodded and she waited as he began casting. The ball of acid exploded just behind the trolls as Andrinor also expelled a blast of the fluid then collapsed. She kicked Cewyr hard and the unicorn bolted forward. Two of the trolls had dissolved into a putrid mess, but the third had lifted a spear made of the same wood that had trapped Riker and was aiming it at Kyrianna's still form.

'The demoness told me Thynitic is having one of those vile amulets made for me.' That was what Kyrianna had told her and Andrinor when they returned to Shokar. That wood could trap a non-corporeal spirit. Could it also be used to draw the spirit from a living person?

She kicked Cewyr again, and the unicorn lunged forward with a shrill neigh. The troll paused and started to turn. He stopped as Conflagration cut through the arm holding the spear and Andrinor's blade pierced his chest.

"Andrinor?" Myrith stared as the young man pulled the sword from the troll and acid dripped from the blade. He was pale and shaking, blood still flowed from the wounds he had received—he wasn't going to last much longer. :*What strength I have, I give to him, My Lady.* That he had forced himself up to face the troll again, was amazing.

She felt herself grow weaker as Andrinor seemed to finally find his balance. A bolt of green lightning streaked past the young man to strike the troll before also striking two of the others. They all dissolved. She fell against Cewyr's neck and the unicorn froze in place. There was a feeling of warmth from the mare's body and Myrith patted her neck in thanks for the healing energy.

She looked up to see Gwideon staring at her. "What did you do?" he asked.

"What was necessary. How are the others?" She slid off Cewyr. Jerietlan was tending to Nirev and Falden was pouring acid on the troll Shydaran had ripped up. The tiger was bleeding from several bad wounds, but backed away when Jerietlan approached. Shydaran growled and shook his body then the wounds began healing slowly. His healing energy was almost gone also.

"How much further?" Myrith glanced at the elf.

"Not far." Raelis was staring at Cewyr. "You have been blessed by the Guardian of the Fields. I am honored to meet one such as you."

Cewyr only nodded then turned to Myrith. "Will you carry Kyri?"

Myrith nodded. She wasn't happy Riker and Cewyr were still in this merging, but it wouldn't do any good for her to demand Riker's appearance right now. She climbed back on the unicorn's back and waited as Gwideon handed Kyrianna up to her. The girl was unconscious and trembling. She was reminded of the spell Thynitic had placed on Andrinor and Falden not that long ago.

"We'll find a way to save you, Kyri," she whispered.

~ * ~

"There is the portal out of the forest," Raelis said pointing to a nearby tree. "Take this." He held out a small pouch. "It is powdered unicorn horn."

"How did you get this?" Falden demanded taking the pouch

and opening it.

"It was given to me by one of the eldest. Just as her sword was given," he said looking at Kyrianna.

"Thank you," Myrith said as Cewyr touched her horn to Raelis' shoulder.

Raelis bowed his head slightly, then stepped aside. Myrith waited as the others went through the portal. "She must find the balance and it must be restored," she heard Raelis say before the portal closed behind her.

Chapter Twelve

Falden held up the pouch Raelis had given him. "I will start the preparations." He paused and looked at Cewyr. "Do you wish to observe?"

Cewyr shook her head.

"Andrinor, you and the others get first use of the showers," Myrith said. "Hendandra, give me a hand getting her out of her armor." She placed Kyrianna on the pallet she had used the night before in the large hall. Jerietlan had said the hall held sanctified magics that would assist with healing; she hoped they would help Kyrianna. Besides that, she was not going to let the girl out of her sight any more than necessary tonight. She had seen others suffering from drug withdrawals. She knew better than to leave Kyrianna alone.

"Do you want something from the dining hall?" Hendandra asked when they finished with Kyrianna.

"Maybe later. Get yourself something, and keep an eye on the tiger so he leaves enough for the rest."

"I'll be back."

"Thank you."

Myrith pulled the blankets up around Kyrianna. The girl was pale and her breathing was coming in shallow gasps. She didn't know anything about this particular drug, but she doubted they had much time left before even the antidote Falden was trying to make wouldn't be able to help. She glanced at Cewyr. The unicorn was next to Kyrianna, her body in close contact with the girl. *That's probably what's keeping Kyri from thrashing and screaming from the pain she has to be feeling.* Whatever the unicorn was doing, she was thankful for it. Not having Kyrianna in obviously severe pain made waiting for Falden a little easier.

"Myrith," Andrinor's voice said from the doorway. "We're done. I'll stay with her, while you get cleaned up."

"I'll wait."

"Lady Lake," Gwideon said. "You must see your own needs. There are others here who can watch her for now."

"Very well." She pulled Conflagration from her back and handed the sheathed weapon to Gwideon. "I won't be long."

"Lady Knight, ye'll be needing help with yer armor," Nirev said.

She stopped and nodded. Kyrianna had been the primary person to help her with the armor, except for the young squire assigned to her while she was at the Coliseum.

She waited as Nirev loosened the straps then helped her in removing the various pieces. "Good, it not be needing any repairs, unlike Andrinor's and Gwideon's. Now, see to getting yerself cleaned up."

"Very well." She headed toward the showers.

~ * ~

"Myrith?" Andrinor's voice pierced the fog in her mind.

She snapped her head up. "What?"

"Falden has finished his work," Andrinor said.

She looked over the shower door at the young man who was looking anywhere but in her direction. "I'll be right there."

Andrinor nodded then hurried out of the area. She waited until she heard the door close before shutting off the water. *How long have I been in here?* She thought as she quickly dried off then threw on a shirt and some pants. The warm water had felt good and she had let it relax her as she stood there, her mind blank.

She was tired. Giving of her own strength and energy to save Andrinor had left her drained. It was only the fact she had been on Cewyr and the unicorn had shared her healing gifts that had kept her from falling into unconsciousness at that point.

She grabbed her pack and ran as a scream echoed off the stones walls. "What's going on?"

"Cewyr removed the magics holding Kyrianna," Falden said. "They would have interfered with the antidote,"

Myrith nodded, her hands clenched tightly as she looked down at Kyrianna. The girl was still screaming and thrashing on the floor.

"Let's get this over with," Myrith said. She motioned Andrinor over to one side of Kyrianna. "We'll need to hold her."

It took her and the young man several minutes to get enough control of Kyrianna to be able to hold her. Falden poured the silver liquid into her throat quickly, then held her mouth closed.

"Now we wait." Falden tapped a finger against Kyrianna's forehead and she went limp. "A low level charm that will let her sleep while the antidote works," he said.

"Watches tonight; myself, Andrinor and Gwideon," Myrith said.

"Lady Lake, I will take the first watch. You get some rest," Gwideon said. "If anything changes," he glanced at Kyrianna, "I will alert you immediately."

Myrith shook her head. "No, it is my responsibility."

"It will be some time while the antidote works," Falden said. "If it does." The last was only a faint whisper.

"Take your rest Lady Lake. There are times when you must let others bear part of the burden. This does not mean you give up your responsibilities; you only allow those who would help to do so."

"Very well." She nodded.

~ * ~

"I didn't know!" Kyrianna sat up suddenly, the image of a dryad still in her mind as she struggled to catch her breath.

"I didn't know," she whispered.

"Kyrianna?"

She looked up to see Gwideon standing next to her, a look of concern creasing his brow. "Another bad dream," she said, glancing around at Andrinor and Myrith standing with readied weapons.

"With everything we have seen and done," Cewyr said, "is it any wonder some of us are having nightmares?"

"No," Myrith said.

Kyrianna took several deep breaths and glanced down at her wrists. The obscuration Grania had placed there was starting to fade. "I didn't know," she said again.

Myrith knelt down next to her. "What was it?"

"It was a water nymph they tortured to create the drug," she said. "I was in a glade next to her pool and she pulled me in." Her voice was labored as she struggled to speak. "I sho...should have known. Sho...should have...have pro...tected...her." She paused and took a deep breath. "Cewyr appeared and the nymph released me. That's when I woke up."

"It was only a dream, Kyri," Myrith said. "There was no way

we could have known or done anything to protect whoever it was they used to create that vile drug."

Kyrianna looked at her friend. There were dark circles around Myrith's eyes and she seemed even more tightly wound than normal.

"Myrith?" Kyrianna asked as she forced herself to her feet.

Myrith didn't answer, only stood, placed her hand on Kyrianna's neck then shook her head and returned to her bed.

"The burden of her responsibilities weighs heavily on Lady Lake," Gwideon said. "It does not help that she almost lost two of her friends today and she would have been helpless to prevent it. That your dreams accuse you of failing one of those your goddess would have you protect only reinforces her concerns."

Kyrianna nodded.

"Go, get some proper rest and lay your demons aside. You didn't know and were deceived by one who knew how to manipulate you and Myrith both." He held his hand out to her.

Kyrianna took the hand and felt a chill pass through her and then the familiar presence of Melissa in her mind. She raised an eyebrow as she looked up at Gwideon.

"She did not need to feel the pain you were suffering."

"Thank you, for protecting her." He only nodded.

Kyrianna rested a hand on Cewyr's neck as they walked through the dining hall and she picked up several pieces of fruit before heading to the shrine.

"What you said before," she whispered. "Are you scared?"

Cewyr shook her head. :*We have had those we care about taken from us. Your 'sister' spent thirty years trapped in a horrid place reliving her brother's betrayal. I myself was embraced by the Guardian of the Fields for forty-six years and allowed, in spirit, to roam her fields—but I was never given form.*

Kyrianna stopped and stepped in front of Cewyr. "What? I thought you had been given life again by the Guardian."

:*No.* She dropped her head and closed her eyes. :*My actions on that day tainted me. I was not given life because of that.*

"You were a foal. How could the Guardian judge you like that?"

:*To give me life after such a deed, even while enspelled, would have shown anything is forgivable. Because of the laws binding her, she could not do such a thing. She protected my soul and I was given the freedom to roam with the herds, but never to be with them.*

:I don't know which would be worse. I knew only misery, while you saw beauty and joy but could never truly share in it, Melissa's voice said.

:It was strange Kyri, Cewyr said. *:I pleaded with the Guardian once to either let me run with the herd or to end my torture. I didn't understand her response at the time; but I think I do now. 'To truly run with them, should you not understand what is in their beating hearts that compels them to do so.'*

Kyrianna closed her eyes and smiled as Cewyr nuzzled her neck. "That tickles," she said with a laugh. She let her face touch Cewyr's and she heard Melissa's voice echo the question she asked.

"But why did she wait thirty years?"

:I am not sure. But, it seems as if she knew I was going to be called someday.

Kyrianna laughed as Cewyr's lips again brushed across her neck. She stepped back as a silence seemed to fill the area of her mind where Cewyr's presence normally was for several heartbeats. "What is it?" she asked.

:The ones who are lost shall find you, Cewyr said. *One with a dark and unyielding heart; the other with a heart in turmoil and distress. They will find you and hopefully they will be able to find their paths out of the darkness as well.*

Kyrianna only stared at the unicorn. *The ones who are lost?* She thought. *Did she mean Brular and me? It doesn't make sense.*

:When did the Guardian say this to you? Melissa asked.

:Some twenty-six years after that foul day.

Kyrianna took step back, her mouth open. "No," she whispered.

:Kyri, how old are you? Melissa asked.

"Twenty."

:She knew. There was warmth in Cewyr's voice as she spoke. *:As did Frayrith—from the moment you were conceived.*

Kyrianna took another step back then turned and ran from the dining hall. She paused at the door to the shrine she had dedicated to Dwycia and Frayrith. Her unicorn horn sword and the red 'tears of Frayrith' rested on the altar. "Myrith, thank you," she whispered. The woman was the only one of the group, except maybe Andrinor she saw taking the time and care to place the items.

She stepped forward and dropped to the floor. "You knew.

You knew Thynitic and Torliana would both come for me. You knew Brular would come for Torliana. You knew Thynitic would take my mother from me. All the misery and pain—you knew and you let it happen." She clenched her fists tightly as her body was wracked with sobs. "Why?"

:*Maybe so you and the others would know the difference between the darkness and the light. I do not presume to understand the rational of the Guardians, much less the gods. However, I trust in their design—as should you.*

"But to be only a puppet...." Kyrianna paused and looked up at Cewyr. The mare tilted her head to the side and seemed to be studying her. "Everything seems preordained. Where is my will?"

:*So, now you have no choices left, is that it? Do you honestly think the gods control everything?*

"It would seem like it."

Cewyr lowered herself to the ground and brushed her muzzle against Kyrianna's cheek. :*If they controlled everything, do you think Thynitic would not have known what was going to happen and have destroyed the others before they reached you?*

Kyrianna nodded. "I agree she would not have let it happen." She wiped at her eyes, brushing away the tears. "So what is it?"

:*Kyri did you not listen to what Frayrith told you in Kilenter. The gods are bound by laws that define their nature. They cannot act outside of those laws; but mortals have a choice. The gods cannot control the future, but they are able to sense its direction and attempt to influence it. It is the choices we make that determine the outcome. It is those choices that will take the world toward the path of darkness or light, order or chaos at crucial moments.*

Cewyr pulled at Kyrianna's hair. :*Thank you for choosing the light.*

Kyrianna shifted around and leaned back against Cewyr, using the unicorn as a pillow. In her mind she heard Melissa begin humming the same song they had played with Tristan. :*Are you trying to make me fall asleep?*

:*No, it's as if it started playing in my head,* Melissa said then giggled. :*Well I don't have a head.* There was a pause. :*Kyri, I think Tristan is summoning me.* There was another pause. :*Maybe he misses you.*

:*Stop that!* Kyrianna said. :*Don't say those things unless you know it is true.*

:*I can ask him.*

Kyrianna took a breath. She knew how he felt, they had told each other before the group left. Why was she thinking like this?

:*Don't!* The word was sharper than she intended and she felt Melissa pull away from her. She forced herself to relax and took a breath before continuing. :*Melissa, tell him about everything that has happened to us since we departed. I would not have you hide anything. Answer any questions he has as best you can*

:*Anything else?* There was a hopeful tone to Melissa's voice.

:*There is one other thing.* Kyrianna took a deep breath as she felt her chest tighten and a chill permeate her soul. :*You must tell him about the amulet and the Reishalli. You must tell him I fear he could be trapped by her vile magic as well.*

:*I will.* Melissa's voice was distant. :*I have to go now.*

"Thank you." Kyrianna let herself drift off to sleep as she waited for Melissa's return.

~ * ~

Kyrianna found herself surrounded by darkness as the sound of a violin and piano flowed through the air.

"He misses you," a woman's voice said. There was something familiar about the voice, but she didn't recognize it. "But, how long do you think he will wait? He seeks to re-establish his family's position and status. Something that will be made easier by the association he now has with King Dracenhalts. An association you brought about. A position that can be strengthened through a marriage alliance to a more powerful house."

Kyrianna's heart skipped and she felt her breath catch at the truth behind the woman's words. "He will wait," she said raising her head. "What we share is more than simple desire."

"Perhaps, perhaps not." The darkness faded as the woman's voice did also.

Kyrianna found herself standing in the guest room of the Duvall house in Raspa. She smiled when she saw the dark blue and silver, elven silk dress hanging on the back of the door. *If this is a dream, then I am going to enjoy it,* she thought as she changed into the gown. She quickly brushed and arranged her hair then touched the sapphire pendant around her neck.

:*Melissa?*

There was no response.

She froze as she opened the door and heard voices in the room below. She couldn't understand what Tristan was saying, but it was followed by a distinctly feminine laugh. She took deep a breath and headed down the stairs to the hall. Staying in the shadows where she wouldn't be seen she slipped behind the statue of Mykaylene that stood near the door.

She felt her eyes burn when she saw Tristan sitting on one of the couches with a young woman of about sixteen years. Across from them was an older couple. The young woman was smiling, her hand resting on Tristan's as he spoke to the older man.

She focused on calming her breathing so she could listen to the conversation.

"Your hospitality tonight has been most generous, Lord Duvall," the older woman said. "Many members of the council have been pleased by House Duvall's recent rise in status and we look forward to seeing you entertain more; as well as attending more functions yourself." She nodded to the girl.

"Grandmother is correct. We will be hosting an informal dinner three days from now. You will attend?"

Tristan nodded and smiled. "I would be honored to accept the invitation."

Kyrianna felt her knees wobble and she grabbed the wall to keep from disturbing the statue. She closed her eyes as Tristan stood and offered his hand to the girl. "You promised to play for us, Caitlin," she heard him say. She opened her eyes and saw the older couple smile and exchange a glance as the girl started to play.

Tristan walked over to the fireplace and placed another piece of wood on the smoldering fire. Kyrianna watched as his gaze moved to the weapons hanging on the wall above the mantel. The first weapon she recognized as the sword they had found at the estate that had belonged to Tristan's grandfather, Rhinehart Duvall. Above that was a two handed sword, with the symbol of Mykaylene prominently displayed on the hilt. Her hand went to her mouth when she saw the weapon hanging above the two swords was the dagger she had given to Tristan before the group left.

Tristan's gaze seemed to linger on the dagger for several heartbeats before he turned his attention back to the girl at the piano. This time, Kyrianna could see the distracted and faraway look in his eyes as he listened to the music. He never glanced at the older couple who were talking quietly to themselves.

Tristan's head jerked up as Caitlin missed several notes of the waltz she had been playing. The girl stood quickly, knocking over the bench as the piano continued playing. He managed to catch her before she tripped. Kyrianna recognized the tune as a badly butchered version of the duet she had shared with Tristan.

"What's going on?" Tristan asked helping the girl away from the piano.

"I don't know. The piano starting playing on its own." She stood shaking behind the couch where her grandparents sat.

"I do not sense anything evil about the instrument. However, perhaps it would be best if we called it a night so I can have it checked by a cleric." He offered the girl his hand as he escorted her to the door.

"We will see you at the dinner, I trust," the older man said.

Tristan only nodded as the gentleman climbed into the coach after the two ladies.

Kyrianna smiled as the door closed and Tristan walked back to the piano. As he approached the music changed to the correct tune.

"Melissa?" Tristan placed his hand on the piano. "Why are you still here?"

Kyrianna stepped out from behind the statue. "Perhaps it is because I am here," she said softly.

"Kyri?" Tristan gathered her into an embrace. "How is this possible?" She placed her hand over his lips and shook her head.

Too bad this is only a dream, Kyrianna thought as Tristan held her and they lost themselves in the music.

After several minutes, they moved closer to the piano. Kyrianna's hand brushed against it and she felt Melissa move back into the necklace as the last notes of the song faded. She looked up into Tristan's eyes and smiled as their lips came together and he pulled her even closer. Her body trembled and she felt her heart skip as his hands slid up to softly caress her ears.

His right hand slid down her neck to her shoulder and she felt him push the collar of her dress to the side as he kissed her neck and shoulder. She took a deep breath and closed her eyes as she leaned into him. Her breath was coming in short gasps and she felt her body flush with warmth.

:Kyri, are you okay? Melissa asked.

"What?" Kyrianna sat up suddenly and gasped as the cool air of the shrine surrounded her.

:Kyri?

"It was only a dream," she said. "Melissa, let it go, please." She stood up and walked to the shower room. There was a bucket of cool water on one of the benches in the room and she splashed her face several times to clear her head before returning to the shrine and some more sleep.

Chapter Thirteen

Myrith waited as Kyrianna completed the meditation that would allow her to see the area they would be traveling through this day. Gwideon stood to the side watching her. Even if she couldn't see his face because of his helm, she could feel the frown she knew was there. They had not spoken beyond his admonishment to rest last night and she didn't understand why he was upset or disappointed in her. Perhaps they would have a chance to talk tonight, depending on what happened this day.

"How far?" she asked glancing at Urric.

"About thirty leagues."

Thirty leagues! She glanced around at the others. They were showing the strain of the previous two days. *We need to get through this place as quickly as possible, but can I push them that fast today?* The distance was only a few leagues further than they had traveled the first day, but half again the distance they had traveled yesterday. She wanted to get to the next portal today, but knew they had to be prepared to fight whatever they would face in Thynitic's citadel when they reached it. Time was critical, but so was being in condition to fight.

"Nothing but grasslands between here and the portal," Kyrianna said, standing up and gesturing to the narrow path that vanished into the tall grass in front of them.

"Lots of things can hide in that," Falden said looking toward Andrinor. "It might be a good idea if we had some sort of over watch."

"There are several areas that appear to have been burned," Kyrianna said.

"Dragons?" Myrith asked.

"Perhaps."

"Andrinor, how long can you remain in your dragon form?"

"Not for the length of time it will take us to travel to the portal."

"Then I would suggest you not use your dragon form, unless it is needed," Gwideon said.

"I be agreeing," Nirev said.

"We will have to remain alert," Myrith said. "Shydaran you and Hendandra scout the area, while Kyrianna and I take the point positions. Gwideon, you and Nirev take the rear and Andrinor you stay with Jerietlan and Falden in the center." She didn't wait for the others as she tapped Riker with her heels and started down the path.

~ * ~

"We are going to need a break soon," Kyrianna said.

Myrith glanced over at her friend and nodded. "In this place, I guess any spot is as good as another."

"Actually any spot may be as dangerous as another. Unless it's something big, we may not know if something is coming up on us. However, Cewyr is tiring and needs a break, and I'm sure the horse Falden summoned is in worse shape unless it has magical enhancements."

Myrith whistled then waved when Hendandra and Shydaran appeared. The tiger nodded his head and started back toward the group. He stopped suddenly and shook, unseating Hendandra as several loud shrieks came from above them. Fire rolled from the sky and the grass around them started burning.

"Drakes," Andrinor yelled.

Myrith felt a wave of cold that heralded Andrinor's change into his dragon form, then the sound of wings as he launched himself into the air. She drew Conflagration as a blast of cold air surrounded them and the flames died down. The area was scorched giving them a bit more open area.

There were five of the drakes overhead and they were swooping down toward them.

"Watch out for the stingers as well as fire attacks," Andrinor called.

Myrith held Conflagration up in acknowledgement then froze as a large black dragon, the largest dragon she had ever seen, appeared in front of Andrinor.

"Tyrus," she heard Andrinor say as the silver dragon lowered his head slightly.

"Myrith, get back into the fight," Kyrianna's voice called.

She jerked her attention back in time to see the tiger jump on one of the drakes, pulling it from the sky and clawing it. Hendandra was dancing around, waiting for an opening. Kyrianna had slid off Cewyr and nocked three arrows to her bow. The unicorn touched the bow just before the girl released the arrows and they struck the drake in the throat. The drake dropped to the ground as Kyrianna dropped the bow and drew her swords. Myrith tapped Riker with her heels and they charged forward to aid Kyrianna.

Behind her, she heard Gwideon and Jerietlan facing one drake while it sounded like Nirev was also fighting one. The last drake was still circling above them.

"Kyri, watch the tail!" she yelled and Kyrianna ducked in time to avoid being hit. The girl's swords flashed and blood flowed from two cuts. It appeared drakes had softer scales than dragons. The drake stretched its head over her, its mouth open as it inhaled. She rose up in her stirrups and thrust as hard as she could forcing Conflagration through its mouth and into its brain.

She twisted out of the way as the drake fell. A shrill neigh caught her attention and she turned to see Cewyr trapped under the drake's tail, Kyrianna hacking at it to free the unicorn.

She glanced around quickly. Gwideon and Jerietlan seemed to be in control of their fight. Nirev was still by himself. She kicked Riker and charged the drake, Conflagration flaring with a brilliant white light as she stuck the drake's neck. Nirev slammed his hammer down, crushing the creature's skull.

She paused and looked up. *Where is Andrinor?* She knew the young man wouldn't immediately attack and had stood by while they had fought other dragon's, but that he hadn't even tried to talk to these drakes was out of character. She frowned when she saw the black dragon still hovering in front of Andrinor and a shimming ball of light surrounding both of them.

There was another shriek as the remaining drake dove.

"Shydaran, bring it down," she yelled.

The tiger roared and leapt into the air with enough force to send him and the drake tumbling several times as his teeth and claws began ripping.

Myrith kicked Riker again and charged the drake.

"Myrith, don't!" Kyrianna yelled.

She ignored the girl and kicked Riker again. As they went by she swung her sword hard.

"No!" Hendandra screamed as the tiger roared.

She spun Riker around and stopped when she saw the gash on the tiger's shoulder. She had hit him—not the drake. The tiger grabbed the back of the drake's neck and shook his head hard. It only took a few shakes, then the drake dropped to the ground.

Myrith sheathed her sword and rode back to the others. Cewyr was back on her feet and Kyrianna was collecting several of the red gems she called Frayrith's Tears. She looked back up at the two dragons above them. The black glanced down at the group, shook his head then vanished. The shimmering light also vanished and she gasped as Andrinor lost his dragon form and fell toward them. "Falden!"

The mage raised his hand and chanted softly. A puff of feathers flew from his hand toward Andrinor and the young man's descent slowed enough he was able to drop lightly to the ground.

"What happened?" Andrinor looked around at the bodies of the drakes. "I was going to talk to them."

"You don't remember changing?" Jerietlan asked.

"No." Andrinor shook his head.

"How about the black dragon that intercepted you?" Myrith said. "I think I heard you say Tyrus."

Andrinor took a step back, his hand right hand going to the dragon scale buckler on his left arm. "I don't remember anything."

Myrith took a deep breath; the last person she would have suspected of withholding information from her was Andrinor. She looked around at the group: Jerietlan appeared to be finished healing the others. Shydaran as usual had taken care of his own wounds. She flinched at the anger she saw in his eyes, even if she understood the reason for it. However, she was surprised to see the same emotion on Hendandra's face as she glared up at her.

Kyrianna pulled a handful of silver hair from one of the wing claws of the drake then patted Cewyr's neck and put the hairs into one of the pouches on her belt.

"If everyone is ready, we should get moving," Myrith said.

"We needed a break before running into these drakes," Kyrianna said looking around at the others. "We need that break even more now."

"But not here," Nirev said. "We not be needing to stay in this area where scavengers will be coming." He looked up at Kyrianna. "Yer a walker of the forest, ye should be knowing that."

"I agree we need a break, but we do need to move away from here." Myrith nodded. "About another hour at a slower pace, then we can rest for a bit." She didn't wait for the others as she turned Riker and moved away from the bodies of the drakes.

~ * ~

Kyrianna raised her hand and motioned for the others to stop. Her vision of the area hadn't shown her this. A rocky plain with scrub trees and bushes was in front of them. They had been riding at a moderate pace for about four hours since their last break and she estimated about another two hours to the portal.

"What's wrong?" Myrith asked.

"This wasn't here before."

"Did we get off the trail?"

"You were riding next to me the entire time. There were no paths off the main one."

"Magic?" Andrinor asked.

"I sense nothing." Falden whispered.

"I see no other way," Myrith said. "We continue on."

Kyrianna shook her head. "I don't like it. This wasn't here before and if the area is changing we have no way to know the portal hasn't also moved. This isn't limbo and it shouldn't be able to change without outside influence."

"What do you want to do? Wait?" Myrith spun around in her saddle. "We wasted enough time, with people late getting back to Irrmar and then taking time for meaningless ceremonies and parties. How much longer do we ask Brular to suffer while he waits for us? How much of her power will Thynitic regain if we keep delaying? No! We continue on!" She turned and kicked Riker.

Kyrianna shook her head again then tapped Cewyr. "We continue on," she said.

"Hold trespassers." A voice echoed against the rocks.

"Our apologies," Myrith said. "We did not intend to trespass. We are following the road and there was no warning."

"There was warning given, by one of your own group. That you did not heed it is your mistake."

Kyrianna brought her bow around and placed it on her lap as she scanned the area for the speaker. There had been an elven tone to the speaker's voice. The accent had reminded her of the Rynial and Taladilith elves of her home.

"Greetings," she called in Taladilith.

"You and your world will be next," the voice said as an elf

appeared in the middle of the area.

Kyrianna stared as a wall of flames surrounded and separated her from the others. The elf had flame red hair and gold eyes. He was one of the Cyral. Only legends remained regarding these elves who left Rhysia millennia ago.

"Who are you?" She called over the roar of the flames.

"Godfeller. All the gods are false and we of the Faithless will destroy them and those stupid enough to follow them. They bring only pain and chaos where they seek to deceive. We offer order and security."

"Godfeller. Ye be facing me!" Nirev's voice echoed against the rocks. "For the murder of the First Hammer and the destruction of the temple of Mulog in Domar, ye be facing me and be answering for those crimes."

"No little man, I will not."

Kyrianna froze at the sound of ringing steel. She steadied herself on Cewyr and readied her long bow. While not normally used from horseback, she was able to balance the tip on her boot and aim in the direction she had seen the elf appear. She muttered a prayer to Frayrith as she drew back then released the arrow.

"You think a weapon blessed by a false god will help you to attack me. You are a fool."

Kyrianna dropped the bow and fell from Cewyr's back as the arrow she had fired drove itself into her shoulder.

"Kyri?" She heard Myrith's voice call.

"I'm fine."

Kyrianna forced herself up when she heard Hendandra's straggled scream. *Chaos! What is happening with the others?* Drawing her swords, she started to dash through the wall of fire. A sudden blow from behind pushed her to the ground and she rolled over to see Cewyr standing over her. The unicorn's eyes were wide and ringed with white. "Cewyr?"

:I sense a great deal of fear in her, Melissa said.

A strident neigh filled the area and Kyrianna stood quickly as she dodged the unicorn's horn aimed at her chest. "Cewyr?"

There was another scream from Hendandra and Kyrianna flinched at the angry roar that came from Shydaran. She could hear Jerietlan cursing loudly and the continued ring of steel on steel. Another lunge from Cewyr sent her back into the wall of fire as the unicorn hit her shoulder.

"Resare take your souls," she heard Gwideon yell as she stepped back again.

Another lunge from Cewyr and this time she felt the horn cut through the chainmail and across her ribs.

There was another neigh and Kyrianna turned to see Riker charging toward Cewyr. The ghostly horse merged with the unicorn and she watched as a bright glow surrounded them. When it faded, the winged unicorn stood there, her head lowered as she turned away from Kyrianna.

:*I'm sorry,* Kyrianna heard Cewyr's voice in her mind.

"I need to borrow her for a moment," Myrith said jumping on Cewyr. She held her sword at the ready and kicked the unicorn. They sprang through the wall of fire and left Kyrianna standing there alone.

There was another roar from the tiger and a few minutes later the walls of fire vanished. Kyrianna looked around. Myrith was kneeling next to Hendandra, who was lying in a large pool of blood. The tiger was pacing behind the knight and Kyrianna knew he was dangerously close to abandoning his disguise despite Shyada's orders.

Jerietlan was using his spear as a staff to lean on as he placed a hand on Andrinor's shoulder. Gwideon stood apart from the others, his armor showing several long gashes she had no doubt had come from Shydaran's claws.

"What happened?" she asked.

"That elf cast something that caused Gwideon to attack the others," Jerietlan said. "You and Myrith were separated from us until she charged through the fire and attacked the elf. He vanished as did the flames and the madness."

"Just like an elf to run away," Nirev said.

Kyrianna ignored the dwarf's comment as she looked around again. "Where is Falden?"

"Here," the mage's voice called.

Kyrianna looked up to see Falden standing on a nearby rock ledge.

"I was transported here and trapped in an anti-magic field," he said.

"I wanted to get to the portal today," Myrith said. "However, at this point we need to stop." She assisted Hendandra to her feet.

"We should only be a few hours, even at a slow pace from

the portal. If we're lucky, we should reach it early tomorrow and be able to pass through and continue on," Kyrianna said. "But I agree, we cannot continue tonight."

Jerietlan nodded and held his shield up and spoke the words that opened the keep.

Chapter Fourteen

Hendandra was still leaning on Myrith when they entered the keep and Kyrianna nodded as the older woman assisted the girl to the showers. She glanced at the men then smiled and followed the other two women. She slipped out of her chainmail then moved to assist Myrith with her armor.

"Hendandra, I thought all your wounds had closed," Myrith said as they watched the water flowing out from the bottom of the shower running bright red.

"They are. This is just what was caked on my body and in my hair," Hendandra said.

"I'm sorry I didn't stop Gwideon sooner."

"Not your fault. You couldn't have known the chaos that elf would cause. Although, I would like to know what he and Kyrianna were discussing while Gwideon was trying to send the rest of us to Resare."

Kyrianna looked up from where she was kneeling to loosen the straps on Myrith's greaves. "He spoke in the language of the twilight elves of my home. He told me his name was Godfeller and he was here to destroy the false gods who deceive others into believing in them and thereby create chaos. He and his people will bring order and security to the worlds. He called them the Faithless."

"Both Andrinor and Falden mentioned the Faithless as well," Myrith said. "Falden said a war with them would be coming."

"Sounds like it may already be beginning, based on Nirev's reaction," Hendandra said.

"He was challenging the elf because he believed he was the one who killed the previous First Hammer and destroyed the temple in Domar," Kyrianna said.

"I'm going to find a place to hide well before that," Hendandra said. "I never want to find myself on the ground with my life pouring out of me again. I'm pretty sure I saw the ghostly eyes of Resare coming for me at one point." She stepped out of the shower and Kyrianna handed her a towel. A long scar marked

Hendandra's body showing where a blade had sliced from her right shoulder across her chest.

"Get some rest," Myrith said. "Once we rescue Brular, I will escort you back to your island where I hope you can find the safety and peace you seek and deserve."

Hendandra threw the towel at Myrith. "Stay away from Justula!" She grabbed her pack, pulled a clean dress out of it and ran out of the room.

"What was that about?"

Kyrianna only shrugged as she stepped into one of the shower stalls. "You would have to ask her." She was sure she knew what the problem was, but she couldn't address it without risking her promise to Hendandra and Feric. She would see if she could find another way to discuss her concerns with Myrith's actions later.

"First Conflagration starts acting like he's upset and disappointed in me, but won't discuss it and now Hendandra gets angry as well. Maybe I should let someone else lead this group."

"Don't look at me; I have my own issues that would create problems."

"At least you have some training and experience with people who are trained to this job. That's a step better than me."

"Myrith..." She let her words trail off. "Perhaps you should find time to talk to Conflagration tonight. Now that we are not in the field, the sword might be willing to discuss his concerns." *Odds are he has the same concerns I have and she'll probably listen better if the admonishment comes from him than me. At least if it comes from Conflagration, she can't accuse me of challenging her authority.*

Kyrianna finished her shower and left the tunic and pants she had been wearing soaking in one of the washbasins. This was something she was glad of, the ability to wash out their clothes each evening. She knew both her and Hendandra and been taking advantage of it.

She reached for her weapons and froze when she didn't feel Melissa's presence in the silver sword. She smiled when she saw the orange and brown gem resting on the table. After today's events, she should have realized Hendandra would want to talk to Feric.

She gathered the rest of her equipment and headed for the scribe's room.

"Hendandra?" she called softly as she closed the door. "Are you alright?"

"No!" Hendandra raised her head slightly and looked at Kyrianna. "I swear Myrith is out to kill Feric. She has expressed her displeasure with him since he and Gwideon joined the group."

"I know her actions were rash, but I don't believe that was truly her intent."

Kyrianna swallowed hard and frowned. She really didn't believe Myrith was trying to kill Shydaran, but the woman's actions had been rash and poorly thought out and had resulted in her seriously hurting the tiger. "Maybe you should talk to her."

"There is no way I can do that without risking upsetting Shyada and I will not let that come between us." She placed her hand on Shydaran's head and stroked the fur.

"I am not defending her actions, but she is doing the best she can under the circumstances," Kyrianna whispered. "She was never trained for this role."

Hendandra removed the wooden ring and threw it at her. "And what if it was Tristan she ran down on the field?"

Kyrianna caught the ring and shivered as she felt Melissa moving from it and through her to the sword.

"I would be just as angry and unwilling to listen as you," Kyrianna whispered. She dropped the ring on the floor and reached for the door.

"If she hurts him again like she did today, I am leaving and with me my husband." Hendandra paused and looked up.

Kyrianna flinched at the anger she saw in Hendandra's eyes as well as the tears.

"She never even acted like she was sorry for hurting him." Her voice dropped to a whisper. "Maybe he is right and we are all blind to what really is important. It seems all that matters to some is conflict and they care not who they call their enemy—only that they claim the side of the righteous."

Kyrianna frowned as Hendandra's words struck a chord in her heart. *Truly, what is the difference between the light and the darkness when they use the same methods and care not about those they hurt?* She remembered Gwideon's words at the Coliseum. 'You showed me what darkness could hide even in those who serve the side of light.' She closed the door as she left the two of them alone. There was a difference—Balthas had intended to hurt, Myrith hadn't.

Perhaps that was the only difference between the two.

Kyrianna walked slowly down the hall to the dining room. Andrinor and Nirev were both there. "The shower will be available soon," she said.

"I hope ye left yer armor in the smithy," Nirev said. "That unicorn ripped a pretty hole in the side of it that be needing repair."

"Yes," she nodded. "Thank you."

"Bah, I don't be seeing anyone else in this group doing it properly and we be needing all of us to get out of this alive."

She smiled as she took the plate of food Andrinor held out to her.

"Cewyr is in the shrine. You should talk to her." He put a couple of apples on the plate. "She refused to eat anything."

"Thanks."

~ * ~

Myrith finished her shower and left her gear in the sleeping chamber. She wore only a long tunic; one that was long enough, it was almost a dress, and carried Conflagration with her as she entered the shrine.

Jerietlan was already there as was Gwideon. Both were deep in prayer. Gwideon, probably seeking penance for attacking the other members of the group today, even if he was affected by some magic on the part of the elf. Jerietlan, because this was one of several sessions he would spend in prayer. She figured it was his way of making sure he had in fact prayed for everyone.

She sat behind Jerietlan with her back against the far wall as she unsheathed Conflagration. :*Tell me what's wrong,* she thought focusing her thoughts on the blade.

:*Your path disturbs me.*

Myrith let her body sag. :*What is it that I do that sits ill?*

:*You ordered the tiger not just into a battle, but a specific action. Then you took direct action that put him at the tip of your blade. You didn't care that he was in your path and at risk.*

:*It was necessary. I needed that thing out of the air before it attacked with its breath weapon. We were badly hurt and there are those who might not have survived such an attack.*

:*You* needed? *The words I* need *have no place in this conversation or even in a knight's duties.* The sword's words were not harsh in their pronouncement only even and specific. :*When one states their needs are higher than another's that is the first step toward the darkness.*

Myrith took a deep breath and let her anger fade before responding. :*Am I to be held accountable for a poor choice of words? The group needed the drake removed.*

:*And the tiger did not do that?* The sword let its voice fade.

:*You think I was wrong. I serve the Battle Maiden. You served a knight of Hellavar, Lord of Fire and Order. I believe she would look differently on my actions.*

Myrith let her words ring loud and defiant in her mind.

:*Tell me Myrith, if Tristan were on the field and locked in a grapple with a powerful being of evil, would you strike even though you might kill another of her servants? And if you did, how would you justify your actions to Kyrianna or Mykaylene?*

:*To defeat evil is the goal of all servants of the light; even if it cost them their own life.* Her words were certain and determined as she thought them.

She heard the sword sigh softly. :*And if it were Mykaylene herself you would strike down; what would be your choice?* There had been no hesitation in the question, as if the sword had expected the answer she had given.

:*Strike a goddess dead? I have no such weapon!* She laughed slightly as if the question were a joke.

:*And if you wielded such a weapon, for they do exist, capable of piercing a god as the Lady of Chaos and Maiden of Battle grappled on the field, what would you do?*

:*The question is ludicrous. It has no answer!* Myrith shouted back in her mind, then realized she had heard her own voice.

"Myrith, are you all right?" Jerietlan asked as he started to stand.

"We have all faced death and our own nightmares this day," Gwideon said from the doorway. "The Sword of Mykaylene seeks answers to questions. It is not for us to question…" he paused. "Or to speak of to the others." He gestured to the door. "If you are finished with your prayers, I suggest we allow the lady some privacy." He dropped a small copper coin on the floor as they left.

:*I still wait for your answer,* Conflagration said breaking the silence.

:*This is insanity. There is no comparison!*

:*So you would judge one servant of light more deserving of your blade than another?* The sword let the comment hang. :*Is that your answer then; that some are more worthy than others of your protection.*

Myrith took another deep breath and tried to still her mind to better listen to what it was Conflagration had just said. :*It is not who we protect from the evil of this world, but that we protect.*

:*Well said. I will speak to you no more on this issue. Everything is a matter of your choice—not mine.*

Myrith stood awkwardly, her mind still reeling from the conversation. *Would I have held back my sword if it had been Tristan or another instead of the tiger?* As she thought about the question, she realized she had already done so when Kyrianna had been held by the demoness that first night, and probably would have done so again this time and that answer disturbed her even more. She knelt in front of the shine, Conflagration grounded in front of her as she bowed her head.

:*My Lady, was I wrong to attack as I did and put the tiger in danger of my blade?*

The answer came quickly. :*Servants of light share the field of battle against those who would do ill to others. It is a sin for them to harm each other, even in the pursuit of vanquishing evil. The greatest enemy is not those of infernal origin, but the losing of the path that all life is sacred and the taking of it must be justified by the creature's misdeeds—not convenience. The ends do not justify the means involved. If they did, then what is there to differentiate the path of darkness from the path of light?*

Myrith swallowed hard as she listened to the goddess' words. Yes, she had been wrong in her actions. Still, there was another question she needed to have answered.

:*Was I wrong to order the tiger to bring down the drake?*

:*No, but you lacked patience and trust in Shydaran to hold or kill his prey. To stand ready with your weapon and wait for an opening would have proven surer of a less costly victory. Instead, you acted rashly and almost killed a member of the group under your protection.*

Acted rashly. The Gatekeeper of Resare warned me about that. '*See you learn to curb your own rashness even as you condemn it in others.*' She nodded. She had acted rashly after ordering the tiger to be in the way of her blade. Therefore she must take responsibility for his blood in that battle. :*Am I still deserving of your exalted blessing?*

:*Brular took upon himself the charge you would ascend to its challenges. He asked I grant you the chance. I cannot say your path has been straight, but the darkness has not touched your heart. You must be wary that your actions be more measured than swift. The place you go will not only seek your life, but your soul. Your failure will not be yours alone, but his as well.*

Myrith let her thoughts return to the here and now then stood and turned toward the doorway.

Myrith nodded when she saw everyone in the dining hall, including the tiger. She didn't summon them, but it seemed they had all decided they needed to eat at the same time.

Hendandra looked up at her, picked up her plate and moved to the far end of the table. She wasn't sure why the girl was mad at her, but she would try to talk to her and apologize for whatever it was. First, though, they had other matters that needed to be attended to and another she knew now she had wronged that she must apologize to.

She pulled Conflagration from his sheath and knelt in front of Shydaran, the weapon held in front of her. The room fell silent and she knew they were watching her wondering what was happening.

"Shydaran, I offer my apologies for my rash actions today." She placed Conflagration on the floor and bowed her head slightly. "I ordered you to attack the drake and then did not trust in you to handle the creature. I charged in without regard for the risk and in doing so put your life at the tip of my blade. I was wrong in my actions and I ask your forgiveness for my lack of patience and lack of trust. I accept your punishment as well."

She waited to see what the tiger's judgment was.

After a moment the tiger stepped forward, then swatted her hard with his paw. The forced knocked her several feet to the side. She heard several chairs being pushed back from the table. "Hold," she said. The tiger hadn't used his claws. Another swat and she was knocked back onto her back, Shydaran standing over him. The tiger's eyes showed his anger, confusion and surprise as he looked down at her. She forced herself to meet those eyes, not showing submission. She was still in charge, but she was willing to accept her responsibility in harming him.

Shydaran nodded and backed off of her.

Myrith stood up and retrieved Conflagration from the floor then sat down at the table. Kyrianna smiled and nodded then slid her a plate of food. Everyone was looking at her and she saw surprise and approval in their eyes. Hendandra was still staring at her, but the smoldering anger that been there earlier had cooled a little.

Was is going on with her? Why would she care about me apologizing to Shydaran?

"Gwideon, before we get to the portal tomorrow, perhaps it would better for Urric to tell us what to expect," Myrith said turning her attention back to where she was.

"The next layer will only be a short visit, though it is one of the least pleasant places to be. You should only be there for about an hour at the longest if you can keep up your pace. The next portal that leads back up to twenty-third is only a few leagues from the one that opens onto the five-forty-fifth."

"What madness be this," Nirev said. "We travel down to the five-forty-fifth to come back up to the twenty-third. This be making no sense."

Andrinor laughed. "Were you really expecting it to make sense? This is the Abyss, a realm of chaos."

"This is the fastest way," Kyrianna asked.

"No," Urric said.

Myrith slammed her fist against the table. "What?"

"If you want the fastest, we enter the nearby demon city and take the portal that opens in the city of the chaos demons where one of the only other two portals to her citadel is located."

"I be preferring this path," Nirev said.

"The only other portal I know of moves from place to place on the plane of limbo. We could spend weeks chasing it."

"What is the twenty-third?" Falden asked.

"Cold beyond imagination. It is the land of absolute ice and frost." The glow in his eye sockets turned toward Jerietlan. "You will need to shield us all from the rigors of that place or we will lose people one frostbitten piece at a time."

Hendandra slapped her hands against the table. "Lovely. Just one uglier death trap after another. I know you said if we can keep up the pace—just what is on the five-forty-fifth that might interfere with our pace."

"It is called the layer of the infinite void." Gwideon shook his head.

"What is that?" Kyrianna asked, her voice quaking.

"Urric, you should have spoken before now," Gwideon said. He let his gaze move around the table, until it locked with Myrith's. "A dark place indeed. It is said to border both the plane of shadow and that of negative energy."

Falden's face went white. "Both. Then…"

"Yes, its denizens are the stuff of nightmares that suck life and pass through even living things," Gwideon said. "We cannot stay for long. Some areas themselves can draw the soul's essence from the body itself. We must make our passage quick."

Myrith glared at the skull on the chain around Gwideon's neck. "You have a funny way of helping us. This is how you pay your penance?"

"I was never asked," Urric said with a cackle.

"Anything else you have left out that we should know about?" Myrith asked.

"What power of note may be found on that layer?" Falden asked.

"None that reside there now. She found the nature of the place robbed her of her guests too quickly," Urric said.

Myrith turned at Kyrianna quick inhale of breath. The girl was visibly shaking. "She?" Kyrianna asked. "Robbed her of her guests too quickly?"

"That is correct. Your lady called it home before she decided Limbo and the sixty-third were more to her liking."

Kyrianna pushed her chair back and stood slowly. "She. Is. Not. My. Lady."

Myrith grabbed Kyrianna's wrist and held it tight. "Kyri, don't let it goad you into doing something rash."

"After your actions today, you have no business cautioning me about rash actions," Kyrianna said jerking her arm away from Myrith.

"Urric, I will see your torment is never ending. You were told to be our guide; we shouldn't have to beg for every scrap of information. Nor do I appreciate your continued harassment of my friend." Myrith spoke slowly and deliberately.

"No," Gwideon said. "His rudeness will be reported. However, as regards the information, he is right; he was not asked until now. He has done nothing wrong and is not subject to any wrong against his contract. What's done is done. We should have asked sooner, but did not." He paused. "Honestly, would it have made a difference?"

"No," Kyrianna's voice was quiet as she spoke.

"If we take another route to the twenty-third? How long would it take?" Myrith asked.

"Just the trip along the twenty-third would be one hundred leagues," Urric said. "With the deep snows that cover that terrain, the horses will only be able to travel maybe a league an hour at best. We cannot afford to spend days on the plane of ice."

"Nor do we have the time available—even if we could," Myrith said.

"I wish we had a way to know what was going on with Brular?" Andrinor said. "Knowledge is important in every battle and even more so where we are going."

Falden looked up. "I agree knowledge is important, but consider where he is, do you really want to know what Thynitic and her demons are doing to him? And what of the risk? Scrying can be as dangerous to the scryer as to the one being watched."

"Jerietlan, didn't Hellavar tell you that you could contact Brular for a short time each day and you would be protected in doing so?" Myrith asked.

"He did. But I have not done so yet."

"Perhaps you should. There are those who may have specific questions for him as well."

Kyrianna nodded her head slowly as Myrith glanced in her direction. "If you are able, please ask him about the amulet Thynitic is having made for me." Her voice caught and she looked away as several of the group turned to look at her.

"Kyri," Falden's voice was soft. "How do you know she is having an amulet made for you?"

"Drezmona told me; and she had no reason to lie to me."

"Other than to cause you torment."

"Jerietlan will you ask him?" Myrith asked.

"I will. I need some time to meditate before attempting to contact him."

Chapter Fifteen

Torliana woke to screaming. She had finished her work on the amulet a few hours prior and collapsed on the small cot in the room. Mixed in with the multitudes of those whose suffering entertained Thynitic and her demons, was another voice, one that seemed to pierce both the physical walls and those she had built around her soul.

"You promised!" she yelled.

The screaming did not subside. She felt his tortured cries in her heart. He had been the only person who had ever cared about her. He had survived the horrors and escaped. Even trapped in her realm, she knew he could escape with the assistance of his fiery servants and comrades, yet he had come back to this cursed place to save her from joining the infinite darkness of the lady.

"And I am the one who trapped him here yet again." She stood up and headed for the hallway that led to Thynitic's throne room. The black glass, she now understood, was not mere decoration to fit the Lady of Chaos' taste, but a symbol of herself. The dark reflective surface was her essence as it portrayed both her soul and nature. It was not she who perverted people to her liking; it was only that she showed them their true selves. Their own wants and wishes unleashed. The chaos of that person's own making.

She stopped to look at her reflection. Her sunken face looked back at her. Her hair cascaded over her shoulders and down her dirty robe. This was her true self. The screaming came again and she closed her eyes and tried to shut it out. When it faded, she saw herself as she was those few days ago as a proud paragon of the chaos that made mortals and demons tremble. She watched the image fade and her current wretched visage looked back out at her again. "Which am I?" she whispered as she turned down the hallway she knew would lead her to Brular.

She saw the two demons who guarded the door. These were not chaos demons, but instead were of the babau caste. They lorded over the manen and other lesser demons and imps, but they were hardly a true power. They could cut a soldier down with their sharp claws easily enough and the acid that dripped off their bodies would melt lesser enchanted weapons. However, she was not some weakling from the prime. She knew their kind and she had little time for them now.

One dared to raise his hand to stop her. She rewarded him with a sudden rush as she dodged his outstretched arm and planted her right foot in his chest. Her skin burned but she ignored the pain as she could still hear Brular's screams. She forced her way through the door and found herself frozen at the scene that confronted her.

She had expected to see Veterak, Thynitic's master of torture. Instead of the great demon, what stood there was a pathetic creature made of once living flesh. His skin taut against his frame as he stood over Brular.

"It is your own fault my skills are not what they should be and that we must keep trying until it is done correctly," the creature said. He lifted a large needle connected to a glowing, flexible tube then jabbed it into Brular's side.

Torliana wasn't sure what angered her more, that Thynitic's promise had been broken or the undead parody of life that stood before her. What was it doing here? Thynitic hated the undead. She saw them as a perversion of the chaos in which she reveled. The Lady of Chaos would never have allowed one such as this to exist on her layer of the Abyss, much less within her very citadel. She took a step forward, then stopped again, her breath caught in her throat as the undead creature lifted a silver knife and cut through the flesh of Brular's left arm to the bone itself. Once the cut was complete, he replaced the knife with a silver saw.

Her anger grew at the pulsing runes that glowed on either side of the cut. She did not know them or the spell they represented, but she understood enough to know they were necromantic in nature. Her manacles were pulsing madly, but it was not the pain that shattered her concentration—it was shock.

The undead creature picked up another large needle and pulled back a tapestry to reveal a man who began to scream as he approached. Without a word, he plunged the needle into the man's chest and the tubing began to throb a deep red as the man shriveled into a desiccated husk.

Torliana collapsed to the floor as she watched Brular's flesh knit back together. Her gaze returned to the prisoner only to see his flesh flake away and the skeleton shatter into a pile of dust on the floor.

"That was the last. I will have to have more brought," the undead creature said with a laugh.

Torliana stood and lunged at the creature. She was unable to stop her momentum as it spun and sliced the air with a flick of steel. He held a dagger at the ready and it was wet with blood that dripped to the floor. Her right cheek felt chill and her teeth ached from the cold in the room.

He smiled as she raised her hand to her cheek and touched the inside of her mouth. She had been wrong to underestimate this one. His blade was so sharp it had opened up her face with her not feeling even the slightest sting.

"Who are you?" she demanded. "The Lady does not tolerate your kind. Why are you here?" Her anger burned in her soul as she struggled to understand what was going on.

"As to my name, I was told not to tell you. As to why," he glanced at Brular. "There is one who needs his skills." He feinted to the side and then moved directly toward her and to her left. Before she could move, he had already moved back. Her face felt cold and she could feel the warm trail of blood that flowed down her cheek. "What a beautiful smile you have."

Torliana saw her reflection in the black glass that walled the room. Her mouth had been neatly slit almost identically on each side. She could see her teeth and the muscles of her jaw that had been spared the blade. She tasted her own blood and more than just a touch of fear that she would not be able to save Brular or herself from this abomination.

She looked back at Brular and saw the tears in his eyes. The tears were not for himself, but for the ones who life had been sucked from them so this undead thing could continue to torment him. She let the anger she felt at this desecration of everything Brular believed fill her as she struggled against the power of the manacles. She felt her own power come to her, stronger than the last time she had defeated the magics binding her. *Too bad she didn't see to binding me with stronger manacles after I was able to defeat them the first time,* Torliana thought. *That was her mistake.* She smiled as she summoned lightning to her hands.

That smile turned to a cry of pain when the undead creature

darted in and neatly severed three fingers from her left hand, disrupting the spell. The power wrapped itself around her, the lightning burning her skin as her opponent waited.

"Enough!" Thynitic's voice was a whip crack in the small room. "Torliana, have you finished the amulet?"

"What does it matter? You have broken your promise."

"You were told I had no further need for the cleric. However, that changed." She reached out and touched Torliana's cheek.

Torliana frowned as she felt the wounds heal. She looked down to see her fingers regrowing on her hand. "Why?"

"I have a need for both his and your power. I need that arm severed from his body. It must be perfectly clean or it is useless to me."

"Why?"

"That I will not tell you, Chosen of Chaos. I have commanded it to be so and so it shall be."

Torliana swallowed. "That abomination has failed in the task several times. He is incompetent as well as disgusting."

"He was once one of the greatest in his art form, my dear, before his encounter with those who condemned him to this." She grinned. "It will just take a while."

Torliana looked from the goddess to the undead thing and then to Brular. He shook his head slightly as if knowing her decision even as she made it. Her movements were quick; she didn't want time to think about what she was doing. She grabbed the needle that still protruded from his side and yanked it free. "No," Brular said. "Don't give in. She is n...." his voice went silent.

"If you wish to save him anymore suffering, be quick," Thynitic said.

She examined the arm and the runes closely. Her initial assumption regarding necromantic magic was confirmed by the aura she felt emanating from them. "I have not seen these before."

"They are magnificent, are they not," the undead creature said. "I have been given the chance to perform my greatest work. He will be magnificent in his evil and the utter chaos he will bring to Chaos' enemies."

"Enough talk," Thynitic said. "I want his arm. We can continue to watch him try to do it properly costing me time and prisoners and you the anguish of Brular's prolonged suffering. Or someone with a steadier hand can complete the task."

Brular shook his head again, his lips moving soundlessly. Torliana placed a hand on his cheek. "It will be done, either by my hand or his. At least this way, I can spare you some pain and suffering as well as others."

She looked up at Thynitic. "Does he need to be awake for this?"

It was the undead creature who answered. "For the magic to be truly strong, yes."

She glanced at the goddess who was still smiling. "You know I no longer want your power. All I want now is to tear that smile from your face."

"Indeed. And it is that, which will make me even stronger."

She turned back to the task. Brular was frozen, unable to move; for that she was thankful. She picked up the silver dagger and looked down at his arm. The table was cut to where his arm was to be severed. She pressed carefully against the line that separated the two sets of identical runes. She knew she had to be quick as the blood would flow and obscure her task. Her mind raced as she realized the task was almost impossible without careful thought. The blood would flow down and cover the markings, making the chance of mistakes even greater. She pulled the blade back a bit and saw Brular relax slightly. Perhaps he thought she had decided to not perform this gruesome task herself. However, that slight relaxation on his part was what she wanted. The blade flashed under his arm and as soon as the point was visible against the mark, she pulled upward until she felt the blade drag against his bone. She pulled the blade up quickly to almost the top of the inside of his arm.

The artery squirted blood with the beat of his heart. She steadied herself, aligned the bottom incision with the top and pushed the blade deep into his flesh.

She swallowed hard, dreading the next part of the task, as she inspected the cut.

If it was not perfect, she would have to do it again and she doubted she would be able to.

She dropped the dagger to the floor and picked up the saw. Silver was hardly the material she would chose for a sharp implement such as this. It dulled too quickly. "This must be what is used?"

"Yes," he replied.

She looked at the edge and saw why the undead creature was having increasing difficulty with the task. The saw was now dull and jagged in too many places. It would be very difficult to make a clean cut that could be followed. "Forgive me," she whispered glancing at Brular. He nodded slightly.

She tested the teeth of the saw with her left hand. She needed the sharpest section to begin the cut. Her heart seemed to stop beating as she concentrated on that search. As soon as she found the only even, sharp section of teeth left on the instrument she brought the saw down toward the exposed bone. She started the cut, before touching the bone and the saw caught and bit deeply. Even with his voice taken from him, she could hear Brular's screams. She fought the tears in her eyes as she worked in quick even strokes so they did not have to start over again—not at this point. It took barely a minute for her complete the task and hand the arm to the undead creature.

She reached for a torch to cauterize the wound.

"No!" Thynitic's voice echoed off the obsidian walls. "The cuts cannot be touched at this point or the magic will be diminished.

"I am to let him bleed to death?"

"Wait," the undead creature said. "And watch."

He pulled another curtain back and Torliana gasped as a lich stepped forward. He was hooded and cloaked. He then pushed the cloak back to reveal the lich was missing his right arm. He placed Brular's arm against the empty shoulder of the lich and spoke very quietly. The runes on Brular's shoulder, the ones on his arm and another set on the lich all glowed. When the glow faded, the arm was attached to the lich and Brular's wound was closed.

"It is done," Torliana said.

"No."

Torliana shook her head as she looked up at the goddess and she nodded toward Brular's left arm.

"Why?"

"He needs a left as well."

Torliana straightened her back and locked her gaze with Thynitic's. "Does it have to be his?"

"No, but it must be from a living person," the undead creature said.

Torliana licked her lips and took a deep breath as she ripped the sleeve from her robes. "Place your runes and be quick," she said.

She handed the knife to the goddess. "He is not capable of performing the task correctly.

Thynitic only smiled as she waited for the runes to be placed.

~ * ~

Torliana turned back toward the goddess after her arm was attached to the lich and he pushed the cowl of his robe back and took a step forward. "This miserable failure is your new mighty servant?" she asked.

One of the lesser demons was assisting Brular to his feet and he stood studying the lich and the runes.

"He is uniquely suited to this task," Thynitic said.

Torliana recalled meeting with the young man this decaying corpse once was in Duvshire. He had sought power and had been easy prey for the Lady. She had just returned from her journey to Nydith where she had called Thynitic's justice down on the dead vessel that had once been her temple. It had not surprised her to learn the clergy of that forsaken place had lost themselves in their games of pain and had abandoned the chaos that was at the heart of the lady. She had retrieved a few relics, including the Book of Chaos, then summoned the demons that destroyed the very foundations of the church. The church collapsed in on itself, much as the *faithful* had done.

Thynitic had directed her to return to Shokar and present the book to a young nobleman. The man lived in some god forgotten little burg, but that hadn't mattered to her. He was the eldest son from a lineage of knights with a strong connection to Mykaylene. The man was hardly old enough to be called that, but he had considerable gold to offer for the book she had brought him. In truth, she had been directed to give him the book; but she felt it would better motivate him to truly pursue the power properly if he invested his money and effort in the book's acquisition. She remembered the look of the shady man who drove the carriage that brought him to the inn where they met. She also remembered seeing a small child playing near the carriage as they closed the deal. The girl had looked back at her from one of the windows of the carriage as it drove away. The memory of those sad eyes seemed so familiar now.

"Suited how?" she asked with a laugh. "He couldn't even kill a simple boy." She regretted the words immediately as she felt Brular's gaze on her.

"This is the woman you returned for?" Thynitic said. "Yes, he failed; not once but twice. However, I do believe he is properly motivated this time."

The lich bowed his head slightly. "The task will be completed as you have directed."

"Good. I have granted you the power you sought, those decades ago, Duvall. But only for a short time." She pointed her finger at Torliana. "You have completed the layering, now you will begin the magics and when they are completed, you will use this to complete the binding." She tossed her a vial of blood.

"You." She pointed to Brular. "I shall not tempt fate with you any longer. You have proven too resourceful in the past to leave in anything but the most secure rooms this citadel has to offer."

Torliana's voice was slow and steady. "You will not harm him."

"Neither I nor any of those the Lady of Chaos commands shall harm him."

Chapter Sixteen

Jerietlan sat on the floor of the main hall and let his thoughts drift as the others gathered around quietly. He felt the other cleric's mind as the link Hellavar had given him was activated; it was guarded. He saw a figure standing before him through strange eyes. The man appeared to be in his forties with a slight build; he was also missing his right arm. Jerietlan cringed at the sight, but knew his time was short. :*Brular, it is Jerietlan, who is he?*

Brular turned, as he did, so did the other man. :*How?*

:*A gift from Hellavar.*

Brular nodded his head once then reached up and touched the ruined flesh of his shoulder. :*I am not sure the reason why she did this, but I suspect you will be the ones who will find out.*

:*I have seen those runes once before,* Jerietlan said. :*Linked life, linked forever.*

:*The arms were given to a lich by the name of Duvall.*

"What!" Jerietlan's startled cry brought him out of the link momentarily.

"Jerietlan?"

"A moment," he said refocusing on the connection with Brular.

:*Brular, I have one more question for you. What of the amulet? Is Thynitic having one made for Kyrianna and how long until it is finished?*

:*The layering is completed, it only needs the final magics cast and the blood to bind it to her. Kyrianna needs to be in a place of protection—a church or a shrine at the least.*

Jerietlan was silent. He didn't want to tell Brular about being here in the Abyss. Even with the ordered control the cleric had, this was information he would probably react to.

:*Jerietlan, your silence betrays some act of foolishness on her part.*

:*You said arms?* He tried to steer the conversation away from the dangerous territory of their trip.

:*Torliana's left arm was taken also.*

Jerietlan's mind was pulled back as the time given to him by Hellavar expired. He swallowed several times before speaking;

then all that came was a strangled cough.

"What did you see?" Myrith asked.

"Misery. Give me some time to explain." He looked up and frowned. "Myrith, I fear we are not ready for the horrors that await us, but we dare not go back." He shook his head. "She removed Brular's right arm and he says she also took one of Torliana's. He doesn't know the reason, but the runes that were etched into his skin were the same as what was on Talon's body."

He looked up at Gwideon. "You said they are used to reestablish a link with the whole of a being."

"Yes," Gwideon said.

"He said they were given to a lich by the name of Duvall."

"No!" Kyrianna's shout echoed off the walls of the hall. "We destroyed him at the estate." She took a slow step back. "Tristan," she whispered.

"Could the lich tap into the magics they both command?" Myrith asked.

"It is possible. But he would not have their knowledge or skill in using them."

"That's a small blessing," Myrith said. "However, it will not stop us. We continue on."

Kyrianna was trembling as she glanced from Myrith to Jerietlan. "What of the amulet?"

"It will be completed soon. He said the layering was already completed—that all that was needed were the final magics and the blood. He said you should be in a protected place."

Kyrianna wrapped her arms around her body and fought the shaking. "She has everything she needs—even the blood."

"No she doesn't," Myrith said. "She doesn't have you." Her voice was strong and even. "And it will be destroyed along with the other."

She nodded slowly at Myrith's words as she turned to walk away from the group.

~ * ~

"Kyrianna!" Andrinor's voice was sharp.

She spun around.

"I think you need a distraction and a way to vent some of that anger and fear you're feeling right now," Andrinor said. "If it will help, you can cross blades with me." He held out the pommel of his sword and smiled.

She looked up at him, her hand going to her long sword. "Agreed, but let's use weapons from the hall—not our magically enhanced blades. I would even suggest changing our armor. This will put us on more even footing as far as equipment and will force us to rely on only our skills."

Andrinor nodded. "Agreed."

Myrith shook her head then turned to Jerietlan. "Make sure they are properly healed when they are through playing games." Jerietlan only nodded.

Kyrianna watched Andrinor closely, judging his movements as he moved to select the only two bladed sword on the wall of the hall. He turned and smiled at her as he began to remove his chain mail.

Her gaze settled on the chain shirt in the room and she lifted it over her head. It was a bit heavier than her elven made armor, but wouldn't be as restrictive as full chain mail would be. She knew she would have to be able to move quickly.

"You be not ready yet?" Nirev called.

She turned and the dwarf nodded across the hall. Her gaze went to the well-muscled, bare chest of Andrinor. He had foregone wearing armor or even a shirt and stood with his sword behind him and against his right arm. A buckler from the wall was strapped to his left forearm. He rolled his head slightly and smiled.

"No armor?" she asked.

"Will I need it?" he asked, smiling.

"Ten gold on the dragon warrior," Falden said.

She shook her head as she heard Melissa laugh in her head. :*You slipped into the necklace again.* She stopped. :*I didn't notice.*

:*Kyri, you are way too distracted. Not a good thing, even in a sparring match.* She paused and her tone became more serious. :*I will not interfere. My father was specific on these matters, but I am here—just in case a blade slips.*

Kyrianna let her shock melt into warmth for the wraith she called sister. :*Thank you.*

"Kyri!" Hendandra's voice echoed in the room. "Stop talking to those voices in your head and get to business." She pulled out her pouch and took out a gem.

"Honestly, what are your chances?"

Kyrianna laughed as she found a long sword on the wall. She

looked for a short sword but found none close by. "Without his armor, I may prove to be some competition for Tormasus' finest warrior." She turned and smirked at Andrinor who only shrugged.

"Less talk," Nirev said.

Kyrianna turned and raised her left hand as a short sword arced through the air toward her. She caught the weapon by its pommel.

"It should be yer steel that be talking." He strode to the center of the hall and motioned for them to join him. "I be the judge of who be the winner and who be the loser," he said. "This be training: not to the death. If I see a blade swung in malice, I be stopping this immediately and ye be explaining it to Myrith." He looked up at Andrinor. "No battle rage or shape changing." He turned to Kyrianna. "No magic from ye or that imp of a girl who be the one ye most likely be talking to before."

Kyrianna nodded. "She has already said she would not aid me."

"Then what be ye waiting for!" He stepped back quickly as Andrinor's blade swung out and over Kyrianna's ducking head. Her blades snapped to the ready. She nodded as Andrinor's blade continued its swing and he caught it in his left hand and balanced it in front of his body. He had only done it to put her on guard.

She knew time was not on her side in this contest. She needed to strike quickly and often to even hope to match him. Her long sword came up quickly in a swing with her right arm across her body and she followed the motion with a swift lunge to her right. She was rewarded with both weapons slapping the muscles of her opponent and drawing thin lines of blood. Unfortunately, she apparently was not able to surprise him with her movement as his buckler blocked the long sword's next swing.

"Not bad," he said as he stepped in, his weapon moving quickly.

His sword was almost dizzying to watch and Kyrianna realized she had never watched him very closely. The movements of his sword were not like a sword at all, but more like a staff and the flat of the blades caught her on one side and then the other in rapid succession. Her own movements betrayed her as she felt one of the blades slap against her back before she found the direction to dive to.

She came in again but used only her first couple of strikes to actually try and hit her opponent; the others she let cover her retreat as his blades started to dance again. She was more successful in deflecting the blades, although she knew she was the weaker of the two in the fight. She didn't even want to think of his draconic strength entering into this match and was thankful Nirev had thought to forbid Andrinor entering one of his battle rages.

The match continued for several minutes as they gauged each other's styles. Kyrianna realized she had the harder task as Andrinor shifted frequently from using the second blade to putting his full power behind the swinging of one blade.

"Chaos!" She heard Hendandra curse. "I bet on the wrong person."

Falden laughed. "Well, blame yourself for raising it to twenty gold on Kyrianna."

Andrinor smiled at the conversation and Kyrianna saw his blades slow a bit. She focused every ounce of her strength as she came in, her blades swinging wildly, and she scored several hits. She let the cheers of the group carry her forward as Andrinor took several steps back.

Her smile dropped as Andrinor looked at her and shook his head. "Chaos!" she whispered as he shifted his grip on his weapon.

Her insides felt like the pudding in the pastries in the dining hall as he hit her twice in rapid succession and she fell to the floor.

"You traded a brief flurry of offense for leaving yourself completely open."

Andrinor extended his hand. "If I had done that in Tormasus, I wouldn't be here today."

Kyrianna felt warmth in the necklace as the pain in her body eased. She took Andrinor's hand and he pulled her back up. "Rash," she said as the others starting laughing. "Stupid, but apparently entertaining."

"I not be having to say who won that bout. Anyone else?"

Silence filled the area. "Ah come on." He turned toward Shydaran. "Anyone be brave enough to go a round with Shydaran?"

Andrinor shook his head and backed up a couple of steps. "I'm sorry, perhaps you missed the little lesson he gave today, by ripping into Gwideon."

Shydaran shook himself, looked up at Andrinor and grinned.

"I have spent some time under his claws," Nirev said. "I be knowing the power they contain. Would anyone here be showing they are better than the cat?"

Hendandra laughed and stepped forward. "I'll go a few rounds with him."

The others looked at her and Kyrianna had to turn away to hide her grin.

"Anyone care to bet I can at least slip away a couple of times," she said.

"Oh, that is worth a few coins," Falden said as he dropped five coins on the bench.

"I deal only in gems," Hendandra said as she began undoing the buttons on her skirt.

"You'll lose that bet, Falden," Kyrianna said.

"And, this advice be from the person who thought she be giving dragon-boy some competition," Nirev said.

"With more discipline she would indeed do so." Andrinor said putting his hand on Kyrianna's shoulder.

"Make it ten gold," Falden said.

Hendandra flashed Kyrianna an impish smile as she walked over. "Can Melissa grow the vines?"

"Of course," she said. She placed her hand on the girl's necklace of leaves and felt Melissa send the power through her.

"Thanks." Hendandra stepped away and her armor reformed as the vines knitted over her body.

Kyrianna sat down and leaned against the wall then opened one of her belt pouches and pulled out several silver-gray strands of hair and began separating them into groups of three. She watched Hendandra and Shydaran as her fingers began braiding the hair together.

"Ye be using magical armor," Nirev said. "That not be quite fair to Shydaran."

"You must be kidding," Hendandra said. "Shydaran carries no equipment and played with Gwideon in the mud today. In all honesty I am still at a disadvantage." She moved to the center of the hall.

Nirev nodded his acceptance then turned to Shydaran. "You, no claws or teeth!"

The tiger ignored the comment as he strolled out.

"Hendandra, just yell if you need help or want out," Andrinor said as he sat next to Kyrianna.

"Begin," Nirev said as he backed away from the two.

Hendandra shifted her feet and waited. Shydaran lunged and she dropped to the floor and tumbled away. Shydaran checked under his paws, but Hendandra wasn't there.

:*Where did she go?* Melissa asked.

"Near the plate mail; in the shadows," Kyrianna whispered.

"Smart girl," Andrinor said.

:*He will find her,* Melissa said.

Kyrianna only nodded.

Shydaran seemed to scan the area where the various suits of armor were placed then dove into it. A blur moved just as the tiger struck. The clanging of metal rang in the hall as did the laughter.

Shydaran now wore a breastplate like a hat and it took all of Kyrianna's concentration to keep her gaze off Hendandra where she stood in a shadow at the far end of the hall. Her fingers paused in the braiding as she waited for Shydaran to make his next move.

The tiger sniffed the air, looked down the hall then sprang. Hendandra jumped also, but was stopped by Shydaran landing only a few feet in front of her.

"Nice kitty," she said as she took a step back. Shydaran moved with her.

He grabbed her with his paw and put her on the ground. Kyrianna lost sight of Hendandra.

:*Is she okay?* Melissa asked.

:*He would never hurt her.*

Falden began laughing loudly and pointing. Kyrianna leaned over to see what he was pointing at. Hendandra was crawling away from Shydaran.

"Lose something?" Nirev asked.

Shydaran turned and looked at Nirev, his eyebrows raised slightly.

"Snitch," Hendandra yelled.

Shydaran pounced again and Hendandra's voice was muffled as she began yelling from under him.

"Hendandra!" Andrinor stood.

"Yuck, cat slobber!"

Kyrianna braided the last set of unicorn hairs together and

tied the group to the base of her long bow. The silver-gray strands shimmered as they reflected the flickering torchlight of the hall. She carefully coiled the three remaining strands of hair, the longest and strongest she had recovered as she watched Andrinor walk toward Hendandra and Shydaran.

He slapped the tiger and laughed. "Come on, let her up." He paused and started laughing even harder as Hendandra crawled from under the tiger.

Her hair was a complete mess and stuck out at strange angles. Her face glistened with moisture. Shydaran licked her again and she slapped his face. "That tickles," she said.

Kyrianna stifled another giggle as Hendandra held out her hand and looked at Falden. The mage deposited a couple of green gems in her hand. "I know it's more than the agreed amount," he said. "The entertainment was worth it."

Kyrianna stood and glanced down at the silver strands in her hand. "I wonder?" she whispered.

"Wonder what?" Andrinor asked.

"Horsehair can be used to make bowstrings; I wonder if unicorn hair would work also."

Andrinor looked at the strands of hair in her hand. "I doubt it will be as easy as it seems. Unicorns are magical creatures; the hair is more delicate than it looks. Although it would be interesting to find out. Maybe it would confer some new magical quality on the bow it is used on."

"I hadn't thought of that?"

"Maybe you should ask Cewyr."

"Maybe I should."

"Kyri, have you talked to her at all this evening about what happened?"

"Not yet."

"Do not let the rage that creature created come between you. You must talk to her."

"I will. Before I retire for the night, I would like to try something, wait here." She picked up her long bow and strung it quickly.

"You want revenge for me beating you?" He took a step back.

"No. I want to see if my skill with the bow would allow me to disarm opponents at range. Particularly those it would take considerable time to take out of a fight."

"That would be a helpful trick; if you have the strength to accomplish it." He pulled out the pommel of his own weapon and the adamantine and cold iron blades appeared. "Let's test your skill," he said. "However, if you miss and hit me, I get to return the favor." He laughed as he moved to the far wall.

"Agreed," Kyrianna said.

She took careful aim as he held the weapon across his body in a standard defensive position. The first arrow hit the pommel precisely between his hands. She again aimed carefully hoping for the same spot. Andrinor looked up at her, surprise evident on his face when the second arrow hit. She noticed the weapon also seemed to vibrate in his hands.

One more solid hit should do it, she thought. She readied another arrow and took a slow careful breath as she sighted along the shaft.

"What are you two doing?" Myrith said behind Kyrianna.

"Chaos!" Kyrianna said as the arrow missed its mark and embedded itself in Andrinor's right arm. She dropped the bow as she turned and dodged behind Myrith.

"I told you what would happen if you missed." He said as he broke the shaft off the arrow. "And you agreed."

Kyrianna stood behind Myrith.

"Andrinor?" Myrith looked at him then back at Kyrianna.

He stopped and glared at Myrith for a second before shifting his gaze to Kyrianna.

"Don't hurt her too badly," Myrith said, stepping to the side. "We need her skill—although it would appear she needs a bit more practice."

Andrinor nodded as he balled up his fist and hit Kyrianna squarely in the chest. She took several unsteady steps back and fell to the floor. "Sorry," she said as she sat up.

Andrinor pulled the arrow from his arm and dropped it on the floor. He picked up Kyrianna's bow and held it out to her. "We can try this again tomorrow night—if you want to risk it."

"We'll see." She stood slowly and took the bow.

Myrith shook her head as she watched Andrinor walk off. "What were you doing and are you okay?"

"I'm fine." Kyrianna coughed several times. "I wanted to see if I had enough skill and strength to damage or break a weapon from a distance with my bow."

"That could be useful. Just be more careful in your practicing."

"If you hadn't interrupted I wouldn't have missed."

"Do you want to take another shot at me for compensation?"

Kyrianna looked at Myrith and shook her head. "I made the agreement and accept the consequences. When will you be starting the watches?"

"In about an hour."

"I'll take the second if that's okay. You can have whoever takes the first find me in the workshop."

"The workshop?"

"I need to do some work on my bow."

"I'll ask Andrinor to take the first watch and I'll be taking the third." She took a deep breath. "There is someone I must speak to again this night."

"I'll see you then." Kyrianna nodded then headed down the hallway. She paused for a moment at the door to the workshop and nodded when she saw Myrith approaching the scribe's room.

~ * ~

Myrith knocked on the door to the scribe's room. She had noted the tiger, *No!* she corrected herself. *His name is Shydaran.* Was sleeping in the room away from the group. With what Kyrianna had told them about the command from his goddess to not reveal himself, she understood why he was remaining separate. But it was also hurting him being seen as a part of group.

"Shydaran," she called cracking the door only a small amount. "May I enter? I must speak with you."

The door was yanked out of her hands and she stepped back at the anger still burning in Hendandra's eyes.

"What do you want?" Hendandra demanded.

"I…" Myrith's mouth went dry as the tiger stood and moved to stand behind the small woman. "I came to talk to him regarding my actions." She bowed her head slightly. "May I came in?"

Hendandra nodded and stepped to the side.

"I do not know what I did to anger you Hendandra, but we can speak at another time. For now, I must speak to Shydaran."

The tiger took a step back and titled his head to the side a bit as he looked at her.

"I know you will not speak to me. I understand you have been commanded to not reveal yourself by Shyada."

There was a low growl from the tiger.

Myrith lowered herself to sit on the floor, putting herself at the disadvantage in front of the tiger. She watched Hendandra move to one of the corners out of the conversation, but not leaving the room. She was surprised when the tiger also lowered himself to the floor, removing the threat of imminent danger, though the danger he presented was still present.

Myrith took a deep breath. "I know I already apologized publically—allowing you to chastise me for my actions, but I wanted to talk to you about today's events and I must explain that because of events in my past, it is very very difficult for me to trust—even myself. Because of this, I find I often rush to judgment and I have very little patience.

"Today, I ordered you to take direct action against those we fought against and you did. Then I acted rashly without consideration of possible consequences and charged into what should have been your battle. In doing so I put your life at risk at the end of my blade. I have already been chastised by Mykaylene and Conflagration when I sought to understand what it was I did wrong. Being who I am, I have always felt the eradication of evil, no matter the cost, was the goal of those who serve the light. I now understand that to properly serve and defeat evil, I cannot take actions that in and of themselves may be evil—the ends do not justify the means."

Myrith looked at the tiger and while she did not see forgiveness in his eyes, the anger seemed to have faded a little. "I make no promises that I will not make mistakes in the future, but I will attempt to consider the consequences before I take action."

She stood up slowly and bowed slightly. "I do not expect your forgiveness but I am truly sorry for what I did and for what I almost did. If you had been killed in the fight with the drake, whether by my hand or the drake's claws, the responsibility would have been mine."

Myrith reached for the door then paused. "I have a small request to make of you. You separate yourself from the rest of the group, isolating yourself in here. I would ask that you spend more time with the group as a whole. While we all now understand that you are more than you seem, it is hard to think of you as anything other than an intelligent animal. By being a part of the group, as you were tonight playing with Hendandra, we begin to think of you are being a part of our group—as one of us."

Shydaran cocked his head to the side and Myrith heard a slight growl.

"Keep in mind, Shyada sent you to us to learn from us, according to what she told Jerietlan. What she wanted you to learn, I have no idea—nor is it my business. But whatever it is, how can you learn it if you are not truly a part of us."

She bowed again. "I will bother you no more this evening." She glanced at Hendandra. "I still do not know what I did to hurt you, but whatever it was I do apologize."

~ * ~

Kyrianna placed the smaller of her two bows in the stand and removed the bowstring. Carefully uncoiling the unicorn hairs, she held them up and lined up the ends of the strands. They were not all the same length, nor were they long enough to make the string out of only these three. She estimated she would need another three hairs woven into these to make the string properly. She knotted the end of the strands together then hooked them to the top of the bow. "Frayrith and Dwycia guide me in this task." While Frayrith favored the long sword, she was also considered a skilled archer as the bow was often the weapon of choice for those who walked the forest paths. Dwycia however was an archer. Kyrianna only hoped the goddesses would bless her experiment with the unicorn hair.

The hair was strong but delicate and Kyrianna spent much of her time making sure the strands remained untangled as she worked slowly. Her fingers were starting to cramp when she finally reached the end of the braid. She plucked a hair from her head to wrap around the strands to prevent them from unraveling during the day. Once the braid was secured, she sat back and began to closely inspect the work done so far for loose or too tight areas or places where the strands had twisted or knotted. The strands shimmered in the light of the room and she could see her patience had paid off; the braiding was smooth and even.

She looked up as Andrinor stepped into the workshop. "Hey," he said. "Weren't you supposed to take the second watch?"

"Andrinor, I'm sorry." She stretched her arms then shook them out as she stood.

"Well," he asked as she shut the door.

"So far so good." Kyrianna said. "I'll work on it again tomorrow. You, go get some rest."

Chapter Seventeen

Kyrianna took a deep breath as she walked into the shrine after her watch. It had been a long day, she was tired but there was at least one more thing she had to do.

"Cewyr?" She whispered the unicorn's name.

:It was happening again. Just like that day.

"I know." She placed her hand on Cewyr's neck. "That thing that called himself Godfeller affected not only you, but Gwideon as well. He almost killed Hendandra before he was stopped."

The unicorn turned her head to look at her, her eyes glistening. *:He shouldn't have been able to affect me like that. Not with the bond we share.*

"Silly horse." She wrapped her arms around Cewyr's neck. "He called himself Godfeller. He destroyed the temple of Mulog in Domar and killed the First Hammer before Nirev. He has the power and probably the will. He targeted you *because* of our bond. And he probably targeted Gwideon because he saw him as the strongest of the group."

:Who are the Cyral? Melissa asked.

:What?

:You thought he might be of the Cyral. Who or what are they?

"I really don't know for sure. They are mentioned in some of the early legends of my home. But they vanished about five thousand years ago—none of the stories I read said why. However they were described as having flame red hair and gold eyes." She focused her thoughts as she tried to block Melissa from hearing them. *There was something else, I remember. Something that tied them to the one called the Consort of Chaos.*

:Kyri?

"It's nothing Melissa," she said.

:Kyri, I'm sorry about today. Cewyr nuzzled her neck. *:Frayrith told me you were the only one who could forgive me as my actions were directed against you.*

Kyrianna shook her head. "There is nothing to forgive. Your actions were not your own. You have done no wrong to me. It is this Godfeller who is at fault." She hugged the mare tightly. "You are my friend and that is all that matters."

:*Do you think you will visit Tristan again tonight,* Melissa asked as a few minutes.

:*After today a few pleasant dreams would be nice,* Kyrianna thought.

She sat next to Cewyr and rubbed her temples as she tried to clear her thoughts. The last dream had been dangerously close to crossing territory she didn't want to cross with Melissa in her mind. She wasn't sure the dreams would continue in the same direction, but the idea Melissa might be there if they did disturbed her.

: *It wasn't a dream,* Melissa said suddenly.

"What? That's impossible. I was here. How could I have been sent there?"

:*I don't know, but it wasn't a dream. When the priest of Resare released me from the summoning, I heard a woman's voice saying I should stay and see what was going to happen. She told me she would make sure I was able to return to you afterwards. I found myself in the piano when Lord Naythor and his family arrived. When his granddaughter started playing I decided it was time for them to leave, she had been flirting with Tristan too much by then. I didn't know you were there.*

"But how is that possible?"

:*Perhaps some magic of the Reishalli?* Cewyr said.

"Perhaps, but it is nothing I have ever heard of." The idea she was being drawn to Tristan was a pleasant one, but she was still concerned about Melissa.

:*Melissa, a person's dreams are usually considered private. Is there any way you can avoid seeing mine?* She asked despite the fact she was sure she already knew the answer.

:*Not really. When you are asleep, there is nowhere for me to go, so I am drawn to your thoughts and dreams.*

:*I understand.* Kyrianna paused and took another breath. :*Maybe I should let you spend your nights with one of the others, or maybe Riker. You could probably transfer into the lance. You're both 'awake' throughout the night and could provide each other company.*

:*Why are you trying to get rid of me!* The little voice sniffed a couple of times.

:*I'm not trying to get rid of you, only prevent a problem. You are only eight years old...*She paused at the snort she heard in her heard. :*I know you have existed for over thirty years as the seasons as measured, but* *based on your life experience and your emotional development you are still only eight.* Her voice took a sterner tone.

:*There are certain things adults do not explain to children, until they believe they are old enough to properly understand them. The question of maidenhood is one of those. Your mother gave you an explanation that while true was also simplistic and appropriate for a child of your age at the time.*

She paused again and her tone softened. :*Little sister, in some ways you are in a bad position, you have the experiences of an eight year old child but you are in thoughts and mind of a twenty year old. You do not have the appropriate perspective to understand properly much of what you are seeing or hearing from me*

:*As far as the question of maidenhood. I am very much afraid that question is going to be answered in a very inappropriate manner for you in my dreams. As you are no longer content to accept the simplistic answer you were given when you were younger, I will try to give you a little better one.*

There was no response from Melissa in her mind, though she could sense the girl waiting.

:*When a man and a woman are in love one of the ways they express that love is in sharing themselves with each other. This type of sharing usually does not take place until after a couple is married, but can take place when both are willing. Kissing and holding hands are only a small aspect of that sharing.* Kyrianna took another deep breath. :*Shyada is the patron of pleasure seekers and there is much pleasure that can be achieved between two who come together. I believe she may be responsible for the direction my dreams are going and I worry they will follow a course she directs. You do not need to know the ways a man and woman come together to share at this time, that is something you will eventually learn. Just know that when a woman has shared herself with a man, she is no longer considered a maiden.*

:*I'm still confused and I know there is something you are not telling me.*

Kyrianna laughed. :*Of course there is something I'm not telling you. I said as much in what I did tell you. However, now is not the time for more detailed explanations. You have a couple of choices for how you pass the night: I can attach the necklace to Cewyr's collar, or we can ask Riker or one of the others. I would prefer Cewyr or Riker myself as I really don't care to explain the reason for the request to anyone else. However, it is your choice and I will honor it.*

:*No matter how embarrassing,* she heard Cewyr whisper in her mind.

"Shut up *horse*," she said slapping the unicorn lightly on the nose.

Kyrianna waited patiently as silence filled the place in her mind where she could normally hear Melissa. Finally, the little girl spoke. :*Can I stay with Hendandra?*

Kyrianna sighed. She had told Melissa she would honor her choice, but that was the last person she really wanted the child to stay with, and was the last person she wanted to explain her situation to. :*Melissa, that is probably not the wisest choice you could make. I worry her dreams could take directions I prefer you not to witness also.*

:*Oh.* The little girl's voice was soft and Kyrianna heard a note of sadness in it. :*I guess I can stay with Riker.*

:*Very well. Let's go ask him.*

:*Don't you think you should ask Myrith first?* Cewyr asked.

Kyrianna froze then slowly turned to face the unicorn. "You're enjoying this, aren't you?"

Cewyr only bobbed her head in answer.

~ * ~

Kyrianna entered the hall to see Myrith and Riker come back in from checking the main doors. The older woman turned and looked at her.

"Shouldn't you be asleep? It has been a long day for all of us. I know Urric's comment didn't sit well with you and then what we learned about Brular and the amulet obviously upset you as well."

"I will be going to sleep shortly, but I have a favor to ask of you and Riker," Kyrianna said.

Myrith raised an eyebrow.

Kyrianna took a deep breath and let her gaze drop to the floor. "My dreams have been very disturbing of late and I would prefer Melissa not stay in my mind while I sleep as she is drawn into those dreams. If you and Riker will allow it, I would ask that she be allowed to pass the nights with him."

Myrith reached out and lifted Kyrianna's chin. "Disturbing? How?"

Kyrianna pulled back a bit and felt her cheeks heat. "First, your answer. I will explain after she transfers. Please." Her voice dropped to a soft plea.

"This should be interesting." Myrith turned to Riker. "Are you willing?"

He bobbed his head and turned slightly, almost presenting the lance to Kyrianna. She drew the silver sword and touched it to the lance. :*Goodnight, Kyri,* Melissa's voice whispered.

:*And you, little sister.* She paused. :*And, thank you.*

"That explanation," Myrith said after Riker moved away from them.

Kyrianna felt her cheeks warm again and she looked down at the floor as she spoke. "I told you I was risking Shyada's anger in telling you about Shydaran. It appears she has been guiding my dreams and they are quickly reaching a point that is very inappropriate for an eight year old to see."

"You've been dreaming about Tristan." It wasn't a question.

Kyrianna looked up and nodded. "I have."

Myrith shook her head. "Back to your bed and your dreams, Rangerette."

"Thank you."

~ * ~

Kyrianna shook her head to clear the fog surrounding her mind. As she finally focused her thoughts, she found herself standing in a grand hall. Numerous people were moving around the room cleaning, arranging decorations and setting up platters of food. She smiled when she saw Tristan talking to a group of guards. He glanced her direction, nodded to the one who appeared to be in charge of the group then moved to join her.

"Kyri, once again you seem to magically appear when I am thinking of you. However, we must find you something more suitable to wear." He turned and waved one of the servants over.

"What's going on?" She asked as she looked around the room at all the activity. She glanced down at herself and saw she was wearing her old leather armor. However, she had none of her other gear or weapons with her.

"King Dracenhalts is visiting Raspa for some trade negotiations with the council. This is his reception."

Kyrianna stared at Tristan. "And, you're in charge of the security," she said.

"Actually, I'm acting as liaison at the king's request."

Kyrianna smiled then leaned forward and gave Tristan a brief kiss on the cheek. "I guess I should be dressed a little better then. However, this appears to be all I brought with me."

"My Lady," the young man who had come over at Tristan's request said as he bowed. "I believe we can find you something suitable to wear, if you'll come with me." Kyrianna glanced at Tristan who smiled and nodded.

The servant led her through the corridors of the hall and to a large dressing and bathing chamber. "If the lady would like to bathe herself, hot water is available and I will send someone with a selection of dresses for her to choose from as well as to help her dress and prepare for the reception." Kyrianna nodded.

He bowed again then backed out of the room, closing the door as he left.

Kyrianna stared at the door for several heartbeats then turned and surveyed the room. A decent sized bath sat in the corner and she could see steam rising from the surface of the water. *Might as well enjoy myself,* she thought as she shed what she was wearing.

The water was hot enough to be comfortable without being scalding and she relaxed as she leaned back and ducked her hair into the water. The next hour passed in a blur as two women arrived to help her. She ended up in a dark green gown with gold stitching that seemed to create as aura as she moved. One of the women spent a long time fussing over her hair while the other applied the cosmetics. Kyrianna sat there in shock—unable to really say anything. Even the night she was presented to the council of Nydith, her father had not allowed her to be waited on like this by any of the servants, nor had she ever really wished to be treated like this.

Kyrianna stared at the face looking back at her, when the women finished. They both knew their art well. Her face was not heavy with cosmetics, only enough to highlight her own features appeared to have been used. While the cosmetics were expertly applied, it was her hair that caught her attention the most.

Her hair had been braided with gold chains holding small green stones that winked in the flickering light of the room. Piled on her head in an elaborate style, she was certain it would fall apart as soon as she moved. "It's beautiful. Thank you." She handed the mirror back to the woman.

"My Lady, the reception has already started, you should return downstairs. Lord Duvall will be looking for you."

"Uh, yes." Kyrianna stood slowly and moved to the door. Before she could reach out to open it, the young man who escorted her to the room stepped in.

"My Lady, I will be happy to escort you back to the hall and have you announced," he said.

"The escort is appreciated, but I do not wish to be announced."

The young man stared at her. "It is the custom."

"That may be, but it is not my custom. Other than Lord Duvall, there is no one here I care to know who I am."

"As you wish."

They entered the hall and Kyrianna began scanning the crowd looking for Tristan. She finally spotted him standing with King Dracenhalts as several of the nobles waited to be introduced to the King of the Dh'Mark realms.

"Did you hear some girl actually showed up in leather armor earlier," Kyrianna heard a voice behind her say. She turned to see a group of about five young women standing there talking as they kept glancing at where the King and Tristan stood.

"I understand Lord Duvall had her escorted from the hall," another said.

"Interesting," an older woman whispered behind Kyrianna. "I understood someone to say the woman who arrived was actually the half-elf Lord Duval has taken an interest in lately."

Kyrianna turned to see a tall woman with dark brown hair and ice blue eyes looking at her. "Do I know you?"

"Not yet, but I believe I know you, Kyrianna Dalynne." The woman held out her hand.

Kyrianna stepped back. "You seem to have me at a disadvantage." She refused to take the woman's hand.

"I am Cassandra Shindar." She lowered her hand.

"You're the one who…" Kyrianna let her voice trail off. This was a serious social function and she would not risk making Tristan look bad by attacking this woman at this time. Besides, Falden deserved the first shot at her.

"You refer to Falden." Cassandra smiled. "He needed a lesson."

"You will excuse me." Kyrianna started to walk away.

"It is an interesting magic that has brought you here, Kyrianna," Cassandra said looking from her to Tristan and back. "Very interesting."

Kyrianna froze in her steps then turned back to fully face the woman. "What do you want?"

"Only to spend some time talking to you. The rest of the

women at these types of functions are usually more interested in talking about fashion, gossiping about others or talking about the latest most eligible bachelor; which at this time is Lord Duvall."

"So I have gathered." Her gaze went back to Tristan. This time he was talking to the girl he had been entertaining the night before.

"Ah, Caitlin Naythor. It is rumored her grandfather refused to allow Lord Hyserian's son to court her in the hope she could gain Lord Duvall's attention. She is considered to be one of the most beautiful girls in Raspa and House Naythor has considerable power on the council." Cassandra smirked as she looked at Kyrianna.

Kyrianna returned the smirk with as sweet a smile as she could muster. "And your point would be?"

"That obviously Lord Duvall cares about things other than beauty and power. You must be careful on your journey, Kyrianna Dalynne, unless you want to see him destroyed from losing you."

Kyrianna gasped lightly. That was almost the same warning she had had last night. "He knows the danger involved in what we do and he understands that this is something I must do. He knows the risks as well as I do."

"In that case I suppose Falden has told you about my warning regarding Torliana."

"He has said nothing to me. What about her?"

"I suggest you talk to Falden. You will probably want an explanation as to why he didn't tell you." Cassandra turned and smiled at a large man who silently appeared at her side. "Kyrianna Dalynne, allow me to introduce my husband Orlundru. He is the Fifth Sword of Tormasus and was your friend Andrinor's trainer for a few days."

Kyrianna nodded her head respectfully. "If you will excuse me." This time she was able to move away from the woman without any more comments.

She threaded her way through the crowd until she finally joined Tristan.

"You look stunning, Kyri. I believe green is more your color than blue," he said.

He gestured toward the King.

"You remember King Dracenhalts."

"Of course." Kyrianna bowed her head as she held her skirts

out and curtsied. "It is an honor to see you again, Majesty," she said.

"Come to tell me of other places where I am slacking in my duty or honor, Lady Kyrianna," the King said with a laugh.

Kyrianna smiled. "Not this time, My Lord. Are there other areas I should be aware of?"

"My Lord, if you will excuse us," Tristan said taking Kyrianna's arm.

"Of course. Thank you for your assistance this evening. I will see you tomorrow at the council," he said give them a slight nod.

Both Kyrianna and Tristan bowed before they left.

Tristan led Kyrianna out of the hall to a secluded part of the garden maze. "What is going on Kyri? How can you be here?" He guided her to a stone bench hidden by the bushes.

Kyrianna shook her head remembering Melissa's words that last night had not been a dream. "As far as I know this is all a dream. Perhaps it is one we are both sharing."

"And that would be your explanation for yesterday as well."

She stared at him for a moment. "What else could it be," she finally said.

"What else indeed." He reached out and placed his hand on her cheek then slowly drew her towards him.

Kyrianna let herself relax as she leaned into him. For several minutes she just sat there, her head resting against his shoulder as he held her. She finally sat back, reached up and turned Tristan's face toward her. This time she was the one to pull him to her and she felt her body tremble as their lips met.

She didn't protest as she felt his hands on her neck loosening the upper laces that held the dress on her shoulders. The cool night air pricked at her skin as the dress started to slide away from her shoulders and down her arms. With the neckline of the dress about midway between her shoulder and elbow, it felt as if her arms were bound to her sides. She gasped softly as Tristan kissed her neck and shoulder, his hands slowly pushing the dress further down.

A small part of her mind wondered at what they were doing. They were not married and weren't even officially engaged, even though she had given him her promise she would return to him. His lips returned to hers and she pushed all thoughts of propriety out of her mind.

~ * ~

"Hey! Come on Kyrianna. It's past time to be up," a voice said as someone shook her.

Kyrianna opened her eyes to see Hendandra leaning over her, a concerned look on the girl's face. "Enough, I'm awake," she said.

"It's about time," Myrith said from the entrance. "As usual you're late. The rest of the group is ready to go."

"Give me couple of minutes to get my gear together."

"You've got five minutes to meet the rest of us at the doors. If you're not ready at that time, we're stepping out and closing the door. You'll be outside the keep in whatever state of unreadiness you happen to be in at that time," Myrith said grinning.

"Very funny. I'll be ready." Kyrianna looked at Hendandra who was gathering some of her equipment together. "Hendandra would you excuse us for a moment? Please."

The girl looked from her to Myrith and frowned. "Are you alright?"

Kyrianna smiled. "I am. I just need to talk to Myrith for a moment."

"I'll be back shortly." Hendandra left the room.

"What's wrong?"

"Did Falden say anything about Cassandra Shindar and Torliana when he got back to Irrmar?" She wiggled into her chainmail and straightened it as she waited.

"He told us Cassandra had told him Torliana must be kept among the living." She handed Kyrianna her sword belt.

"Why?" She lifted the unicorn horn sword from the altar and slid it into its scabbard.

"That is something you will need to ask Falden. You ready?"

Kyrianna grabbed her pack and bedroll. "Let me drop these in my chest as we leave." She paused and looked at Cewyr. "Come on horse."

Cewyr bumped her with her nose. :*Stop calling me a horse*, she said.

Riker was waiting as they entered the hall and Kyrianna touched the lance attached to his gear and felt the familiar chill of Melissa moving through her body. :*Good morning, sister*, she asked. :*How was your night?*

Kyrianna mounted Cewyr and followed the others out of the hall as she waited for Melissa's answer.

Chapter Eighteen

Brular woke from his sleep. He was disorientated in the complete darkness and silence of the area he was in. He could feel nothing—all sensation had been taken from him in this place. Despite being trapped in this prison, his mind remained active. He still wasn't sure which of the two Ladies of Chaos Torliana had been serving all these years. Was it Carrinna or was it Thynitic? She thought she served Thynitic, but he suspected it was Carrinna who brought the chaos storm down on Mount Veri. Had Torliana been deceived by Carrinna after she answered Thynitic's call to follow the path of chaos, or had it been Carrinna the entire time?

The other question: just how much power did Carrinna have? Thynitic had indicated she no longer knew which plots were hers and which were Carrinna's. Did the demons who served Thynitic know which of the two they were dealing with each day? And, did it truly matter? Both were dedicated to chaos and pain. Although, based on what he had read in the book Thynitic had given him, pain had not always been a part of her makeup. Perhaps if Neysinil could be restored, then Thynitic could also.

He blinked several times as the darkness of his cell was flooded with light and he saw an image form on the wall. He frowned as the image formed into an area of twilight and fog and he saw Myrith astride Riker with another warrior standing next to them. Myrith glanced behind her as colors swirled in the air and Kyrianna and Cewyr appeared.

A portal? He studied the shadows made up the area as more of the group appeared through the portal. *What foolish thing have you done, Myrith?*

He turned his attention to the armor of the warrior standing next to Myrith and Riker. He shook his head when he recognized the runes—they were unmistakable—he was one of the Grey. *No! You fools, you came after me. Why would you do that and risk yourselves in an impossible task?*

He searched the image looking for clues as to where the group was. The rest of the group appeared through the portal and the gray fog began swirling around them. When it faded a set of gates appeared and Myrith fell to the ground as Riker was pulled from under her and through the gates. Kyrianna's face went white and she fell against Cewyr's neck as a ghostly form flowed from her body toward the gates.

You fools! he thought. *You came to the five-forty-fifth. You have no idea what you've risked.* The five-forty-fifth; he knew that layer. Thynitic had inhabited it for a while, but it had proven too dangerous, as it would suck the life from those who stayed there for too long. But, to protect her domain, she had removed all but one primary portal to the sixty-third. There were only a handful of paths to that portal and this was considered the least dangerous of those. The question now, was it Thynitic or Carrinna the group would be facing here?

~ * ~

"Melissa!" Kyrianna screamed the wraith's name as she drew her swords and slid off Cewyr. She cringed at the screams that echoed in the fog surrounding them. Riker's neighs were in counterpoint to the girl's screams. The pain in their voices tore at her heart. Both she and Myrith had a duty to protect their ghostly companions and they had both just failed in that duty. She took several steps forward, only to find herself blocked by Conflagration as flames sheathed the blade.

"Wait" Myrith whispered. "We need to know what we are facing here before we charge in."

"Myrith, are those...?" Hendandra pointed at a rusty set of gates that appeared several yards in front of them.

"The estate," Kyrianna said. "Frayrith, no." Her voice was harsh and she found it hard to catch her breath as she stared at the figure in front of the gates.

"Kyri?" Myrith asked.

"Mikyl." Her voice was only a whisper.

"Can you hear them?" he asked. "It's almost like being home."

"Mikyl!" Kyrianna screamed the lich's name as she started toward the gates.

Mikyl smiled and raised his hands. "A gift for the happy couple."

"Kyri!" Andrinor grabbed the girl as several bolts of arcane force struck her.

"Let me go!"

:*He's not there,* Cewyr's voice said in her mind.

"What?" Kyrianna spun to face the unicorn.

"This one is an illusion," Cewyr said. "There is a shimmer about sixty yards in that direction." She nodded with her horn.

Kyrianna sheathed her swords and readied her bow, watching as Myrith and Gwideon moved in the direction the unicorn had indicated.

:*I cannot see it well enough to direct your aim,* Cewyr said as she bushed Kyrianna's neck.

Kyrianna listened to Falden chanting softly. She knew the spell he was calling on and smiled as a figure was outlined in a soft purple glow. She had her target and raised her bow.

Kyrianna's arrow went wide as Mikyl raised his hands and the sleeves of his robes fell back. He only smiled as a black bolt of force leapt from one hand to strike her and another flew from the other to strike Andrinor. She knew that black bolt and the hand that cast it—Torliana. She could only stare at the mocking smile on Mikyl's face as he looked at her.

She half-turned as Andrinor roared and she saw him change into a silver dragon and launch himself into the air. His claws wrapped themselves around Mikyl and he dove back to the ground, carrying the lich. He roared again, ice falling in shards around them when he landed and Mikyl vanished.

"Why didn't his magic hurt either of us," Andrinor asked after he changed back from his dragon form.

"There are spells that will allow magic to strike another by targeting someone close to them," Falden said.

"For the happy couple," Kyrianna whispered.

"What?" Myrith asked.

"Before the first bolt hit me, he said, 'A gift for the happy couple.' That spell was meant for Tristan!" She turned toward the gates. Melissa's screams pierced the air. "Mikyl!"

There was no answer as the gates swung open.

Myrith stopped as the building that appeared in front of them burst into flames.

Melissa and Riker's cries grew louder as the fire rose.

"The servants' quarters," Kyrianna said.

Andrinor pushed through the group and grabbed the chain

that held the doors. The chain snapped and the doors flew open, knocking him back several steps. A figured clothed only in flames rushed toward Falden.

Sword cuts from both Myrith and Gwideon don't even slow the figure as it embraced Falden and then merged with the mage.

A red glow surrounded Falden and balls of flame appeared in his hand as he looked around at the others. "Child of ice," he said his voice sounding more like Mikyl's than his own. "Let's see how you fair against my flames." The flames leapt from his hand to strike Andrinor, surrounding the young man in a whirlwind of fire.

"Jerietlan, douse the flames!" Myrith yelled as Andrinor dropped to the ground and began writhing and screaming in pain.

Kyrianna raised her bow and Myrith stepped between her and Falden. "He is still our friend."

Kyrianna lowered her bow.

"Fools. For the sake of a perceived friendship, you risk losing another friend," Falden said. Flames danced around him then shot out to surround Hendandra who screamed and fell to the ground. Water flowed from Nirev's hands to douse the flames around Hendandra even as Gwideon was throwing his cloak over her. He helped her up and held a vial of a glowing blue liquid for her to drink.

Shydaran roared and leapt at Falden from behind, knocking the mage to the ground. He pinned Falden, keeping him face down and preventing him from casting again.

"How do we get whatever that thing is out of Falden?" Myrith asked.

Kyrianna moved away from the group now standing around Falden. "Mikyl, you are a coward. Stealing power from others and then hiding behind that power instead of facing us directly. If you want to get to Tristan, you are going to have to go through me."

"If I want to get to Tristan, I can also use my *sister*, Melissa." Mikyl's voice echoed in the area.

"Chaos take you!"

"I already serve chaos; your curse means nothing—Daughter of Chaos."

Kyrianna risked a quick glance at the group with Falden. Shydaran was growling softly and a brilliant glow surrounded the mage. "I see you still do not face us yourself. Are you afraid? We did defeat you once before and we will do so again."

"Kyri, that's enough," Myrith said. "You put Tristan at risk with your taunting. Is that what you want?"

"Is that thing out of Falden?" She spoke softly; pitching her voice so hopefully only Myrith would hear her.

Myrith nodded.

Kyrianna readied her swords. "Let's find our friends."

~ * ~

Myrith looked at the doors of the stable and took a deep breath. Riker's neighs continued and now she could hear the rattling of chains and the stomping of his hooves. Despite her desire to charge through the doors, she knew they needed to be cautious.

"I'll check the other set of doors," Hendandra said. "Just keep anything that may be interested in eating me distracted and over here." She moved away from the group and Shydaran followed her. Hendandra paused, glanced back at the group and grinned.

"Wonder if that spider will be there as well?"

"I'm sure it will be something far worse," Myrith said.

Several minutes later, Shydaran walked up to Cewyr and the unicorn lowered her head to touch him with her horn.

"He said Riker is in his stall and there is some sort of shadow thing guarding him," Cewyr said. "There doesn't appear to be anything else in the area."

Myrith took several steps toward the stable then jumped back as a large scythe swept across the ground striking the wall of the stable, collapsing it. One of the trees moved and she looked up and up at the giant who stepped forward. The tiny head on the thing's shoulders was that of the stableman—Creed Lawton.

"Why have you returned to my stables?" The giant's voice echoed in the emptiness of the area.

"We seek only to retrieve our friends and will then leave," Myrith said.

"This is where those you seek belong. It is their home." He moved to stand in front of the door, his scythe blocking the path around to the stable.

"You seek to hold them against their will," Myrith said.

"That doesn't matter. This is where they belong, and this is where they will stay."

"I think not." Myrith raised Conflagration and white flames

surrounded the blades.

Several arrows flew past Myrith's head to strike the handle of Creed's scythe. The giant laughed and swept the blade at the group. Myrith dodged to the side and found herself tripping on one of the tree roots. Conflagration's flames faded as she fought to maintain her balance.

"Get in close to him," Gwideon said. "Inside the arc of his weapon."

Myrith let herself drop to the ground as the blade swept over her. If Creed was focusing on her, he was ignoring the others. She rolled toward the giant, Conflagration quiet in her hand. As soon as she was close enough, she swung the blade and slashed across the front of the giant's legs. The blade didn't seem to cut very deep and there was no reaction from Creed. She jumped to her feet and Conflagration flared to life.

"Let's see 'em fight this," Nirev said. "Stand ready Lady Knight." The dwarf pulled a sword from his back and held it up.

Myrith nodded as the Sword of the Giant King caught Creed's attention.

"Foolish dwarf, that weapon only works against a true giant," Creed said.

"Then attack me," Nirev challenged.

She smiled as several bolts of arcane force struck the giant followed by more arrows. Creed Lawton looked down at her, but he didn't move his weapon.

"Yer body be that of a giant, foolish specter, and it be bound by the magic of this blade."

Myrith glanced at Nirev. When he had attacked the giant in Torliana's domain, he had been frozen in place by the blade also. How was he able to continue taunting the stable master like this? She would worry about it later.

She nodded to Andrinor who stepped up next to her and swung his sword at the giant's arm, aiming for the wrist. Myrith balanced Conflagration in her hands and swung hard at the giant's legs. Gwideon was behind the giant and she saw him swing at the other leg. Several bolts of arcane force again struck the giant's chest.

"Move back!" Jerietlan yelled.

Myrith backed up slowly staying next to Nirev and Andrinor as they moved away from the giant. A rain of fire fell on the giant and he screamed as it surrounded him.

Several more bolts of arcane force hit the giant and he fell back crashing into the stable. A shrill neigh pierced the air and Myrith charged into the rumble. "Riker," she yelled.

Another neigh.

"Myrith, over here," Hendandra's voice called.

Riker was in the same stall they had originally found him in. Chains were draped over his body, and they rattled as he stamped his hooves on the floor. She dropped Conflagration and ran to the horse. She took a few seconds to stoke Riker's neck, calming him as Andrinor grabbed one of the chains.

The young man smiled as he seemed to focus his strength on the chain and twisted. There was a loud snap and Myrith began unwinding the chains from around the horse.

When the last chain fell, Riker shook himself and brushed his muzzle against her cheek. "I'm sorry," she whispered.

:*You couldn't have known what would happen when you stepped through the portal. To me or Melissa.*

Melissa! The name hit her like a blow from Nirev's hammer. In her concern over Riker, she had forgotten about the child.

"Kyri?" she looked around, but her friend was gone. "Kyri!"

Hendandra picked something up from the ground and held it out. "Myrith."

She took the unicorn figurine from Hendandra. "The maze," she said. "She went there without us." Myrith knew her friend's rashness would probably get her killed someday. *Mykaylene, please don't let it be today,* she prayed. *Don't let it be today.*

~ * ~

"Kyri!" Myrith dropped Conflagration and stared. Kyrianna was trapped in a tangle of grass and vines while a huge mastiff stood ready to lunge. The creature was as tall as a large war horse and easily three times as massive. It was trembling as it tried to reach Kyrianna and she was reminded of the mastiff that attacked Tristan in the maze—held back by the magic of the collar it wore. But, what was holding this abomination back now. She raised her hands and whispered the words to a spell she had been given during her meditations that morning. Glittering shards of diamond dust flew from her body and she dropped to her knees as the power fueling this magic was drawn from her own strength.

"Lady Lake…." Whatever else Gwideon was going to say was cut off by a girl's pain filled scream. A scream that itself was cut off abruptly.

"Melissa!" Kyrianna called as the dog leapt at her. Myrith grabbed Conflagration and forced herself to her feet then stopped as Shydaran pounced on the dog and splinters of wood began flying as his claws tore into it. She turned toward Kyrianna to see Hendandra and Jerietlan working to free her from the vines. Gwideon was holding the girl's silver sword, the symbol of Resare pressed against the metal.

Andrinor and Nirev stood ready to attack the dog, but the tangle that was the tiger and the dog together wasn't allowing them a target.

Mykaylene, what happened? There was no answer, only a disapproving silence in her mind.

:Myrith.

She turned to see Riker nosing at something on the ground. She walked over and picked up the unicorn figurine. "Cewyr," she whispered.

The mare appeared in front of her and bowed her head. "I tried to stop her," she said. "I'm sorry."

Myrith placed a hand on the unicorn's neck. "She is too rash for her own good. There is no fault on you for that." She glanced back at Kyrianna.

Gwideon was handing the sword to Kyrianna, who was now free of the vines.

The dog was a pile of splinters and Jerietlan was tending to Andrinor and Nirev. Shydaran was watching the cleric as Hendandra seemed to be pulling splinters from the tiger's body. *It acts like it hates all of us, except her. With the threats Drezmona made, perhaps it's good the tiger likes her—maybe he will protect her from the demoness' son.*

"Jerietlan, when you are through, let's set up the keep, I believe we all need some rest," Myrith said.

Kyrianna was still pale and her hands trembled as held the sword. "Melissa?" Myrith asked.

"She's back with me." Kyrianna didn't look away from the sword.

"Good. We have our friends back. Now, we get some rest and prepare for tomorrow."

Chapter Nineteen

Myrith waited as Kyrianna tended to Cewyr. "I'm sorry," she heard the girl whisper as she started brushing the unicorn's mane. The silver gray strands shimmered in the dim light of the stable area creating a halo around Kyrianna and the unicorn.

"When Jerietlan talked to Brular, you said she had everything she needed, even the blood. How?" Myrith asked.

Kyrianna looked up. "Remember when she appeared?" Her hand went to her face. "She scratched my face with her nail and caught the blood in her hand."

"Then if she's finished casting the magics…" Her voice trailed off.

"After she finishes casting the required magics, when I die, my soul will be trapped in the amulet."

"It's not going to happen." Myrith held out her hand. "You have my word and I believe Andrinor's on that." She frowned as Kyrianna ignored her hand and turned her attention back to grooming Cewyr. The unicorn didn't look like she needed to be brushed out, but perhaps the ordinariness of the task was something Kyrianna needed.

"Don't forget to get something to eat," Myrith said. "I will also ask Andrinor about splitting your watch with me tonight."

"There is no need."

"Perhaps not, but that is the way it will be." She turned and left the area passing Jerietlan. She stopped at the door to listen.

"Falden believes Mikyl cast a spell commonly referred to as Love's Pain. It allows one person to be attacked through another, if there is a strong connection, like love, between them."

"Is there any way to prevent Tristan from being attacked again?"

"There are magics that will allow me to protect you from specific spells. However, they do not last very long and are limited. I believe I can shield you from this spell and thereby protect Tristan as well. Love's Pain is a complicated spell as it is cast on one person in combination with other spells in order to attack another. I cannot guarantee it will work."

"I understand."

Myrith heard Jerietlan turn and start toward the door. She left the area before he could see her.

~ * ~

"Jerietlan." Kyrianna stepped into the dining hall. "You mentioned being able to shield me from Mikyl's spell that allows him to attack Tristan. Is there a way to protect Melissa and Riker so they can't be taken away from us like they were today?"

"I doubt an actual spell was used," Gwideon said. "This area is a replica of the place where they were trapped as spirits for thirty years. There is an affinity, a connection, between them and this place that drew them back to the places where they were killed."

"So this can continue to happen to them?" Myrith asked.

"I don't know. I hope as soon as we get into the house proper, the risk will be minimized. It is also possible that with the stable and its guardian destroyed as well as the maze and its guardian, they will no longer be at risk. Unfortunately, there is no way to know at this point."

Gwideon paused and glanced from Kyrianna to Myrith and back. "There is another way to protect them."

"What would that be?"

"Carry them each in a piece of the spirit wood."

Kyrianna took a step back. "Trap her in the wood, like she was trapped in that creature we fought. That is not an acceptable option."

"I agree." Myrith felt her hand tighten on her sword.

"Then I will ask Resare to protect them, if he is able, so nothing else happens to them in this vile place."

"Thank you," Myrith said. She frowned when Kyrianna didn't say anything only turned and left the area.

Gwideon placed a hand on her shoulder. "She carries guilt for almost losing Melissa today."

"She couldn't stop what happened." She started to go after Kyrianna.

"True. And do you not feel some guilt because of Riker?"

Myrith nodded. It wasn't their fault Mikyl had been able to take their friends from them, but protecting them was their responsibility.

The sound of splintering wood caught her attention and she raised an eyebrow as she stepped into the main hall. Andrinor had set up one of the practice dummies and was now hacking it to pieces. There was no pattern, only anger.

"I be not understanding the reasons why he, Kyrianna and yerself be so upset over today," Nirev said beside her.

Myrith glanced down at the dwarf.

"Yea, we were surprised by what we found here. But, we defeated the creatures Mikyl sent against us. We rescued yer horse and the girl. None of us saw the ghostly eyes of Resare. We be one step closer to reaching Brular. None of this be making any sense. We should be celebrating the victory—not mourning something that didn't happen."

"Humans have a tendency to get angry when they lose control over a situation."

Nirev looked up at her and nodded. "I be understanding that, but tell me Lady Knight; at what point be we ever having control in this situation?"

She stared at him and leaned back a bit as she realized he was correct. They were following a path laid out for them by someone else. Trusting a guide who was serving penance for some unknown crime. They moved blindly from one portal to another facing chaos spawned demons. Nirev was right—they had never been in control.

"Ah, ye see it also."

She nodded.

"We be not in control, but that be different from being controlled. As long as that be not happening, we be fine." He slapped her on the back. "Take yer rest Lady Knight—tomorrow will be long."

"And you as well, First Hammer."

She watched Andrinor destroy another practice dummy and shook her head. Anger was an emotion that could control someone if they didn't control or tame it. She hoped Andrinor was able to tame his.

She began loosening the buckles on her armor as she headed to the shrine to meditate before her watch.

~ * ~

Myrith raised her head when she heard Kyrianna's light step.

She wasn't sure how much time had passed as she had been reviewing the events of this day in her mind. Events that had almost cost her Riker. Then there was something about her attack on the dog bothering her. It seemed Gwideon had been about to warn her of something when she cast the spell and then Melissa's scream of pain. She stood and moved to the opening.

Kyrianna was stripping off her own armor. Myrith watched as the girl placed the unicorn horn sword on the small altar along with the red gems she had been collecting.

"Kyri." Myrith felt her throat catch. "If you and Melissa are willing I wish to speak to her for a moment."

Kyrianna looked at her for several seconds, then nodded and drew the silver sword and handed it to her.

As she took hold of the sword, she could hear the sound of a child crying.

"Melissa?"

"She can hear your thoughts. There is no need for you to speak aloud," Kyrianna said.

"I will return her shortly." Myrith walked back to the area dedicated to Mykaylene, the sword held before her as she slowly knelt before the altar.

:*Melissa, are you still whole?*

:*I don't know,* Melissa said between her sobs. :*It was like I was reliving that day, only worse. Mikyl...*She started crying again.

Myrith waited a few heartbeats, unsure what to say to the child. She knew what she wanted to ask, but was worried about the effect it might have.

:*Melissa,* she hesitated as she formed the question in her mind. :*Were you trapped inside that abomination?*

:*Yes.*

:*Then it was you preventing it from attacking Kyri.*

:*Yes. It was difficult, but I was able to exert a little control over it.*

:*Thank you.* She took a deep breath as she finally found the courage to ask the question she had meant to ask. :*When...when I cast the spell...*Her thoughts trailed off.

:*Yes, Myrith, I was also hurt by it. I remember the pain, like something was cutting and tearing at my soul. There was a brilliant light surrounding me, then nothing until I found myself back in the sword with Gwideon holding it.*

:*Melissa, I'm sorry. I didn't...I wasn't thinking...I never thought...*

Her thoughts trailed off again. She should have waited to see what Gwideon was going to say before blinding casting the spell. She wasn't thinking only reacting rashly, without knowledge. The Gatekeeper was right, she needed to recognize and control her own rashness before she condemned it in others. Yesterday, her lack of trust in others and lack of patience had almost cost Shydaran his life, today…

:*Myrith?* Melissa's voice seemed far away and small.

:*I'm sorry. Oh, Mykaylene, I am sorry.*

:*Take me back to Kyri…please.*

Myrith didn't answer as she stood and carried the sword back to Kyrianna. She refused to look at her friend as she handed her the sword. "Mykaylene, what have I done? What have I done?" she muttered as she returned to the area dedicated to the Maiden of Battle.

~ * ~

Kyrianna frowned at Myrith's muttered comment as she walked away, but she didn't say anything. Her concern over Melissa was growing. She could sense the girl's presence in the sword, but there was only a cold silence in her mind in the place where Melissa normally whispered.

:*Melissa?*

:*Kyri, what happened after Myrith attacked the dog?*

:*Gwideon grabbed the sword and began whispering something I couldn't understand. Jerietlan said he was pleading with Resare to protect an innocent soul.*

:*How long did it take?*

:*Melissa, what are you talking about?* Kyrianna felt an icy hand grip her heart.

:*How long?* Melissa's voice was demanding. :*How long before Gwideon said I had returned to the sword?*

:*It took several minutes. Shydaran had almost shredded the creature by that time. Melissa what's wrong?*

:*While she was talking to me, Myrith realized that by attacking the dog, she might have actually been able to destroy me. She didn't say it, but I could sense where her thoughts were going.*

"What?" Kyrianna almost dropped the sword. :*She realized what?*

:*That her attack could have destroyed me. Kyri, I think she almost did.*

:*Gwideon,* Kyrianna thought. :*It was only through his intercession with Resare that you were spared. Oh, Melissa.* Kyrianna pictured herself hugging Melissa and she felt the girl return the hug. :*Thank you, Resare, for protecting her.*

Kyrianna glanced toward the shrine to Mykaylene and shook her head. Myrith's tendency to rush into battle without thinking about the risks to others was going to cost them all one of these. Thankfully, this wasn't the day.

Kyrianna looked up as Cewyr entered the area. "I'm sorry," she said. "I could say I was trying to protect you from Mikyl, but that wouldn't be completely true. I was angry at you for trying to stop me from confronting him."

The mare lowered herself to the ground and wrapped her neck around Kyrianna. :*I knew why you were doing it. Both the primary reason and the one that was at the bottom of your emotions at that time. I felt your anger and your worry as well as your love.*

Kyrianna leaned back against the unicorn and let herself finally relax. She smiled when she heard Melissa humming lightly. :*Feeling better?*

:*Yes.*

:*Good.* Kyrianna felt sleep starting to claim her and she wondered if she would again visit Tristan. That brought another thought. She had had Melissa spend the previous night with Riker to protect her, but the girl had told her staying with the spectral horse had been difficult because of their natures. After today's events, she didn't want to ask the child to stay with one of the others either.

:*Are you wanting to get rid of me again?*

:*No, Melissa, but there are things I am concerned about. Perhaps I should ask Shyada to not bring Tristan and I together tonight and let you and I share other pleasant dreams.*

:*Go to sleep.* Melissa started humming again.

Kyrianna found herself standing on the road outside the Duvall house in Raspa. "Melissa," she whispered.

:*I'm here.* There was a pause. :*I'm sure he's fine. You would have known otherwise.*

:*I know, but I'm still worried.* Kyrianna glanced down at her attire and was surprised to see she was wearing only a simple linen dress.

"Tristan?" She stepped just inside the door of the house and held her breath.

"Kyri?" Tristan stood up from the chair he had been sitting in and turned to face her.

She felt her heart stop. He was pale, limping and his left arm was bandaged. "Tristan?" *Oh Frayrith, please let Jerietlan be able to block this vile magic tomorrow. He should not suffer like this because of me.* She stared at him as he stood there. She closed her eyes as she saw Mikyl in her mind and heard his mocking statement about the happy couple.

"Kyri?" He squeezed her hands tightly and she opened her eyes to see the concern on his face.

"I'm sorry. A bad memory that will not go away any time soon," she whispered.

He led her to the couch then knelt down in front of her on the floor. "Tell me everything."

"Mikyl. We've run into Mikyl," she said. "He...he's..." She stopped, her throat tight as she struggled to find the words.

Tristan reached up and cupped her cheek in his hand. "Take your time."

She refused to look at him as she continued. "He has recreated a nightmare version of the estate where we are and we are having to fight our way through it again." She sat silently for several minutes, waiting for him to say something.

"Your friends defeated him once before, you can do it again."

"He's much stronger now; his magic is being augmented by Thynitic." Her hand went to the sapphire necklace he had given her.

"Kyri?"

"Your injuries...the magic that attacked you. That was Mikyl, attacking you through me. I'm sorry."

"Now that I know what is happening, I can take appropriate precautions." He paused. "There's something else."

"He...he...he took Melissa from me." She flinched as his hand tightened painfully on hers, but she didn't pull it. "We were able to get her back, but I couldn't protect her from him."

Tristan released her hand and reached for the necklace. She didn't protest as he removed it from her neck and held it for several minutes.

"It wasn't your fault." He refastened the necklace around her neck.

She looked at him and shook her head. "I should have protected her better."

Tristan moved to sit next to her and lifted her chin so she had to look at him. "You had no way of knowing he was going to be there or what he was going to do. It wasn't your fault." He reached out and pushed her hair back behind her ears.

She leaned her head against his hand as his fingers caressed her ears. "How can I protect her from him when we have to face him again?"

"That I cannot tell you. But, I trust you to do what you can; as does Melissa."

Kyrianna nodded and smiled at Tristan as his hand caressed her cheek, wiping away the tears. "May I never lose that trust," she whispered. She turned her head slightly and kissed the palm of Tristan's hand. The sword calluses on his hand were in sharp contrast to what she remembered of the nobles of her own home. Most were trained in the use of the rapier or other light blades, but other than those like her father who had earned their titles through their actions, none had the calluses that showed they trained regularly or used their weapons for anything other than mock duels.

His hand slid up to caress her ear and she gasped softly. In her mind, she heard Melissa humming.

She pulled away and shook her head. *I asked Shyada in the waking world to shield Melissa, perhaps I need to ask her here in the dreams she has created*, Kyrianna thought.

"What's wrong?"

"I need to visit a shrine to Shyada. There is something I must ask of her at this time."

Tristan looked at her, his brows creased with concern for a moment then he nodded. "I know where the shrine is." He stood up and offered her his hand.

~ * ~

Kyrianna watched as the stable boy saddled a grey gelding. The horse tossed his head not wanting to be bridled.

"He's still a bit headstrong," Tristan said. "I bought him a few days ago as a present for Melissa—for when you return."

"With a proper trainer he should settle down enough by then to be a proper mount for young lady." Kyrianna watched as the

stable master came over and handed Tristan the reins to his chestnut horse. The older man then turned to the grey, dismissed the
stable boy and began talking to the young gelding.

"Sterling was only introduced to a rider a few days ago. While
he is able to be ridden by most riders, he is still a bit head shy regarding the bridle," Tristan said. "Seems he doesn't like anything
touching his ears, unlike a certain half-elf I know."

"And that half-elf is very particular about who or what
touches her ears." Kyrianna shook her hair out, causing it to cover
her ears.

:*Melissa, what do you think about Sterling?*

:*He's pretty, but I don't know if I will be able to ride him.*

Kyrianna chuckled. :*With me and Cewyr to teach you, you'll be the
best rider in Raspa.*

The stable master had unbuckled the straps of the headstall
and was now coaxing the gelding into opening his mouth. Once
the bit was in his mouth, the horse seemed to settle down as the
stable master carefully buckled the headstall. When he finished, he
reached up and ruffled the horse's ears then offered him a piece of
an apple before he could react.

"I like him," Kyrianna said, "he cares about how the horse
feels."

"That's why I employ him. I do want your opinion on Sterling as well."

The stable master led the gray over after offering him a few
more pieces of apple. He held the horse's bridle as Tristan offered
Kyrianna a hand up. She looked at him and only shook her head
as she waved him off and swung up into the saddle. She leaned
over and adjusted the stirrups, then held her hand out.

"I assume he still has a light mouth," she said taking the reins.

"Yes, My Lady."

"Good."

"Come on, you can try his paces on the way to the shrine."
Tristan mounted his horse.

Kyrianna followed Tristan through the streets of Raspa. As
they rode, she tested Sterling's responses to rein and knee commands. The gelding moved and responded well. He still tossed his
head and seemed to worry about the headstall, but it was more a
show of annoyance than true rebellion.

Sterling stopped and Kyrianna smiled at the gray tabby cat

that sat in the road, looking at her. The cat stood and stretched before walking toward the right side of the road. At the edge of the road, it stopped, looked back over its shoulder, and meowed.

"Seems she want us to follow her," Tristan said. "You were seeking Shyada, perhaps she was sent by the goddess to meet you."

"Perhaps." Kyrianna slid off Sterling and watched as the cat walked up to the door of a house and sat on the step, again looking over her shoulder at them. "Do you know this house?"

"It is the home of my foster grandparents. The couple who raised my father after…" his voice trailed off.

:They raised Christian. Melissa's voice was excited. *:Can we visit them? Please?*

"Melissa would like to visit them. While I don't know how much time we will have together, I do not care to ignore so obvious a sign either." She glanced at the cat, who was still sitting on the step, her tail curled around her front paws as she watched them.

"We should at least pay our respects. Perhaps Melissa can visit with them while you conduct your business at the shrine. And I know they would like to meet you as well."

Kyrianna felt her cheeks warm at the smile Tristan gave her. *Thank you,* she thought glancing down. The cat blinked slowly then nodded and walked away, her tail held high in the air.

:Kyri? What was that about? Melissa asked.

:The possible answer to a prayer, little sister. The possible answer to a prayer.

Tristan looped the reins of both horses over the porch railing, then knocked on the door. A moment later an older woman opened the door and grinned when she saw Tristan standing there. "Tristan," she said. "And this must be Kyrianna." She held her hands out.

"Grandmother, this is Lady Kyrianna Dalynne of Nydith," Tristan said.

"Welcome to our home, Lady Dalynne." She bowed her head slightly.

"I thank you for your welcome. Please call me Kyri."

"I'm Cornelia and my husband is Tabran," she said escorting the two of them into the sitting where her husband was.

The older gentleman stood and grasped Tristan's hand with

both of his. "About time you brought her to meet us. I kept expecting to hear the announcement of your engagement without having met the lady."

"I'm sorry, but other obligations have interfered," Tristan said.

Cornelia came back into the room carrying a tray with a pitcher and several glasses on it. Kyrianna jumped up. "Let me take that for you," she said.

The older woman shook her head. "You are our guest. Please sit."

Kyrianna took her seat and watched as the woman filled the glasses with a pale orange liquid. The house was small, and in what appeared to be an older and poorer area of Raspa. She looked around at the furnishings; none were of high quality, although they were well made and comfortable. These were people who had what they needed and wanted but not the trappings of luxury or nobility. She had originally been concerned to see where Tristan's grandparents lived. She had an idea of the wealth and position Tristan had, and that he would leave the people who had taken in the frightened orphaned boy who was his father in a place like this bothered her. But she could see this was where these people wanted to be. They were happy and she had no doubt Tristan made sure they had what they wanted. "So when are the banns to be posted?"

"Grandfather!"

"Tabran! That was an impolite question to ask at this time," Cornelia said.

"That it may be, but anyone with a pair of eyes can tell they will be posted," he said. "Even though he told us about everyone in the group that accompanied him to the estate, young lady, there was always something in his voice when he talked about you." Tabran smiled at Kyrianna.

"We did find it interesting he never told us much about you other than what he knew from the estate," Cornelia said.

"We really didn't have time to trade histories at that time," Kyrianna said.

"Then tell us about yourself," Tabran said.

Kyrianna took a deep breath, glanced at Tristan then smiled as she told them about her family and her life.

"Kyri, we do have other business to attend to." Tristan interrupted before she could tell them about being exiled and the things that had happened since that time.

Kyrianna's hand went to the necklace. "We do have one other person to introduce," she said. :*Sister, can you manifest; even for a short time?*

:*I think so.*

"This is Melissa," Tristan said when the girl appeared.

"Christian was your brother," Cornelia said.

Melissa nodded as she faded back into the necklace.

"I'm sorry," Kyrianna said lifting the necklace from around her neck. "She cannot manifest for very long at this time." She held the necklace out. "However, she is able to possess objects and her spirit has found a temporary home in this necklace. She has expressed a desire to learn more about her brother's life. If you are willing, I would like to leave her in your care for a while so she can talk to you about him." The woman took the necklace slowly.

"If you are in contact with the necklace, she can communicate with you and you with her."

:*Melissa, you behave yourself,* Kyrianna told the girl before she released the necklace.

"She said to tell you that you should listen to your own advice," Cornelia said.

"We will return as soon as we are able." Tristan offered his hand to Kyrianna.

~ * ~

Kyrianna pulled back sharply on the reins causing Sterling to neigh and toss his head in protest as they approached a large marble building.

"Sorry." She patted his neck then looked back up at the building and frowned.

"This can't be the right place," she said.

"The shrine itself is to the right of the building." Tristan pointed to a smaller building next to the larger one.

"Then what is that?"

"It's a brothel." He didn't look at her.

"A brothel?" Kyrianna tapped Sterling with her heels and pulled him up in front of Tristan's horse, blocking the path. "And, just how is it you are so certain that is what it is?"

Tristan grinned as he started to guide his horse around her. "You can blame Laraf."

"Oh no." She reached out and grabbed hold of his horse's bridle. "You don't get out of the question that easily, Tristan Duvall."

"When Laraf and I returned to Raspa, this was one of the places he brought me when we were gathering information."

"Gathering information?" Kyrianna grinned and batted her eyelids. "That could be considered another name for pillow talk."

Tristan took a deep breath and frowned. "Neither of us was ever involved in pillow talk," he said. "Besides, Mykaylene would never approve of that kind of activity. And neither would a certain woman that I care about."

Kyrianna felt her cheeks warm and she nodded and released her hold on the bridle.

~ * ~

One of the priestesses stepped forward when they entered the shrine. "Lady Kyrianna, you have been expected. Would you please follow me? Lord Duvall you must wait here."

Tristan grabbed Kyrianna's arm. "I don't like this. I would prefer we not be separated. How does she know who you are and why would she be expecting you?"

"I was expecting something like this," Kyrianna said. "You wait here, I'll be fine."

Tristan released her arm. "Don't be too long."

She nodded then followed the priestess to another room.

"You have guessed correctly, Kyrianna," the woman said. "For your insult to Feric and Shyada, the goddess has enhanced the bond you share with Lord Duvall. You are indeed being brought here, and your passions are being enflamed during this time, so you can feel what it is like to be denied something you crave—just as you denied Feric." The priestess walked around her slowly. "This will continue until you make the proper offering at one of Shyada's shrines." She grinned.

Kyrianna bowed her head. "I stand by my actions, but I also accept Shyada's punishment for my insult. However, what of Melissa? She is still only a child and should not be subjected to the direction these visits are taking."

"Shyada was also an orphan and cares deeply for those who

have lost their parents. The copy of the necklace you left with your mate's grandparents will remain with them and she will be taken there during your visits."

"Thank you for providing that for her." Kyrianna grinned. "I suppose making the offering during one of these visits will not suffice."

"Correct. It must be done when the two of you are truly together." She paused and cocked her head to the side. "Your mate is growing anxious. However, before you are properly reunited, I believe a game is in order."

Kyrianna cocked an eyebrow. "What kind of game?"

"We will see just how well your mate knows you. You will be in this room with two other women and he will have to determine which is the real Kyrianna. You are not allowed to say or do anything to identify yourself. Are you willing to test him?"

"I am."

The priestess opened a wardrobe and removed a simple linen dress. "Remove everything you are wearing and put this on."

Kyrianna took the dress and looked around the room. She paused and turned back to the priestess who only gave her a small smile. There was no dressing screen in the room and Kyrianna frowned as she started to remove her clothing. It didn't bother her to bathe with Myrith or Hendandra or to even have to sleep in the same area with the men of their group, yet changing in front of this woman did.

She hurried into the dress as one of the younger girls came in, gathered her stuff and carried it out of the room. A few minutes later, two other women dressed identically to Kyrianna came in. Both appeared to be human and although they were about the same height and build as Kyrianna, they weren't very much like her in appearance. Another girl came in and handed each of the two women a potion vial then left.

The women drank the potions and their appearances began to shift until they looked like mirror images. The priestess motioned for them to stand next to Kyrianna then moved back to the wardrobe and removed a small bottle. The aroma of oranges and cinnamon wafted from the bottle as the priestess applied the perfume to each of them.

The first girl came back into the room leading a blindfolded Tristan. Kyrianna smiled as she thought back to how she had tied the black silk cloth over his eyes when they traveled from Raspa to Irrmar and his comment about being kidnapped by two beautiful women.

"Lord Duvall," the priestess said. "Shyada has determined a little game is in order to see how well you know Lady Kyrianna. Your lady is in this room with two others and you must correctly determine which of the three she is. You will remain blindfolded and she is not allowed to speak or do anything else to identify herself to you. As an additional challenge, keep in mind what you do to one, you are required to do to all."

"How do I know Kyri is actually in this room at this time?" Tristan raised his head slightly.

"Lady Kyrianna, calm your mate."

"Tristan," Kyrianna said. "I am here."

Tristan nodded.

"You both understand the rules. Neither is to speak from this point forward." She stepped closer to Tristan. "Any reward or punishment you may receive from this will be provided by your Lady, so think carefully about your decision and what methods you use to arrive at it."

Kyrianna watched as the girl led Tristan to the first woman and he reached out and took her hands in his. After a minute, the girl led him to the next woman and then to Kyrianna. She fought to control her reactions as his fingers slid lightly over the palm of her left hand and then the tips of the first two fingers of her right hand. *He's checking for archer's calluses,* she thought.

She stood quietly as Tristan moved back down the line returning to her again, this time he reached up to her face and let his fingers caress her cheek. As his fingers slid down her cheek and across her lips, she felt herself wanting to lean into his hand and had to fight not to react to his touch as the priestess watched her.

Tristan move back down the line and Kyrianna swallowed as she watched him step back and shake his head. He stood there for several minutes, waiting. When he stepped forward, his hands moved to the sides of the woman's face and pushed her hair behind her ears. His fingers slid slowly over the tips down the back of her ears and down her cheeks so his hands met in front of her lips.

He seemed more confident as he moved to the next woman and did the same thing to her ears. Kyrianna glanced at the priestess and saw the warning in her eyes when Tristan moved to her. She caught her breath, again having to fight her body's reactions. As Tristan's hands moved over her ears, she saw him smile.

"You have made your decision?"

Tristan nodded.

"You may speak."

"These ears are so distinctive and wonderful to caress with one's fingers," he said.

Kyrianna kissed his fingers.

"You have made the correct choice." The priestess removed the blindfold then motioned the others out of the room.

"If either of you speak this visit is concluded."

Kyrianna nodded and waited as the priestess left the room and closed the door.

She smiled at Tristan then placed a finger on his lips and shook her head, before he could say anything. His hands returned to her ears and she took a deep breath and let her head roll side to side pressing into his hands.

Her hands slipped under his tunic and she let her nails drag slowly across his chest as he stepped forward and his lips caressed her left ear. "I lo…"

"No!" Kyrianna fought the tears as she found herself back in the shrine.

:We were making cookies, she heard Melissa say.

Kyrianna jumped up, removed the necklace and tossed it over Cewyr's horn. She ran to the showers and dunked her head under the cool water. She could still feel his lips on her ears and his voice whispering, "I love you."

She stood there for several minutes letting the scene replay in her mind as the cool water washed over her. "I love you too," she whispered as she sank to the floor under the running water and cried.

Chapter Twenty

"Thank you for your assistance," Kyrianna said when Jerietlan finished casting the spell he had promised her.

"I pray it works as we hope it will." He bowed slightly then walked away to join Andrinor.

Kyrianna grinned at Andrinor when she saw Jerietlan's hand moving in the same pattern as they had in his spell for her. Someone the young warrior cared about had also been attacked by Mikyl. *No wonder he was so angry last night,* she thought.

:*You didn't assist Myrith with her armor this morning,* Melissa said.

:*She left the shrine and didn't seem interested in my help.*

:*You didn't even ask.*

Kyrianna glanced at Myrith standing near the door, waiting for the rest of the group. Her armor, while on properly, was loose as many of the straps had not been tightly buckled. Kyrianna took a step toward her, but stopped when Myrith looked at her then turned away.

She still needs to sort through what happened and almost happened yesterday. She thought when she realized Riker was not standing there. *She dismissed him; she doesn't want to risk him being trapped again. I'll give her a day before I talk to her. I'm not letting her do what I did and pull away from everyone and risk losing herself. We can't afford to lose her.* She paused and looked around the rest of the group. *We can't afford to lose anyone.*

The doors to the keep opened into darkness and Conflagration flared brightly in Myrith's hands as they stepped out. The black fog rolled away from them to show they were back in front of the closed gates to the estate.

"This is where we were yesterday," Hendandra said. "I hope we don't have to go through the exact same stuff again."

"Melissa is still here." Kyrianna rested her hand on the silver sword.

"Kyri." Myrith drew her long sword and held it out. "Perhaps it would be best to not use Melissa's sword in this place."

:*Sister?*

:How can I help you, if I'm not in the weapon you are using?
:Your presence adds an enchantment to the blade?
:Yes.

Kyrianna nodded, it made sense. Jerietlan had told her shortly after they left the estate the blade was considered blessed after Melissa's tears had fallen on it. It hadn't been a spell the girl had used, but it was her presence itself. *:It is not worth the risk to you in this place. I'm not leaving you behind, but I think Myrith is correct. I should use her sword and not put you at additional risk.*

There a silence for several heartbeats before the girl spoke again. *:I understand.*

Kyrianna took the sword from Myrith. "Thank you," she said.

Myrith gave her a curt nod then her attention went back to the gate.

"Urric, do we have to go this direction or is there another path to the portal on this layer or even a different portal?" Falden asked. "Why should we worry about Mikyl, if we don't have to?"

"After what he did to our friends yesterday, I be wanting a piece of his hide." Nirev slapped his hammer.

"We can't leave him in a position to attack us from behind," Andrinor said.

"I will not leave him," Kyrianna said. "As long as he exists, he is a direct danger to Tristan and Melissa."

"Three who seek revenge or retribution; two who openly admit it and a third who couches his words in strategy," Urric said. "Remember, Retribution is one of Thynitic's domains and this is an area where she holds power." The eye sockets glowed brightly for a moment. "There is only one portal on this plane to the next one we seek. Unfortunately, even I do not know its precise location. It is hidden in the chaos of this place even better than the one on limbo is hidden. I can sense it is close, but suspect it will not manifest itself until after you have defeated this Mikyl. As long as his power controls this area, you will be forced to play whatever game he desires."

"Is it his power, Thynitic's or the power that has been stolen from Brular and Torliana?" Jerietlan asked. "All but one of those will dissipate when he is defeated. If the goddess has hidden the portal, we may not be able to find it."

"We are not here for revenge or retribution. If there is another way to reach Brular, without facing Mikyl, I am willing to take it. If he comes after us, or our friends, we will deal with him at that time. For now, the most important thing is to get to Brular. Everything else is secondary."

Myrith turned to look at the skull on Gwideon's chest. "However, if there is no other way, then we will do what we must." She raised Conflagration. "Mikyl!"

Silence was the only answer they received.

The black fog thickened around them and Hendandra screamed as a tendril reached for her. She jumped and twisted in the air, landing on Shydaran as several quills flew from the bracer on her wrist to embed themselves in the black substance.

"Do not let the fog touch you," Gwideon called. "This plane borders the plane of negative energy and the fog is a manifestation of that energy. It is capable of devouring souls."

"Then we have no choice but to travel where Mikyl wants us to," Myrith said.

The fog rolled back several feet as the gates swung open. Striding out to meet the group was a recreation of the armored guardian of the chapel on the estate.

:*Melissa.* Kyrianna's hand went to the necklace. :*What was the password for the guardian?*

:*The guardian?*

"The chapel guardian." Kyrianna didn't realize she had spoken aloud until Myrith turned to look at her. "Melissa, what was the password?"

The fog closed in on the guardian, preventing them from being able to move around it.

Kyrianna felt herself being pushed back by a sudden rush of cold air. Andrinor had changed into a dragon and his wings were beating. She smiled as the fog around the guardian moved back from the force of the air.

:*Kyri, the password was 'For Mykaylene's Glory'.*

:*Thank you.*

Kyrianna dropped the sword Myrith had given her and drew her own silver sword. The hilt chilled as Melissa moved into the weapon from the necklace. "For Mykaylene's Glory." She raised the sword in salute.

The guardian raised his sword also, returning the salute, then appeared to freeze in place.

"So the blasted walking suit of armor be not attacking us. We still be needing to deal with the fog," Nirev said.

"We have no way of knowing which way to go in this," Falden said. "If this is a recreation of the estate grounds, we could end up walking off the cliff into the sea. Something, none of us would want to do."

Andrinor roared and began beating his wings again.

"We need to figure something out soon," Hendandra said. "This stuff is getting closer." Her sword gleamed in the twilight created by the walls of black fog.

"Kyri." Myrith turned toward her. "You were able to see the route through the Rock Palace and features of other areas, will the same magic help here? Maybe even let you see where the portal is."

"I don't know." She sheathed her sword and knelt on the ground brushing the area with her hand. "I need several minutes to cast the magic involved."

"Shydaran and I will watch your back," Hendandra said.

Kyrianna nodded as the tiger moved behind her, a low growl coming from his throat.

"I think not." Mikyl's voice was soft as he began chanting.

"Chaos!" Kyrianna shouted as she was whipped by the swirling dirt that surrounded her and the others. She staggered to her feet, holding Myrith's sword and stumbled back into Shydaran.

"Watch it." Hendandra's voice was high pitched and quavering.

Kyrianna spun around, the sword held high, so she wouldn't risk hitting her friend. "No!" she screamed as several black tendrils reached out to grab the smaller woman and drag her into the darkness.

Shydaran roared and was surrounded by a golden light before he plunged into the fog.

Kyrianna dropped her sword as one of the tendrils wrapped itself around her wrist. The thing didn't pull on her, only seemed to be holding her in place.

"Kyri!" Myrith's voice echoed in the small area.

Kyrianna shook her head. "Find Hendandra. It's not hurting me." She watched as Myrith and Nirev charged into the fog after the tiger followed by Jerietlan and Falden.

"At least, not yet," she whispered.

Andrinor launched himself into the air and Kyrianna fell to

the ground from the force his wings generated. *At least, the wind generated by Mikyl seems to have stopped,* she thought.

She felt a hand on her shoulder and she looked up to see Gwideon standing there. They were the only ones left the in the area. "They will need your protection in that stuff," she said.

"And what about you?"

She picked up the fallen sword again and held it in her free hand. "I will be fine."

He squeezed her shoulder again and she felt warmth flow from his hand to her body. He nodded then vanished into the fog.

Kyrianna felt her strength being sapped. "Cewyr," she said softly. The unicorn didn't appear.

:Kyri, she stepped out with us and she wouldn't have left with the others, Melissa said.

:I know.

~ * ~

Myrith held Conflagration high as his flames changed from their normal blazing colors to a brilliant white. The fog retreated away from the flames and she found herself in an open area with the others. Shydaran was standing over Hendandra, still glowing. Whatever protections he had shielded himself with were now protecting her as well. The girl was curled up on the ground not moving, several tendrils of the black substance still clung to her arms.

Falden stood close to the tiger, his staff also glowing brightly. Jerietlan was kneeling next to Nirev's body. The cleric looked up at her and shook his head. The dwarf was covered by the black substance, almost like it was a shroud. In a way, it was. She spun around at the sound of movement behind her and stopped short of bringing Conflagration down on Gwideon's head. She smiled and he nodded as she shifted the weapon away from him. "Can anything be done for Nirev?" She turned back to face Jerietlan.

"No," Gwideon said. "As I said earlier, the shadows that make up this manifestation drain the soul away from the body. It cannot be recalled."

"Are you saying his soul will not be able to find its way to Mulog's hall?" Jerietlan asked.

"It is doubtful."

"His soul was protected," Falden said. The mage pointed his staff at Nirev's hammer. The weapon was glowing.

"We need to remove the hammer from this place," Gwideon said. "His soul will remain trapped there as long as we are here."

Myrith looked up as a loud roar came from Andrinor. She watched him fold his wings and drop toward them. As he entered the area, the black fog reached out and entangled him, trying to pull him into it. She charged forward with Conflagration blazing. She heard both Gwideon and Falden chanting and two balls of brilliant light erupted on either side of Andrinor. The black fog retreated a small amount, but didn't release its hold on the silver dragon.

With measured movements, she swung Conflagration as close to Andrinor as she dared to cut the tendrils clinging to him. Gwideon stood on the other side, and handled Drinker with the same precision. She had to give the young man credit as he held his body completely still as they worked. The only sign of agitation or anger was his tail swinging back and forth preventing the tendrils from taking hold of it.

As soon as the last tendril was cut, Andrinor changed back into his human form and knelt next to Nirev's body.

Myrith glanced back at Shydaran, surprised the tiger hadn't moved. He hadn't shirked away from a fight before; in fact he seemed to relish combat. But, this time he had left them to defend Andrinor without his help. Hendandra moaned and shifted on the ground and the tiger nosed at her cheek. *He was more interested in protecting her than the fight,* Myrith thought. *Why?* She pushed the question away as something to think about later. Right now, they needed to regroup and mourn Nirev.

"Jerietlan," she called. "Set up the keep. We are done for today."

"Kyri?" Gwideon's voice was low.

"Chaos!" Myrith spun around and took off through the black fog. How could she have forgotten about Kyrianna?

~ * ~

"Your friends left you here, alone," Mikyl said.

Kyrianna looked up to the see the lich standing several feet from her. She grabbed Myrith's sword and started to stand, but the tendril around her wrist pulled her back to the ground.

"You're lucky, I have control over these shadows," Mikyl said. "Otherwise you would be dead by now. Your soul devoured by them. And Melissa's as well." He took a step forward. "However, there is another who would be very upset if that happened." Another step. He raised a black twisted metal wand. "If that happened your soul would be lost, unable to be held by the amulet she made for you."

Made? Kyrianna gasped and felt herself start to shake at his words. *She has completed the amulet.* She jerked her arm as hard as she could against the tendril holding it. It only tightened as another one wrapped around her other wrist.

"Give the Lady of Chaos my regards," Mikyl said. A bolt of lightning streaked from the wand to strike Kyrianna in the chest.

"No!" Myrith's scream echoed in the area.

Kyrianna's skin tingled and burned as the lightning danced around her. She fought the muscles contractions and forced her back as straight as she could.

Conflagration cut through the wand and lightning exploded around Mikyl. The lich dropped the remaining piece of metal then vanished.

"Thank you," Kyrianna said as Myrith cut through the black tendrils. She reached down and picked up the unicorn figure from the ground. "Cewyr," she whispered.

The unicorn appeared and placed her horn on Kyrianna's shoulder. "I don't know how he did it, but he was able to dismiss me as if he were the one who summoned me. He shouldn't have been able to do that."

"Brular created the figurine, he may have a connection because of that," Myrith said.

"He still shouldn't have been able to dismiss her," Kyrianna said. "Melissa, Tristan and now Cewyr, I will not let him continue to strike at those closest to me."

"Myrith," Jerietlan's voice came from behind them.

Kyrianna turned and saw the keep doors open. "Are we done for today?"

Myrith nodded. "We lost Nirev," she whispered.

"No! Chaos take it! No!"

"Where is Nirev's body?" Myrith asked.

"Gwideon wouldn't let us touch it to bring it," Andrinor said. "Falden burned it."

"It was encased by the black material and would have devoured the soul of any who touched it," Gwideon said.

"Then you did the correct thing." Myrith glanced around at the others. "Who has his hammer?"

"I do," Andrinor said. He strode into the keep without saying anything else.

Kyrianna followed the rest of the group as they trailed behind Andrinor to the area of the shrine dedicated to Mulog. The young warrior placed the hammer in a small niche in the front of the statue. Both the hammer and statue glowed brightly for several seconds then the light faded.

"May the Great Mother spread her wings over you and guide you to the halls of Mulog," Andrinor said. He turned and knelt down in front of Hendandra. "Are you well?"

She nodded.

"Then his death has meaning."

"I'm sorry," Hendandra whispered.

"You have nothing to apologize for Hendandra," Kyrianna said. "However Thynitic and Mikyl have much to answer for." She paused and glanced around at the others. "Etewyn, Laraf and now Nirev."

"And then there's Bukon," Myrith said. "He was taken by the portal the demon in that first temple opened." She placed her hand on Andrinor's shoulder. "We cannot continue to dwell on these things. Take time to mourn tonight, but tomorrow we must be focused on the task. We cannot let Mikyl separate us as he did today and we must find our way to the portal—we cannot continue to allow Brular to remain in torment while we delay."

~ * ~

Myrith watched as the others left the area. Kyrianna still stood staring at the hammer. "It wasn't Hendandra's fault—it was mine," she said.

"And why do you say that?"

Kyrianna turned and looked up at her. "Mikyl wanted to separate me from the rest of you. He said he had control over the shadows, as he called them, in that area—otherwise they would have destroyed my soul. He then said there was one who would be upset if that happened. He told me to give his regards to the Lady of Chaos before he used the wand." She took a deep breath and dropped her head. "He had the shadows take Hendandra because he knew several of the stronger members of the group would go after her." She looked up. "He died as a warrior—which is as it should be. He will be received by Mulog with honor." She left the room.

~ * ~

Myrith wandered through the keep, not sure what to do. Gwideon was in the shrine dedicated to Resare. She understood he would spend the night in vigil for Nirev. Hendandra had vanished into the scribe's room with the tiger. Her curiosity got the best of her and she stood outside the room for several minutes trying to hear something—anything that might explain why Shydaran and Hendandra were getting along so well, when the tiger had made it clear, with his actions that he hated all of them. She heard nothing from the room, and decided against confronting them. This was not the time.

She assumed Falden was in the lab—he seemed to find the solitude of that room to be preferable to spending time with the others. She frowned as she approached Jerietlan who was sitting on his bed staring at the floor. "Jerietlan." She spoke softly as she sat on the edge of the bed.

"Another friend lost? Is it really worth it? Why are we trying to challenge a goddess?"

"To rescue a friend from being tormented by her." Myrith placed her hand over one of his.

He looked up and nodded. "And, to prevent her from claiming another," he said.

"Nirev would have said it was worth it and so do I—even if I must pay the same cost."

"Be prepared tomorrow. I intend for us to leave this layer." Myrith stood. "One way or another."

Jerietlan nodded. "I'll be ready."

Myrith paused at the dining hall and picked up two mugs of ale then walked to the shrine. Andrinor was kneeling in the area he had dedicated to Ghainaess. She tapped her foot once to let him know someone was there.

Andrinor turned his head slightly and gave a quick nod before turning back for several minutes. Myrith continued to wait until he stood and faced her.

"I would ask you to join me in honoring the memory of our fallen comrade," she said holding out one of the mugs.

"The warriors of my home frown on the idea of getting drunk before a known battle, it dulls the reflexes and senses," Andrinor said. "However, as you ask this to honor Nirev, to whom I did owe a rematch of our last contest, I agree. It is an appropriate way to honor his life." He took the mug and gestured toward the dining hall.

Myrith smiled as the young warrior led the way.

~ * ~

Kyrianna glanced in the dining hall and grinned when she saw Myrith and Andrinor. "To Nirev." They both lifted their mugs and drained them.

"Fighter, Cleric, First Hammer of Mulog and creator of kindling from animated carriages," Myrith said with a laugh.

Kyrianna paused for a moment at the sound of Myrith's laughter. It was one of very few times she had heard the woman laugh, and as usual she was surprised by its lightness. It was one of the few elven traits Myrith could not suppress. She cringed as the two of them started trying to sing a dwarven drinking song. Neither of them actually spoke the language and it appeared they were trying to remember the words Nirev had sung and failing. Still, she had no doubts; Nirev would be pleased with the attempt.

"Kyri," Andrinor called. "Join us in a toast to the First Hammer." His words were slurred and he swayed a bit as he stood and held out a mug for her.

She sighed as took the mug. She didn't care for the taste of ale, but she wouldn't risk insulting Andrinor or Myrith by refusing. "To Nirev, First Hammer of Mulog," she said raising the mug.

She slammed the mug on the table along with the other two then slipped through the archway to the great hall. She saw Cewyr standing in the corner and walked over to her. "We need to talk," she said softly.

Cewyr followed her into the stables where Kyrianna picked up a brush and began working on her silver-gray coat. "I am worried about tomorrow. Mikyl has shown he is able to dismiss you without having been the one to call you. If we are separated somehow, he could dismiss you and claim the figurine."

Cewyr nickered softly before she spoke. :*I do not want to leave you, Kyri. I have been charged with being your companion and to help protect you from her.*

"But if Mikyl is able to dismiss you, then you are not with me either." She set aside the brush, picked up a comb and began combing out the long thick mane.

For several minutes, they stood there not talking with only the rhythm of the comb breaking the silence; as well as the occasional outburst from the dining hall. Kyrianna jumped when she heard music in her head. Cewyr neighed as the comb caught and pulled at a small tangle in her tail. "Sorry," Kyrianna whispered.

:*Melissa?*

:*It is Tristan.*

:*Melissa, be careful. Mikyl is getting stronger and targeting those around me. Perhaps it would be best if you stayed with Tristan—at least for now.*

:*Are you trying to get rid of me?*

:*No! I just don't want to risk losing you again. If you were caught traveling between the planes by Mikyl or Thynitic…* her thoughts trailed off.

:*I have to go.* Melissa's voice faded. :*I'll be careful.*

Kyrianna finished combing out Cewyr's tail and carefully tucked the strands that had come loose into her belt pouch. She poured some oats into the bucket in the stall and checked the water pail. Drawing the silver sword she sat in the corner and waited for Melissa to return.

~ * ~

Myrith looked up at Andrinor as he poured more ale into their mugs. So far, the young man had matched her drink for drink and seemed to be handling it as well as, if not better than she.

Between them they had finished almost all the ale produced by the hall that night as they told tales of Nirev and sang the songs they had heard him sing many times.

"This is the last of the ale," Andrinor said standing and lifting his mug high.

Myrith copied his pose. "We have shared tales of his courage and skill in battle," she said. "We have sung the songs of his race. We shall miss his hammer and his ax. We shall miss his company. He was our companion and our friend."

"May he find his place in the halls of his god," Andrinor said. "Hail Nirev, First Hammer of Mulog."

They both drained their mugs and slammed them down on the table. Myrith paused when she saw the mug they had set aside at Nirev's usual place was also empty. She knew neither of them had touched the mug and yet it had been drained. She glanced up at Andrinor and saw him looking at the empty mug also. "Nirev's spirit was able to join us in at least one round," Myrith said.

Andrinor nodded as he sat back down and let his head drop to the table.

I'll have to remember to talk to Jerietlan in the morning, Myrith thought as she fell back into the chair and slumped forward against the table.

~ * ~

After Melissa returned, Kyrianna went to the workroom to work on the bowstring. She had one hair from Cewyr's tail she felt would be strong enough and after a couple of false starts she managed to get it woven into the others properly so it was secure. The other hairs she had obtained, she braided together and tied to the hilt of the silver sword like a ribbon.

Finished with her work, for now, she left the workshop and walked through the keep checking on the others. Falden was asleep on a pallet in the lab and Hendandra and Shydaran were in the scribe's room. The fire had died down, but a low growl from Shydaran told her not to bother with building it back up. She shook her head when she saw Andrinor and Myrith asleep at the table in the dining hall. Gwideon didn't even acknowledge her when she stepped into the shrine and she left him to his vigil for Nirev. Jerietlan had finally gone to sleep and she pulled a blanket around him before stepping into the great hall. Cewyr was in a corner watching her. It didn't appear Myrith had called Riker back yet, as the ghost horse wasn't there.

She patted Cewyr on the neck, then headed back out to the stable area. After making sure the doors were properly barred she leaned back against the unicorn, her sword drawn and ready. If anything came through the doors they would know.

Chapter Twenty-One

Kyrianna found herself in the courtyard of a large house. She glanced down at her clothes to see she was dressed in an elegant copper-colored gown with gold stitching.

"I see you made it," a familiar voice said behind her.

Kyrianna turned to see Cassandra Shindar watching her. "Don't look so confused, Kyrianna. I had nothing to with this. As I said the other day, it is an interesting magic bringing you here. Knowing that, I was expecting you." Cassandra smiled as she slowly walked around Kyrianna.

"If you will excuse me." Kyrianna lifted the hem of her skirts and turned toward the house.

"If you walk up there by yourself, you will not be allowed to enter," Cassandra said.

"How do you know?"

"Silly girl. This is the manor of Lord and Lady Naythor. While Lord Duvall was one of those invited to the dinner tonight, you were not. And, since you did nothing to hide your presence at the reception for King Dracenhalts the other night, both Lady Naythor and her granddaughter Caitlin are well aware of who Lord Duvall vanished from the hall with. You will not be welcomed by either of them." Cassandra paused and smiled again. "However, if you will stay with me through the dinner and promise to answer a few simple questions, I will help you to gain entrance so you can meet with Lord Duvall later this evening."

"What types of questions?" Kyrianna took a step back. She looked toward the manor entrance where she saw Tristan dismounting from his chestnut horse and being greeted by Caitlin Naythor. The girl took his arm and escorted him into the large house. "And, how will you be able to gain me entrance, if I will be recognized?"

Cassandra reached down, grabbed Kyrianna's left hand and brought it up. "Here I was starting to think there was more to you than most of the other empty-headed noblewomen in this town. Perhaps I was wrong," she said tightening her hand around Kyrianna's wrist. "You wear a ring that allows you to alter your appearance—use it."

Kyrianna jerked her hand away from the mage and silently thumbed the ring as she concentrated on changing her features so she appeared to be human. She studied the woman standing in front of her and willed her face to more closely match hers.

"It would seem I now have a younger sister," Cassandra said. "Interesting. Now you need a different name. Something similar to your own so you don't make any mistakes. Arianna should suffice."

Kyrianna only nodded.

"Good. Keep your mouth shut unless someone asks you something directly. I will do the talking." Cassandra gestured to a nearby open carriage. "After you, Arianna."

Kyrianna climbed up into the carriage and smoothed her skirts as she sat down.

Cassandra followed her up and nodded to the driver who slapped the reins and guided the horses to the front of the house.

"Lady Shindar." Lord Naythor offered her his hand as she stepped down from the carriage. "Welcome."

"My thanks for the invitation. My husband was called back to Tormasus this morning and sends his regrets that he is unable to attend." She motioned for Kyrianna to step down from the carriage. "I hope you do not mind that I asked my sister Arianna to accompany me this evening."

"Of course not." He offered Kyrianna his hand as she stepped down.

Kyrianna smiled and nodded respectfully as she exited the carriage. "Thank you Lord Naythor," she whispered.

Kyrianna followed Cassandra into the house as the woman moved confidently through the small gathering. She caught her breath when she saw Tristan standing with Caitlin Naythor. The young woman had her arm wrapped possessively around Tristan's.

"I suggest you behave," Cassandra whispered. "Think of this as trying to pass through an enemy camp."

Kyrianna jerked her head to the side and glared at Cassandra who only smiled. The woman had no way of knowing that another mage had also suggested disguises to pass through an enemy camp. One who had acted as an ally only to turn on her.

Kyrianna stayed close to Cassandra as they mingled with the

other guests. She frequently found herself glancing at Caitlin and Tristan. Each time she looked in their direction, she felt her heart stop for a second and her breath catch.

The dinner was served as a buffet so people could more easily move around and engage in conversation. Even though she wanted to move closer to where Caitlin was holding court with her friends, she found herself staying by Cassandra's side. Every time she started to move toward the group around the girl, her attention was drawn away by something. The problem was she couldn't seem to identify what it was that was grabbing her attention each time.

Time seemed to blur as did the faces of the people Cassandra spoke to. Kyrianna wanted out of this place, it was too closed and the people all seemed to have different agendas and plots. This was a world she was familiar with, but since she had left her home, she had never missed this part of her previous life. Her gaze went to Tristan who was laughing at some joke Caitlin had told her group of admirers. This was his world; a world she had been forced to abandon; a world she wasn't sure she wanted to return to.

Cassandra touched her elbow and guided her out to the garden. Kyrianna hesitated and tried to take a step back as the woman led her toward a hedge maze in the far corner of the garden. She glanced back at the house as Cassandra whispered something.

Kyrianna shook her head slightly and followed the woman into the maze.

~ * ~

"Now, Kyrianna Dalynne, you will answer a few questions for me. When we are done, I will send a message to Lord Duvall that you are waiting here to meet him." Cassandra guided her to one of the stone benches in the maze. She waved her hand and darkness covered the entrance to the area where they were.

Kyrianna shook her head, trying to clear it of the fog that filled it. The air held a chill to it and she shivered as she watched Cassandra pacing in front of her.

"Tell me about Thynitic and what she did to you," Cassandra said suddenly.

"That is none of your business." Kyrianna started to stand, but found herself frozen as Cassandra waved her hand in her direction.

"As a member of the Circle, I have decided that it is my business. You will share the information I want, either voluntarily or I will force it. I don't have time to play games with you. There is too much at stake." Cassandra paused as she looked down at her.

Kyrianna only glared; she had managed to force Thynitic, who was a goddess, out of her mind and she would fight this woman with every ounce of her strength and will.

"Stubborn and foolish." Cassandra snapped her fingers and a scroll appeared in her hand. She stepped back as Kyrianna again tried to stand and was held by the mage's magic. She smiled as she began reading the scroll.

"No!" Kyrianna fought the probing she felt in her mind. "No." Her voice became a soft whimper.

"Thynitic," Cassandra said.

Kyrianna shuddered as images flashed in her mind and she felt something shifting through them; studying them. The voice she had heard while in the interrogation chamber with her brother, the swirling portal that pulled her from her home. The shifting scenes skipped quickly through the planar temple, pausing only as Kyrianna felt herself being drawn to the symbol of Thynitic; again at the chaos demon who referred to two of the daughters working together and her statement about the Daughter of Chaos. The scenes continued and paused again at the shrine in the basement of the Duvall estate. The image of the shrine was held there for several seconds and Kyrianna again felt herself being drawn toward the altar and Thynitic's symbol on the wall.

The scene vanished and Kyrianna found herself surrounded by blackness and a familiar voice whispering, "Just as your mother served me, you shall also."

"No!" Kyrianna screamed as she briefly fought her way out of Cassandra's control.

"Interesting, but I am not through with you." Cassandra closed her eyes in concentration and raised both of her hands.

"Please, no more." Kyrianna's voice was only a weak whimper as she felt the probing in her mind again.

She felt herself shudder violently as images of the dream she had been sent by both Thynitic and Torliana filled her memory. Images of her mother destroying the elven community, images of the ranger Cewyr and the unicorn filly—both dead. Then came images of Andrinor and Falden after she challenged Thynitic to prove her power and the goddess had trapped them both in severe pain.

Her eyes were burning as the images flashed, showing the torment she had suffered at Torliana's hands. "Chaos, no. Not again," she whimpered as the scene shifted to the clearing in Kilenter and her mother facing the group of Rynial.

Blackness surrounded her again then cleared as she watched Torliana and Brular when he had been drawn into the Abyss by the demons. She saw Torliana attempting to renounce her allegiance to Thynitic, followed by the arrival of Myrith and the others. She could sense Cassandra's interest when the comet struck Thynitic and she was actually hurt by the attack. She wanted to scream as she again was forced to watch the demon take Brular's head and the many-armed demon that appeared behind Hendandra; her six swords ready to attack the girl.

She heard her voice as she called on Thynitic and felt her power fill her as she used it to dismiss the demons, heal her friends and open the portal back to Shokar. She had tried to convince them to leave. However, Andrinor and Myrith had shown how stubborn they both were as they refused to leave her. It had taken her several tries to force the goddess out of her mind before the demon had pulled her through the portal to the Abyss.

The images finally faded and Kyrianna found herself back in the hedge maze with Cassandra.

"Very interesting and informative." Cassandra paused then nodded. "I see you still have not talked to Falden, so I will give you this warning. Torliana must be left among the living."

Kyrianna jerked her head up. "After what she did to me, you expect me to let her live?"

"There is great danger coming to Shokar and Thynitic will need a vessel to channel her power through. If it is not Torliana, then it will be another she favors." Cassandra's gaze locked with Kyrianna's. "I do not care how many of your friends I have to kill in order to drag you back to her. If Torliana is not among the living then I will see that *you* serve the Lady as her Chosen."

Cassandra cocked her head to the side and nodded. "Lord Duvall has received the message and is on his way here. I will take my leave at this time." With a snap of her fingers, Cassandra vanished from the area.

Kyrianna felt her strength leave her and she leaned back against the backrest and pulled her feet up onto the bench as she felt tears welling up in her eyes. She had tried to put the pain of her experiences behind her so she could focus on the task at hand—getting to Brular and rescuing him from Thynitic. Now she had a new worry. Cassandra was not the type to make idle threats—only promises. If Torliana was killed, then Cassandra would do whatever it took to force her into serving Thynitic.

She looked up as Tristan stepped through the veil of darkness that still covered the entrance to the area.

"Excuse me," he said. "I must have the wrong area." He started to leave.

"Tristan, wait." Kyrianna thumbed the ring and willed it to dispel the magic cloaking her appearance.

"Kyri?"

"A ring that allows me to alter my appearance. There are times when it is wisest to not appear as who I really am," she said.

"But if this is a dream, why do you need it."

Kyrianna shook her head. "These are more than just shared dreams. In some ways, they are real. Melissa told you about the Reishalli the first time you summoned her."

Tristan nodded. "She did, but I didn't really understand it."

Kyrianna smiled and held out her hand. She pulled Tristan toward her then leaned against his shoulder as he sat next to her on the bench. "Reishalli means Soul Weaving in the language of the Taladilith or twilight elves of my home. It is similar to the human concept of soul mates, but with a much deeper connection. The elves of Rhysia explain the Reishalli as two souls joining together to form one soul shared by two bodies."

"And this is what is bringing us together?" Tristan wrapped his arm around her shoulder.

"Yes and no. This is not something I was ever told could happen with the Reishalli. However…" Kyrianna let her voice trail off and she took a deep breath. "However, I managed to offend Shyada and she has enhanced the bond so this is happening. The idea, I believe, is to punish me for the offense. This will continue until such time as I return to Shokar and make a 'proper' offering at one of her shrines. It was suggested my mate and I visit the pools at the Great Grove in Irrmar."

Tristan pulled away slightly and Kyrianna turned so she could look at him. He was frowning as he looked at her. "And, how did you manage to offend a goddess other than Thynitic."

She shook her head. "Sorry, that is between Shyada and me."

"And was that why you needed to visit the shrine yesterday?"

"No, that visit was made for Melissa. With the direction our visits have been going I was concerned she would receive more of an explanation regarding the issue of maidenhood than she needs at this time. It was Shyada who guided us to your grandparent's home. Now, when I visit you each night, she is transported to the copy of the necklace that was left with your grandmother so she can visit with them."

Tristan stood up and stepped away from her. Kyrianna felt her breath catch in her throat and she stared at his back in the silence. She realized she had made a mistake in telling him these were more than shared dreams. He was a knight serving a goddess whom he had told her frowned on the type of activities they had come close to participating in during her visits. Her own questions about the propriety of the situation came back to her as she sat there waiting for him to say something.

"Kyri," he said softly. "I thought these were just dreams. Granted they seemed to be very real, but I assumed that was because I was thinking about you so strongly. Now, you tell me they are more than dreams, more than even shared dreams. That this is real, that in some way you are here with me." He turned back to look at her.

"Yes." She stood and reached out to take his hands in hers.

He gripped her hands and held them tight. "We are not formally engaged and yet our behavior has been...," he stopped and looked away. "There is no excuse for my behavior."

"Other than our feelings for each other." Kyrianna stepped closer and rose up on her toes a bit to let her lips touch his. "I have given you my promise, Tristan. All you have to do is ask."

He smiled and wrapped his arms around her and pulled her close. "It is not quite that simple. There are certain customs that must be observed. I should talk to your father and to Cewyr as well."

"You will have a hard time speaking to my father as I am not from this world."

"As you well know, there are ways to travel to the other worlds." He slid his hands up her back then lightly touched the tips of her ears.

Kyrianna gasped as a shiver went through her body and she leaned in closer to him. Cassandra Shindar's voice in her mind caused her to jerk away from him. *You must be careful on your journey, Kyrianna Dalynne unless you want to see him destroyed from losing you.* It was what the woman had told her at the reception for King Dracenhalts two nights ago.

"Kyri? What's wrong?"

"Cassandra Shindar told me at the reception to be careful on this journey unless I wanted to see you destroyed from losing me. Tonight, she warned me if anything happened to Torliana she would see I was taken back to Thynitic." Kyrianna sat back down on the bench. "Before she sent the message that told you I was waiting here, she used some sort of magic on me so she could see everything Thynitic has done to me. I had to relive those images and torments, including...including...." Her breath caught and she clenched her hands tightly.

Tristan knelt down and took both her hands in his as he looked up at her.

"Including?"

"Including how Torliana used her magic to create a connection between my mother and I so my mother suffered the same torment and pain I did at that witch's hands." The words were coming out in a rush. "Including having to watch the vision Thynitic sent me of how she had my mother killed—again."

Tristan moved to sit on the bench, gathered her into his arms and held her as she cried.

After several minutes, Kyrianna looked up at him and smiled softly. "I love you," she whispered.

Tristan pushed her hair back from her face and let his hands rest on her face.

"And I love you."

Kyrianna felt her body flush with warmth at Tristan's words and she leaned forward and let her lips brush against his.

"Kyri...." Tristan pulled away slightly.

"Hush." She placed a finger on his lips. "We both know our feelings. There is nothing wrong in what we are doing." She let her hand slide to his cheek and leaned in again. This time she was more insistent as her lips met his and she didn't let him pull away.

~ * ~

:Kyri? Kyrianna heard Melissa's voice in her head.

"Chaos." Kyrianna sat up. "I'm sorry Melissa." She removed the necklace, tossed it over Cewyr's horn and headed for the showers.

She stood under the cool water for several minutes. She knew she had made a mistake telling Tristan these were more than dreams. Until a formal engagement was announced, she had no doubt he was going to follow the dictates of propriety more closely when they were together. She also had no doubts that every time she was with him, her feelings would grow stronger. She could be with him and still not with him, Shyada had seen to that. Now there was another barrier separating them until such time as they could be together as a true couple.

She stepped out of the shower and took a deep breath. The rest of the group was still resting so she went to the shrine to begin her morning meditations. She needed to center herself for the coming day. She called to Cewyr in her mind and the unicorn met her in the shrine.

~ * ~

Myrith looked around as she and Andrinor stepped out of the dining hall that morning. There was no one in the great hall. She stalked through the hall, her boots echoing loudly. She stopped at the doors to the keep and spun back around. "No watches were set last night!" She frowned as her voice echoed. Andrinor cringed slightly, and her own head felt like the echo was bouncing in her own skull as well.

Gwideon had told her he would be spending the night in vigil in the shrine, as was his custom when a comrade fell. And if her memory served her, Myrith wasn't sure she could trust her memory of the night's activities, Kyrianna had joined them in at least one of the many toasts made to Nirev. The girl should have had the presence of mind to see to the watches when she realized Myrith would not be doing it.

She headed for the shrine and paused at the entrance as she glanced toward the area Kyrianna had dedicated to Frayrith and Dwycia. The girl was fully dressed and appeared to be completing her morning prayers. After several minutes, Kyrianna stood and turned toward her.

"Morning. How's your head today?"

"I'll be talking to Jerietlan in a few minutes. Right now, I need to talk to you."

Kyrianna cocked her head to the side as she picked up the unicorn horn sword from the altar and sheathed it. "What's wrong?"

"Why were no watches posted last night?"

"Excuse me?" Kyrianna stared at her. "I believe the person normally responsible for that was drunk and unconscious in the dining hall; along with one of those normally assigned to take a watch. Perhaps you should ask *her* why that detail wasn't taken care of before she decided to drink herself into a stupor."

Kyrianna started to step around her, but Myrith grabbed her arm. "I'm not done."

"I am. See to your head and your morning prayers, Myrith. Nothing happened during the night. The only time we have had a problem here was with the whip and I brought that in from the outside. You have Falden checking everything we bring into the keep now, we should be safe here."

"That is not the point. You know we normally set watches to be sure. Why didn't you do so last night?"

"And who was to stand those watches? You dismissed Riker, Gwideon was in vigil, and both you and Andrinor were drunk and unconscious. You want Falden or Hendandra to stand a watch? Or how about Shydaran? While I am sure he is capable of handling most anything—do you trust him? Do you trust any of us for that matter?" Kyrianna jerked away from her and stalked out of the shrine.

"You still haven't answered my question about the watches," Myrith called.

Myrith started to go after Kyrianna but was stopped by Cewyr stepping in front of her and laying her horn on her shoulder. "Leave her be. Both she and I spent the night in front of the doors with them barred in such a way we would be alerted and awakened if anything tried to come through them," Cewyr said.

"Then why didn't she tell me that?"

"She has other things on her mind, such as having learned what you failed to tell her about Cassandra Shindar." Cewyr turned and left her standing there.

Myrith shook her head and went to find Jerietlan so he could see to her head. She saw the cleric in the dining hall already tending to Andrinor. The young man nodded as she approached the cleric. Jerietlan chanted softly then placed a hand on her shoulder.

"Thank you. We will be ready to go in about an hour or so, after everyone has had time to meditate and pray," Myrith said.

Jerietlan nodded. "I will ensure everyone is aware of that."

"Thank you," Myrith left the dining hall and headed back to the shrine.

Chapter Twenty-Two

Kyrianna glanced at Myrith, but the woman refused to meet her eyes as she spoke quietly to Falden. The woman probably knew about the threats and thought to protect her from the knowledge, thinking she had other things to worry about, like the amulet. Of course the question then became, if Myrith would have stopped her from killing Torliana if it came to it or if her arrogance let her assume they could deal with Cassandra when it became necessary.

Myrith opened the doors and stepped out into the same darkness that had greeted them yesterday. Kyrianna blinked as a brilliant light flared from Conflagration creating a small area free of the black fog.

"It's about time." Mikyl's voice echoed around them.

:*You forgot to talk to Jerietlan this morning,* Melissa whispered.

"Chaos."

"For one who is fighting against chaos so strongly, it is interesting that you call on it so much." Mikyl appeared in front of Kyrianna. "You have an appointment to keep with the *true* Lady of Chaos, but first, she has charged me with ridding her of these pests." He gestured to the rest of the group as Conflagration cut through his arm.

Laughter filled area. "Do you think I am stupid enough to give you a chance at me? No, I will take care of you one by one then watch as the daughter falls into chaos."

"Do not let your ego cause you to fail—again," a woman's voice said from the darkness. "Finish them. You have the power—but do you have the will to use it? Finish them all—including the daughter."

A wall of dancing blades surrounded the group as streams of fire began pouring from the sky. Shydaran knocked Hendandra to the ground and stood over her as he roared. The fire appeared to hit a barrier and flowed to the ground outside the blades.

"Thank you Shydaran," Myrith said. "We need to get out of here and find Mikyl."

She spun on Jerietlan. "Set up the keep so we can escape this trap."

Jerietlan raised the shield. "I seek...." He dropped the shield and his hands went to his throat. Only a garbled strangle came out.

"Shyada's pet may have redirected the fire, but how long can he keep it up?" Mikyl laughed again. "Here is another challenge for you to stop."

"Return to your home," Kyrianna said to Cewyr as the circle of blades began tightening around the group. She picked up the unicorn figurine and tucked it into her belt pouch then readied both of her swords. It was going to be a deadly dance; one she hoped they could survive. She heard the ringing of metal as others of the group also began parrying the spinning blades. If they were lucky, maybe they could start knocking the blades out of the circle.

"Kyri," Falden called. "Do you have a couple of strands of unicorn hair?"

Kyrianna missed a parry and took a deep cut to her arm as she tried to twist away from the blades. "Why?"

"They will add power to the spell I am trying to cast."

Kyrianna brought her long sword up as she shifted the silver sword back. "On the hilt. Be quick."

"Thank you." He tapped the sword hilt then began chanting.

She snapped the sword back in time to catch one of the blades that would have opened her stomach. She ignored the wind that began whipping around her as Falden's voice rose in volume. There was a loud pop behind her and the wind rushed past her and exploded against the circle of dancing blades. As soon as the blades vanished, a curtain of fire formed around them.

"Your other protector grows weak," Mikyl said.

Kyrianna turned to see Shydaran on the ground, his breathing labored.

Hendandra had a hand on his paw as she whispered to him in the halfling language.

"We need to take Mikyl out of this fight," Myrith said. "But how? I doubt any of us can pass through that fire and still be able to fight." She grabbed Andrinor's arm as he started for the flowing fire. "It will probably kill you," she said.

"My shield," Jerietlan said. "It is big enough two people could use it as a barrier and it might withstand the fire if we move quickly."

Myrith picked up the shield, shifting her hands so they were inside the protection.

"One moment," Jerietlan said. He whispered a quick spell, then touched Myrith's shoulder as well as his own chest then the shield. "A little extra protection—just in case." He stepped in close to Myrith and grasped the shield. "Let's go."

Kyrianna watched them vanish through the curtain. The fire flow was so thick she couldn't see their shadows once they were through. "Frayrith guide them," she whispered.

"Kyri," can you help him?" Hendandra's voice was weak.

She looked down at Shydaran and saw he was trembling. She dropped to her knees and placed her hands on his body willing her strength and healing energy into the tiger. The trembling slowed and his breathing eased. "I'm sorry, that's all I can do."

The fire suddenly vanished and Kyrianna jumped up, her swords in her hands as she scanned the area. Myrith and Jerietlan stood near the body of Mikyl. "For what he did to Melissa and Tristan, he's mine." Kyrianna took several steps forward.

Myrith shook her head then plunged Conflagration into Mikyl's chest. A pale blue light surrounded the lich and his body crumbled into dust.

"She must have wanted to give him a stronger reason than her displeasure to not fail," Jerietlan said. "That was the talisman I spoke of the last time we faced him." He raised his symbol of Mykaylene and a silver light fell on the ashes of Mikyl's body consuming them.

The black fog vanished, leaving them in a desolate gray landscape, without any landmarks to guide them. "Urric," Myrith said. "The portal?"

"I still cannot sense it."

"Let's get some rest. Maybe Kyrianna will be able to locate it tomorrow."

Jerietlan raised his shield then stopped as a shadowy figure appeared in the distance. "He was only a pawn," a woman's voice said. "A way to finally break the fire cleric's faith."

"No!" Kyrianna yelled. She turned to Myrith. "It wasn't you who stopped the fire spell, it was Brular."

"Indeed, Lady Kyrianna," another voice said. The man, who was sheathed in fire, turned toward the other figure. "Be gone from this place. These are under my protection at this time." The figure vanished. "It was his power that called the firestorm down on you and sustained it for as long as it did. It was his renunciation of his faith and power that ended Mikyl's ability to use that power."

"What?" Kyrianna dropped to her knees as she stared at the man before her. "Why?"

"I cannot get you into her citadel; however I can open a portal to the keep of the demoness Drezmona, which guards the only gate to Thynitic's citadel." He paused for a moment. "If you wish me to."

"Yes!" Andrinor said. "The quicker we can get there the better."

"True as time is even shorter now. However," he glanced around at the group. "Perhaps you should rest first." He vanished.

Jerietlan again raised the shield and recited the opening words.

~ * ~

"Come on," Myrith said looking around. "We need to rest and plan."

The group began moving slowly into the keep and Myrith stopped and turned toward Kyrianna, who was still kneeling on the ground, crying.

"Kyri?" Myrith approached her friend. "Come on." She reached down, placed a hand under Kyrianna's arm and pulled her to her feet. "There may still be time to save him, but we have to be ready."

"Why did he do it? Even at his darkest, he never lost his faith. Why?"

"He must have thought it was necessary. He was too ordered, too deliberate in his actions to act in a rash manner. He must have thought there was no other way." She wrapped her arm around Kyrianna and half carried the girl into the keep.

Andrinor closed the doors behind Kyrianna and Myrith.

Myrith ignored the looks of concern on the faces of the others as she guided Kyrianna to a chair in the dining hall. The girl dropped her head on the table.

The group finished their meal in silence and Myrith watched as they each drifted away from the table into other areas of the keep. She knew tomorrow would be rough on them all and only hoped each of them would be able to take some rest this evening.

She would talk to Gwideon and Andrinor about the watches later.

"Kyri?" She said when the girl finally stood up from the table.

"Let me know when you want me to take my watch. I'll be in the workshop for a while, then the shrine."

Myrith nodded. That Kyrianna was going to work on whatever project she had going in the workroom was a good sign. The girl had appeared to be more upset than any of the others over what had happened. She knew Kyrianna felt she owed Brular a personal debt, and Myrith was still worried about her. The girl tried to fight her streak of rashness at times; but, when she was emotional, like she was now, it seemed to dominate her actions. Then there was the issue of the threats Drezmona had made regarding Hendandra. They would be entering her keep tomorrow and they would have to deal with the demoness and her son. Things were coming together too quickly. With Brular's renunciation, he would now be vulnerable to Thynitic and Torliana. The threats against Hendandra. Drezmona's assertion her son was also Myrith's half-brother. Then there was Kyrianna and the amulet, which was probably completed by now. All it would take to trap the girl; would be her death.

Myrith stood up and headed for the shrine. She wasn't going to allow that to happen, no more than she was going to allow Drezmona's son to have Hendandra. No matter it cost her own life, neither of those things were going to happen to her friends.

Chapter Twenty-Three

Her watch completed, Kyrianna sat in the shrine, the ring she had been given by the Master of the Flames at the temple in Irmar rested in her palm as she stared at it. Brular had traded places with her while Torliana held her in order to give her time to rest and strengthen her will to face Thynitic. He had written the contract with Torliana knowing he wasn't going to attack the group, as she demanded, and he would be sent back to Thynitic. She wasn't sure why he had done it, although she suspected he was trying to save Torliana. She had seen the woman try to renounce the Lady of Chaos and be taken away by Thynitic's demons. Thynitic had Brular beheaded by one of her chaos demons as Kyrianna watched because the goddess believed he had helped Jerietlan when he called the comet down on her. Now, Brular had finally given in to her. After over two decades in her clutches prior to this, he had finally succumbed and renounced the god he had followed so faithfully.

Tears flowed down her check and she clutched the ring tightly, feeling the warmth trapped within it. "Why?" *Frayrith, why? He fought her for over twenty years and did not falter. What made him give in this time?*

:Kyri, he never recognized Torliana was in love with him before, Melissa whispered. *:Remember what Frayrith told you in Kilenter? That what he did not realize about Torliana protected him. He had a fortress of scripture and no emotions to betray him. She warned you Thynitic had found that crack and was chipping away at the stone even then. She told you that while he was fighting hard, he would lose.*

:He called me Missy. Kyrianna could hear Melissa crying softly. *:That was the nickname my tutor used. The power he held scared me, but I could also sense the control he had over that power,* Melissa said.

"I will not abandon him. We brought him back from the darkness once. I will do whatever it takes to bring him back again," Kyrianna said. She slipped the ring back on her finger then drew the dagger that had once belonged to Brular and made a careful cut across the palm of her hand. "With my own blood, I swear to do whatever I have to, to save him, Just as he has done for me and my friends."

:*Kyri! What are you doing?* Melissa's voice held a note of panic in it. :*Do you realize what that oath could cost you? Brular made the same type of oath to save Torliana from Thynitic and look what has happened to him.*

"Yes, Melissa, I do realize what it might cost. Let's just hope it doesn't come to that."

Kyrianna closed her eyes as she leaned back against Cewyr. The unicorn didn't say anything to her about her oath, but she could feel her unhappiness and concern. She knew Cewyr wouldn't try to dissuade her from this path, no more than Tristan had tried to stop her from bringing the whip or wanting to seek revenge for the death of her mother. He had expressed his concern, but had still offered his support and love. She could feel Cewyr's silent disapproval in her mind, but she could also sense her love and support. She knew the oath she had just made might cost her her very soul if it came to it, but she also knew her friends would do everything they could to save her—even from herself.

As she finally started to drift off to sleep, Kyrianna found her thoughts turning to Tristan. Even if they survived this journey, her oath could still prevent her from returning to him.

~ * ~

She found herself standing in the familiar courtyard of her family's home in Nydith. She looked around in surprise at the neighs coming from the stables and the sound of ringing metal in the practice yard. *What am I doing here?* She looked down and saw she was dressed in a plain but serviceable chain shirt, nothing like the elven chain she normally wore. She was also missing her weapons. She shook her head as she headed for the main doors of the house then stopped suddenly.

Last night Tristan had been upset about finding out their visits were more than just shared dreams; that they were real. He had pulled away from her because of that information and had mentioned he needed speak to her father as well as Cewyr before they went any further. "Chaos!" she whispered. "He found a way to visit Father."

She turned and moved as quietly as she could to the back of the house. There were several guardsmen in the back practicing in the open ring and she could hear the ringing of swords in the sallee as well.

She tried to slip into the group unnoticed, but stopped as one of the spectators in the yard called to her.

"Kyrianna! Welcome home," Tynal called as he waved to her.

Several of them turned and waved as well. She paused and walked over to the guardsman who had been one of those on the northern gate the day she had been exiled.

"Do you know where my father is?" She spoke softly as the others returned to their practice.

"He is in the training sallee with a nobleman I have never seen before."

Kyrianna smiled. *Of course, Father would want to test his skills,* she thought. She grinned as she looked at Tynal. "Let me borrow your sword and helm," she said.

"You have never wanted to use a full helm before. Why now?" Tynal picked up his helm from the pile of equipment next to him then handed her his sword.

"I want to surprise them." She settled the helm over her head and Tynal reached out to adjust it slightly.

"Anything else?"

"Anyone have a short sword." She tested the balance of the long sword Tynal had given her.

"Hang on." Tynal whispered something to the younger man next to him, who drew his sword and handed it to Kyrianna.

She turned toward the sallee.

"Kyrianna, wait. If you open your mouth to challenge one of them, your voice will be recognized," Tynal said. "Let me do it for you."

Kyrianna nodded then gestured to the doorway.

"Lord Brygan," Tynal called from the door. "One of the new recruits wishes to test her blades against your guest, if he is willing. It seems she does not find the other recruits to be enough of a challenge, yet she is hesitant to challenge him herself."

Kyrianna took a deep breath as her father's laughter echoed in the building. "Do you believe this recruit is good enough to challenge my guest, Tynal?" he finally asked.

Tynal laughed also. "I believe one or both of them will receive an interesting lesson, My Lord."

"Lord Tristan, do you accept this, perhaps foolish, challenge on the part of this recruit?"

Kyrianna smiled under her helm as Tristan drew his sword and moved to the center of the ring. Tristan saluted her father then turned to face her as she approached. She knew she probably didn't have a chance of beating Tristan, but the match could be fun and she doubted he would embarrass her as badly as Andrinor had. She stepped into the ring and turned to face her father, bringing the long sword up in salute. She then turned to face Tristan and saluted him as she settled into a defensive position.

Tristan returned the salute then took a slow step forward, moving to the side to circle her. She moved lightly, both of her swords held at the ready as she turned with him. Very slowly and carefully, she inched closer to Tristan as they circled each other. It was a trick her father had taught her. She started weaving the blades in a pattern in front of her body, hoping to keep Tristan distracted from her movements. He was a trained observer; this trick would be harder to pull on him than others she had done it to.

She finally got to the distance she wanted then moved quickly to engage Tristan's blade. She swung her long sword high, letting his blade catch it as she jabbed with the short sword. The point of the second blade slid along his ribs, not damaging the armor, but still ringing to let them know the hit had been scored.

Tristan shifted his weight slightly and brought his shield in to catch her in the chest forcing her off balance as she tried to step back and recover from the swings.

She ducked under his swing and swung her long sword at his back as she came back up. He twisted and caught the blow on his shield. He came under her swing with a jab of his own.

Kyrianna gasped as Tristan's blade hit and slid along her side. There was more power in the blow than she had anticipated. She backpedaled quickly, watching Tristan's movements.

"That was entertaining, but I think you need to remove that helm, young lady." Brygan stepped between them. "Did you forget who taught you to wield two swords? Or did you think I wouldn't recognize your fighting style, Kyrianna?"

"Kyri?" Tristan dropped the sword he was holding as he stared at her.

"That wasn't fair," Kyrianna said as she removed the helm then handed it and the two swords to Tynal. "You should have let us finish."

"I think not. There was too much anger in your movements, no matter how hard you tried to hide it." Brygan turned toward Tristan. "I believe the three of us should go into the house," he said.

Tristan picked up his sword and sheathed it as he stepped up next to Kyrianna.

"That wasn't a very nice trick. What if I had hurt you?"

"Then you could pay for the healer." She rose up on her toes and gave him a light kiss on the cheek then followed her father out of the sallee and into the house.

"I want to know how it is you are here, Kyrianna," Brygan said as Kyrianna and Tristan sat down.

"It is the Reishalli."

"This is still not normal even for the Soul Weaving."

"I know. The bond has been *enhanced* by one of the goddesses of Tristan's home so that when I sleep, we are brought together."

"Interesting. You made no mention of the Reishalli, Lord Tristan in your request to court my daughter. Why is that?"

"My Lord," Tristan said softly. "I am from another land and do not fully understand the customs of yours. All I know for sure in this matter is that I love Kyrianna and wish to marry her."

"And do you feel the same way, Kyri?" Brygan looked at his daughter.

"I do," Kyrianna said.

"Then I cannot say no to this. However, I don't like the idea you may be leaving Rhysia for good. You are my daughter and your place is here," Brygan said.

Kyrianna stood up and moved to kneel next to her father's chair. She took his hands in hers as she looked up at him. "I will visit as often as I can. A part of me will always be here," she said.

Brygan looked down at his daughter. "To think, I was so worried about you and that streak of impulsiveness that is such a part of you. You have made me very proud of you, Kyri." He leaned forward and kissed her forehead. "You are so much like your mother."

Kyrianna felt a cold shiver go down her spine at the mention of her mother. There were things she would never tell him about her travels. He knew how Torliana had bound Kyrianna and her mother together, but she would never tell him how the Lady of Chaos had forced her to watch her mother's death.

Brygan stood up, held his hand out to Kyrianna and pulled her to her feet. He then held his other hand out to Tristan. As he reached for the older man's hand, Brygan pulled Kyrianna's hand slightly so he was placing it into Tristan's. "As long as you protect and love her, my blessings go with you," Brygan said softly. "If you ever deliberately hurt her, my wrath will find you."

Tristan bowed his head. "May I always prove worthy of the treasure you have entrusted me with," he said.

Kyrianna found herself unable to speak, as she looked at Tristan and her father.

"Now as you two probably have a limited time, perhaps I should give you time together," Brygan said with a smile.

"Can I borrow Smoke and another horse for Tristan?" Kyrianna asked. "I would like to show him Kilenter."

Brygan nodded. "He can borrow Black Sun."

Kyrianna jerked her head up to stare at her father. "Black Sun?"

"If I am going to entrust him with you, surely I can trust him with my horse."

"Give me a moment to change into something more appropriate for a ride." Kyrianna gave Tristan's hand a squeeze as she turned and darted out of the main room and through the halls to her room.

Kyrianna paused as she entered what had been her room while she was growing up in this house. The canopy-covered bed was no longer covered in the stuff she had thrown out of the wardrobe and chests as she had packed that last day. She opened the wardrobe to find everything back in its place hanging neatly; waiting for her return as if she had never left. "Mother," she whispered as she stumbled back to sit on the edge of the bed.

"Kyri?" Tristan's voice called from the doorway. "Are you okay?"

She glanced over at him and nodded. Tristan had already removed his armor and was dressed in simple riding leathers. It was a set she recognized has having belonged to her brother Erudus a few years ago. "I left this room a mess when I left. Mother must have been the one to straighten it." She stood and moved to the dressing table where a small portrait of an elven woman and Brygan sat.

"Your mother? I see where your beauty comes from," Tristan

whispered in her ear.

"Everyone always said I look more like my father, except for my ears."

Tristan fingers touched the tips of her ears and she sighed as she leaned against him. "You have her eyes and her smile," he said.

Tristan stepped away. "Your father is having the horses readied, don't be long."

She nodded again and moved back to the wardrobe to find a set of riding clothes to wear.

~ * ~

Kyrianna exited the house to see Erudus standing next to his horse talking to Tristan and Brygan. The look on his face was one of suspicion and concern. "Erudus," she called as she walked up.

"There you are, Kyri." He glanced at Tristan as he draped an arm protectively over Kyrianna's shoulder.

She laughed as she ducked out from under her brother's arm and quickly mounted Smokemist. The gray gelding danced a bit as she gathered the reins, but quickly settled down.

"Father, what is the current fine for galloping a horse through the city streets?" She turned Smoke to face the gate.

"They raised it to fifty gold, per rider," he said.

"Oh, never mind." She looked at Tristan and smiled as she nodded toward the gate.

The two of them kept the horses to a walk as they made their way to the northern gate. As soon as they exited, Kyrianna looked at Tristan. "Catch me if you can." She kicked Smokemist and the horse bolted down the road.

Tristan caught up to Kyrianna as they reached the edge of the forest. She slowed her horse as they passed under the trees and into the artificial twilight. She led him along the main path until she came to a small game trail that turned to the south.

"You remember this path, Smoke?" Kyrianna leaned forward as she spoke to the horse.

Tristan remained silent as she guided him to the small clearing with the clear pond where she had first encountered the avatar of Frayrith. She slid off Smokemist and tied his reins to the branch of a small tree. Tristan did the same with Black Sun.

"This is the place where I met the avatar of Frayrith," Kyrianna said as she looked down at her wrists. She reached out and touched the dagger Tristan was wearing. "She touched the blade with her horn then touched my wrist."

Tristan placed his hand over Kyrianna's. "Then this is a sacred spot for you. Thank you for sharing it with me."

Kyrianna smiled as she pulled her hand away and carefully walked over to the pond. She knelt beside the water and motioned Tristan over. As he joined her, she pointed out the cloven-hoof prints of a unicorn. "One of her children still visits this place," she said. "That is a good sign."

Kyrianna stood and brushed the dirt off her skirts as she moved to stand near a bush that was dead and twisted. Here the ground was barren with no sign of any animal tracks across it. "The Lady's touch has left this place damaged as well," she said softly.

"Excuse me? The Lady's touch?"

Kyrianna turned back to face Tristan as she quickly moved away from the barren patch of ground. "This is the spot where the portal opened that pulled me away from my home and into the temple where I met Myrith and the others. A portal I now believe was opened by Thynitic."

"Despite everything you suffered and all the pain and torment, there is still at least one reason to be glad she opened that portal." Tristan wrapped his arms around Kyrianna.

"And what would that be?" She cocked her head to the side.

"By opening that portal and taking you away from here, you found your way to Shokar and I found you." He held her tightly as he kissed her.

As their lips parted Kyrianna felt warmth surge through her body. "So, now that you have my father's blessing will you ask formally?"

Tristan released his hold and took a step back. "I still want Cewyr's blessing on this, Kyri. She is a unicorn and while you have told me you do not have to make a choice in this, I have to know she accepts this as well. She was given to you by your goddess through the cleric Brular, I cannot ignore her."

Kyrianna frowned as she looked up at him. "There is no way you will get to talk to her before we return, if we return." She dropped her head.

He reached out and lifted her chin with hand. "Kyri, don't say that. You will return. You have a powerful group and Thynitic was weakened. You will make it back."

"But will we succeed. Tristan, today we fought Mikyl and to protect us from the power he was wielding, Brular renounced his faith."

"What? How can that be?"

Kyrianna slowly told Tristan about the battle with the lich, the perversion that been perpetrated by the placing of Torliana and Brular's arms on Mikyl's body to give him access to their powers. She told him about the circle of blades, the firestorm and about learning Brular had renounced his faith. As she finished she glanced down the palm of her right hand then clenched it tightly.

Tristan grabbed her hand. "What is this?" He slowly pried her fist open and stared at the scar.

"I swore an oath that I will do whatever it takes to save Brular, just as he has done for us."

"Kyri, are you mad? Please tell me you didn't do this on hallowed ground."

She looked away. "I was in the shrine I dedicated to Frayrith and Dwycia, in the shield keep."

Tristan only stared at her, not saying anything as she turned away. "I'm sorry, Tristan," she whispered. "I owe him too much to not do everything possible to save him. He said once that power always exists, just not the will to use it. My will is resolved in this."

She turned back to face Tristan. "I'm sorry," she whispered.

"You must be true to your beliefs and your heart. I would never want to change that—for to do so would change who you are. And, while I do not want to lose you, for you to change who you are would be an even greater loss." Tristan reached into a small pouch at his belt and pulled out a gold ring. He dropped down on one knee and looked up at Kyrianna. "Lady Kyrianna Dalynne, I formally ask that you accept this token of my love and I hope you will marry me when you return to Shokar."

Kyrianna stood there for a moment, tears streaming down her face as she looked at Tristan and the ring he was holding. She slipped the ring that allowed her to alter her appearance off her left hand and Tristan carefully placed the gold ring on in its place. She gasped and dropped to her knees in front of Tristan as she stared at the ring. It was the same ring he had taken from the body of his grandmother and given to the group. The same ring they had sold, along with its mate, to get equipment for the journey. She had completely forgotten that these had been his grandparents' wedding rings.

"Cassandra Shindar returned them to me. She sent them with a request that I consider an offer she wishes to make regarding buying the estate." Tristan showed her the second ring on his own hand.

"Tristan, for as long as this moment lasts, I want to forget about Thynitic and the Abyss. I want to forget about Torliana and what she has done to me and my friends. I want to forget about Mikyl and the evil he did. All I want to think about is us and this moment."

Kyrianna reached out and pulled Tristan toward her, her lips seeking his. "I only hope Shyada lets me take the ring back with me," she said as he held her.

Kyrianna relaxed in Tristan's arms as she felt him lean forward and gently kiss her ears. His hand moved to her shoulder and she took a deep breath as he pushed the tunic off her shoulder and kissed her neck and shoulder.

She reached for the ties on the side of the tunic she was wearing then swore as her eyes opened and she found herself back in the shrine.

She didn't even wait for Melissa's comments as she removed the necklace and dropped it over Cewyr's horn and hurried to the shower.

As the cool water splashed over her head, she glanced at her left hand and smiled. "Thank you, Shyada." The gold band Tristan had given her was still on her hand.

She returned to the shrine a few minutes later, and retrieved the necklace. "Melissa, can you tell what ring I now wear on my left hand?" She asked as she put the sapphire necklace around her neck.

:*Kyri, that's my mother's wedding ring. I thought you and the others sold it. How did you…Tristan!*

:*Yes, little sister. Tristan gave it to me tonight and Shyada was kind enough to let me bring it back with me.*

"By the way, Cewyr when we make it back, he wants to talk to you about this before we get married. He feels he needs your approval as well as my father's, which he got today."

:He has Frayrith's approval as is evident by the Soul Weaving. However, I will talk to him and put him at ease. First thing though, we have to survive this place and return to Shokar, Cewyr's voice said in her mind.

"I don't think I can sleep anymore," Kyrianna said. "I'm going to get some more work done in the workshop."

Chapter Twenty-Four

The same desolate gray landscape greeted the group the next morning. Once the doors to the keep closed, the figure of Hellavar appeared.

Kyrianna mounted Cewyr as the portal appeared before them. She frowned at the open expanse of grassland they found on the other side. About three hundred yards from where they exited the portal was a fortress. Demons patrolled the parapets.

"I don't like this," Kyrianna said. "We will be out in the open, with no way to hide our approach."

"I don't see any other way to get to there," Myrith said. "We will have to stay alert."

Kyrianna slid off Cewyr and drew her bow. The unicorn moved to the opposite side of the group as the tiger, while Andrinor dropped back with Kyrianna to the rear, his double bladed sword at the ready. Jerietlan, Falden and Hendandra stayed in the middle of the group, while Myrith and Gwideon took the lead.

"Head's up!" Kyrianna snapped her bow up and scanned the area.

"What?" Myrith called back.

"I thought I saw something move near the fortress."

"Hendandra?"

"Sorry nothing."

"Stand ready for a few minutes," Myrith said.

Kyrianna shook her head as they waited. "Must have been a bird or a heat mirage." She lowered her bow. They were still about a hundred yards from the fortress. Maybe they would make it without drawing the attention of the demons guarding it.

They had only taken a couple of steps, when Kyrianna felt a wave of dizziness hit her. She tried to shake her head to clear it, but couldn't move. The others also seemed to be frozen in their tracks as well. She lost focus and everything began spinning then faded into a gray fog.

~ * ~

"Your group has made it further than I would have believed possible," Drezmona said. The demoness walked around the group, paused in front of Myrith and smiled. Shydaran growled low in his throat and she laughed. "You should reconsider that threat." She nodded toward one of the chaos demons standing behind her holding a sword to Hendandra's throat.

Shydaran took a slow step back, but continued to growl as his gaze followed the demoness.

"Ah, Andrinor. A pity you didn't accept my previous offer. No matter I have you, or will have you, now." She shook her head. "Just like before, there will be consequences if you try to change forms. In this case, those manacles you are wearing will cut through your wrists and my commander will be able to add a set of dragon claws to his collection.

Andrinor only glared at her.

Drezmona pointed toward Cewyr. "Dismiss her or I will have my demons disembowel her in front of you."

Kyrianna hesitated, trying to find her voice. Several of the demons moved toward the unicorn, their claws extended.

"Return to your home." The words came out in a rush and Kyrianna felt her heart racing as one of the demons dove at the unicorn, just before she vanished.

Drezmona reached down and picked up the figurine. "It is useless in this form." She dropped the figurine back on the ground.

Kyrianna took a step forward, then dropped to her knees from the searing pain that traveled through her body. The manacles on her wrists were glowing brightly.

Drezmona grabbed her arm and pulled Kyrianna back to her feet. "Behave or the pain will grow worse." She looked at the others. "Attempt to cast any magics or do anything you have not been directed to and the magic in the manacles will cause great pain. Each time they activate, the pain will increase." Her hand moved to Kyrianna's necklace and jerked it from her neck.

"No!" Kyrianna tried to grab for the necklace, then screamed as lightning sparked from the manacles to surround her.

"I warned you."

"Leave her alone, Demoness." Myrith reached for Conflagration only to have the blade evaporate under her hand.

Andrinor turned toward Myrith and was surrounded by a circle of flames.

"Enough," Myrith said. "We understand."

"Really." Drezmona took Kyrianna's hand and again pulled her to her feet.

"Please," Kyrianna whispered as she felt Drezmona pull the gold ring from her finger.

The demoness held up the ring. "I believe you are correct, Myrith." She dropped the ring and smiled at Kyrianna. "Pity, I thought you were stronger than this. Perhaps Thynitic is wrong in placing so much value on you."

The demons moved to surround the group.

"I want this one," Drezmona pointed to Andrinor, "kept separate from the others." She turned toward Myrith. "Mordamien will want to speak to that one. The rest..." She paused and glanced at Kyrianna. "As long as this one remains alive, you may do whatever you wish to them." Her wings flapped several times and she vanished.

Kyrianna didn't move as one of the demons grabbed her arms and held them behind her back. *Cewyr, Melissa, Tristan.* Her mind kept repeating the names even as darkness claimed her.

~ * ~

Kyrianna slowly opened her eyes to see a shimmering veil surrounding her. Her arms were pulled over her head and she winced at the pain in her shoulders. She saw Andrinor bound to the wall opposite her, also surrounded by a similar energy cage. Not far from the young man, all of the group's weapons were piled on the floor. She glanced to her left and saw Falden bound to the wall several feet away.

"Welcome sister," a voice above them said. "Give her sword back and bring her."

Kyrianna tried to turn her head to see the person speaking. All she could see was a small ledge. Two of the demons grabbed Myrith and carried her to the ledge. Another picked up Conflagration from the pile of weapons and followed.

The larger demon appeared in the room, still holding Hendandra and another appeared with Shydaran. The tiger spun and his claws ripped into the body of the demon with him.

"Hold!" the large demon said.

Kyrianna's let her gaze scan the area again. At least twelve demons were positioned along a walkway that circled the room.

She heard Falden chanting softly and glanced toward him. The mage's face was twisted in pain and concentration. He was fighting the magic of the manacles' in order to cast.

"Change, servant of Shyada, or I will cut her into pieces."

Kyrianna jerked her attention back to the demon holding Hendandra.

Shydaran growled and took a step forward.

The demon's blade cut into Hendandra's neck and blood began dripping on the floor.

"One piece at a time, until you take your true form."

Shydaran's head dropped and his body shimmered for a moment, then he was standing there as a halfling—as Feric.

Kyrianna shook her head slowly. He had been forced into a choice he never wanted to make—to betray his wife or betray his goddess. Even if Shyada forgave him, would he forgive himself?

Falden's voice froze in its chanting and she smiled as a half-elven woman stepped from behind the demon and smiled at Feric.

She reached up and touched Hendandra's neck and the bleeding stopped. The girl slipped from the demon's grasp and ran to hug Feric.

"But I disobeyed you," Feric said.

"You did it for her—because of love. That is no renunciation," Shyada said. "It is part of why I sent you here." She smiled. "But there are other lessons for you to learn. You have another choice to make." She moved to stand next to Kyrianna. "You can stay and fight for these or you can return to Justula." She raised her hand and Kyrianna felt tears in her eyes when the figurine of Cewyr, her necklace and ring appeared next to her feet.

"I cannot interfere further," Shyada said. "You have to finish this yourselves."

"Thank you," Kyrianna whispered.

Feric's form shimmered again and a large reptile stood in front of the demon. His tail pushed Hendandra behind him as his teeth reached for the demon.

Falden's chanting resumed and a sudden blast of power launched bolts of energy at the other demons on the walkway. The explosions shattered the stones sending rocks and debris flying through the room. A large piece of stone hit Kyrianna in the temple sending her into darkness.

~ * ~

Myrith stood up from the body of the half-demon and looked down at the ring she had taken from his hand. A simple copper band with a moonstone. Etched on the stone was a familiar crest—one she hadn't seen since she left the Silver Dragon—the symbol of Lavial. She still didn't believe Mordamien's claims they were related any more than she had believed those same claims when Drezmona had made them not that long ago. "By all the gods, has it only been fourteen days since we retrieved Kyri from the demoness?"

She glanced again at the body. At least with his attention on her, Mordamien had been too busy to concern himself with Hendandra. *Hendandra,* she thought. *The others!* She had heard the explosions from the room below this one, but had been dealing with Mordamien and unable to do anything. She had been torn between wanting to go help them and staying here. Mykaylene had whispered in her mind to trust her companions and deal with her own immediate threat. Kyrianna had asked her just two nights ago if she trusted any of them and she had been unable to answer. Today she had been forced to let them to fight their battle while she had been occupied with her own.

She walked out onto the balcony and looked down at the group. Falden stood in the middle of the room, tendrils of energy snaking from his hands to the manacles binding the other members of the group to the wall. There was a male halfling standing with Hendandra, his arm around her waist. Even with the worry that creased Hendandra's face when she saw Myrith looking at her, there was relief in the shy smile she gave her.

So this is who you really are, Shydaran, she thought.

Myrith stepped back into the room and glanced around, there was no obvious door and she didn't feel like searching for one at this time. She returned to the balcony, hopped over the edge and dropped to the floor. She winced, but managed to keep from verbalizing the pain she felt in her knees and back. The drop combined with the weight of her armor, probably made her little stunt a bit stupid. Still, it was better than spending too much time searching for a hidden exit or worse waiting for one of the others to come find her.

How? Myrith thought when she saw Kyrianna hugging Cewyr.

It doesn't matter, at least they're safe. She looked around. :*Mykaylene, you were right. Forgive me for not learning to trust them sooner.*

Thing was she had trusted them at one time. She remembered how she had relied on Kyrianna almost like a second at the estate. How she had willingly asked for advice and listened to it from them. It had been the events in that nightmare place of Torliana's that caused her to lose faith in her companions. She had come to believe every time they questioned something they were challenging her; there had been hard feelings between them at times and secrets. She had seen every secret as a personal attack against her leadership. *Lady of Chaos indeed.* She had seen what Thynitic had done to Kyrianna with her constant whispering in her friend's mind, now she understood what the base chaos of that place had done to her as well.

She looked around again, they had succeeded in their fight and she in hers—perhaps together they would have a chance to rescue Brular.

Kyrianna walked over and seemed to be studying her. "Are you alright?"

"Fine. What about the rest?"

Kyrianna nodded. "Falden defeated the magic on his manacles and released a storm of arcane energy that destroyed the demons guarding the walls. It was as if the struggle of fighting the manacles increased his raw power ten-fold or more. Or perhaps he has been tempering his power. Whatever the reason, all I know is I'm glad that power was unleashed on the demons and not on us." Kyrianna shuddered. "Everyone seems to be fine. Shydaran took out the main demon, and Falden took care of the rest then released us."

Myrith glanced at Hendandra and the halfling with her. "And…"

Kyrianna nodded. "The demon forced Shydaran to assume his true form by continuing to threaten Hendandra. Shyada appeared, healed her and forgave him for disobeying her. Seems she was pleased by his reasons for doing so."

"So you knew about him all along?" Myrith tried to fight the anger she felt at the deception, but she saw Kyrianna's eyes flash in defiance then relax.

"I did. However, as I told you the first night when you wanted everyone subjected to the anti-magic field, I considered myself bound by Shyada's command as well as a promise made to Feric to not reveal his secret."

"Feric?"

"His real name. He did not want to use it while he was disguised."

"And, I suppose Hendandra knew also." She glanced again at the girl who had not left the halfling's side.

Kyrianna nodded. "She met him on the island." She paused for several seconds. "He is one of the protectors of the island and would not have left except Shyada directed him to join us. I don't think she realized immediately he was Shydaran until just before we left. Although, he was the one who defended her in the Coliseum."

"I thought the rules of combat for that stated it must be a member of the accused's house or family."

"Myrith, she told you the chief made her a member of the tribe. He is one of the protectors of the island and a member of the same tribe—that counts as a member of the same house," Kyrianna said quickly.

Myrith frowned. "I guess that also explains why he seems so protective of her as well."

"Myrith who was that and what did he mean by calling you sister?" Kyrianna asked as the rest of the group joined them.

Myrith paused for a moment, then remembered Kyrianna would have very little if any recollection of the things Drezmona had told them.

"The demoness, Drezmona, told me she had a son who was my half-brother," Myrith said. "That was the person who spoke. He claimed to be her son and therefore my brother."

"You don't believe them," Kyrianna said.

"I do not."

Kyrianna nodded and appeared to be lost in thought for several seconds. "When we are able to have some privacy, Melissa has something she wishes me to tell you," Kyrianna whispered. "She will not tell me what it is at this time; she says it will have to wait until no one else is around."

Myrith frowned but nodded. She glanced around the room, there were no obvious doors or passages. "Hendandra, looks like we will need your skills to find our way out of this place."

Hendandra nodded then began checking the walls.

Myrith waited as the rest of the group gathered their weapons. Kyrianna was again hugging the unicorn. "How...?" she asked.

"Shyada," Kyrianna said.

"I thought you were in trouble with her."

"I am, but that is a separate issue."

Myrith nodded. "She has my thanks also for returning her and Melissa to you."

She reached down and lifted the girl's left hand. "Tristan?" Kyrianna only smiled.

"There are several hidden doors," Hendandra said.

"Pick one," Myrith said.

Hendandra opened one of the doors. Myrith gestured at the darkness. "After you."

Hendandra smiled and led the way into the tunnel.

~ * ~

"The portal is behind those boulders."

Myrith spun to face Gwideon and Urric.

"This portal will lead you to Thynitic's citadel," Urric said. "It is the only one that leads straight there instead of depositing you somewhere at random or even on Limbo as she has considerable control there."

"How can anyone control Limbo?" Jerietlan said. "It is a place of eternal chaos."

"Even in chaos there is a spark of order," Kyrianna said. "There has to be; otherwise chaos would destroy even itself."

Myrith jerked her head around to stare at Kyrianna. "Kyri?" It bothered her to hear the girl speaking so casually on this subject.

"It is an ancient saying that seemed appropriate."

Myrith looked around the small room. The wall of boulders almost filled the area. It would take several hours for them to clear them from the portal.

"Well, do we press on or do we wait?" Andrinor reached for one of the boulders.

"We wait. Tomorrow we enter the citadel of a goddess. We must all be rested and prepared." Myrith turned to Jerietlan.

"Actually," Feric said. "I can deal with this easily myself." He paused. "However, I do believe it would be better done in the morning."

"I agree. If Drezmona is working against Thynitic, and it seems she may be," Gwideon said. "Then this was probably done to prevent the Lady from sending her own demons against this fortress. If there is a guard on the other side, we will have to fight them and then her forces will be alerted to our presence."

"They will be alerted whether we take care of the boulders tonight or in the morning," Andrinor said.

"True," Kyrianna said. "But do we want to give them a night to prepare for us after we clear the portal. Or do we want to be able to clear it and then continue moving? Thynitic knows we are coming, let's not give her any advantages."

Myrith looked at Feric. "You are sure you can handle this and still be ready to fight?"

Feric nodded.

"We wait until morning," Myrith said. "Let's move back to that last room to set up the keep." She smiled at the grin on Hendandra's face. The last room they had checked before this one had been a storeroom filled with gems and other valuables.

Chapter Twenty-Five

The shield hung in the air for a moment before the familiar doors of the keep appeared. Myrith waited as the others gathered the gold and gems from the room and carried them into the storeroom. Once they were done, Falden cast several spells and declared the items claimed as safe.

Myrith shook her head as Hendandra began muttering about the work that would be involved in dividing the treasure up. She returned to the main doors and barred them for the night before joining the others in the dining hall. She grinned when Kyrianna raised a glass of the elven wine.

"My com..." Myrith paused and looked around at the group. "My friends." Yes, that was more appropriate. This group of people had become her friends; the only real friends she had ever had in her life. They had made their feelings and belief in her known at the Coliseum in Irrmar when they had all been ready to face the ranks of clerics and knights for her. "My friends," she said again. "Tomorrow we enter the citadel of Thynitic herself. We go there for one purpose and one purpose only—the release of Brular." She glanced at Kyrianna. "We do not go for revenge; though several of us here have cause to seek it. For any of us to seek revenge, here at the place where she is strongest, is to risk falling into her grasp." She saw the slight nods of agreement from everyone except Kyrianna. There was anger burning in the girl's dark green eyes. She continued to stare at Kyrianna until she finally bowed her head slightly. *Good*, she thought. *Now, if she will only remember that when we face Thynitic.*

"Everyone refresh themselves tonight and rest well. Tomorrow we must act together and move swiftly through her citadel to find Brular and then we must escape back to Shokar." She turned toward Gwideon. "Urric, I assume you know how we are to return to Shokar," she said.

"Through the appropriate portal and there are many in her citadel," Urric said. "I will have to wait and see where we are after we get to the fire cleric."

Myrith nodded. "Now, I believe an introduction is in order." She turned toward Hendandra and Feric.

Hendandra stood and pulled on Feric's arm so he stood beside her. "This is Feric," she said. "He is a druid of Shyada and is one of those entrusted with protecting the isle of Justula. He was directed to join us on our quest by Shyada herself." She looked around. "Feric, I believe you know the others already." Feric only nodded without saying anything.

Myrith raised her glass. "Welcome to our group." She glanced around again then sat down to enjoy the food of the hall and the simple companionship of her friends.

~ * ~

Myrith sat in the dining hall after the others had dispersed for the night holding the signet ring. She looked closely at the design. The background was a swirling mass of color, the image they had come to associate with Thynitic and on top of that was a rearing unicorn. The unicorn on the ring was dark gray in color with a blood-red horn. She remembered the crest of the Overlord as being more of a silver-grey, like Cewyr with the golden horn appearing more bloodstained than solid red.

Myrith gasped as she looked up from the ring. She had never made the connection before, even though it had been in front of her this entire time. The unicorn Brular, as Ashe, had summoned for Kyrianna had the same coloring as the unicorn crest of Lavial. Was there a connection and if so what was it?

She walked slowly to the shrine. She wasn't sure she wanted to tell Kyrianna about this. The girl had enough to worry about; she didn't need to start trying to see connections between Cewyr and Lavial in addition to everything else. She dropped the ring back in the pouch and stepped into the area dedicated to Mykaylene. No, she wouldn't tell Kyrianna about this at this time. Maybe later, if necessary, but not right now.

~ * ~

Kyrianna sat and looked at the bowstring for several minutes before beginning her work for that night. There was only a small amount that needed to be done, but she wanted to make sure the string was done correctly. For almost an hour, she let her fingers carefully feel and check every braid and splice in the string. It was smooth and felt seamless to her fingers.

With a silent prayer of thanks to Frayrith and Dwycia she began braiding the final section. As she attached the end of the bowstring to the bow, it appeared to sparkle for a moment. She held the bow carefully, testing its weight and balance in her hands. She then brought it up and pulled the string back. The tension was correct. She slowly relaxed the string, not allowing it to be released without an arrow nocked. Even if there were no magical properties from the unicorn hair, it was still a good string and should be stronger than a normal one.

~ * ~

"Late again." Myrith grinned as she entered the workroom.

"My watch?" Kyrianna picked up the bow.

"It is. Everyone else seems to be asleep, perhaps now Melissa can tell me what she wanted to discuss.

Kyrianna nodded as the two of them walked to the main hall. She held the silver sword out and waited for Myrith to place her hand on it.

Myrith waited while Cewyr moved to stand between them and the doors then touched the sword.

:*Good evening, Myrith,* she heard Melissa say after they were all in contact.

:*Good evening, Melissa.*

:*Myrith, I understand from what I have heard and seen that you do not believe the claims made by Drezmona and Mordamien. There is a spell I can cast that can verify the truth of the matter. It has the ability to verify if people are related. It can also be used to verify a specific bloodline or find unusual elements in a person's blood.*

:*You may cast your spell, Melissa. However, it will make no difference to me if their claims are true or not. It changes nothing.*

:*I would not expect it to change you. I do this only to prevent our enemy from having knowledge we do not. It is always better to know the whole truth. It is half-truths that give credence to lies.*

:*Very well.*

Myrith glanced up at Kyrianna who remained quiet during the conversation. The girl's face was expressionless and Myrith wondered what she was thinking.

:*Yes, you are related to Mordamien. There's something else here though.* There was a pause. :*Myrith, you have traces of divine blood in your own.*

How is that possible?

Myrith didn't answer immediately, her mind was still denying what Mordamien had told her. His statement that she, like him, was descended from Thynitic and because of that she was also a Daughter of Chaos. She glanced again at Kyrianna then looked away. The last thing she wanted to do was tell her friend about this, but she wasn't going to lie when asked so pointedly. However, that didn't mean she had to tell everything.

:Mordamien told me I was a descendant of Thynitic. However, I don't believe it.

She frowned when she heard Melissa chanting.

:Myrith, Melissa said slowly, *:it's true.*

"You're a descendent of Thynitic?" Kyrianna let go of the sword and took several steps back.

Myrith sighed. This was what she was afraid would happen. Mordamien had made it a point to call her a Daughter of Chaos. The demon in the first temple had made reference to two of the daughters working together. Brular had told Kyrianna her mother's title was Daughter of Chaos and Skylar had called Kyrianna a Daughter of Chaos. For a second, her mind also flashed on the image of Mordamien's ring and she glanced at Cewyr.

She tried to force all of that from her mind. She didn't need her friend falling apart before they entered Thynitic's citadel. That would make her all the more vulnerable to the goddess. "Kyri, that doesn't change anything," she said. "Would it change who you are if Thynitic was in your ancestry?" She tightened her hand on the sword, she hadn't meant to say it that way and she frowned as she heard Melissa chanting again. There was a small gasp from the wraith, then she was silent.

"I guess it wouldn't," Kyrianna said. "I grew up in a place where I was judged because my mother was an elf; I shouldn't have reacted like that because of something you have no control over. I apologize."

Myrith nodded and held out her free hand.

:Melissa if you just cast the spell again and got the answer I think you did, please do not say anything to Kyri at this time.

There was a long pause. *:I understand.* Another pause. *:Myrith, I saw your thoughts about the ring and Cewyr. You should also know Torliana had a book Brular called the Book of Chaos and it had the same unicorn on the cover.*

That was the connection! Myrith stared at Kyrianna. The silver-gray unicorn was tied to Thynitic in some way. But how? And did it also tie Kyrianna to Thynitic?

"Myrith?"

"Sorry." She handed the sword to Kyrianna then looked away.

"Divine blood," Kyrianna said.

"What?" Myrith jerked her head back.

"Divine blood. Next thing you know we will be dedicating a shrine to you." She smiled.

"Sure you will." She turned and walked away. *Two Daughters of Chaos, one serving a goddess of order. The other apparently destined to serve the Lady of Chaos, no matter how she fights against it. One of us will probably end up killing the other one day.*

~ * ~

Her watch completed, Kyrianna sat in the shrine holding the short bow. The string had a silver shimmer to it that matched the shimmering of Cewyr's mane and tail. She wondered how brightly the string would reflect in sunlight or even moonlight. She had rechecked the braiding and splices and found the string was now seamless. The magic of the unicorn hair, or a blessing from the goddesses—she wasn't sure, but she was glad it had happened.

She stood and carried the bow to the altar and laid it with her sword and the red 'tears' she had been collecting. "Frayrith guide us through the chaos we will face tomorrow. Help us to restore the order that is so desperately needed."

She bowed her head as she knelt before the altar, her thoughts on Kilenter, her home and Tristan. She felt Cewyr's soft muzzle on her neck and she opened her eyes to see herself in the clearing in Kilenter.

"Frayrith," she whispered as a pure white unicorn stepped from the trees.

The unicorn stood silently for a moment, then was surrounded by a bright light. Kyrianna look up to see a tall elven woman standing there with golden skin, silver hair and midnight black eyes.

"Daughter, your words are wiser than even you could have guessed." The goddess sat on the ground across from Kyrianna. "For even in the heart of chaos there is a spark of order. That is the contradiction of chaos and the thing that keeps chaos from destroying everything. Just as Brular must be redeemed and restored to Shokar, so must Thynitic be redeemed and restored to Rhysia. However, that time is not yet."

Kyrianna felt her jaw drop as she looked at the goddess. "Thynitic redeemed?"

"Yes, child: Redemption, rededication and rebirth. Over the eons she has existed, her own chaotic nature and the manipulations of others have twisted her into a parody of what she once was. You must accept your ties to the Lady of Chaos, so you can complete what has been started."

"No! I will not accept her." Kyrianna stood up and turned away from Frayrith to find her path blocked by a ghostly figure. "Mother." She felt herself shaking as she stared at the figure in front of her.

"You must listen to Frayrith." Arielle's voice was as soft and delicate as her form was wispy.

"I cannot accept her. Not after what she has done."

"Frayrith did not say you would have to accept Thynitic; only that you would have to accept your ties to her."

"I don't understand." Kyrianna held her hands out.

"Nor are you meant to—at this time." Frayrith took one of Kyrianna's hands.

"You have another appointment to keep this night. You should return." Arielle smiled. "He is a very nice young man."

"Thank you," Kyrianna whispered as her mother faded away and the goddess transformed back into a unicorn.

The unicorn reared up in salute then spun on her hind legs and darted out of the clearing. Kyrianna wiped her hand across her eyes as the forest of Kilenter faded back into the shrine.

She settled back against Cewyr's side. The unicorn was already asleep and only snorted softly as she leaned against her.

:*Melissa can you hum your mother's song for me please?*

:*Of course.* There was a pause. :*Kyri, we enter Thynitic's citadel tomorrow.* Another pause. :*I'm scared.*

:*So am I. However, we have to see this through. Apparently, there is more at stake here, than we may ever know if we are successful.*

:*Enjoy your visit with Tristan* The girl giggled then started humming.

Kyrianna smiled as she closed her eyes. She hoped it wouldn't be the last time she saw Tristan.

She opened her eyes to find herself again in the guest room of the Duvall house in Raspa. The room was immaculately clean with none of the items she had left there anywhere in sight. She frowned when she found the wardrobe empty except for a stack of soft towels and bed linens. The last time she was here, her blue dress had been cleaned and hung on the back of the door. What was going on? She brushed at the simple linen dress she was wearing.

She stepped out of the room and glanced around; there were several more doorways—all closed. She debated checking the other rooms, but stopped when she heard voices downstairs; Tristan and another man. She moved silently down the stairs to the sitting room.

"Ah, she did make it." Cassandra Shindar stood up, along with a well-muscle man who nodded politely.

Tristan stood and turned toward Kyrianna. He held out his hand and guided her to the chair he had been sitting in.

"I see my gift has been put to good use." Cassandra reached for Kyrianna's left hand.

Kyrianna jerked her hand away from the woman.

"It has," Tristan said. "Kyri, we will only be a few more minutes if you would prefer to wait in the garden."

Kyrianna took a deep breath. "I'll be fine." She looked at the gentleman with Cassandra. "My apologies for interrupting."

"No need to apologize, Lady Kyrianna. My wife told me to expect your arrival." He held his hand out. "I am Orlundru Shindar, Fifth Sword of Tormasus. We met briefly at the reception for King Dracenhalts."

Kyrianna nodded. "My friend Andrinor speaks very highly of you, sir."

"The dragon warrior is well then?"

"He is."

"Please relay my respects and regards for his successful return."

"I will."

Tristan handed the papers back to Cassandra. "If that is all?"

She looked at the papers. "I believe that settles the matter. I will have a courier deliver the draft tomorrow." Cassandra handed a copy of the papers back to Tristan, rolled up the rest then stood.

Both Tristan and Orlundru stood. Tristan clasped hands with Orlundru as Cassandra moved to an open area and held up a crystal rod. "With your permission, Lord Duvall," she said.

"Of course."

"One last thing: Kyrianna, be careful tomorrow and do not forget my warning." She placed her arm around her husband's and broke the rod before Kyrianna could say anything.

"Kyri?" Tristan spun back to face her.

"Tomorrow we expect to enter Thynitic's citadel. Cassandra was reminding me to not let anything happen to Torliana." She looked away from him. "After what she did to me, why did you agree to sell her the estate?"

Tristan grabbed her hands and knelt in front of her. "Kyri, I understand your feelings regarding her because of what she did. However, she is on the council of mages of Gormanghast and her husband is the Fifth Sword of Tormasus. Politically, I could not ignore or risk insulting her."

Kyrianna started to pull her hands away from Tristan but felt him tighten his grip.

"Lady Kyrianna, I love you and would never intentionally hurt you. I have no desire to ever return to the estate and have no reason to hold on to the property. In addition to a generous offer for the estate she did locate and return my grandparent's wedding rings. Lord Shindar has agreed to provide for the defense of Duvshire as well as training for the local guardsmen."

Kyrianna nodded. "I'm sorry. I understand."

"And I am sorry also. It would have been better if we had been able to conclude our business before you arrived. However, it was Cassandra who set the time for our meeting."

"Probably because she wanted to have the chance to give me that last warning."

"Enough of this." Tristan stood and pulled Kyrianna to her feet and hugged her tightly. "I want to show you something." He released her and held out his hand.

Together they went back up the stairs. Tristan grinned when they reached one of the closed doors. "Close your eyes," he said as he reached for the handle.

Kyrianna smiled as she followed Tristan's instructions. Tristan took her hands and she let him guide her into the room. He let go after a moment and she heard another set of doors opening.

"You can open them."

She opened her eyes to find herself in a large bedroom, before her was an open wardrobe filled with dresses and other clothes—much of it her own from Nydith. On a table next to the wardrobe was a swatch of deep blue cloth that shimmered with silver threads.

"Blue is the traditional color for weddings in the church of Mykaylene," Tristan said. "I hope you have no objections that I have already commissioned a dressmaker to begin work on the dress."

"Only if you don't mind having a second ceremony on Rhysia performed according to the rituals of Frayrith." Kyrianna picked up the cloth and held it against her cheek.

Tristan placed his hand over hers and gently pulled the cloth from under her hand, letting it barely touch the skin, as it kissed the tip of her ear.

Kyrianna gasped as a flash of warmth flooded through her body. "Tristan, please don't. Not unless…" She let her voice trail off.

Tristan didn't say anything as he let both of his hands slide over her ears. He then tilted her face up and leaned close as he kissed her.

Kyrianna wrapped her arms around him and held him tightly as he tried to pull away. She rose up on her toes as her lips found his. She was determined this time the moment wasn't going to get away. They had been very lucky today and she knew it would take even greater luck for them to survive tomorrow. She wasn't going to let this chance be missed by either of them.

When their lips parted, she stepped back and reached for the ties on the back and shoulders of her dress. She smiled as the dress slid over her shoulders and to the floor.

Tristan only stared at her, his eyes wide.

She took a step forward. "Tristan, I go to face Thynitic tomorrow. I don't want to lose this, because I may not get this opportunity again."

Tristan placed his fingers on her lips. "Don't even think such a thing. I have your promise that you will return and you have my promise as well."

She shivered as his hands moved to her ears, over the tips then down her neck, and over her shoulders to rest on her back.

"Are you sure?" His lips brushed her ears lightly.

She sighed and leaned against him as his lips found her neck.

"No!" Kyrianna screamed as the room faded and she found herself back in the keep.

:Kyri? Melissa's voice whispered in her head.

"Just a bad dream," Kyrianna said as Myrith came running, Conflagration aflame in her hand.

Myrith looked at her and frowned slightly. "I thought your dreams had you visiting Tristan. This wasn't some sending of Thynitic's was it?"

Kyrianna stood slowly and shook her head. She removed the sapphire necklace and placed it over Cewyr's horn. "No, nothing like that. It was more a bad time to myself here instead of there. Excuse me." She pushed past the older woman and headed for the shower.

She head Myrith's light laughter just as the water started and grinned also in spite of her anger at having her visit stopped when it was. As the cool water washed over her, Kyrianna found herself relaxing. All she had to do was survive tomorrow and then convince Tristan to visit the pools at the grove in Irrmar and this torture would end.

Chapter Twenty-Six

Myrith stood with Conflagration at the ready as Feric shifted into a large animal with sharp claws. He resembled a badger, but he was almost as large as a tiger. Not his normal tiger shape, which was as large as a war horse, but a normal tiger. Feric began digging through the boulders and she grinned when Gwideon and Kyrianna had to dodge pieces of flying rock.

"You should dismiss her." Myrith placed a hand on Cewyr's shoulder. "We don't know yet what we will be facing. You can summon her if needed."

Cewyr snapped at Myrith's hand, her teeth just missing the skin. "I would prefer us not be separated at this time."

"Trust us to protect her—even from herself."

Cewyr nodded.

"Return to your home," Kyrianna whispered. She picked up the figurine then held it out to Myrith. "Please."

Myrith took the figurine. "Only until we get back to Shokar. She is your responsibility."

"I know and I do this to protect her." Kyrianna's hand went to the necklace.

"If something happens. I will make sure Melissa is returned to Tristan. But for now, she will be happiest where she is."

Kyrianna nodded.

"Myrith," Hendandra called.

She turned to see the area in front of the portal cleared. She spun back around at the sound of Kyrianna's weapons being drawn from their sheaths. "Kyri?" The girl ignored her and started for the portal.

"Kyri!" Myrith stepped in front of her friend.

"I have a score to settle with Thynitic." She stepped around Myrith.

Myrith shook her head as Kyrianna stepped through the portal. "Let's go."

She stopped as Kyrianna was thrown back into the room. She caught the girl before she hit the floor. Her arms and face were badly burned where there were no protections and the metal of her chain mail was fused in several areas.

She looked up at Jerietlan. "Take care of her, but make sure the sting remains."

The cleric nodded then placed his hand on Kyrianna's arm. "Falden, look at these," he said.

"Fire, lightning *and* acid. Each one makes a distinctive type of burn—this shows all three." He pointed to different areas on Kyrianna's arm.

"So there are at least two barriers within the portal. One that caused Kyri's injuries and another that forced her back through." Myrith frowned. "Urric is there another way?"

"At this point no—unless you want to backtrack and then risk having to find your way to Thynitic's citadel from several leagues away. This is the only one that opens into her citadel."

"Fine. How do we get through the portal?"

"That will depend on the specific spell we are facing," Falden said. "There are a number of spells that can produce these types of effects, but each one takes something different to cancel it out. I can cast the appropriate magics for the ones I am aware of. However, I do not think it wise to waste power by guessing. Plus without knowing which order they are placed in, it is possible we will not be able to remove them all."

"Gwideon, may I borrow Urric," Hendandra asked.

"What are you thinking?" Feric grabbed her hand.

"By holding the skull and pushing him slowly into the portal, he might be able to identify the magics."

"Hendandra?" Kyrianna pulled her arm away from Jerietlan.

"I swore to come on this journey to help a friend and I haven't done anything yet."

"Other than almost dying," Feric said.

"While I agree that using Urric in this manner might be an excellent idea, this is too dangerous, little one," Andrinor said. "You have little more knowledge of magic than Kyrianna or I. Let those, like Falden who have the knowledge do this."

"And if I need both hands to cast the counter magics? How do I hold the skull and cast?"

"This is something I can do," Hendandra said. "Urric can talk and let me know how close we are to the barrier and what it is without risking further injury."

"If you are willing." Gwideon lifted the chain holding the skull from around his neck, then detached it from the skull. The skull returned to full size as he handed it to Hendandra.

She took the skull and nodded. Falden stood next to her as she slowly extended the hand holding the skull into the portal.

"Hold." Urric's voice was distorted, but understandable. "It is a shifting curtain of colors. Red, black, blue, green and yellow."

"This is the spell that hurt Kyrianna. There will be another spell that forced her back through the portal." Falden turned to look at Kyrianna. "Be glad you were only touched by the red, blue and green colors. The black would have killed you instantly and the yellow would have trapped you in a diamond prison."

Myrith held up a small mirror as Kyrianna's hand went to her face. "No scars, Rangerette. You'll still be beautiful for your wedding day."

Kyrianna nodded.

"One of these days you will learn to control that impulsiveness," Andrinor said.

"Be quiet. I need to concentrate." Falden turned back to face the portal. His hand slid along Hendandra's arm and into the portal. After a moment, he began chanting and his other arm entered the portal.

"Wait," Urric's gravelly voice said. "There is someone in the other room.

Falden pulled his hands out of the portal and clasped them together tightly. Energy arced from his body into the walls, causing rocks and debris to fall to the floor.

"Once the casting was starting, the power had to go somewhere," he said. He placed a hand on the outside of the portal. "Bring him out."

Hendandra pulled Urric out of the portal and handed the skull back to Gwideon.

The portal shimmered then an image formed. An elf woman with long black hair stood in the room facing the portal from that side. "It was Kyrianna who tried to enter." She passed her hand in front of her then turned to the side. "Leave," she said.

"My Lady?" a voice asked.

"The danger from the other side has been removed. You are dismissed."

"Yes, My Lady."

"What is she doing?" Myrith moved closer to Falden.

"Be quiet," Falden whispered. "I am not sure if she can hear us. I am confident I have blocked her seeing into this room—but sound is different."

Myrith nodded then reached out and grabbed Kyrianna's arm as the girl started to step past her. She shook her head when the girl looked at her, and ignored the pleading in her friend's eyes.

The woman on the other side moved slowly around the room.

"She is dismissing and dispelling the magics that are in that room," Falden whispered.

The woman paused and turned back to face the portal. "Welcome to my citadel, my daughter," she said then vanished.

"Kyri?" Myrith's grip tightened when she heard the girl's sword hit the floor.

"My daughter." Kyrianna jerked away from her and took a step back. "That was Thynitic." She shook her head. "You said Mordamien called you a Daughter of Chaos. Melissa confirmed you are a descendant of Thynitic." She paused and took a deep breath. "She was talking about me—does that mean...?" She darted toward the portal.

"Stop her!" Myrith grabbed Kyrianna's weapons from the floor and started after the girl.

~ * ~

The room they had seen through the portal was not the one they stepped into.

"Her nature is chaos," Urric said. "The rooms and passages change and move." Kyrianna moved slowly to the steps leading up to two thrones.

"I thought there was only one throne before," Andrinor said. "Is this the correct place?"

"Kyri?" Myrith placed a hand on Kyrianna's shoulder. The girl ignored her as she climbed the steps.

Kyrianna paused behind the thrones and placed a hand on each one. As she did, a symbol glowed on each one. Myrith recognized the multi-colored portal of Thynitic and the flame symbol they had seen in the first temple. "Chaos and Order," Kyrianna said. "The Lady and the Consort. The balance must be restored."

Myrith frowned as the words came from Kyrianna's throat,

but it was not her voice.

"It is from chaos we are born." Kyrianna spoke the words slowly. "Chaos gives life and creates change. It is only through chaos that we can see the truth. Chaos and passion call all to them. Mercy and retribution should only be meted out when deserved; not when dictated. Embrace passion, mercy and retribution. Embrace chaos. Embrace life."

"Kyrianna!" Myrith snapped the name.

Kyrianna jerked her head up. Without a pause she pulled her bow up and released an arrow over Myrith's shoulder.

Myrith dropped both of Kyrianna's swords, drew Conflagration and spun around at the cry of pain that came from behind her. A small imp lay of the floor, the arrow through its shoulder.

Andrinor reached down and picked up the imp. "Now we have a guide," he said.

Kyrianna shouldered her bow, reached down and picked up her swords then headed out of the room.

"Kyrianna!" Myrith started after the girl. This couldn't be good. Kyrianna was acting like she was being controlled. And it had occurred after she entered this place. She sheathed Conflagration and drew the small dagger she carried in her belt. The same dagger she had started to draw when Kyrianna was forced to call on Thynitic before.

"Kyri!" She called the girl's name and hurried after her. She turned the dagger in her hand as she caught up to her friend. Kyrianna's steps slowed and she waited for Myrith.

"We need to hurry," Kyrianna said. "The balance is almost lost."

"Lead the way." Myrith let Kyrianna get a step ahead of her, then raised the hilt of the dagger and brought it down hard on the back of her friend's head. She dropped the dagger and caught Kyrianna as the girl collapsed.

"Myrith?" Jerietlan helped her lower Kyrianna to the floor.

"I don't like the way she was acting."

The imp Andrinor was holding started laughing. "She was the one who could have guided you through the chaos. The one destined to serve. Now, you have destroyed the balance and chaos will reign unchallenged." His high-pitched voice squeaked as Andrinor tightened his grip.

"You will guide us." Andrinor slammed the imp's head into

the floor twice then held him up and shook him.

"The balance is lost. There is nothing you can do to stop it. I will guide you."

Myrith ignored the imp and sat next to Kyrianna, waiting for her friend to wake up. She wasn't sure what she was going to tell her. She didn't want to lie, but she also didn't want to tell her she had been the one to hit her.

"Thank you." Kyrianna's voice was harsh. "You?"

"Yes." Myrith stood then held her hand out to Kyrianna. "You were acting like you were being controlled and I wasn't going to let that continue." She paused. "Thynitic?"

"I don't know." Kyrianna rubbed her head. "It didn't feel like her, but at the same time it did." She looked at the others.

"Where is the cleric of Hellavar?" Andrinor looked at the imp.

"I do not have that knowledge."

"Then I suggest you grow more intelligent." Andrinor slammed the imp's head against the floor.

"I can take you to one who might be able to tell you where he is." The imp pointed to one of the hallways.

Andrinor held the imp out in front of him, his hand tight around its throat. "If you lead us into a trap, it will be you who triggers it."

"You cannot stop what has started. I will guide you."

They moved quickly through the corridors, following the imp's direction.

"Where are you leading us," Myrith asked when they paused at an intersection with another corridor.

"To one who might be able to tell you where the cleric of Hellavar is held." The imp pointed to a door. "She is there."

Hendandra checked the door several times. "How do you open the door?"

The imp laughed again. "You have to have proper access." He pointed to a small panel next to the door.

Andrinor slammed the imp into the wall and the imp went silent. He held up the imp's hand and pressed it against the plate. "That didn't work," he said when nothing happened. He flung the imp into the far wall and nodded as it slid to the floor. "I believe his usefulness is at an end."

Kyrianna took a deep breath and started to raise her hand to the plate. Myrith reached across in front of her, her hand pressing the plate first. The door slid open.

"Myrith?" Gwideon asked as the entered the room.

"Not now," she whispered.

Gwideon nodded.

"What is all this?" Hendandra was standing in front of a bench with various items scattered across it. Falden walked over and nodded. "Someone was crafting something here. However, it looks like they destroyed whatever it was." He pointed to a small smelting pot.

"I destroyed the amulet meant for Kyrianna," a woman's voice said behind them.

Myrith spun around in time to see Kyrianna standing with her sword raised and held to Torliana's throat.

"Why?" Kyrianna's voice was harsh.

"Not for you." Torliana took a step back. "Because he wouldn't have wanted to see another person trapped in this way."

Kyrianna nodded then touched Torliana's shoulder with the tip of the unicorn horn sword. The woman screamed and fell to the floor. Her hand going to the shoulder where her other arm was missing. "The balance must be properly restored." Kyrianna took a step back.

Myrith placed her hand on Kyrianna's. The girl's voice had the same tone and quality it had earlier.

Kyrianna shook her head. "Don't worry."

Myrith looked at her and frowned. "I always worry."

Torliana pushed herself up from the floor and rubbed the arm that had regrown.

"Why?"

"Not for you," Kyrianna said. "Where is Brular?"

"She said she was having him taken to one of the most secure areas. I have not seen him since the lich was sent to deal with you."

"Can you find him?" Myrith asked.

Torliana closed her eyes for several minutes. "Yes." She started to raise her hands and stopped as Kyrianna's sword was against her throat again. "I have very little power left, but this is the only way to reach him."

"I don't trust her," Andrinor said.

"Neither do I," Myrith said. "But do we have a choice?"

Torliana smiled and waited for Kyrianna to lower her sword. There was a pop and the group found themselves in a small room, an area of darkness floating over their heads.

"He is there." Torliana pointed at the floating darkness.

"Can you dispel whatever that is?" Myrith looked up at the darkness and frowned. It was half again her height away from them and there was nothing in the room to stand on. Not that she really wanted to risk anyone entering the area.

"No. It took my remaining power to bring us here." She walked around the room slowly, Kyrianna staying close to her. "That area allows no light, no sound or any other sensation and he has been there for several days."

"I have an idea." Andrinor stood directly below the area. "Myrith," he looked up at the area, "if Gwideon and I lift you up, you might be able to reach him and pull him out of the area."

"If the area allows no light, sound or other sensation, how will you know you have him?" Hendandra asked.

"We keep trying."

Myrith let Andrinor and Gwideon lift her up so she was standing on their shoulders. As soon as her head entered the area she lost all sense of direction. The darkness was absolute and she couldn't even hear her own breathing. However, she could feel where Andrinor and Gwideon held her legs. With a silent prayer to Mykaylene, she reached out into the darkness and thought she felt something brush her hands. She grabbed whatever it was and twisted her feet. Andrinor and Gwideon pulled her out of the darkness and she breathed a sigh of relief when she saw she had hold of a man's arm. "Falden," she said looking at the mage.

He nodded and she felt herself floating toward the floor as she pulled Brular from the darkness.

"You should never have come to this place," Brular said.

"We would never abandon a friend." Myrith clasped his arm.

Kyrianna stepped over, raised her sword and touched his shoulder. "The balance must be restored," she said.

Brular winced, but remained standing as the magic took hold. "Thank you," he said. He glanced at Torliana, then back at Kyrianna a look of surprise on his face.

She turned away.

"How do we get out of here and back to Shokar?" Hendandra asked.

"I dare not try and open a portal in this place," Falden said.

"Teleportation is the only way in or out of this cell," Torliana said. "It is one of the most secure in her citadel." She looked at Kyrianna. "Your sword." She held out her hand.

Kyrianna took a step back. "I am not giving you a weapon."

"Your sword was created from the horn of one of the eldest of Kilenter. In case you haven't noticed, the unicorns of Kilenter have a unique ability to teleport within the forest. It is possible I can tap into that power and open a doorway to another part of the citadel."

Kyrianna shook her head and held her hand out to Myrith.

Myrith nodded and handed her the unicorn figurine.

"Cewyr," Kyrianna whispered. The unicorn appeared.

"Her ability is restricted to the forests," Torliana said.

Cewyr touched the woman with her horn. "Cast your spell," she said.

A small area in the wall shimmered. "Hurry," Torliana said.

The group found themselves in a corridor.

"Good. There is a portal to Shokar at the end of this hallway," Torliana said.

"Where is the amulet holding Brular's soul?" Andrinor said.

Torliana pulled a small amulet from under her robes. "She gave it to me to hold. This way I would know if anything happened to him. She knew I wouldn't destroy it as I couldn't risk destroying that part of his soul."

Andrinor snatched the amulet from her. "I made an oath to see that thing destroyed."

"Wait!" Torliana stepped in front of him. "If it is not done properly, you will destroy the part of the soul it contains."

"The amulet must be destroyed by a weapon that is considered sanctified," Gwideon said.

Myrith started to draw Conflagration.

"No Lady Lake." Gwideon placed a hand on her arm. "Conflagration is a powerful weapon in service to a deity, but it is not considered sanctified. There are only two weapons in this group that can be used. Kyrianna's silver sword, and then only if Melissa is in the blade at the time and Andrinor's bone blade. The amulet must also be placed in an area that negates magic. Passing through that field could be dangerous for Melissa, so it is best if it is Andrinor's weapon."

Falden took the amulet and chanted for several minutes then dropped it to the floor. "Andrinor."

The warrior brought the blade down, shattering the metal of the amulet. Two tendrils of mist snaked out from the remains to float back to Brular and Torliana. "Which way to the portal?"

"Straight ahead."

"How is it, I don't know about this portal?" Urric asked.

"Because you are a fool," Torliana said.

"What I don't understand is why it has been so easy since we got to this place," Hendandra said. "There was that woman, who appeared to be Thynitic, dispelling the magics guarding the portal into this place. Then we find an empty throne room, with only a single imp watching it. One that takes us straight to Torliana. Who in turn takes us straight to Brular. Now, all we have to do is get to a portal to take us back to Shokar. Something, doesn't make sense."

"It's chaos," Kyrianna said. "It doesn't have to make sense."

"There is more going on with Thynitic than is apparent at this time," Brular said.

"I think your concern that this was going to be too easy has been heard," Andrinor said.

"There is a saying among the thieves' guild," Kyrianna said. "When you look for a guard, you will find one. Apparently we have found the demons we were expecting." She grabbed Hendandra and put her on Feric's back after he shifted into his tiger form.

"Get to the portal," she said.

Andrinor stuck the pommel of his sword in his belt and moved to the center of the corridor. "Watch the other corridors," he said.

Myrith moved to the right as Gwideon moved to the left. She heard Falden chanting. Conflagration flared in her hands as several demons appeared in the corridor she was watching. Behind her, she heard Andrinor roar followed by a blast of cold air.

There was another explosion.

"The corridor to the portal is cleared," Kyrianna called. "Feric and Hendandra should be there. Falden, Jerietlan, Brular, Torliana move."

"Grey," Brular called. "These others will not understand why you came here, but I do."

Myrith risked a glance over her shoulder to see Brular holding up a small vial.

Torliana had stopped and was staring at him.

"I will have your word that you will give whatever it takes for them to escape."

"You have it." Gwideon's voice echoed in the corridor and Myrith felt her heart stop for a moment.

"Good." Brular raised the vial.

An arrow flew past Myrith.

"Watch your back," Kyrianna said.

Andrinor released another blast of cold air as Myrith spun around catching the blade of the demon closest to her.

"Go!" Gwideon yelled. "I will hold them." He held a rolled parchment out to her. "Get the rest to safety."

:Remember what Riker asked you? Myrith heard Conflagration's gravelly voice in her head as she grabbed the parchment and herded the rest of the group toward the portal.

She glanced back to see Gwideon surrounded by the demons. She had told Riker she would allow Gwideon to hold the line so they could escape if that was the knight's wish. At the time she had spoken those words, she had been sure it would never come to that—now it had and she had been forced to face that situation, it was something she would never do again. She had succeeded in what she needed to do—rescue Brular and get the others back to Shokar. But, the cost had again been too high.

Chapter Twenty-Seven

"Gwideon?" Andrinor looked at Myrith as she stepped through the portal.

She only shook her head.

Kyrianna was standing guard next to Torliana who was kneeling next to the body of an old man. "He took a potion that counteracted all the potions of long life he had taken in the past," she said. "That was the release Gwideon was sent to provide for him."

"We released him from his torment and Resare claimed his soul." Myrith looked at Torliana. "He was a cleric of Hellavar, the Lord of Fire. I assume a pyre would be appropriate."

Torliana nodded.

Myrith left Kyrianna with the woman and helped Andrinor gather the wood and build the pyre. With care she placed the body on the platform and waited as Torliana walked around it repositioning and straightening the wood. When she was finished, Torliana stepped back, placed her hands together then fanned them out as fire shot from her body to ignite the wood. It was the same gesture Rynalana had used in the temple in Irrmar to light the fire pits.

Myrith frowned as Hendandra and Feric left the area while the rest stood and watched the fire burn. Tears continued to fall down Torliana's face as she focused only on the fire. Without any warning, she collapsed on the ground. Myrith looked at Kyrianna who only shrugged.

Feric and Hendandra walked back to the group, a third person with them, dressed in simple robes. Myrith noticed gray now scattered in Feric's hair.

"Brular?" Jerietlan asked.

"I am he," the man said. "Thanks to these two, I have been brought back and Lord Hellavar has again blessed me." He stopped and looked down at Torliana. "I owe each of you as well, for bringing us out of that place."

Myrith shook her head. "You owe us nothing. There are none here who would have willingly left a comrade to that torment."

He nodded and turned to Kyrianna. "I sense there is something you would ask of me."

Kyrianna smiled. "I ask not for me but for another." She drew the silver sword and held it out. "Melissa was killed by her brother, Mikyl, when she was just a child. She spent thirty years trapped in pain and chaos. I would ask that she be restored."

Brular smiled as he took the sword. Mist flowed from the weapon and solidified into the form of a small child.

"Melissa." Kyrianna gathered the girl in her arms and hugged her. She looked up at Brular. "Thank you," she said.

He only nodded and turned back to where Torliana lay.

"What will you do with her?"

"We will try to bring her back from the darkness—as we did you," Myrith said.

"Her actions have shown me she is not completely lost."

"Leave her with me. I was and am her Keeper. It is my responsibility to redeem what has been lost."

Myrith nodded.

"No!" Kyrianna yelled.

Myrith turned as an arrow flew past her to impale the ground next to Torliana's head. "She will return to Rhysia with me. She will face the council of Nydith for her crimes against a member of a noble house of that city."

"Kyri?"

The girl ignored her and focused on Brular. "You may have forgiven and absolved her of her crimes against you and the temple at Mount Veri. However, you do not have the jurisdiction to do so with my accusations. These crimes did not occur against a citizen of Shokar or within these realms. I demand my rights under Nydith law."

"I agree with Kyrianna." Andrinor moved to stand next to her.

"As do I," Jerietlan said.

"Kyri." Myrith looked at her and held her hands out. "If there is a chance to save her from Thynitic's chaos and darkness, isn't that better than seeking retribution."

"Retribution?" Kyrianna's voce rose in volume. "Retribution? If I was after retribution, I would have killed her when we found her. I am demanding justice. She is guilty of the kidnapping and torture of a member of House Dalynne."

Myrith nodded took a step forward and placed her hand on Kyrianna's shoulder. "Are you sure you are truly seeking justice over retribution. For you to say you are only seeking justice, you would have to be seeking a fair hearing before the council of Nydith." She paused. "Kyrianna Dalynne, can you swear to me, that as an elf, Torliana will receive a fair hearing before the council?"

Kyrianna took several steps back and dropped her head.

"I'm waiting for your answer, Rangerette."

"Kyrianna." Brular whispered her name as he stood next to Myrith.

Kyrianna shook her head, still not looking up at Myrith. "I cannot make that guarantee."

Myrith reached out and lifted Kyrianna's chin so she would have to look at her. "I wouldn't let you be the one to kill Mikyl, because you were being driven by a need for revenge and retribution and I will not let you fall into the same trap here. You have been touched by Thynitic; even wielded her power. This means you remain vulnerable to her. Don't let yourself be drawn in."

"Am I supposed to just forget what she did to me?" Kyrianna jerked her head away from Myrith. "Am I supposed to forget how she bound my mother and I together so she suffered the same pain and torment I did. Am I supposed to forget how Thynitic used that connection to convince my mother she would see I was released if she would return to her?" Kyrianna's voice broke. "Am I supposed to forget how I had to watch as a group of midnight elves killed my mother and I could do nothing?" She looked from Myrith to Brular. "You may be able to forgive, I cannot."

"There is something else you should consider, Kyrianna;" Falden said.

"Cassandra Shindar of the Circle of Mages in Gormanghast. Do you want to be hunted by her and the other members of the Circle? If you take Torliana back to Nydith and she faces the council, what would be the most likely sentence?"

"She would be executed."

"And in that case, Thynitic would no longer have a Chosen. The Circle is preparing for something; something even the gods have been preparing to face. That is the reason they are choosing from among their followers those who will hold their highest blessings and power. If Torliana is no longer among the living, she can no longer serve as Thynitic's Chosen. Cassandra was adamant that someone would serve. As you have a connection to the Lady of Chaos, then it will be you. Even if she and the others on the Circle have to destroy the rest of us to accomplish it, she will see you taken to Thynitic." Falden looked at Kyrianna. "Would you knowingly put those you call your friends into the position of having to fight the Circle of Mages? You say you cannot forgive what she has done. Would it be easier to forgive yourself if Cassandra succeeded in killing any of us—even if she did not succeed in returning you to Thynitic?"

"And if Brular succeeds in bringing her back from the darkness she has embraced, who is to say she will serve as Thynitic's Chosen then," Andrinor aid. "Either way Kyri ends up facing Cassandra."

"We will deal with Cassandra if the need arises," Myrith said. "Her threats are not pertinent to this discussion."

"I do not ask you to forgive her as I have," Brular said. "Nor, can I absolve her of the crimes she has committed against you. However, you saw what hatred and a need for vengeance twisted me into when we met. Do not start down that road, it only leads to darkness."

"While I consider you one of my dearest friends, she will never be welcome around me. If she ever attempts to hurt me or my friends again, I will not hesitate. Not even for the sake of our friendship." Kyrianna crossed her arms over her chest and stared at Brular.

"I understand. I will do everything I can to prevent that from ever happening."

Kyrianna took several deep breaths then dropped her head. "I withdraw my claim—for now," she whispered.

Myrith nodded. "Let's go home."

Falden nodded and raised his hands. A portal opened showing the garden at the house in Irrmar.

Myrith smiled. When they originally met, all any of them wanted was to go home. She waited as the rest stepped through then followed them. They had much to mourn as well as celebrate, but for now they were home.

About the Author

A native Texan, Carol found her way to her current home in Colorado by way of a five-year detour in The Nederlands - courtesy of her husband Tim and the US Air Force.

An avid reader at a young age, her strong desire to write came from her love of (her husband calls it her obsession with) Star Trek. It was this early love of Star Trek that led her to the Science Fiction and Fantasy genres.

In addition to her writing she has worked as a receptionist/office manager for two veterinary clinics, a deputy sheriff in El Paso County Colorado and for the Professional Bull Riders.

She has been published in various anthologies and magazines including "Creature Fantastic", PanGaia Magazine, "Stories of Strength", Baen's Universe, Tales of the Talisman and Kepler's Dozen. Her books include: *Call of Chaos, Chaos Embraced, The Road into Chaos*, and *Chaos Challenged*.

Carol has also edited several anthologies for Sky Warrior Books including: "Zombiefied", "These Vampires Don't Sparkle", and "The Dragon's Hoard".

In addition to her own writing, she is the editor and publisher of the online e-zines: The Lorelei Signal and Sorcerous Signals as well as running her own micro-press - WolfSinger Publications.

Answer the Call

Call of Chaos - Book One: The Chaos Reigns Saga

The exiled daughter of a minor noble, Kyrianna Dalynne, finds herself trapped in a temple dedicated to Thynitic, The Lady of Chaos. She and her companions, are charged with finding an ancient artifact before the ones guarding the portals out will allow them to leave. As their search continues, Kyrianna begins to question if there was a specific reason she and the others were brought to this place.

After the guardians claim the artifact has been secured, they offer to open the portals to allow the group to return to their homes. Instead of the familiar forest of Kilenter, Kyrianna finds herself in another world. Her companions from the temple arrive several days after her.

When one of the members is accused of murder, they are tasked with assisting Tristan Duvall, who must face the demons and ghosts of his family's past in order to claim his birthright as a nobleman of the city of Raspa. Kyrianna finds herself attracted to the young man and facing the difficult decision of accepting his invitation to remain with him or return to her own home.

Now Available from WolfSinger Publications

Chaos Embraced – Book Two: The Chaos Reigns Saga

Nowhere in all the worlds or planes is there no pain, torment or chaos. All we can do is accept those strikes which cannot be avoided and give back chaos and pain to those who offend. Kindness should be the only companion to pain and will increase the intensity of suffering and the chaos surrounding us. Do not ignore the sudden whim of compassion; let it always come, but only seldom as to give those who suffer a sense of hope. Hope is consort to chaos and torment is their offspring. Unending torment destroys pain and this in turn destroys the chaos that nurtures us. Act alluring to trap those who would never seek the Lady on their own. Confuse those that think they know the ways of the world around them. Bring pain and torment not only to those who enjoy it, or to those who deserve it, but also to the innocent and those who do not anticipate it. The lash, fire and cold are the three physical pains that never fail the devout. Love, jealousy and hatred are the three pains that should follow in the footsteps of her devout. Spread Thynitic's theology whenever pain is meted out and chaos swirls. Wherever pain is, there is Thynitic. Wherever chaos is, there is Thynitic. Embrace the pain and chaos. Embrace Thynitic.

Trapped in a place where they are constantly faced with new opponents and challenges, Kyrianna and her friends, will also have to face the Goddess Thynitic and her Chosen Torliana.

Kyrianna finds Thynitic whispering in her mind, calling her deeper into the chaos. In order to save her friends from the evil goddess, will she finally Embrace the Chaos and accept her place as a Daughter of Chaos or will she succeed in renouncing Thynitic forever? And if she does, what will the cost be?

Now Available from WolfSinger Publications

Seeds of Chaos – Book Five: The Chaos Reigns Saga

"At this time you and your friends are safe from my plots and machinations." This is the promise Thynitic gives to Kyrianna after the group returns from rescuing Brular. Even with the Lady of Chaos 'ignoring' the group they find they are still not able to return to the lives they once had.

Falden must face Cassandra in a mage duel as he seeks acknowledgement and justice for the Blooded. Andrinor seeks to fulfill his vow to Ghainaess to restore her children to Shokar.

Myrith and Jerietlan are faced with cleansing the corruption that had taken hold in the Coliseum. Brular seeks to restore Mt. Veri and to also help Torliana find her balance even as he must allow her to return to Thynitic's service.

And during all this there are those (both among gods and mortals who are preparing for the return of the Faithless)

But before all this starts there are two weddings to celebrate.

Coming 2016 from WolfSinger Publications

www.ingramcontent.com/pod-product-compliance
Lightning Source LLC
Chambersburg PA
CBHW061556170626
46811CB00001B/224